AMONG THE GODS

Books by
Lynn Austin
FROM BETHANY HOUSE PUBLISHERS

All She Ever Wanted

Eve's Daughters

Hidden Places

Wings of Refuge

REFINER'S FIRE

Candle in the Darkness

Fire by Night

A Light to My Path

CHRONICLES OF THE KINGS

Gods and Kings

Song of Redemption

The Strength of His Hand

Faith of My Fathers

Among the Gods

www.lynnaustin.org

CHRONICLES
of the
KINGS

AMONG THE GODS

LYNN AUSTIN

BETHANY HOUSE PUBLISHERS
Minneapolis, Minnesota

Among the Gods
Copyright © 2006
Lynn Austin

Cover design by DesignWorks Group

Unidentified scripture quotations are from the HOLY BIBLE, NEW INTERNATIONAL VERSION®. Copyright © 1973, 1978, 1984 by International Bible Society. Used by permission of Zondervan Publishing House. All rights reserved.

The scripture quotation identified NRSV is from the New Revised Standard Version of the Bible, copyright 1989 by the Division of Christian Education of the National Council of Churches of Christ in the U.S.A. Used by permission. All rights reserved.

All rights reserved. No part of this publication may be reproduced, stored in a retrieval system, or transmitted in any form or by any means—electronic, mechanical, photocopying, recording, or otherwise—without the prior written permission of the publisher and copyright owners.

Published by Bethany House Publishers
11400 Hampshire Avenue South
Bloomington, Minnesota 55438

Bethany House Publishers is a division of
Baker Publishing Group, Grand Rapids, Michigan.

Printed in the United States of America

ISBN-13: 978-0-7642-2993-0
ISBN-10: 0-7642-2993-1

Library of Congress Cataloging-in-Publication Data

Austin, Lynn N.
   Among the gods / Lynn Austin.
      p. cm. — (Chronicles of the kings ; bk. 5)
   ISBN 0-7642-2993-1 (pbk.)
   1. Manasseh, King of Judah—Fiction. 2. Bible. O.T. Kings—History of Biblical events—Fiction. 3. Israel—Kings and rulers—Fiction. 4. Religious fiction. I. Title. II. Series; Austin, Lynn N. Chronicles of the kings ; bk.5.
   PS3551.U839A84   2006
   813'.54—dc22

                                                                2006008821

Dedicated to my Canadian friends:
Illa Barber, Alma Barkman, Sharon Bowering,
Dianne Darch, Lynda Kvist, Estella Muyinda,
Heidi Toews, and Jan Wiebe.
You were with me at the start of this race.
Thanks for cheering all the way to the finish line.

The Lord is my strength and my song;
he has become my salvation.
He is my God, and I will praise him,
my father's God, and I will exalt him. . . .
Who among the gods is like you, O Lord?
Who is like you—majestic in holiness,
awesome in glory, working wonders?

EXODUS 15:2, 11

LYNN AUSTIN is a three-time Christy Award winner for her historical novels *Hidden Places, Candle in the Darkness,* and *Fire by Night.* In addition to writing, Lynn is a popular speaker at conferences, retreats, and various church and school events. She and her husband have three children and make their home in Illinois.

Prologue

"I HATE WAITING," Joshua mumbled under his breath. "There's nothing worse than waiting." He would give anything to get this meeting over with and learn what his future was going to be, but as the morning slowly crawled toward afternoon, he feared he wasn't going to get his wish.

He glanced at the tall, dark-skinned sentries standing guard at the door to Pharaoh's throne room, then turned his attention back to the multicolored murals decorating the walls of the anteroom. They depicted scenes of the pharaohs' many conquests and the glories of Egypt's ancient past. Memories of Joshua's own past and of the loved ones he had lost were too painful to dwell on for very long, and he stared at the forbidden Egyptian images to push those memories from his thoughts. Violence and bloodshed marred his present life as a fugitive, and he was eager to leave that life behind him. He bore the scars of it on his face, the pain and guilt of it in his heart. He was no longer certain what God wanted of him or what the future would bring; perhaps before the day ended he would find out.

Prince Amariah fidgeted beside him as they waited, looking worried. "I wish they would hurry up and summon us," he said. "I hate being surrounded by all these images and idols. How can you even look at them?"

Joshua glanced at Amariah, then at the delegation of chief priests and Levites who had accompanied them to Pharaoh's palace. With no place to rest their eyes without sinning, they stared at the floor, silent and nervous. "If Pharaoh allows us to stay in Egypt, we'll be living among these gods all the time," Joshua told the prince. "You'd better get used to them."

Joshua understood the shock the Judean exiles were experiencing. In the month since he and more than three hundred priests and Levites and their families had made their daring escape from Jerusalem at Passover, their euphoria had slowly ebbed away as they began to comprehend all that they had lost. For many of the priests, the physical separation from the Promised Land had been as painful and traumatic as severing a limb. Abandoning Solomon's Temple on God's holy mountain left them stunned with grief. For centuries, God's deliverance from Egyptian slavery at Passover had defined who they were as a people, yet now God had apparently reversed His redemption plan and returned them all to Egypt. Joshua couldn't promise them that the sojourn would be temporary.

At last the massive door swung open and a chamberlain beckoned to them. "Pharaoh will see you now." Joshua touched the leather eye patch he wore, making certain it was still in place over his sightless right eye; then he and the delegation followed Prince Amariah into the throne room.

Dust motes danced in thin beams of sunlight as Pharaoh's slaves fanned the air with palm branches. The palace wore a faded look of aging glory—the paint dingy gray, the plaster flaking in spots, the air musty with the scent of damp stone. Joshua stifled a cough as he bowed low before Pharaoh Taharqo, the third Nubian king to reign as Pharaoh of Upper and Lower Egypt. Taharqo had the flawless ebony skin, broad nose, and full lips of his Cushite ancestors, but his impassive features revealed nothing of his response to the Judeans' request for sanctuary in Egypt. When Joshua first presented their petition a week ago, he had told Pharaoh that he and Amariah were former officials in King Manasseh's government; he hadn't disclosed the fact that Amariah was a royal prince of the House of David.

"Pharaoh has considered your request for political asylum," Taharqo's spokesman began. The sheet of papyrus crackled like dry twigs as he carefully unrolled it. Clean-shaven, bare-chested, and dressed in a white linen kilt, he and the other Egyptians standing on the dais beside Pharaoh gazed down at the Judeans' bearded faces and long robes with obvious distaste. "His Majesty offers you the following terms of refuge. You will have two days to either accept them or to leave Egyptian territory permanently."

Prince Amariah nodded slightly. "We understand, my lord."

There was little doubt in Joshua's mind that the terms would be acceptable. The priests had consulted God's will before their escape using the Urim and Thummim, and God had made it clear that it was His will for this remnant of believers to find sanctuary in Egypt. Isaiah's prophecy confirmed it.

"Pharaoh Taharqo has generously granted you a portion of land on which to establish your exiled Jewish community. You may erect an altar there to worship your god." One of the chief priests standing behind Joshua expelled a sigh of relief. "We have three seasons in Egypt," the official continued. "You have arrived during *shemu,* our harvest time. Therefore, Pharaoh has graciously agreed to provide your followers with grain, oil, and enough food supplies to last through *akhet,* when the Nile River will flood once more. We use that season for building, since no farm work can be done. That will give you four months to settle into your new homes before *peret,* the season of plowing and sowing."

"We are very grateful," Prince Amariah said, bowing again.

Joshua knew this offer had nothing to do with generosity. Pharaoh would surely demand something from them in return. "How may we repay Pharaoh for his benevolence?" he asked.

"The land deeded to you is on an island in the Nile River known as Elephantine," the spokesman said. "It is an important military outpost, and Pharaoh expects it to remain so. The terms of the treaty are these: First, Pharaoh requires all the young men of your community to enter into military training in order to staff Pharaoh's fortress on Elephantine."

The demand stunned Joshua. He couldn't believe that Pharaoh would require military duty. The priests and Levites would never agree to it.

"Second, this Jewish garrison will come to Pharaoh's defense if

Egypt is attacked by a foreign nation. Third, you will join with Pharaoh's other armed forces if our great god Amon-Ra should decree that the Egyptian empire must expand . . . even if this means going to war against your former countrymen in Judah."

"We aren't soldiers—" one of the chief priests began before Pharaoh's spokesman cut him off.

"Pharaoh knows who you are: experts on Jewish Law and displaced priests without a temple."

"Then why would he want us to command a military garrison?"

The hall fell silent, as if the Judean priest had committed a grave sin by questioning Pharaoh's decision. Pharaoh himself finally broke the silence.

"Because I am a student of history," he said. It was the first time he had spoken to them on either visit, and his voice resounded powerfully in the great throne room. "Twenty years ago when Pharaoh Shabako reigned, you Judeans accomplished something no other nation has ever done—including ours. You defeated Sennacherib and his entire Assyrian army. Your king Hezekiah made it very clear that the victory was not won by his own sword but by the sword of Yahweh, his god. Now you come to me claiming to be true priests of Yahweh. You ask to build an altar to him in Egypt. I have granted your request. But in return, I ask that Yahweh's military power be made available to me."

One of the chief priests started to protest, but Joshua stopped him with a warning look. "Where is Elephantine Island located, my lord?" he asked the Egyptian official.

When Pharaoh's spokesman replied, his cold smile offered Joshua the first hint of his fate. "You will find it's a considerable distance upstream from here, near the first cataract of the Nile, approximately four hundred miles due south. The journey requires a week's travel by boat."

Joshua nodded, struggling to prevent his shock and disappointment from registering on his face. One of the priests behind him moaned. They all knew without consulting a map that they were being exiled to the extreme southern border of Egypt, much farther from home than any of them ever imagined. Joshua glanced at Prince Amariah and saw stunned disbelief reflected on his face. It was the prince's duty to respond for the group, but he seemed incapable of answering. Joshua stepped forward.

"Your Majesty Pharaoh Taharqo, please accept our gratitude for your abundant generosity," he said. "But we won't require two days to reach a decision; we gratefully accept all of your terms."

The priest beside Joshua inhaled sharply. *"What!"*

Amariah gaped at him in alarm. "Joshua, wait. We can't—"

"I know what I'm doing," he whispered. "Trust me."

The Egyptian official studied the murmuring priests with an expression of boredom. "Since it seems there is some disagreement among you, the chamberlain will escort you to the hallway to continue your discussion. Pharaoh has other petitioners waiting."

The delegation was quickly ushered from the room. The chief priests turned on Joshua as soon as they reached the outer doors, everyone talking at the same time. "What were you thinking? We can't possibly accept such conditions! This isn't an offer of asylum; it's military enlistment and banishment."

"We aren't soldiers, Joshua," one of the chief priests said. "Our sons are dedicated to God's service, not Pharaoh's. And Yahweh won't be manipulated like a graven idol to fight for the Egyptians."

"Besides," Amariah said, "we can't ask our people to move so far into the interior of Egypt. We've already moved them three hundred miles from home as it is."

Joshua folded his arms across his chest as he battled to restrain his temper. "Did you imagine that the Egyptians would offer us the well-watered plains of Goshen, like they offered Joseph and our ancestors?"

"I'm sure many of us saw the lush, green lands of the delta and did think that," Amariah said. "How am I supposed to tell everyone that we're moving to the border of Cush? We both know from our studies with Lord Shebna what the land is like down there—beyond the narrow strip of flood plain there's nothing but Sahara desert. We won't be able to plant vineyards or olive groves in that climate or—"

Joshua gestured impatiently. "I know all of this, and I also know that Yahweh doesn't make mistakes. If He wants us to be trained as warriors, then it must be for a good reason. I'm not any happier than you are about moving to an island four hundred miles farther upstream. But don't you see how perfectly it fulfills Isaiah's prophecy? 'There will be an altar to the Lord in the heart of Egypt, and a monument to the Lord at its border.'"

The priests stared at him, uncomprehending. "Listen, we thought this prophecy meant that there would be *two* shrines, one in the middle of Egypt and one at the border," he explained. "But if we build our altar on Elephantine Island it will fulfill *both* conditions at the same time. The island is on the southern border of Egypt, but it's also close to Cush—and Pharaoh Taharqo's empire consists of Egypt and Cush. Therefore, Elephantine Island is right in the heart of that empire."

Amariah closed his eyes. "But it's so far from home," he said softly.

"Yes, but it's also an island. Can't you see God's wisdom in giving us an island, all to ourselves? We can live separate lives—holy lives. Not contaminated by all of this." He gestured to the images painted on the walls.

No one spoke for a moment. Joshua drew a deep breath. "We're going back in there, and we're telling Pharaoh that we accept his terms. Any objections?"

When no one uttered a sound, Joshua caught his first glimpse of his future, and he neither liked nor understood it. He would be a soldier in Pharaoh's army, stationed on the island of Elephantine, more than seven hundred miles from his home in Jerusalem.

Part One

You have abandoned your people,

the house of Jacob.

They are full of superstitions from the East. . . .

They bow down to the work of their hands. . . .

Go into the rocks, hide in the ground

from dread of the Lord and

the splendor of his majesty!

ISAIAH 2: 6, 8, 10

I

WANING CANDLELIGHT BATHED the family dinner table with a sleepy glow as the Passover meal drew to a close. But Joshua shifted restlessly in his seat as he listened to the familiar story of deliverance. This was the first Passover that his community of exiles had celebrated since escaping from Jerusalem a year ago, and the festive meal stirred unwelcome memories.

"'Give thanks to the Lord, for he is good,'" Joshua's older brother Jerimoth recited, "'his love endures forever.... In my anguish I cried to the Lord, and he answered by setting me free.'"

Joshua didn't feel free. He would never feel free until his enemy, King Manasseh, was dead. He swallowed a sip of his wine and said, "I wonder if Manasseh is celebrating Passover tonight in Jerusalem." Jerimoth turned to him in surprise, as if the king's name had been a bucket of cold water dashed across their festive table.

"What difference does it make, Joshua? I thank God for the privilege of celebrating with my family for the first time in our new home." Jerimoth spread his arms wide as if to embrace all the family members and friends gathered around the table. He had worked hard to turn the musty, mud-brick dwelling on Elephantine Island into a comfortable home for his wife and children; he and Joshua had built a compound of adjoining mud-brick houses with a common courtyard for their extended family. Their sister Tirza lived in one of the houses with her husband, Joel, the high priest. Joshua shared a third house with his mother, Jerusha, and his sister Dinah. Joshua loved his sister, but every time he looked at Dinah he was reminded of Manasseh and how he had held her captive, made her his concubine, then sacrificed her son to Molech.

The servant girl, Miriam, and her brother Nathan also shared Joshua's home. Miriam did more than her share of the work, but her presence was another irritant to Joshua, a daily reminder of how his stupid mistakes had caused the death of Maki, Miriam's father.

"Am I the only one who sees how insane all this is?" Joshua asked. "We're thanking God for delivering us from the Egyptians while living in the heart of Egypt!" He looked to the others gathered around the low table for confirmation, but they returned his gaze with embarrassed silence. "I don't mean to spoil your fun, but we've been stuck here for a year already. I guess I'm getting a little tired of waiting for God to act."

He sat back in his seat again, resting his chin on his hand, covering his scarred face with his fingers. He was self-conscious about his disfigurement; the wide, jagged scar stretched down the right side of his face from above his eyebrow to his jaw, leaving him with only a ragged beard on that side. Every now and then, he would touch the leather patch to reassure himself that it was still in place over his ravaged eye. Prince Amariah said the wound made him look older, battle-hardened, tough. Joshua was the community's hero, and the young soldiers-in-training stood in awe of him, even though he was only a few years older than they were. They had chosen the ox—Joshua's nickname—as the island regiment's symbol, decorating their banners and shields with it.

"I apologize to my esteemed guests for my brother's behavior," Jerimoth said with a tight smile. "Please, allow me to refill your cup, Your Majesty."

Joshua's impatience soared as Prince Amariah held out his own cup to Jerimoth instead of demanding to be served. Even though the priests had anointed Amariah as their king and the rightful heir to King David's throne, he lacked the assertive bearing and authority of a true king. Joshua knew that he, not the prince, was the island's true leader in every respect.

Jerimoth turned to his other guest. "Would you like some more wine, Colonel Hadad?"

"It's excellent—but no thanks," Hadad replied. He was yet another reminder to Joshua of all that he had lost. Hadad's grandfather, Shebna, had served with Joshua's father as the king's top two officials until King Manasseh had begun his bloody purge. Because of Hadad's extensive military training in Jerusalem, he had been given command of the garrison with the rank of colonel. He had abandoned strong drink after their escape and had worked hard for the past year to turn the Levites' scholarly sons into an active fighting force, skilled with spear, bow, and sword.

As Joshua watched, Hadad wiped the palms of his hands on his thighs for what seemed like the hundredth time. Why was he acting so nervous tonight? He'd been a frequent guest at their family's table, so it couldn't be shyness. Joshua noticed that Hadad had scarcely touched his meal. "Is something the matter with your food?" he asked.

"No, nothing. I've eaten my fill, that's all." Hadad turned to Jerimoth, their host, and a smile spread across his handsome face. "I want to thank you again for inviting me tonight. I've never known what it is to be part of a large family, having lived alone with my grandfather most of my life."

"You're always welcome in our home, Hadad, you know that. And now, if you know the words, please sing the closing hymn with us."

Joshua didn't join in with the others as they sang. Instead he watched Hadad carefully, certain that he had something on his mind. Jerimoth ended the Passover celebration with a prayer, and the women left the room to clean up the kitchen and put the sleepy children to bed. Hadad rose to his feet.

"There's something I'd like to say," he began, confirming Joshua's suspicions. All the men turned to Hadad as he expelled the air from his lungs with an uneasy laugh. "Phew! This is worse than going into battle. My stomach feels like I'm back on board the ship that brought us here."

"You're among friends," Jerimoth assured him. "Please, tell us what's on your mind."

Hadad nodded, grinning nervously. "What I want to say is that my life really began a year ago at Passover. Before then I didn't know who I was or what I wanted to do with my life. But ever since our escape from Jerusalem I've finally found meaning and purpose here in Egypt. I enjoy my work at the garrison. Military command suits me, and I think I've finally earned a good name for myself. Now I lack only one thing to make my life complete." His voice grew hushed. "To marry the woman I love. Jerimoth, I'm asking you, as head of this family, for your sister Dinah's hand in marriage."

Hadad's request was so unexpected that it took Joshua a moment to digest it. Hadad couldn't be serious! Surely everyone knew why such a marriage was impossible. But before Joshua could react, Jerimoth's face split into a wide grin as if he was about to accept Hadad's proposal. "My dear friend Hadad, I'd be honored to—"

"Jerimoth, stop!" Joshua sprang to his feet, cutting off his brother's words. "You can't let him marry Dinah!"

"Joshua, if this is a joke—"

"It's not a joke," he told his brother. "I assumed you knew. I assumed all of you knew. . . . Dinah has to marry Prince Amariah."

"What?" Hadad looked as though Joshua had punched him in the stomach. "What are you talking about?"

"Dinah was once part of King Manasseh's harem," Joshua explained. "She bore his son. Now she belongs to the House of David. Anyone who marries her will be challenging Manasseh's right to rule and officially claiming the throne of Judah. She has to marry Prince Amariah."

Hadad's hands knotted into fists. "She isn't a piece of property that gets passed from one man to the next! You can't force Dinah to marry him!"

Joshua took an aggressive stance to match Hadad's. "It's not up to you or me to decide. It's written in God's Law."

"Just a minute," Prince Amariah said, rising from his seat. "Don't I have any say in this?"

"No. You don't," Joshua told him. "God is the one who put royal blood in your veins. This is His plan for revenge. The only choice you have is whether you're going to fight for your father's throne or let Manasseh have it."

"I'm not certain I have a right to my father's throne," Amariah said. "Manasseh is the firstborn and—"

"Manasseh forfeited his right when he committed idolatry," Joshua retorted. "He sacrificed his *own son*! If your father were alive, who do you think he would choose as his successor? You or your brother?"

"I–I see your point." Amariah shrank back, as if fearful of Joshua's anger.

Hadad grabbed the prince's arms. "Amariah, no! Don't listen to him. You're my friend! You know Dinah cares for me, not you. Ask her! Bring her in here and ask her who she wants to marry."

"What she wants doesn't matter," Joshua said.

"It certainly does matter!" Jerimoth told him. "Abba never would have forced Dinah to marry against her will, and neither will we! Of course we'll ask her." He rose and hurried from the room, returning a few minutes later with Dinah in tow. She looked uneasy as she entered the room full of arguing men. Then Joshua saw her expression soften as she looked up at Hadad. Joshua hadn't realized that their feelings for each other had grown since Hadad had helped Dinah escape from Jerusalem a year ago. He should have paid closer attention.

"Dinah, please," Hadad begged. "Tell Joshua how we feel about each other. He's trying to prevent us from being married."

Joshua interrupted before she could reply. He couldn't let her spoil God's flawless plan. "I can see that you have feelings for him, Dinah, but your responsibilities to God and to our family must come first."

"I . . . I don't understand."

He took a step toward her, barely able to control his voice as his anger welled up along with his memories. "Do you remember the night Manasseh's men killed our grandfather in cold blood? Do you remember how helpless you felt because you couldn't fight back? You had to watch them beat a gentle, defenseless old man to death, and you couldn't help him!"

Dinah's hands went to her face. "I'm sorry . . . I couldn't . . ."

"Joshua, stop this!" Jerimoth said.

"No, I won't stop. None of us has spoken to her about Manasseh for almost a year, but our silence doesn't erase what he did. Dinah needs to remember it—all of it—before she decides who she wants to marry." Joshua gripped her wrists and pulled her hands away from her face, forcing her to look at him.

"Manasseh murdered our father, too. Abba did nothing wrong, nothing to deserve execution, but Manasseh lashed his back open with a bone-tipped whip, then pummeled him beyond recognition with his stones."

"*Stop . . . !*" Jerimoth begged. He had witnessed their father's torture, and Joshua knew it was cruel to remind him of it, yet he continued just the same.

"Manasseh raped you, Dinah. He held you captive for a year, and he raped you—how many times? Then he took your newborn son away from you, and he—"

"Enough, Joshua! That's enough!" Jerimoth shouted. "I won't allow this in my house!" His face was white as he pushed Joshua aside and gathered Dinah into his arms. "What are you doing to her? To all of us?"

"I'm reminding her of the facts. If Dinah wants to let Manasseh get away with murder and rape, then she can go ahead and marry Hadad. But if she wants to avenge her son's death—and our father's death and Grandpa's death—then she can fight back by marrying Amariah."

"No," Hadad moaned. "No, don't listen to him, Dinah."

"Look, we all want to fight Manasseh," Jerimoth said. "That's why we're here in Egypt. But we'll fight him by preserving our faith and our heritage. For now, that's all Yahweh has asked us to do. Revenge is God's to repay, not ours."

"And Dinah is God's instrument of revenge," Joshua said, "whether she likes it or not. Why do you think He allowed her to be rescued?"

"But I helped rescue her, remember?" Hadad asked. "She loves me. Tell him, Dinah. Tell him what you already told me."

Joshua watched, ready to intervene, as Dinah turned to Hadad again. "I-I'm sorry," she whispered. "I never should have promised you. . . . Joshua's right. I can't marry you."

"No . . ." Hadad shook his head in stunned disbelief. "No . . . please don't do this, Dinah."

"I do love you," she told him as her tears fell. "But I hate Manasseh even more. He killed my son. I need to marry Prince Amariah."

Hadad closed his eyes. Joshua watched him warily, afraid of what he might do. When Hadad was able to speak again, he faced Joshua, his voice trembling with rage. "I'll kill you for this, Joshua! As God is my witness, you'll pay for what you've done!" He stormed from the house, letting the door slam behind him like an explosion.

Miriam felt the shock waves in the kitchen as Hadad left the house, slamming the door. She had never celebrated the Feast of Passover before and had looked forward to it for weeks. Now the night had ended in ruin. She and the other women had heard every word of the argument, and as soon as Hadad left, Jerusha had taken Dinah to another room to calm her. Miriam knew that Dinah loved Hadad, not the prince, and she hoped Jerusha would talk some sense into her daughter.

Miriam wished she could flee to another room, too, and escape from the men's angry shouts, but she had work to do. She drew a calming breath, then entered the main room to finish clearing the table. She hoped that the argument would end now that Hadad was gone, but Joshua's face was still filled with anger. He stood poised as if for a fight as Jerimoth continued to plead with him.

"Joshua, don't force Dinah and Amariah to marry. It's wrong."

"I'm not forcing them. They're free to make their own decisions." He turned to the prince as if challenging him. "Amariah, did I force you to come with us to Egypt? You aren't naïve; you must have known when you left Jerusalem that siding with me meant fighting Manasseh."

"I don't know what I thought," Amariah mumbled. "I just wanted to get away from my brother. I hated what he was doing, and I wanted no part in it. I never chose to—"

"Did you leave my potsherd with the symbol of the ox where Manasseh would find it?"

"Yes, but—"

"Then you made your decision. You've cast your lot with me, and I'm Manasseh's sworn enemy."

"How has this turned into talk of enemies and hatred?" Jerimoth asked with a groan. "We were celebrating Passover . . . there was a proposal of marriage. . . . Please, Joshua. Let's stop all of this."

Joshua ignored him. Miriam knew that kind, gentle Jerimoth could never hope to win against Joshua's relentless anger. No one could.

"It's up to you, Amariah," Joshua said. "Are you willing to marry our sister or not?"

Miriam stopped stacking the dishes and bowls and looked up. Joshua stood in front of the prince, as if challenging him to a duel, his arms folded defiantly across his chest. Amariah's head was lowered in defeat. Miriam longed to enter the fight, to plead for Hadad's rights and urge the prince to do the same, but she knew her place.

"Dinah is a very beautiful woman," Amariah finally said. "I would have to be a fool to refuse to marry her. But Hadad is my friend. He loves her. I can't do this to him."

"You have to," Joshua said. "It's the Law."

"What law?" Jerimoth asked. "There is no such law."

"Yes! If an older brother dies without an heir, his younger brother must marry his wife in order to provide one. Dinah's first son by Amariah will be considered Manasseh's heir, and heir to the throne."

"But my brother isn't dead."

"He's dead in God's eyes!"

The prince exhaled, shaking his head. "Hadad is my friend," he repeated. "The only reason he got involved in this mess was to help rescue me. He risked his life. He'll never forgive me if I marry the woman he loves. You heard what he said."

Miriam saw the anguish on Amariah's face and looked away. Joshua turned away from him, too. "There are other women for Hadad to marry," he said. "He'll get over her."

"For shame, Joshua!" Jerimoth said. "You of all people should understand how Hadad feels after what happened with you and Yael!"

Miriam watched to see what Joshua's reaction would be to the name of the woman he had once loved and lost, but he had his back turned. It was the first time since they'd moved to Egypt that Miriam had heard anyone dare to mention Yael's name. Everyone who knew Joshua feared his anger, which was always barely contained. They avoided provoking him, keeping their distance from him as if he were a hungry lion on a leash.

When Joshua answered, his voice was as hard as iron. "Yes. I do know how Hadad feels. But I got over it."

"Did you?" Jerimoth asked. "Then why have you refused to discuss any of the offers of betrothal that have been made this past year?"

The news stunned Miriam. Several of the chief elders had visited their house, but Miriam had no idea it was to talk to Joshua about their daughters. It made sense to her now. Joshua governed the island; naturally the elders would seek to promote themselves by marrying into this powerful family. And it underscored the truth that she still struggled to accept: She would never be considered a suitable wife for him. Joshua would never return her love.

"We're discussing Dinah's betrothal, not mine," Joshua said. "What are you going to do, Amariah? You need to decide."

The prince gaped at him. "Now? Tonight? But Hadad—"

"Dinah has already consented to marry *you*, not Hadad."

Jerimoth banged his fist on the table. "Joshua, stop this!" He was usually so soft-spoken. Miriam had never seen him this angry. "Revenge is the wrong reason for two people to be married!"

"It isn't revenge. It's the Law."

"I know the Law as well as you do, and so does the prince. You're twisting it around to suit your own purposes because you're blinded by hatred. And Dinah allowed hatred to color her judgment, too. Please, Your Majesty, don't let Joshua blind you. You'll be making a terrible mistake."

Miriam gathered the last of the dishes, hoping that Joshua and Amariah would both listen to Jerimoth and end this argument. But a moment later she heard Joshua say, "It would be easier on everyone if you had the wedding as soon as possible."

"Are you certain that's what Dinah wants?" Amariah asked.

"She wants another son, a royal heir, and you're the only one who can give it to her. We can arrange the betrothal right now. Miriam, ask Dinah to come here."

Miriam didn't move, hoping the prince would refuse.

"What about a dowry?" Amariah asked. "Don't I have to—?"

"Give me your signet ring as a pledge. Miriam, go get Dinah," he said again.

Miriam hesitated, looking up at the prince to see if that was what he really wanted. Amariah nodded slightly, then bit his lip as he slowly twisted the royal ring from his finger.

"Don't do this," she heard Jerimoth say as she slowly walked from the room. "Take a day or two and think about what you're doing . . . please."

As Miriam approached one of the bedrooms she could hear Jerusha and Dinah talking inside. She knocked on their door. "Dinah?" she called. "Joshua would like to speak with you again."

Dinah appeared calm as she opened the door and returned to the main room with Miriam. Amariah stood waiting for her, holding out a cup of betrothal to her. "I pledge my life to you, Dinah," he said in a shaking voice. "Will you have me?"

Don't do it, Miriam silently pleaded. This wasn't right. Dinah should accept Hadad's proposal, not the prince's. Hadad loved her and she loved him. But Dinah took the cup Amariah offered her and drank from it, then gave it back to him. He drained the remainder. They were betrothed.

Miriam's stomach knotted when she saw the look of satisfaction on Joshua's face. She loved him, but what he had just done was wrong. She left the dishes where they lay and fled to the courtyard behind the house.

Outside, a gentle breeze blew inland from the river, bringing air that was clean and cool, faintly tinged with the aroma of roasted lamb. Miriam inhaled deeply, as if to cleanse away the ugliness of what she had just witnessed. Could it really be God's will for Dinah to marry the prince when she loved Hadad? Joshua had said that the

Law required it, but Lady Jerusha always spoke of God as a loving Father whose laws were just and fair. Tonight Miriam had a hard time understanding why a God of love would force two people to marry this way.

She heard the back door open and turned to see Dinah standing on the step. "I need to ask a favor, Miriam."

"What is it?"

Dinah's eyes filled with tears and for a moment she couldn't speak. For the past few weeks she had seemed so happy, as if the painful memories of her captivity had finally healed. But tonight's events had erased Dinah's joy, and her face wore the same lifeless expression that Joshua's usually did. She moved toward Miriam like a figure in a dream. "Hadad will be waiting for me down by the river. We've been meeting there every night. It probably wasn't proper, but we met the first time by accident and then . . ." She smiled faintly. "And then it got to be a habit."

"Dinah, if you're in love with him, don't—"

"Love doesn't matter. I loved my grandfather, but it was my fault that they murdered him. He wouldn't have known where Joshua was that night if I hadn't told him. And I loved my son, my sweet little Naphtali, but it was my fault that Manasseh killed him, too. I should have tried harder to escape while he was still safe inside me. Now I owe it to both of them and to Abba to avenge all their deaths."

"It seems wrong to marry someone for revenge."

"It isn't revenge. It's the Law."

"But Jerimoth said—"

"I'm going to marry Prince Amariah. Would you please give this back to Hadad for me?" Dinah opened her fist, reluctantly it seemed, and handed Miriam a ring. The smooth metal was warm from Dinah's palm. Miriam remembered the anguish in Hadad's voice as he'd pleaded with Dinah, and Miriam tried to give it back to her.

"This is wrong, Dinah. If you took Hadad's ring, then you made a pledge—"

"I made a mistake. I never should have accepted his ring . . . but it once belonged to my father. He wore it when he was secretary of state. And after Abba was promoted, Hadad's grandfather wore it."

Miriam recognized the symbol of the House of David engraved on the signet ring. The heavy gold shone with a warm glow, like a summer sun behind hazy clouds. She took Dinah's hand in both of hers and tried to push the ring back into it. "Don't do this to Hadad. Don't make him suffer because of King Manasseh's crimes. Hadad risked his life to rescue you, and he's worked so hard ever since we moved here to make a name for himself and be worthy of you."

"That doesn't matter." Dinah's face turned hard and Miriam saw her resolve. "If you won't give it to him, I'll ask a servant to do it."

Miriam knew it would be kinder for Hadad to hear the news from her than from a stranger. She sighed in resignation. "All right . . . I'll do it. But you're making a terrible mistake."

She turned her back on Dinah and strode out through the gate, longing to get this terrible task over with and to get as far away from this house of turmoil as she could. Her steps slowed as she neared the riverbank, following the sound of lapping water. Miriam had lived all her life in dry, arid places, and after nearly a year in Egypt she still hadn't grown tired of the lovely sound. It reminded her of distant laughter. She remembered how their laughter had filled the room tonight as the family shared the Passover feast, until their joy had been shattered when Joshua brought vengeance and hatred into the room.

She was still thinking about Joshua when she looked up and saw someone pacing in the shadows by the water's edge. Miriam recognized Hadad by his broad shoulders and muscular stance. He saw her approaching and ran forward to meet her.

"Dinah?"

"No, Hadad, it's me—Miriam." He stopped short and waited for her to reach him, his arms hanging from his slumped shoulders as if anchored by heavy weights. "Dinah isn't coming," Miriam said.

"Did she send you?"

Miriam nodded. "She asked me to give you this. . . ." She lifted Hadad's fist and gently opened it, laying the ring in his palm. Hadad's knuckles turned white as he squeezed his fingers around the ring, then pressed his fist to his heart.

"How could Joshua do this to us?" He looked up into the black sky, as if pleading with the stars for an answer, his face twisting with pain. "I've been waiting a year to marry Dinah. I fell in love with her when we were trapped inside Asherah's booth, wondering if we were going to live or die.... I haven't known very much love in my life. Dinah was all that I had."

"I'm so sorry," Miriam murmured. "I don't know what to say." She wanted to run far into the night rather than witness Hadad's despair. It was so hard to watch this strong man suffer.

Hadad's voice trembled when he spoke again. "I tried to make something of my life so I'd be worthy of her. I wasn't born with a name, but I earned one ... I *earned* one, Miriam! I worked hard to make this island our home, training the men to be soldiers, helping Joshua and Amariah run this outpost. I considered them my brothers, my friends. But real friends would never do this to someone, would they? They wouldn't take away the only person I've ever loved."

"No, they wouldn't," she said. "What Joshua did was wrong." Hadad's grief forced Miriam to acknowledge Joshua's cruelty. He had betrayed his friend. She loved Joshua, but Miriam realized that while most of the people in their community had been healing from their wounds this past year, Joshua's need for revenge had been growing and festering. Tonight his hatred had hurt three innocent people who loved him. No, four people—because in revealing what was inside his heart, Joshua had hurt Miriam, as well. She couldn't face Hadad.

"I think you should know something else," she said, staring at the ground. "Just before I left the house, Amariah and Dinah sealed their betrothal."

"No ..." Hadad moaned. The night seemed to fall silent for a moment—the whisper of reeds, the chirp of frogs, the hum of insects all hushed in the face of Hadad's grief. Miriam felt as though she had fired a fatal arrow and watched it strike its mark.

"I swear before God, they'll pay for this," he breathed.

"Is that all any of you can think about?" Miriam shouted. She grabbed his arms and tried to shake some sense into him, but he was as immovable as a pillar. "Revenge isn't the answer, Hadad. It's the cause! It will only bring more misery, more pain. This circle has no end!"

He looked down at the ring in his hand, then closed his fingers around it again and drew back his arm to hurl it into the Nile.

"No, don't!" Miriam cried. She lunged to seize his upraised fist, halting his momentum. "Don't do it, Hadad. That ring belonged to your grandfather."

He hesitated a moment, then slowly lowered his arm, gazing into the dark water as if his thoughts were far away. At last he slipped the ring onto his finger.

"Thank you," he whispered. He swiped at his tears with the heel of his hand. "You have a tender heart, Miriam. Don't give it away to someone who doesn't deserve it. Or worse, to someone who will poison it."

Miriam knew that he meant Joshua, and she wondered how he had guessed that she loved him. Was her love that transparent? But before she could speak again, Hadad walked away from her into the night.

2

"THIS IS THE WAY A FESTIVAL should be celebrated," Manasseh said. He lounged on his throne in the Temple courtyard, presiding in splendor over the midnight orgy. His palace administrator, Zerah, sat at his side. Manasseh watched as frenzied worshipers spilled over the edges of the plaza and into the streets below the Temple Mount, dodging animal remains and spirit shrines as they whirled in ecstasy, mumbling spells and incantations. Many of them wore nothing but tattooed symbols and splattered blood, and he wondered how they kept warm on such a chilly spring night.

"Behold our future," Zerah said with his arms spread wide. "The ritual acts performed tonight will ensure plentiful crops and herds in the year to come."

Manasseh watched three young maidens chase a goat that had broken free from its tether. "This is much more to my liking than sitting at a dull dinner table," he said, "eating roast lamb and dredging up stories of the past."

"Nothing will be denied you at this celebration, Your Majesty. Remember, you're free to enjoy everything!"

Manasseh had long grown accustomed to indulging in practices that his Torah instructors used to call perversions. He remembered feeling shocked when Zerah first proposed them a year ago, but now they seemed ordinary, almost boring, and he constantly sought greater thrills. How easy it all had been once he freed himself from the false guilt that the priests had imposed on him, once he recognized that no one had the right to tell him how to live. He alone was responsible for deciding what was right and wrong. "I can't imagine why I ever let anyone tell me what to do," he said.

Zerah smiled. He sliced off another thick chunk of meat from the platter in front of them and fed it to Manasseh. The king sighed with delight. It was cooked the way he liked it, roasted in its own juices, still pink in the middle. He mopped up some of the blood from the platter with his bread.

"It's hard to believe a year has passed," Zerah said, "since the Levites left and the Temple was restored to its rightful priests."

"I don't miss the Levites in the least. Good riddance to them." Manasseh raised his wine goblet in salute, then drained it to the bottom. "Besides, all the property and wealth they left behind has greatly increased my treasury accounts."

"Doesn't it make more sense to worship God in all his many forms—Baal, Asherah, Molech?" Zerah asked.

"I can scarcely recall doing it differently."

As he rose from his seat, Manasseh suddenly remembered that this was also the anniversary of the night Dinah had stabbed him. Horror at his own vulnerability still gripped him whenever he caught a glimpse of the ugly, jagged scar on his stomach. He felt a sudden chill at the thought that he might have died, and he strode across the courtyard to seek the warmth of the bonfire, holding out his hands to the flames. Above him, dark, hulking clouds hung suspended in the sky, blotting the constellations from sight.

"That's how I feel," he mumbled.

Zerah, who had followed him, bent his head closer to hear above the clamor of music and squeals of drunken laughter. "Pardon, Your Majesty?"

"I feel like there's a dark cloud hanging over my head. It's been a year, you know. A full year of not knowing where Joshua is or what he's planning to do next."

Zerah gave a grunt of exasperation. "You shouldn't allow your enemy to rob you of a night of pleasure."

"He's plotting against me, I know he is. He has my brother, the Ark of the Covenant, my concubine . . . What more does he need?"

"We have informants watching all the borders, Your Majesty. We would know about it the moment his forces crossed into Judean territory."

Manasseh gripped Zerah's arm, pulling him closer until their faces were just inches apart. "How? You can't guard every road. And what if he doesn't use the roads? What if he cuts through the Judean wilderness? How are you going to guard against that?"

"We'll know it. The omens will warn us."

"We didn't know it the last time!" He pushed Zerah away again. "Besides, for all we know, my guards might be part of their conspiracy. How did Joshua get past them before? He came right into my palace and left his calling card!"

Zerah spread his hands in a soothing gesture. "You're right. We need an advantage. The gods know everything, Your Majesty, so we will seek their help. Then we'll perform a curse to—"

"Your curses haven't been working."

"Maybe we need stronger, more powerful magic on our side." Zerah's close-set eyes narrowed in thought. Manasseh knew the look. He was measuring his words, searching for a way to propose something shocking. "There are deeper levels of sorcery, Your Majesty. I know their mysteries . . . but I'm not certain you're ready for them."

Fear crawled up Manasseh's spine. The spirits Zerah already had conjured up for him seemed powerful and barely under the priest's control. Manasseh could scarcely imagine even deeper levels of witchcraft. But he couldn't deny the spirits' power or his own fascination with it. He would do anything to defeat Joshua.

"I'm ready," Manasseh said. "Tell me how and when."

Dinah sat in the courtyard of her home, surrounded by her bridesmaids, waiting for her groom, Prince Amariah, to appear. Their wedding had all the trappings that Dinah had dreamed about as a girl, yet she was barely able to hold back her tears. This wasn't a celebration but a somber, joyless affair. Each time she glanced at her mother or her brother Jerimoth, she saw dismay and disapproval in their averted eyes and lowered heads. They had tried to talk Dinah out of marrying Amariah right up until the moment she had dressed in her finest gown.

"This marriage won't change anything," Jerusha had said, pleading with her. "It won't bring any of our loved ones back."

"Manasseh has to pay for what he did," Dinah insisted.

"Then let God avenge his crimes," Jerimoth said. "He's the Judge of all the earth."

"Leave her alone," Joshua said. "This *is* God's plan for vengeance." He was the only one who supported Dinah's decision, and he had set all these plans in motion. But now that the day had finally arrived, Joshua didn't seem very joyful, either. He was continually on edge, and Dinah knew he was watching for Hadad, worrying about the threats he had made.

"I have soldiers guarding all the docks in case he tries to return to the island," Joshua told her.

"I'm not going to change my mind," she assured him, "even if Hadad does come back." Each time she'd thought of Hadad, Dinah had nearly lost her nerve, wondering how she could live the rest of her life without the man she loved. But then she would force herself to relive each moment of her year with Manasseh, remembering how his soldiers had beaten her grandfather to death, picturing her son's tiny face. She resolved to pledge her life to Manasseh's brother in revenge.

The evening air felt warm as Dinah waited, the sky above the courtyard dotted with the first few stars. Suddenly a shout went up. "The bridegroom comes!" She saw torches bobbing and heard the music of flutes and tambourines as Amariah's procession arrived at her gate. Dinah lowered the veil over her face, thankful that it would also hide her tears. She thought of King Manasseh as she watched his brother enter the torchlit courtyard. Prince Amariah slowly walked across the cobblestones and stopped in front of her chair. He looked pale and somber, not at all like a joyful, expectant groom. He reached for her hand and drew her to her feet. Dinah's knees shook as she looked up at him.

Amariah was so tall he towered above her. He was more than a head taller than Manasseh, half a head taller than Hadad. King Manasseh had been compact and sinewy, Hadad brawny and muscular. But Amariah was lanky and awkward, unsure of himself, and not nearly as good-looking as either of the other two men. Nothing about him stood out as extraordinary. His hair and beard didn't have quite enough copper in them to be auburn, his eyes were an undistinguished hazel. Dinah felt nothing toward him except a faint loathing for reminding her of Manasseh.

As she stood beneath the wedding canopy beside him, Dinah glanced at the courtyard gates one last time, searching for Hadad, wondering if he would force his way past the guards and carry her away. Hadad was a skilled warrior; Amariah would never be able to stop him if Hadad decided to fight for her. Joshua probably couldn't win against him, either. But Hadad didn't come to her rescue.

Dinah brought her attention back to the ceremony and dutifully recited her wedding vows. Then it was over. She was Amariah's wife.

All of Elephantine Island's most important families had been invited to the marriage supper, held in the courtyard of the home Prince Amariah had prepared for her. The feasting and music and laughter lasted long into the night, but Dinah enjoyed none of it. She found herself dreading the moment her husband would take her to their marriage chamber. She wondered if she could go through with it.

Finally Amariah stood and reached for her hand. Dinah's legs felt heavy and leaden as she allowed him to lead her to their bridal chamber. The sounds of the marriage supper faded in the distance as Amariah closed the door behind them. As she smelled the fragrant aroma of perfumed sheets and remembered her nights in Manasseh's bedchamber, panic welled up inside her until she could scarcely breathe.

"You are a beautiful bride, Dinah," Amariah said. The sound of his voice, so different from his brother's, brought her back to the present.

"Thank you, my lord." Gradually, her panic subsided as she remembered what Joshua had told her: She would have another son; she was doing God's will. She looked up into Amariah's eyes. They were wide and long-lashed like Manasseh's and nearly the same color, but they lacked his startling flashes of topaz; they also lacked his glint of cruelty. She thought of Hadad's eyes—deep, vivid brown like rich loam—and remembered the love she had seen reflected in them. Then she remembered the pain that had replaced it, pain she had caused. Tears came to her eyes.

"It's not too late to change your mind," Amariah said softly. He had been studying her, as well. "We don't have to go through with this."

She brushed away her tears. "I haven't changed my mind."

"What's wrong, then?"

"I . . . I'm just so sorry that I had to hurt Hadad."

"I know. I am, too." He folded his arms across his chest awkwardly, as if he didn't know what else to do with them. She had expected him to embrace her, but he hesitated. They were both silent for a moment. Dinah could hear the distant strains of music from the wedding feast and the swish of palm branches against the window shutters.

"I've been thinking about both of our fathers all day," Amariah said. "Your father raised me after mine died. I loved him and Abba both." He leaned against the door and sighed. "Joshua is convinced that this is what they would have wanted—that it's what they would have expected us to do. But I'm still not sure. I never wanted to be king, you know. I still don't."

"Then why did you agree to marry me?"

"Joshua said it was what you wanted, and I . . . I wanted to make it up to you, somehow . . . for what Manasseh did to you."

"What your brother did wasn't your fault. There wasn't anything you could have done."

"I'm not sure that's true, because I didn't even try." He unfolded his arms, gesturing fervently as if his hands could convey his feelings better than mere words. She noticed that he had graceful, artistic hands with long, slender fingers. "I should have done something to stop Manasseh from killing your father and Rabbi Isaiah. They didn't even get a fair trial. And when Manasseh started worshiping all those idols, I should have known where it would all lead. I should have tried to save your son. I'm sorry." He folded his arms again as if in defeat, tucking his hands out of sight.

"I blame myself, not you," she said, but he didn't seem to hear her.

"I want to make it up to you, Dinah . . . and so if I can give you another child, an heir to David's throne like your first son, then that's what I want to do."

His unselfishness touched her. But in spite of the bond of guilt they shared, in spite of the matching wounds Manasseh had inflicted on each of them, she didn't love Amariah. She doubted if she ever would. Dinah was barely twenty years old, Amariah twenty-one. They might be married to each other for a long time. The thought of all those empty years stretching ahead of them exhausted her.

Every moment she had spent with Hadad had seemed charged with energy and excitement, making Dinah feel breathless and alive. She smiled, remembering his broad, handsome face and dazzling smile. He was her savior, strong and vigorous yet surprisingly tender. An angel, she had told him, sent by God to rescue her.

"It's still not too late," Amariah said softly. "Our marriage isn't official . . . until we . . ."

But Dinah knew that it was too late. Hadad was gone. She needed to focus instead on Manasseh—on her need for revenge. She took a step closer to Amariah. "We're doing the right thing," she said. "Neither of us was able to stop Manasseh. Now we're finally fighting back."

Amariah nodded and carefully drew her into his arms. His embrace felt formal and unnatural. She remembered how comfortable she had felt in Hadad's brawny arms, held against his broad, solid chest.

Finally Amariah bent to kiss her. Dinah glimpsed the deep sorrow in his eyes before he closed them and wondered if it mirrored her own.

3

JOSHUA PACED RESTLESSLY IN THE COURTYARD of the military outpost, waiting for the recruits to assemble for their training in hand-to-hand combat. He seemed to spend far too much of his time in limbo—waiting for Amariah to reach a decision, waiting for these young men to solidify into a fighting force, waiting for God's signal that the day of His revenge against King Manasseh had finally arrived.

"Come on, let's go! Take your places!" he shouted. The recruits moved lethargically in the morning heat. It was well before noon, but the sun already felt hot on Joshua's back, the desert breeze moving across his bare arms and legs like warm water.

A few weeks ago it had been Hadad's job to instruct these men, but after he'd disappeared, the task had fallen to Joshua. He felt no satisfaction in the knowledge that the men looked up to him or had named their regiment in his honor. He wasn't as patient with them as Hadad had been, and the setbacks they'd experienced after the change in leadership frustrated him. He gazed at the row of straw practice dummies in front of him and saw that someone had sketched an ox on one of the dummies' tunics, over the place where the heart would be. He glanced at the gate one last time, wishing that Hadad would miraculously appear and take over this job, yet he feared the terrible consequences if he did return.

Joshua straightened his shoulders and faced the assembled men. It seemed a lifetime ago that he and Manasseh had trained together like this, and he recalled how much he had hated his own military training. He removed his dagger from its sheath and repeated the words his instructors had once taught him. "Your point of entry is below your enemy's rib cage, left-hand side. Put all your weight behind the knife, not just your arm muscles." The straw crunched as Joshua plunged his knife into the dummy to demonstrate. "Stab in, then twist up to pierce—"

Without warning, the terror-filled eyes of the young guard Joshua had stabbed to death reappeared in his mind. A shudder rocked through him. He released the knife as if it had just emerged from a forge, and stared at his hand as if expecting to see blood. The young soldiers watching him grew utterly still.

He cleared his throat, but his voice still sounded strangled when he spoke. "You twist up to . . . to pierce your enemy's heart." He gazed into the distance above their heads, afraid to look at them, afraid to see that they were the same age as the guard he had killed. The boy wouldn't have died if Joshua had remembered to disarm him. Joshua struggled against narrowing air passages to draw a breath. The air wheezed through his lungs when he spoke.

"Have any of you ever killed a man?" he asked, still gazing past them. "No, of course you haven't. . . . It's not—" Joshua shuddered again as he relived the moment that the second guard ran his sword through Maki's body. "It's . . . it's not . . ."

He closed his eyes. It was his fault that Maki had died. Joshua had blundered out of the house too soon. He had no memory of killing the second guard in retaliation, but he would never forget what the man's body had looked like after he'd hacked him to death. "God forgive me," he murmured. He felt the silent scrutiny of his men. He was their hero, the leader who had orchestrated their deliverance from Judah. His present behavior must appear strange to them. He cleared his throat again.

"Killing a man isn't the same as stabbing a sack of straw," he said at last. "For one thing, there will be blood—more than you can imagine. And it's warm. . . . It never occurred to me that blood would be so warm. . . ."

He had to get a hold of himself, get on with the exercises. He shook his head. "But when you're in combat, you will either kill or be killed. You'll do what you need to do." He yanked his knife from the straw and slipped it into the sheath at his belt, angry with himself for sounding so apologetic. "Go ahead, start practicing."

Joshua stood back, still shaken, and watched the recruits attack the straw dummies. The familiar sounds transported him to Jerusalem, and for a moment he was training with General Benjamin again in the courtyard outside the palace. He recalled Manasseh's steely concentration as he attacked the straw figures, the gleam of zeal in his eyes.

"Whose face do you see on that straw man that makes you so eager to kill him?" Joshua had once asked him. Manasseh had glared at him without answering.

Joshua had grimly endured his own military training, always eager to return to his academic studies. But Manasseh had reveled in their combat sessions, quickly surpassing Joshua in skill and speed. If they were to fight hand-to-hand now, if Joshua's rage overpowered him again, he wondered which of them would win.

"Joshua . . . Excuse me, Joshua?"

He returned to the present with a jolt, surprised to see one of the city scribes standing in front of him. How long had the man been waiting?

"I'm sorry. Did you need me for something?" Joshua asked.

"The city elders want to speak with you right away. Can you come?"

Joshua placed one of the older recruits in charge of the exercises and followed the scribe to the square where the elders met to dispense justice. It wasn't unusual for them to call for Joshua, often sending for him when they were unable to reach a decision. But as he approached he was surprised to see Miriam's ten-year-old brother, Nathan, standing in the center of the group. A guard held the boy's thin arms pinned behind his back, but Nathan's chin was raised in stubborn contempt.

"What's going on?" Joshua asked.

"We're sorry to disturb you," the chief elder said, "but you're the boy's legal guardian, aren't you?"

"Yes.... Is there a problem?"

"I'm afraid so. One of the vendors in the marketplace caught him stealing. He ran off with about twenty shekels of silver."

White-hot anger rushed through Joshua. He grabbed Nathan's bony shoulders and shook him slightly. "Is this true, Nathan?" Nathan stared defiantly at Joshua without answering. "I asked you a question. Answer me!"

Nathan's eyes narrowed with cool disdain. "Make me."

Joshua raised his hand to slap him, then stopped himself in time. Nathan's disrespect was shameful, but Joshua didn't want to make things worse by losing his temper. Then another thought occurred to him. "Why aren't you in school, studying with the rabbi?"

When Nathan gave a snort of contempt and spat on the ground, it took every ounce of restraint Joshua had to keep from striking him. He turned, instead, to one of the elders.

"Please tell Nathan the punishment for stealing."

"It's fifteen lashes."

"Fifteen lashes, Nathan. Are you going to answer my questions, or shall I assume by your silence that you're guilty and let the elders flog you?"

The boy folded his arms across his chest and raised his chin to stare Joshua in the face. "Why don't you flog me yourself?"

At that moment, Joshua was angry enough to do it. Nathan was humiliating him, challenging his authority in front of the city elders. Joshua was the second-ranking official of this island community; how would it look if he couldn't control a skinny ten-year-old boy? His jaw clenched in anger.

"Is there proof of his guilt?" he asked the elders.

"Yes, there were several witnesses."

"Did the vendor get his silver back?"

The chief elder held up a leather pouch. "It was all here when they caught the boy."

"Then if you'll agree to release him into my custody, I'll see that he is properly punished."

"That's fine with us, my lord." The elders seemed relieved that they wouldn't have to deal with Nathan. Joshua grabbed the boy by the back of his tunic and hauled him away. He wanted to take him someplace where no one could overhear them—and where Nathan's disrespect couldn't further humiliate him. He marched Nathan to the pits outside the village where the laborers mixed mud and straw to make bricks. It was approaching the hottest hour of the day, and the area was deserted as the workers took their break. Joshua pushed Nathan down on a bale of straw and stood over him, his hands on his hips.

"What do you have to say for yourself?"

Nathan said nothing.

"You'd better start talking or—"

"Or what?" When Nathan lifted his chin with a sneer of defiance, Joshua slapped him, unable to tolerate any more of the boy's contempt. Nathan grinned. "It takes a big, tough man to hit a defenseless kid, doesn't it?"

Joshua stared at the red mark he had made on Nathan's cheek and battled to keep his rage under control. For some reason, Nathan seemed to want him to lose his temper.

"You deserve a lot more than a slap," Joshua said. "You owe me for what you did today. You owe me an explanation and an apology."

Nathan sprang to his feet. "I don't owe you anything!"

Joshua pushed him down again. "You were nothing but a worthless thief when I took you in, and in spite of all the breaks you've been given, it seems that you're still a worthless thief. I fed you, tried to educate you, made you part of my family—and look how you've shown your gratitude: you skip classes, rob vendors in broad daylight, humiliate me in public. After everything I've done for you."

"I never asked you to do any of it!"

"No? Then why didn't you leave two years ago? Why stay under my roof? Why accept the food and the clothing I've given you?"

"Because I had no place else to go, thanks to you."

"Thanks to *me*?"

"You're the wanted criminal, not me. If it hadn't been for you, I'd still be living in Jerusalem, not on this filthy rathole of an island in the middle of nowhere!"

"You call this a rathole? I guess you've forgotten what your house in Jerusalem looked like? Or how your own mother treated you?"

"It was better than this! You treat my sister and me like the dirt beneath your feet!"

Nathan's words stunned Joshua. "How can you say that?"

"Because it's the truth! The only reason you gave Miriam and me a home in the first place was because you killed her father."

Joshua went cold all over. "What did you say?"

"I know what really happened to Maki. Mattan told me. It was *your* fault that the soldier killed him. You ran out of the door and opened your big fat mouth too soon."

Joshua stared at Nathan, too stunned to speak. It was true—Maki's death was Joshua's fault. But he'd never imagined that anyone else knew the truth.

"Everyone around here thinks you're such a big hero," Nathan continued. "But I wonder what they'd say if they knew the truth. If they knew that Maki died because you screwed up!"

Joshua grabbed Nathan by his upper arms and lifted him off the ground, shaking him. "Shut up, you little—!"

"Go ahead, hit me. I dare you. When they ask me about the bruises, I'll tell Miriam and everyone else what really happened to her father."

Joshua's entire body trembled. He released Nathan, then turned and quickly strode away, well aware of what he might do to the boy if he lost control. He headed blindly toward the riverbank, then stumbled aimlessly around the deserted docks, trying not to imagine what would happen to his reputation if Nathan carried out his threat.

Joshua told himself to stay calm. He could easily explain about Maki. He'd made an honest mistake in a moment of panic. He had been upset after killing the first guard because he had never killed anyone before. He had overreacted when he saw that the second guard had caught little Mattan. But even as Joshua replayed the events in his mind, he knew his excuses would sound feeble after so much time had passed. He would risk losing the entire community's respect for not confessing right away as he should have, instead of waiting two years. They might wonder what else he was hiding.

And the men might be reluctant to follow his leadership, afraid that he'd panic again in the heat of battle and cost someone else his life.

Sweat soaked Joshua's clothes, but he knew it wasn't from the sun's heat. He walked for a long time, wandering blindly around the island until he ended up back at the mud pits, where he'd started. Nathan was gone, but the workers had returned to their labors, standing knee-deep in ooze as they mixed mud and straw with their bare feet.

The only way to save his reputation, Joshua decided, was to win back Nathan's trust and friendship. But how could he do that? Joshua didn't know anything about raising a son. He never should have agreed to adopt Nathan in the first place. He should have let his brother, Jerimoth, assume responsibility for Nathan as he had for Miriam's younger brother, Mattan. Now it was too late.

Not knowing what else to do, Joshua headed for the market square to ask Jerimoth's advice. He found his brother in his booth bargaining with a customer over the price of a bolt of cloth. Joshua ducked beneath the welcome shade of the canopy and waited for the men to finish their haggling.

"I need some advice," Joshua said when the customer was gone. "I'm having problems with Nathan, and I need to know how you handle Mattan."

Jerimoth pulled up two rush-bottomed stools and motioned for Joshua to sit. "It's no mystery," he said. "Whenever I'm stuck, I simply ask myself what Abba would do."

His words made Joshua feel worse. Abba wouldn't have lost his temper. He wouldn't have slapped Nathan or threatened him. Joshua remembered how he and Manasseh had once skipped classes to go for a walk in the rain. Afterward, he had experienced Abba's deep disappointment but not his anger. His father had never struck Joshua in his life. He gave a sigh of frustration.

"I'm not very good at being a father."

Jerimoth motioned to the seat a second time. "Sit. Tell me what happened."

Joshua didn't realize how drained he felt until he sank onto the stool. Jerimoth handed him a skin of water, and Joshua took a long drink, wiping his mouth with his fist.

"The elders called me to the square a while ago," he began. "They caught Nathan stealing. He's been skipping classes, too."

"What did you do?"

"I tried to question him, reprimand him.... But he was so rude to me, so disrespectful. And I don't understand why. After all that I've done for that kid! I've given him everything—"

"Except yourself."

Joshua felt his temper flare. "I'm a very busy man, Jerimoth. I'm responsible for everyone on this island."

"Exactly."

"So you're saying Nathan's behavior is my fault?"

"No, I'm saying that because you've been too busy to be a father to him, maybe this is his way of getting your attention."

"By humiliating me in front of the city elders?"

"Did it work? Did he get your attention?"

"Yeah, I guess he did," he said with a sigh. "But some of the things Nathan said to me . . . and the way he said them . . . it was as if he hates me."

"Were you loving in return? Remember, 'Better a patient man than a warrior, a man who controls his temper than one who takes a city.'"

Joshua shook his head dismally. "No, I lost my temper and slapped him." The memory shamed him, even though Nathan had deserved it. He looked up at his brother again. "Now what? Where do I go from here? To tell you the truth, I'm so disgusted with the kid, I can't even stand to look at him. There's nothing worse than a thief and a liar."

"What did he lie about?"

Joshua realized that Nathan hadn't lied. But if the boy decided to tell everyone the truth about Maki, Joshua would have to accuse him of lying in order to save his own reputation. Then he remembered that Mattan also knew the truth—and Mattan was Jerimoth's adopted son. Something cold writhed through Joshua's stomach as he saw the web of lies that threatened to ensnare him.

"Nathan refused to admit that he stole the silver," he said at last. "But he didn't deny it, either. There were too many witnesses. And he wasn't repentant at all. He wouldn't offer an excuse or an apology."

Jerimoth exhaled. "Look, Josh. Why don't you try to spend a little more time with him? Take him to work with you. Ask him what he wants to do with his life if he isn't interested in studying with the Levites."

"It's not that easy! It's . . . it's not! He's a difficult kid. So insolent and—"

"You almost sound like you're afraid of him."

Joshua looked away. He *was* afraid of Nathan—afraid he would expose the truth.

"He's a ten-year-old boy," Jerimoth continued. "He simply needs a little attention, that's all."

"Yeah . . . I guess you're right," Joshua mumbled. "Thanks for your time. I should go."

He stopped at Nathan's school on the way home and learned more bad news. Nathan was insolent toward his instructors, undisciplined in his studies. He seldom completed his work and often skipped class. But Joshua had no idea how to punish Nathan for this behavior without running the risk that the boy would retaliate.

When Joshua finally arrived home that night, he approached Miriam warily, worried that Nathan had decided to tell her the truth about her father's death. But Miriam acted no differently than usual toward him, and he guessed that Nathan hadn't carried out his threat—yet. He would likely dangle his knowledge of how Maki had died over Joshua's head as long as he could in order to get away with even more. The fear of blackmail made Joshua desperate to make peace with the boy at all costs.

"Have you seen Nathan?" he asked Miriam.

"He's out back in the courtyard." Miriam stopped Joshua as he headed toward the door. "Did something happen today? Is Nathan in some kind of trouble? He seemed upset when he came home, but he wouldn't tell me what was wrong."

"I'll talk to him." Joshua knew he hadn't answered Miriam's question, and he hated himself for being a coward, for valuing his reputation above the truth. It chilled him to think that once he started lying he would have to tell more lies and half-truths to conceal the first one.

He found Nathan sitting on a bench outside the door, carving a chunk of wood with a knife. The boy was very clever with his hands, shaving the soft wood in even, graceful strokes. Joshua sat down on the back step opposite him and watched him work for a few minutes. But when he recognized the head of a hippopotamus taking shape beneath Nathan's fingers, his anger rekindled. The boy knew that the Torah forbade him to make an image of any living thing. What was he doing? Joshua saw Nathan's concentration, the loving care he gave each stroke of the knife, and he barely restrained his temper, certain that Nathan was making the image to spite him. Finally, he could no longer hold back his words.

"Nathan . . ." The boy continued to whittle without responding or looking up. "Nathan, look at me." When he did, Joshua saw contempt in his eyes. Nathan knew he had the upper hand. Joshua reminded himself that he had come to make amends, not start another confrontation. "We need to talk about what happened today."

Nathan looked down again and resumed his work. But when he turned the wood over to carve the other side, Joshua was shocked to see that the figure had the body of a woman, the hands and feet of a lion. It was the Egyptian goddess Taweret. He gritted his teeth, furious with the boy's audacity.

"Have the rabbis taught you the Ten Commandments, Nathan?"

"Yeah, they taught me."

"Then you know that the second commandment forbids us to worship idols."

"I'm not worshiping this, am I?" Nathan spat out each word.

It was all Joshua could do to keep from striking him again. He tried to decide what his own father would do, but he couldn't even imagine it. No one in his family had ever been so disrespectful and rebellious. In one swift move, Joshua grabbed the wood and the knife out of Nathan's hands, startling him.

"Hey! Give those back!"

"You can't carve idols, Nathan. And you can't steal, and you can't defy me as you've been doing. I'll have to punish you for all three things. But that's not why I came out here." He drew a deep breath, swallowing back his anger. "I came to apologize to you." Nathan stared, his mouth open in surprise. "I'm sorry that I haven't spent very much time with you like a . . . like a father should." As soon as he said the words, Joshua realized that he didn't think of himself as Nathan's father. He didn't want to be "Abba" to him the way Jerimoth was to Mattan. Or the way his own father had been. Undoubtedly, Nathan knew it, too.

"I don't need a father. I can take care of myself."

"Well, too bad. You're stuck with me." When Nathan made a face, Joshua threw down the wood and grabbed Nathan's chin in his hand. "No more of that, Nathan! You will treat me with respect, understand?"

For the first time, the boy showed a ripple of fear. He nodded slightly, and Joshua released him.

"I talked to the rabbi today. He said you've been missing a lot of classes lately. Want to tell me why?"

"Because I hate it. I don't need to learn all those stupid laws and things."

"Do you plan on making a living by stealing for the rest your life?"

"I'm going to be a soldier."

"You will be one when you're old enough, but in the meantime you're going to study the Law with the rabbis like I did." Joshua regretted his harsh tone the moment he'd spoken. It wasn't the way his father would have said it. He saw rebellion flare in Nathan's eyes.

"You can't make me!"

"Yes I can." He drew a deep breath. "But I'm not going to force you." Again, he saw surprise on Nathan's face. "If you want, you can come to the building site with me after your lessons. We've almost finished preparing the courtyard for the sacrifices and—"

"I don't care about the stupid sacrifices, either."

Joshua reached the end of his patience. He couldn't befriend this little brat. He didn't even want to try. He stood and turned to leave. "If that's the way you want it, Nathan, fine. Since you don't want me to be a father to you, and you don't want to study, then you can go work for a living and pay me for your room and board."

"I'll tell Miriam and everyone else how you—"

He whirled around and gripped Nathan's shoulders, hard enough to bruise him and, he hoped, hard enough to scare him. "Go ahead. Just try it. Who do you think they'll believe—a respected official like me or a dirty little thief like you?"

"They may not believe me, but they'll believe Mattan."

He released Nathan, fear crawling all over Joshua at the thought of everything he could lose. In his desperation, he could think of only one way to silence Nathan's threats and save himself. He scooped up the idol and hurried into the house, quickly gathering Nathan's meager belongings.

"What are you doing? What's going on?" Miriam asked as she watched him. He didn't reply. When he finished tying Nathan's things in a bundle, he carried them across the courtyard to Jerimoth's house and thrust the idol Nathan had made into his brother's hands.

"Nathan carved this. It's the Egyptian goddess Taweret." Jerimoth stared, open-mouthed. "I'm taking Nathan to the mainland to live with the Egyptians," Joshua told him.

"Wait . . . you can't just drop the child on the mainland and forget about him!"

"I know that," Joshua said, even though it was exactly what he longed to do. "I know an Egyptian man who operates a forge over there. We get some of our equipment from him. I'm going to arrange an apprenticeship for Nathan with him."

"Joshua, he's only a boy. . . ."

"A boy who carves idols!" he shouted, gesturing to the figure in Jerimoth's hands. "We can't tolerate an idolater living under our roof."

4

As soon as Hadad crossed the border into Judah, he felt a rush of emotion that was soul-deep. He was home. He hadn't realized how much he'd missed Judah's rolling green hills and rock-strewn valleys until he was gazing at them once again.

Everything looked so wonderfully familiar—and yet so very different. The farther he journeyed into his country's heartland, the more changes he noticed. Roadside shrines now dotted the road to Jerusalem, piled with offerings to the Baals, the carved idols draped with charms and amulets. Every hill he passed seemed to have become a high place with a sacred grove and Asherah poles and altars to the starry hosts. In one village Hadad saw the townspeople gathered to dedicate a new building, and he watched in horror as the remains of a sacrificed child were enshrined in one wall to ensure prosperity. Hadad had never been very religious, but this wickedness appalled him. It had happened so fast. And it was so widespread.

He ate his evening meal at an inn in Beth Shemesh, but he had made up his mind not to spend the night within the walled city. When he rose to leave, the owner stopped him, urging him to stay. "The roads aren't safe to travel after dark," he told Hadad.

"There are still a few hours of twilight, and I need to go a little farther. I don't mind sleeping in a barn if I have to."

"You'll find no place to stay in the countryside," the innkeeper warned. "Judean farmers no longer extend hospitality to passing strangers. They'll run you off with threats and curses . . . or worse."

Hadad wondered if the man was telling the truth or trying to gain his business. "What would they have to fear from me?" he asked.

"They fear the night, and if you're smart, you will, too. You'll risk the worst sort of assault if you sleep anywhere except behind a locked door at night. That's when the worship at the shrines takes place." Hadad gazed at him blankly. "The male shrine prostitutes," the man said in a whisper. "Believe me, you don't want to be out there after dark."

"If Judah is so unsafe, why doesn't the king do something about it?"

The innkeeper gave a snort of laughter. "Who do you think is behind it all? Listen, I'm warning you for your own good—wait until tomorrow to finish your journey."

"But tomorrow is the Sabbath. I won't be able to travel on that day."

"How long have you been away from Judah?" the man asked, eyeing Hadad curiously. "The Sabbath laws haven't been enforced for more than a year."

In the end, Hadad took the man's advice and spent the night at the inn. His goal was much too important to jeopardize by taking foolish risks. He arrived in Jerusalem on the Sabbath and saw that the innkeeper had told the truth. The city gates stood wide open to trade and travel, and merchants and shoppers crowded the streets, buying and selling goods. It might have been any other day of the week. Hadad was glad he wouldn't be delayed, eager to finish what he had come to do.

He walked straight up the hill to the king's palace, where he'd once lived with his grandfather, but Hadad barely recognized his former home. King Manasseh had constructed so many barricades, it resembled a fortress. Hadad couldn't get past the first gate without submitting to a thorough search.

"State your name and your business," the guard demanded.

"I'd like an audience with King Manasseh." The guard laughed and would have quickly turned him away, but Hadad knew how to gain entrance. He held out his fist, displaying his grandfather's signet ring with the emblem of the House of David. The guards let him pass to someone higher in authority. Hadad did the same with each new official he faced, refusing to give his name or state his business, displaying his ring and demanding an audience with the king.

At last he stood before Lord Zerah, the palace administrator—a stranger wearing Lord Eliakim's sash, keys, and signet ring—the second-highest official in the nation. Hadad had known most of King Manasseh's nobles and officials, but he'd never seen this man before. His close-set eyes beneath sharply peaked brows made him look cross-eyed.

"I want an audience with King Manasseh," Hadad said.

"First tell me who you are and what your petition is."

"My name is Hadad." He pulled his grandfather's ring from his finger and handed it to Zerah. "Give this to the king. It will tell him who I am. I've come to discuss his enemy, Joshua ben Eliakim."

Lord Zerah disappeared with the ring, and while Hadad waited, surrounded by four palace guards, he searched in vain for a reminder of the home he'd once known. The palace he remembered had been filled with sunlight and mountain air and the constant bustle of activity. But now, with so many of the windows and doorways boarded, it was a place of darkened hallways and trapped smells. When a chamberlain finally summoned him, Hadad wasn't ushered into the throne room, as he'd expected, but into the private chambers he had once shared with his grandfather.

Hadad's throat tightened until he could scarcely swallow as memories of Shebna washed over him. He recalled his grandfather's crisp, accented voice; the way he stood with arms akimbo; the proud way he walked, head held high. Manasseh and the cross-eyed administrator sat watching Hadad, the guards hovering close.

"Where did you get this ring?" Manasseh asked. He toyed with it, tossing it lightly into the air and catching it again.

Hadad cleared his throat. "It belonged to my grandfather, Lord Shebna. He was King Hezekiah's secretary of state—as well as yours. We lived in these rooms."

Manasseh studied him like a cat watching a mouse, then

abruptly tossed the ring to him. Hadad caught it in his fist and slipped it onto his finger.

"I remember you, Hadad. You studied with my brother Amariah."

"That's right."

"When you and your grandfather vanished into the night a few years ago, I was forced to conclude that you were also part of Eliakim's conspiracy."

Hadad shook his head. "My grandfather was never a traitor, just wise enough to leave the country and avoid arrest. I went with him."

"Where have you been hiding all this time?"

Hadad quickly grew impatient. After the long journey, the endless waiting, and the innumerable searches, he wanted to get down to business. "What difference does it make where I've been? I'm back now. Don't you want to know why?"

Manasseh's strange eyes flared like a bonfire, and the guards on either side of Hadad gripped his arms. "Where is your traitorous grandfather?"

Hadad forced himself to be patient. "My grandfather died of a stroke shortly after we left Jerusalem."

"Can you prove that you and Shebna weren't involved in Isaiah's plot?"

"Can you prove that we were?"

Manasseh gripped the armrests as he bristled with anger. The palace administrator covered the king's hand with his own, caressing it to soothe him. A shiver ran down Hadad's spine at their casual intimacy. These were evil men. There were no other words to describe them. Hadad understood why Prince Amariah had been so anxious to flee his brother's palace. He also knew he had found the source of the moral decline he had witnessed throughout Judah.

Manasseh looked the same—handsome chiseled features, eerie golden eyes, hard muscles beneath his tunic. Yet he appeared totally different—unpredictable, unstable, with a gleam of crazed madness in his eye. He sat forward in his seat, as if poised to spring from it and tear open Hadad's throat.

"What do you want, Hadad?"

"Nothing. But I have something you want very badly." He waited, forcing Manasseh to ask.

"And what is that?"

"Joshua ben Eliakim."

Manasseh's eyes flamed again. "I'm listening."

"I know where he is. And where your brother Amariah is, as well. I can deliver them both to you."

"Where? How?"

"They're in hiding at the moment, but Joshua would return to Judah in a heartbeat if he thought there was a chance to assassinate you. If you lay a trap, I'll convince him to walk into it."

Manasseh's eyes seemed to bore through Hadad. "How do I know you weren't sent by Joshua to lay a trap for me?"

"You won't even have to leave your palace. Stay here with all your bodyguards. Send a decoy in your place."

Manasseh leaned back in his chair, silently stroking his beard. "What do you think, Zerah?" he asked.

The palace administrator had been watching King Manasseh's every move with fascination, but now he turned his gaze to Hadad. "What's in it for you?" Zerah asked. "What do you want out of this deal?"

The question of payment had never occurred to Hadad. He still had plenty of gold from his grandfather. And he certainly didn't want a position of power in Manasseh's evil government. His reward would be Dinah. She was the only prize he coveted. But Hadad would never tell King Manasseh the truth. Dinah had once been the king's concubine.

"Revenge," he said quietly. "Same as you. I want to watch Joshua die."

"If you know where he is, then why don't you kill him yourself?"

Indeed, why not? Joshua wasn't surrounded by dozens of guards, as Manasseh was. Hadad could easily slip onto the island after dark and kill both Joshua and Amariah while they slept, then escape with Dinah. Instead, he had come to Jerusalem.

"Because it would be too easy, too merciful to kill him myself," Hadad finally replied. Anger and passion made his voice quiver.

"You'll make him suffer, King Manasseh. Joshua hates you with every ounce of strength he has. The knowledge that you won, that he died by your hands, will torture him more than I ever could." Hadad curled his hands into fists. He felt the guards tighten their grip on his arms as his muscles flexed.

"Why do you hate Joshua?" Manasseh asked.

"He stole something that belonged to me."

"What did he take?"

Hadad clenched his jaw, remembering. "Do you want me to deliver him to you, or don't you?"

"What about my concubine? He has Dinah, too, doesn't he? I want her back, as well."

Hadad hadn't expected Manasseh to ask for Dinah. According to Hadad's plan, Joshua and Amariah would both die and he would escape somewhere—maybe back to Moab—to live with Dinah on his grandfather's gold. He swallowed hard.

"Dinah is dead. She died of a fever when Joshua was hiding in the swampland near Gaza."

Several emotions played across Manasseh's face, but sorrow wasn't one of them. He turned to his administrator. "What do you think, Zerah?"

Hadad tried not to flinch under Zerah's intense scrutiny. Hadad knew nothing about the man, but the look in Zerah's eyes told him that he was perversely wicked, without conscience.

"I think you should lock Hadad in prison until we find out whether or not he is telling the truth," Zerah said.

Manasseh nodded to the four guards surrounding Hadad. "Can you beat the truth out of him?"

"Yes, Your Majesty."

"Do it."

Hadad's first whiff of the airless hole made him gag. He had time for only a fleeting glimpse of his fellow prisoners in the palace dungeon before the guards disappeared up the stairs with the torches and left the prison in total darkness. He thought he had counted about five other men crowded into the tiny cell, some shackled hand and foot, others unfettered like himself.

The guards had stripped Hadad of his outer robe and sandals, and the sodden straw felt warm and mushy beneath his bare feet. He leaned against the barred door, determined he would collapse from exhaustion before he would sit in his own filth, much less lie down in it.

Someone in the corner on his right was moaning in agony. The sound was continuous, unending. Hadad waited for his eyes to adjust to the gloom, but it never happened. The darkness in the cell was total. He sensed someone standing very close to him, felt the moisture of breath on his face.

"Who are you?" a voice rasped. "Who did you kill?"

"No one," Hadad mumbled. "Get away from me."

"Where shall I go? Through the bars? Or maybe I can float up near the ceiling for a while." His laughter had the timbre of insanity.

"You want space?" another voice in the darkness asked. "Why don't you put that old man over there out of his misery and take his space?"

"What's wrong with him?" Hadad asked. He heard several people chuckle.

"You'll find out soon enough," the voice nearby said. "They torture everyone in this cell sooner or later."

"Yeah, sooner or later." The voice came from someone sitting near Hadad's feet. "If you confess, you'll die sooner. If you don't confess, you'll die later." Everyone but Hadad laughed.

For the first time, Hadad realized that he might die in this stinking hole. The knowledge should have staggered him, but he felt nothing—no fear, no regrets . . . nor did he long to cling to life at all costs. He realized then that he had no reason to live. Everything that usually drove a man—love, work, friendship, dreams of the future—had all been stolen from him. Even if King Manasseh set him free, Hadad had no desire to begin a new life all over again without Dinah. He had started a new life in Egypt and had ended up in this dungeon. All he wanted was vengeance—to make his enemies pay for stealing Dinah away from him—or death.

Hadad leaned his back against the door and smiled, but no one saw him in the darkness. "They can't kill me," he murmured. They couldn't kill someone who was already dead.

Time must have passed, but living in eternal darkness, Hadad had no way to mark its passing. He might have been imprisoned for days or weeks or even years. The guards occasionally delivered meals of rotting food and stale water, but Hadad allowed the other prisoners to fight over his portions.

When Hadad had long since given up standing, the old prisoner's moans finally ended in a death rattle. The guards didn't remove the man's body right away, and Hadad heard his cellmates fighting over his ragged tunic, hoping for a scrap of cloth for warmth against the dungeon's cold nights. Then the other prisoners took turns sitting on the corpse, using it for a bench to avoid the filthy floor.

Every so often the guards dragged one of the prisoners away to be tortured. They didn't take him far; Hadad could hear the muffled blows, the agonized screams, the guards' laughter. The prisoner always returned unconscious. Hadad knew that the suspense of waiting for his turn had been carefully calculated to heighten his fear, but he felt strangely unafraid.

By the time the guards came for him, Hadad no longer cared what they did to him. He had retreated to a safe, dark place inside his soul where no one could ever hurt him again. He had searched hard for that place after his grandfather had died, hoping that strong wine might lead him to it, but now he knew that it could only be reached when all hope had finally died. His closest friends had betrayed him. He'd lost his home, his work, the woman he loved. He sat in a dark, stinking prison cell, surrounded by suffering and madness, hunger and thirst and cold. What more could anyone do to him?

The fact that he showed no fear, that he uttered no sound as the guards beat him, seemed to infuriate them. He heard none of their threats, felt none of their blows, because nothing could ever hurt him as much as Dinah's betrayal had. He saw her face, heard her words over and over in his mind . . . and Hadad welcomed death.

Two weeks after he had locked Hadad in prison, King Manasseh summoned the warden to his throne room. "Well, what have you learned from the man? Is Hadad telling the truth?"

"We've learned nothing, Your Majesty. He refuses to talk."

"Even when you tortured him? Threatened to kill him?"

"He doesn't seem to care if he lives or dies."

"I find that hard to believe," Manasseh said. "Everyone fears death."

The warden shrugged. "Not this prisoner, Your Majesty."

"What about the informant you placed in his cell?" Zerah asked. "What does he report?"

"He says that Hadad has eaten almost nothing since we locked him up. He doesn't seem to sleep, either. And he hasn't said more than half a dozen words to anyone, even his fellow prisoners."

Manasseh turned to Zerah in amazement. "What do you make of this?"

"Perhaps Hadad is telling the truth after all. If so, then the gods have answered your prayers, my lord. You asked for a decisive victory over your enemy; maybe it will come through this man."

Manasseh felt the thrill of triumph. He had finally won the gods' favor. His prayers had been answered. He would defeat Joshua at last.

"Take Hadad out of prison and clean him up," Manasseh told the warden. "I'm going up to the Temple to make a thank offering. I'll see him in the secretary's chambers—his old chambers, where he lived with Shebna—when I'm finished."

Manasseh climbed the walkway to the Temple, bursting with praise. The gods had sent Hadad in answer to his prayers. He would finally prevail against his enemy. Manasseh made an extravagant offering in return, and his only petition to the gods was for Joshua's death.

When he returned to his palace a few hours later, Manasseh found Hadad sitting stiffly on the window seat, as if in great pain. Manasseh was amazed at how much weight he had lost in two weeks, how changed his appearance was. Hadad's face was purpled with bruises, his left eye swollen nearly shut, his nose bent where it had recently been broken. He didn't rise when the king and Zerah entered or try to bow down to them. He appeared too weak to stand. Yet the warden said Hadad had never begged for mercy. Manasseh had remembered Shebna's grandson as carefree and undisciplined, and he wondered what had happened in his life to produce the man who now sat before him.

"So, Hadad. You've had a taste of my prison; now I offer you a taste of my palace. What would you like first? I'll send you anything you want . . . sumptuous food, excellent wine, someone to warm your bed . . ."

"I want to watch Joshua die." Hadad's speech was slurred as he tried to speak through lips that were cracked and swollen. "Set a trap for him. I'll make certain he walks into it."

Manasseh realized that Hadad's pain wasn't caused by his physical condition but by a hatred deeper than his own. Hadad was a driven man, so obsessed with revenge that he had withstood prison and torture and returned to this room not a weakened man but a stronger one. Manasseh felt a ripple of pleasure and fear. He stood in awe of such obsession. "Tell us your plan," he said.

Hadad leaned forward, and the hatred in his eyes mesmerized Manasseh. "Announce that you'll preside over a feast in one of the towns west of Jerusalem. Make sure your procession will have to travel through the narrow mountain pass on the Beth Shemesh Road to get there. I'll convince Joshua to set up an ambush at the pass. But your forces will infiltrate the area first, surrounding him completely. When he attacks the procession, which will be a decoy, your soldiers will move in, cutting off his escape."

"How many men will he have?" Manasseh asked.

"I can make sure that his army will be small and inexperienced. He'll probably order them to distract your guards, then retreat. I'm certain that he'll try to assassinate you himself. If you use a covered sedan chair, with guards waiting inside, you might take him alive."

"What about Amariah?"

Hadad's eyes glimmered with hatred. "Do you want him dead or alive?"

Manasseh smiled. "I'll let you decide, Hadad. You deserve a small reward after surviving my prison."

"I'll deliver what's left of him to you."

"I thought you and my brother were friends. What happened?"

"He chose to become my enemy."

"When would you like this ambush to take place?" Zerah asked.

Manasseh glanced at his advisor and fought a twinge of jealousy when he saw the greedy way Zerah eyed Hadad. Manasseh understood why. As weak as Hadad was, his hatred gave him an aura of strength and power.

"I'll need a month to return to where Joshua is hiding in Egypt and plant the idea in his head," Hadad said. "Joshua will probably want a few months to make plans and train his men. Why don't we say the New Moon Festival, four months from now."

"How will you convince him to follow your plan?" Manasseh asked. "If you and he are enemies, won't he suspect that it's a trap?"

"Joshua is my enemy. I never said that I was his enemy."

Again, Manasseh saw Hadad's powerful hatred and felt the grip of awe. "What did Joshua do to you?" he asked in a hushed voice.

Hadad stared at him, through him. "He cut out my heart. Now I want the chance to cut out his."

5

JOSHUA HURRIED THROUGH BREAKFAST, his mind on the full day of work ahead of him. A supply ship was arriving from the north today with a shipment of military weapons from Pharaoh. And there was always more work to be done on the altar site. He pushed himself away from the table and stood, so abruptly that he nearly bumped into Miriam, who had been hovering behind him.

"Sorry," he mumbled.

"No, I . . . I've been waiting to speak with you, my lord. I need to ask a favor."

"Can you make it fast? I'm in a hurry."

"It's about Nathan."

Joshua's stomach clenched at the mention of his name. "What about him?"

"He's been living away from home for two months now. Hasn't he been punished enough? He's just a boy."

Joshua's life had been peaceful without Nathan and the threat of blackmail hanging over him. He didn't want Nathan to come back.

"I sent him away because he wouldn't live by the rules of this house. How can I be certain that he's ready to live by them now?"

"Because he's suffered enough, my lord, being separated from Mattan and me."

"He's not suffering, he's learning what it means to work. The apprenticeship will do him good. He didn't want to go to school; he refused to obey or respect me. There was no other alternative than to make him earn his keep."

"Please give him another chance."

Joshua couldn't meet her gaze. He stared past her through the open doorway to the courtyard beyond. "I've given him plenty of chances. I even offered to let him work with me if he didn't want to study with the Levites, but he refused. I won't take him back until he apologizes."

"He's too proud. He'll never take the first step and come to you. Please . . ."

"I'm sorry." Joshua spread his hands. "There's nothing I can do." He hurried away before she could plead with him further.

Miriam and her brother aroused too many disturbing feelings in Joshua—guilt over Maki's death, shame because of the mistakes he had made, fear of being exposed. He could forget all of these emotions if Miriam stayed in the background and if he didn't have to deal with Nathan. And that's exactly what he intended to do.

He left the house and walked to the work site, but Miriam's pleas lingered like a bitter taste on his tongue long after he arrived at the new worship area. The Levites were building an outdoor enclosure where the exiles could assemble and the priests could offer sacrifices, but today the sight of the huge unfinished courtyard aligned toward Jerusalem depressed Joshua further.

The new worship site was an alien place, so unlike the Temple in Jerusalem atop Mount Zion, with its clean air and panoramic views. This courtyard was cramped and dingy-looking; all the incense in Egypt couldn't erase the pungent, fishy smell of the nearby river. Countless setbacks and supply problems continued to delay their work, so after more than a year of waiting, the priests were still unable to offer more than the daily sacrifices. Joshua hadn't been able to make an offering for his sins or find relief from the guilt that plagued him. Maybe once the site was finished and he'd made his guilt offering, he'd be ready to deal with Nathan again.

He tried to push aside these thoughts as he bent to inspect the foundation trench for the enclosure's walls. Engrossed in his work, he didn't hear the approaching footsteps.

"Hello, Joshua."

He looked up, then stood abruptly. Hadad stood a few feet away. Without thinking, Joshua gripped the hilt of the dagger he wore at his hip.

"You won't need your weapon," Hadad said quietly. "I'm not armed."

He lifted his hands in surrender, but Joshua still felt uneasy. Hadad had left the island spouting threats, swearing vengeance. Joshua remembered being angry enough to kill someone after learning that Yael had married another man, and he knew he had good reason to fear Hadad. Or was it only his conscience confronting him with the truth of how he had wronged his friend?

Joshua released the knife but balanced his weight on the balls of his feet in readiness. "When did you get back?" he asked Hadad.

"This morning. I came on the supply boat."

Hadad looked several pounds thinner than when he had left, with a lean hardness that often comes from suffering. Joshua noticed a ridge on his nose that made it look as though it had been recently broken, and a scar on his upper lip that he didn't think had been there before.

"We need to talk," Hadad said.

Joshua brushed the dirt off his hands and folded his arms across his chest. "I'm listening."

"I want Amariah to hear what I have to say, too."

"He's up at the fortress. We can talk there."

Joshua allowed Hadad to lead the way, but as they silently walked the short distance to the outpost, Joshua's mind spun with all the questions that Hadad's return raised. Instinct warned him not to trust Hadad, and he considered sending soldiers to Amariah's house to guard Dinah. He stopped walking when they reached the outer gate.

"You were furious when you left, Hadad. You made some pretty serious threats. I can't let you near Amariah until I'm certain you're unarmed."

"You're welcome to search me," Hadad said. He turned to face the wall, resting his palms against it. Joshua searched him, carefully patting his clothing and inspecting the folds of his robes. He found no weapons.

"Shall we go in now?" Hadad said when he was finished. Joshua tried to read the expression on his face but couldn't. There was something very wrong. Hadad showed no anger, no wariness . . . no emotion at all.

They found Prince Amariah inside the courtyard, watching as several dozen recruits sparred with one another and offering occasional words of advice and encouragement. Hadad gave a humorless laugh. "You've got to be kidding. You've got the *prince* coaching them? He would have flunked his own training if he hadn't been the king's son."

"We had no choice after you left," Joshua said irritably. "I've had to divide my time between helping here and supervising the altar's construction."

Amariah turned as they approached, and Joshua saw his surprise and fear when he spotted Hadad. Hadad spread his arms wide as he strode toward Amariah, as if to embrace him, but Joshua quickly moved between them, holding Hadad at bay.

"Amariah, how are you, my brother?" Hadad asked.

"I'm well. And you?" Amariah gazed at him, wide-eyed. Joshua nodded to reassure him.

"We need to talk," Hadad said. "Can you spare a few minutes?"

Amariah exhaled. "All right. Let's go inside."

The prince led the way to an empty guard room and sank onto a bench as if his legs wouldn't hold him any longer. Joshua followed with Hadad. Although he knew Hadad wasn't armed, it didn't ease his distrust. He stayed alert, ready to defend himself or the prince. When Hadad refused a seat, pacing restlessly in the small room, Joshua also remained standing.

"I'll admit I was angry when I left," Hadad began. "In many ways, I still am. But I've had a lot of time to think about everything these past few months, and there's no way I can undo what's already happened." He halted in front of Amariah and their eyes met. "Are you and Dinah married?"

Amariah looked at the floor. "Yes. We are."

"I thought so." Hadad turned his back and crossed the room to stare out of the window, gripping the shutter latch so hard that Joshua saw his knuckles turn white. He waited, watching Hadad carefully. Finally Hadad turned to face them again.

"I went back to Judah," he said. "At first I intended to stay there, but everything's changed. It's a very dangerous place now. Entirely pagan. I can't live there anymore among all that idolatry. And so I decided . . ." He paused, and Joshua saw him swallow hard. "I decided that if I have to give up Dinah, then I want my loss to count for something."

Joshua's fingers gripped the leather sheath that held his dagger. "What does that mean, Hadad?"

"I want to put Dinah's son on Judah's throne. I want to do that much for her. It would be a waste for her to live her life here in Egypt while Manasseh leads our country into ruin. I would have lost her for nothing. But if we got rid of Manasseh, and Amariah became king, Dinah could take her rightful place by his side. Her son would reign someday. I'm prepared to fight for that. And I've worked out a plan to do it."

Joshua didn't believe him. Hadad was Amariah's enemy, his rival; why would he help the prince recapture the throne? For Dinah's sake? It didn't ring true. Hadad wasn't that noble. Joshua suspected he was lying, but he had no basis for his suspicion except his gut reaction.

"What's in it for you?" he asked.

"I want my grandfather's job as secretary of state when Amariah is king. I figured you would probably be palace administrator, right?"

Hadad's answer seemed too quick, too rehearsed. Joshua pulled out a chair and swung it around, straddling it. He rested his forearms on the back and laced his fingers together. "Tell us your plan."

"King Manasseh is building a shrine to the sun god at Beth Shemesh."

"What?" Amariah asked. "The *sun god*?"

"That's not unusual," Hadad said. "He has pagan shrines all over Judah now. But I found out that he will be going to Beth Shemesh for the dedication ceremony during the New Moon Festival a few months from now." Hadad paced, not looking at either of them as he talked. "That means he'll have to take the Beth Shemesh Road from Jerusalem and go through the narrow mountain pass near there. If we lay an ambush—"

"I saw one of Manasseh's processions," Joshua said. "He was very heavily guarded."

"True. But we could attack from well-entrenched positions above the road. His men would be in the open, without cover and with no way to escape. We'd also have the advantage of surprise."

Joshua's pulse quickened with excitement, and for a moment he forgot his caution as he realized what Hadad was proposing. They could kill Manasseh! The ambush might work! Attacking the procession at that narrow pass was a brilliant strategy. The king's guards would have no escape or protection. Once Joshua got close to Manasseh, he could finally get revenge.

"How many men do you think we would need?" he asked.

"If they're excellent archers, not many. We could kill half the guards in the first round, before Manasseh's men have a chance to string their bows."

"Won't they be on the alert coming through that pass?"

"Even if they are, it won't do them any good. We'll dig positions on the ridge above them the night before, then lie in wait."

"But doesn't Manasseh have guards at all the borders, watching for me?"

"I didn't see any. Nobody stopped me. Besides, we wouldn't enter the country as soldiers. We could use one of your brother's caravans to smuggle our men and weapons into the country."

Joshua's mind raced ahead, analyzing Hadad's scheme. It was a simple plan, but it just might work. General Benjamin had once taught him that the simplest plans were often the best. Joshua couldn't spot any obvious flaws, and the exhilarating prospect of revenge stole his breath from him.

"Are you certain that Amariah is still Manasseh's only heir?" he asked.

"I'm positive. There has been no announcement of a royal heir. I checked."

"Good. Then once Manasseh is dead—"

"No!" Amariah was on his feet. "I won't let you do it. Manasseh is God's anointed king. It's wrong to kill him."

Joshua's anger soared at the prince's naïveté. "He would have killed you in an instant once his heir was born."

"That's still no reason for us to kill him."

"We have a hundred reasons to kill him," Joshua shouted. "Do you have any idea how much innocent blood he has shed, how much evil he has done?"

"Yahweh is Manasseh's judge, not us. We should wait for Him to bring justice."

"We're Yahweh's instruments of justice! That's why He sent us here to be trained as soldiers. Remember your disbelief when Pharaoh first told us we'd all have to serve in his army? Can't you see how God's plan is finally coming together? I've waited a long time for this chance!"

"No," Amariah insisted, "this is wrong. I don't want any part in Hadad's plan. I'm the island's leader, and I refuse to condone it."

The stubbornness in his voice surprised Joshua. He signaled to Amariah's servant. "Go get me a Torah scroll," Joshua told him. "I need to show Prince Amariah something."

They all waited uneasily while the servant went on his errand. When the man returned with the scroll, Joshua rolled through it until he found the passage he wanted. He read the words aloud: "'If your very own brother . . . secretly entices you, saying, "Let us go and worship other gods" . . . do not yield to him or listen to him.'"

"I don't care what it says, we can't—"

"'Do not spare him or shield him,'" Joshua continued, cutting Amariah off. "'You must certainly put him to death . . . and then the hands of all the people—'"

"No! I won't listen to this." Amariah turned his back.

Joshua raised his voice to a shout, drowning Amariah's protests. "'Stone him to death, because he tried to turn you away from the Lord your God. . . . Then all Israel will hear and be afraid, and no one among you will do such an evil thing again.'" He shoved the scroll into Amariah's hands. "Here. Read it yourself."

"He's my brother. Could you kill Jerimoth if he—"

"We're not talking about Jerimoth, we're talking about Manasseh—the man who murdered my father and my grandfather, the man who tortured God's prophet to death, the man who raped your wife and murdered her child!"

"I know, but—"

"You told me yourself how Manasseh tried to force you to participate in his pagan rituals—Asherah poles, divination, witchcraft, sodomy. How much more will it take to convince you that he deserves to die? This is a God-given opportunity. How can we refuse it?"

Amariah thrust the scroll back into Joshua's hands. "I'm telling you I can't do it. I *won't* do it!"

"You don't have to," Joshua said softly. "I'll kill him myself." He glared at the prince in silent confrontation while Hadad leaned against the window ledge, watching them.

"So do we have a deal?" Hadad finally asked.

Joshua nodded, his eyes still riveted on the prince, daring him to contradict. "We'll need a squad of commando fighters to draw the guards away from the king. Help me choose the best men, Hadad. Help me train them."

"Are you sure you trust me with a weapon?"

When Joshua looked at Hadad and tried to read his face, he couldn't. Once again Joshua felt the chill of uncertainty. He hesitated, carefully weighing his suspicions about Hadad's motives against the opportunity for revenge against Manasseh. His hatred, his burning need for vengeance, won the battle.

"I need your help, Hadad, so I'll have to trust you. We'll only have a few months to prepare."

"All right," he said quietly. "But this island isn't very big. It will be easier for me if I could live here without seeing your sister."

Joshua understood. He often saw Yael, the woman he had loved, with her husband and year-old son. Yael was pregnant again. "You can move into your old rooms in the barracks," Joshua told him. "Dinah lives . . ." A whisper of doubt stopped him again. He shrugged it aside, remembering his goal to kill Manasseh. "Dinah lives on the other side of the island."

Hadad's brief smile lacked emotion. "If everything goes according to plan, we'll all be living in the palace in Jerusalem again, won't we, my brothers?"

6

AMARIAH PACED ACROSS THE MAIN ROOM of his house, exasperation pushing his patience to the limit. "No, Joshua. I already told you. I don't want any guards lurking around here. This is my home. Either you trust Hadad or you don't. And since you're going ahead with your assassination plans, that obviously means you've decided to trust him."

"The guards would be for Dinah's sake," Joshua began.

"She's *my* wife. It's *my* job to protect her!"

Joshua raised his hands in a gesture of surrender. "All right, I didn't mean to offend you. Sorry."

But Amariah knew by the cold expression on Joshua's face that his refusal to order extra guards had angered Joshua. He might as well risk angering him further. "Before you leave, Joshua . . . I've been thinking. I'd feel better about this assassination business if you'd ask the priests to consult the Urim and Thummim about it."

Joshua took a step toward him. Amariah recognized the move as one Joshua always made when he wanted to intimidate an opponent. The maneuver didn't surprise Amariah, but his pulse quickened all the same. Joshua was not as tall as Amariah was, but the barely controlled anger that had ruled his life these past two years frightened everyone who knew him. His dark eye patch and rugged scar gave him an added ferocity.

"In the first place, we don't have the Urim and Thummim," Joshua said. "We left it behind when we fled Jerusalem. And in the second place, we wouldn't need to consult it even if we did. The Torah makes it very clear that your brother deserves to die."

"Then why not trust God to deal with him instead of avenging him yourself? According to the king's chronicles, David had two opportunities to kill King Saul, who was just as guilty of disobeying God as my brother is. But David refused to lay a hand on God's anointed king. And in due time, God took Saul's life and placed David on the throne."

"You're right, Amariah," Joshua said coldly. "David didn't need to kill Saul. God sent his enemies, the Philistines, to do it." His voice rose to a shout. "And I'm Manasseh's enemy! God is sending me to kill him!"

Amariah saw that it was no use. He couldn't compete with Joshua's agile mind and bitter tongue. "I have one more question, then," Amariah said quietly. "How do you know that Hadad isn't leading you into a trap?"

The question seemed to take Joshua by surprise. He paused, stroking his ragged beard. "I suppose it's something I ought to consider...." But before Joshua had time to weigh the possibility, Dinah interrupted, hurrying in from the courtyard to embrace her brother.

"Joshua! I thought I heard your voice. What brings you here?"

Amariah held his breath, silently hoping that Joshua wouldn't tell her the truth or try to convince her to surround their house with guards. She already knew that Hadad had returned; he didn't want her to live in fear of him.

"Oh, nothing important," Joshua said with a shrug. "But as long as I have you both together, we need to talk about your heir. Dinah, it's vitally important for you to get pregnant within the next few months. Before our mission, if possible."

Dinah nodded her head, murmuring apologetically, but Amariah was too stunned to speak, outraged that Joshua would dare to interfere in his married life. As Joshua continued to explain the urgent need for an heir, Amariah finally found his voice.

"Get out of my house!"

"What?"

Dinah laid her hand on his arm. "Amariah, please..."

"I want him to leave. Now!"

Joshua stared hard at him for a moment, his anger smoldering like banked coals. Amariah braced himself for an explosion, but it never came. Joshua simply shrugged. "Whatever you say, Your Majesty." He kissed his sister's cheek and strode away without another word.

But Amariah couldn't shrug it off that easily. Joshua's demands had infuriated him. How dare he interfere in their married life, violating their intimacy, commanding them to produce a son? Amariah was so angry that it took him a moment to realize Dinah had been speaking to him. "I'm sorry," he told her. "What did you say?"

"I said the servants have your evening meal on the table."

But Amariah couldn't eat, sickened by Joshua's audacity. Was this the way the rest of his life would be, with Joshua giving all the orders, dictating his every move? Amariah had longed to escape from Manasseh's authority and live his own life, make his own decisions. But he had merely exchanged one taskmaster for another.

"I'm not hungry," he told Dinah. "I need to get some air." He left the house and started walking—anywhere, nowhere.

The worst thing about living on an island, he quickly discovered, was that he couldn't walk very far without coming to the end of it. And the worst thing about being that island's leader was meeting people who wanted to talk when the last thing in the world he felt like doing was talking. After barely an hour, he gave up the search for solitude and returned home.

As the evening wore on and the servants retired to their own homes for the night, Amariah found himself dreading the moment when he would have to go to bed with his wife. He sat in the main room of his house alone, watching as evening faded into night and the room's familiar furnishings disappeared into the shadows, wishing he could disappear along with them. His life was not his own. He wondered if it ever would be.

He wasn't sure how long he had been sitting in the dark when a beam of light flickered in the gloom and Dinah entered, carrying a small lamp. He shaded his eyes with his hand, shielding them from the lamp's glow and from her scrutiny.

"Oh . . . I wondered if you'd fallen asleep out here," she said.

"No. I'm awake."

"Why don't you come to bed?"

Amariah sighed and rubbed his eyes. "All right." He slowly pulled himself to his feet and started to follow her, then stopped. Joshua had demanded an heir and she was determined to obey him. The thought sickened Amariah.

"Dinah, wait."

She turned to him. The light was between them, and she studied his face. "What's wrong?"

"It's supposed to be an act of love," he said softly, "but it's not. They've turned it into an act of vengeance."

She lowered her head, and her dark hair fell around her face, hiding her eyes. Amariah took the lamp from her and set it on a stand, then reached for her hand.

"Come with me, Dinah."

"Where?"

He led her through the door and out into the narrow street without answering. A transparent moon bathed the warm night with light and formed pale gray shadows beneath their feet. He walked with her toward the river, to a sandy stretch of shoreline where he knew there was little danger of crocodiles. An abandoned rowboat lay upside down on the beach, and Amariah pulled Dinah down beside him on the warm sand so they could lean their backs against it.

"Look," he whispered, pointing. At the end of the beach where the marshlands began, a crane poked its head from among the reeds, then ventured cautiously forward. A moment later his mate followed, tottering on stick-legs almost too fragile to support her. Their gossamer feathers glowed in the moonlight.

"They're beautiful," Dinah murmured.

"I wish we were like them," Amariah said. "They're free."

They watched the cranes wade farther into the river, away from the marsh; then the birds suddenly took flight, soaring magnificently toward the mainland, wings outstretched. Amariah longed to do the same, to open his heart like wings, to freely soar.

"What's your favorite color, Dinah?" he asked when the birds were out of sight.

"My favorite color? Why?"

"Because I need to know." He swallowed the lump in his throat and began again. "When we lived in my brother's palace in Jerusalem, our lives weren't our own. We belonged to Manasseh. He controlled where we went, who we saw, what we did . . . and I realized tonight that he still controls us. We married each other because of him. I'm supposed to rule this island because of him. You're supposed to have a baby because of him. Our lives still aren't our own, Dinah. No one ever asks us what *we* want."

He tossed the weathered piece of driftwood he had been toying with into the water. It washed toward him on the waves several times, bobbing in the moonlight, before floating out of sight.

"I have my father's blood in my veins—King David's blood. According to Joshua, that means I'm obligated to stop Manasseh. Obligated to father your son. Obligated to be king. But I'm more than Hezekiah's son, more than Manasseh's brother, more than David's heir. I'm a man—Amariah. I'm myself, separate from everyone's obligations and expectations. Why do I have to define my life in terms of filling a need? Can't I have a purpose of my own choosing?"

He put his hand to his face, pressing his fingers against his closed eyes. Then he looked at Dinah again. She had unpinned her hair for the night before they'd left the house, and the breeze blew wisps of it across her face.

"And what about you, Dinah? Are you merely the means by which I claim my brother's throne? Are you only Manasseh's concubine? Amariah's wife? The mother of the future king?" He brushed her hair away from her eyes in a gesture of tenderness that he seldom dared to express. "You're a woman—a flesh and blood person, with real feelings and needs. Don't you have any dreams and hopes? Or is revenge the only one?" He saw confusion and pain in her eyes, and he turned away from her to stare into the water again.

"I know you didn't marry me because you love me. The real Amariah doesn't matter to you. I never did. I'm Manasseh's brother, your means of revenge. That's all our marriage is based on, do you realize that? Revenge. What was meant to be the most tender act of love between a man and woman is merely an act of vengeance for us."

Dinah shuddered. He wondered if it was from the cool night air or from his words. "I'm sorry," she whispered after a moment. "But what else can we do?"

"I don't know. . . . I don't expect you to ever love me, but can't we at least . . . ?" He stopped, unable to find the words he wanted.

She turned his face toward hers. "Tell me."

"Can't we at least be ourselves with each other? Can't we give each other that one gift, even if no one else does? Everyone else might think of us as 'Manasseh's brother' and 'Manasseh's concubine,' but I can let you be just 'Dinah' to me. And you can let me be 'Amariah.' Maybe someday you'll fall in love with the real Amariah, maybe not. It doesn't matter. I'd be happy just to know . . . to know that you liked me for myself." He took her hands in his. "No matter how everyone else defines us, we need to hang on to the small haven we can create for each other and not let them take it away from us."

She let go of his hand to wipe her tears. "How?" she whispered. "How do we do that?"

"We've already begun. We've left their bedroom, left their expectations for us . . . and we're here—on a sandy beach, with warm water and starlight. When we were watching the cranes a few minutes ago, we weren't thinking about Manasseh or revenge or anything else except how beautiful they were, how perfect they looked in the moonlight. We need to forget about everything else when we're together. Forget the past and all that Manasseh has done to us, forget the future—producing an heir, governing the nation. We can live right now—in the present. I want that to be the only thing that's real to us." He waited until her eyes met his. "What do you want to do *now*, this very moment?"

"I don't know."

"Well, I know what I want to do." He stood and kicked off his sandals, then shrugged off his outer robe and waded into the river in his tunic. "The water's warm, Dinah. It feels like silk. Come on, try it."

He held out his hand to her and waited. After a moment, she untied her sandals and waded out to him, lifting her skirts above her knees. They walked together along the shore, the water lapping around their ankles.

"I want to learn the names of all the birds and all the trees and all the stars," Amariah said. "I want to play the lyre again and compose songs like I used to do. Maybe I'll sing one of them for you sometime."

"I'd like that very much."

He stopped walking and faced her. "What's your favorite color?"

Dinah's eyes met his, and it seemed as if she finally saw him for himself. "Green," she said softly.

"That's my favorite color, too." He smiled. It felt good to smile. He couldn't remember the last time that he had. He took her hand in his, twining their fingers together. "Green . . . like the trees and the fields and the grass."

7

THE SOUND OF CLASHING SWORDS RANG in Joshua's ears as he stood in the courtyard of the fort watching Hadad drill his troops. The men revered Hadad and had welcomed him back with great enthusiasm. He was an excellent commander and always eager to join in with their sparring. As each day passed, Joshua felt less suspicious of him.

When Hadad spotted Joshua watching, he quickly ordered his men to form ranks, then strode to where Joshua waited. "I weeded out all but the best," Hadad said, still breathless with exertion. "Here's our top sixty men."

"Do they know about our mission?"

Hadad shook his head. "I'll let you tell them."

Joshua straightened his eye patch as he stepped in front of the assembly. The murmuring quickly fell silent. "I'm told that you're the best," he began. "And for the mission Colonel Hadad and I are planning, we'll need the best. But this is a volunteer assignment. Like Gideon's small, elite corps, we'll be up against much greater odds—some would say impossible odds. So I'll tell you the same thing Gideon told his troops: Anyone who is uncertain, anyone who has commitments to his family or spouse, anyone who is uncomfortable with this mission for any reason is free to go. No one will think any less of you. This may not be your battle, that's all."

He studied their faces. They all looked much too young. "For those of you who decide to volunteer, I can assure you that your job will be dangerous. Some of you may die." As he paused, he saw their zeal and also their admiration and awe of him. "Our goal," he said quietly, "is to assassinate King Manasseh." Shock and surprise rippled across the courtyard like a wave. He waited until it ebbed. "When Manasseh is dead, our families can all return home. Judah will be our homeland once again."

As a spontaneous cheer went up, Joshua realized that they were almost as homesick for Judah as he was. They had lived more than a year in Egypt, but for Joshua, more than two years had passed since the night he had left his father's house to eat dinner with Yael and had never returned.

"Take the next few days to think it over," he continued. "If you decide to volunteer, we'll only have about three months to train and develop the teamwork we'll need before we begin our journey north. Three days from now, Colonel Hadad will draw up a final roster of volunteers. Until then, you're dismissed."

As the courtyard emptied, he motioned for Hadad to follow him inside. "We need to finish planning the final details of the mission," Joshua said. "I've persuaded Amariah to join us."

"Has he finally decided to come with us?"

"No, but I convinced him that the assassination is going to take place, with or without his cooperation, so he may as well listen in on our plans."

The prince was already waiting for them in the small room overlooking the practice yard, gazing out of the window like a prisoner. Joshua wondered if he'd been watching Hadad's soldiers drilling. Amariah kept his back turned as Joshua and Hadad took their places on opposite sides of a small table.

"How many men do you think will volunteer?" Joshua asked.

Hadad stroked his smooth chin. "I'm hoping only about half."

"Half! That won't be enough. We'll need at least forty men. I'd prefer all sixty."

"That's too many," Hadad said. "We can't smuggle that many men into the country without arousing suspicion, not to mention hiding them all at the ambush site."

"I saw one of Manasseh's processions a year ago," Joshua said. "He has dozens of bodyguards with him. And his troops are experienced. Ours aren't."

"We can do it with twenty men, Joshua."

"No, that's not enough!" Joshua's temper slipped from his grasp, and as he struggled to recapture it, Amariah suddenly turned to face them.

"Why don't you argue about it after you see how many men volunteer?"

Joshua gaped at the prince in surprise. "That's a good idea," he said after a moment. He took another moment to gather his thoughts, then asked, "What else do we need to decide, Hadad?"

"I scouted out a site for the ambush before I left Judah and found a place along the road west of Jerusalem that I think will work." He spread out a piece of parchment on the table in front of them, sketching as he talked. "The road curves around a hill, like this. Manasseh's men won't be able to see our ambush ahead of time, but we can watch their approach from the top of the ridge. On the other side of the road is a sheer drop-off. They'll have no escape."

Joshua's pulse quickened at the prospect of revenge. "I think I remember that place. Go on."

"We'll wait until Manasseh rounds the curve, then our archers will fire the first volley from the top of the hill, taking out as many bodyguards as possible."

"Tell them to concentrate their fire on the guards surrounding the king," Joshua said.

"Right. We'll split our forces into thirds—the archers on top of the hill will make one group, those setting up the ambush around the curve will make the second, and the third will dig in along the road to cut off the king's retreat after the ambush."

"I want to kill Manasseh myself," Joshua said.

"I figured you would." When Hadad smiled slightly, Joshua recognized something familiar in his expression, something he couldn't quite define.

"Listen, Hadad, once Manasseh is dead, I want all our men to scatter. There's no sense risking their lives against a superior foe any longer than we need to."

"Are you sure that's what you want? You'll be putting yourself at greater risk."

"I'm positive," Joshua said. "You can devise a signal that will tell our men when to retreat. And we'll need a location where we can regroup later."

"The logical place would be the hideout where Amariah will be waiting."

"I don't want any part of this," Amariah said from his place near the window ledge. "I'll be waiting right here in Egypt."

"We won't involve you in the battle," Hadad said, "but we'll need to anoint you as king immediately. We can't wait several months for you to travel back to Jerusalem from Egypt."

"Hadad is right," Joshua said. "The country can't be without a leader that long. You'll need to assume power immediately as the rightful heir." He saw a look of dismay cross Amariah's face at the prospect of becoming king, and Joshua's anger soared. "You're coming with us! This is God's will!" he shouted. When Amariah didn't reply, Joshua signaled for Hadad to continue.

"I found a small cave in the area. It's right about here on the map. Amariah can wait there with Dinah while—"

Joshua leaped to his feet. "Dinah? Who said anything about Dinah?"

"Absolutely not!" Amariah cried at the same time. "Dinah stays here until I'm well established in Jerusalem and all the turmoil has died down!"

Hadad's rage exploded. He shoved the table away from him, scattering everything on it and startling everyone into silence. "You said you needed Dinah to solidify Amariah's claim to the throne! Was that a lie? Now all of a sudden you don't need her anymore?"

Joshua knew he had to defuse the situation quickly and saw only one way to do it. He couldn't let his plans fall apart now. "Hadad is right. Dinah needs to come with us."

"No!" Amariah shouted. "How can you even think about endangering her life? I won't allow it!" He turned to storm from the room, but Joshua grabbed him by the arm and hauled him back.

"Do you think for one minute that I would do anything to endanger my sister's life?"

"I love her more than both of you do," Hadad said. "You know I won't let anything happen to her."

Amariah's face was pale. "Dinah stays here, or I stay here, too."

Once again, Joshua felt his anger slipping from his grasp. If he had to, he would shackle Amariah and carry him to Judah in a sack. Then he thought of a more reasonable idea. "I think we ought to let Dinah decide if she wants to come or not."

"No! She's my wife! I decide what happens to her, and I say she stays here. What does she know about fighting battles and fleeing from danger? You can't expect her to travel with an army or camp out with a bunch of men."

"I'll ask Miriam to accompany us and take care of Dinah," Joshua said. "Miriam is resourceful. She's helped me twice now, and she's proven that she can stay calm and think on her feet."

"No," Hadad said suddenly. "It's not fair to use Miriam to fight any more of our battles."

Joshua stared at him in surprise, wondering why he was so concerned about her. "I'll only use her if she volunteers, okay?" Joshua said. "Like the rest of our troops."

"Why should she volunteer? What's in it for her?" Hadad asked. "She'll agree because she's good-hearted, but you've never done anything in return for all her help except provide food and a roof over her head."

"How can you say that? I've made her part of my family—"

"She saved your life, Joshua—twice! For that you've allowed her the honor of being your family's servant!"

"That's unfair."

"Is it? If she's really part of your family, why haven't you been as concerned about finding her a respectable husband as you were about finding one for Dinah?"

"I guess it never occurred to me. She seems a little young."

"That's because you still see her as the child she was two years ago. She's a grown woman, Joshua. Take a good look at her for once."

Joshua recalled Nathan's accusation that he treated Miriam like dirt, and the dull ache of guilt returned. Hadad was right. He still thought of Miriam as a servant, as Maki's daughter, and he never gave her a moment's thought until he needed her. Joshua knew he needed her now.

"I'll admit there's a lot of truth to what you're saying, Hadad."

"Well, don't use her again. Stop taking her for granted. Before you ask her to volunteer, have the decency to tell her what's in it for her besides a thank-you."

Joshua saw his simple plan growing more complicated by the minute. He needed to focus on his goal and concentrate all his energies on killing Manasseh. Perhaps in time the other details would straighten out by themselves.

Miriam stared into the muddy waters of the Nile as she stood on the dock, waiting for the ferry that would take her to the mainland to see her brother Nathan. In a few days she would be traveling to Judah on these flood-swollen waters, and she needed to say good-bye to him before she left. As the seabirds swooped above her, crying raucously, she wondered again what miracle had made Joshua suddenly notice her and ask for her help. She watched the ferry approach, remembering how earnest his handsome face had been as he'd warned her of the dangers she would face. He couldn't have known that she would walk into Sheol itself for him. As she moved to get in line with the other passengers, someone called her name.

"Miriam . . . wait!"

She turned, surprised to see Hadad hurrying toward her. Miriam knew that he'd returned to Elephantine Island almost four months ago, but she hadn't seen him since that terrible Passover night when he'd asked for Dinah's hand. The changes she saw in him now startled her. She'd known him drunk and sober, angry and content, in love and in pain, but something about the haunted emptiness she saw in his eyes frightened her now. And she'd never been afraid of Hadad before.

"Did Joshua tell you we're leaving for Judah in a few days?" he asked without a word of greeting.

"Yes, he asked me to go with him."

Hadad cursed. "Is that what he said? Go with *him*?" His anger alarmed Miriam. She took a step back.

"Not exactly. I'm going to accompany Dinah. We're the only women who are going, and—"

Hadad kicked a discarded piece of sacking and sent it flying into the water, accompanied by more curses. "Don't do it, Miriam! Don't go!"

"Why not? What are you so angry about, Hadad?"

"He's using you, and he has no right to do that. I know because he used me the same way. When he needs something he makes you think you're his friend, but the truth is, he considers himself superior to you and me. We're beneath him."

"Because we have no name?"

Hadad nodded. For a brief moment his eyes lost their empty look as they searched hers. "I know you're in love with him, Miriam."

"I am not!" She looked away, her cheeks burning.

"Don't try to deny it. I figured out the truth a long time ago—when you followed Jerimoth's caravan from Moab to Jerusalem. I was there when Joshua raged at you for tagging along. I heard all the terrible things he said to you. Yet you still risked your life to wade through all that carnage at the Temple and drag him out of there."

Miriam stared at the ground, ashamed. She thought no one else but Jerusha knew of her love for Joshua. She couldn't look at Hadad, but he lifted her chin, forcing her to face him.

"He isn't worthy of you, Miriam. Your motives are pure; you're helping him because you're in love with him. But he's only using you. There's no room in his heart for you or anyone else. Did he tell you what will happen if our mission is successful? If he assassinates King Manasseh?"

"He said we'd be able to move back home again and—"

"What about you? What did he promise you for helping him?"

Miriam was ashamed to feel tears brimming in her eyes. "Hadad, don't. Please."

"Once Amariah is king, Joshua will be his palace administrator, the second highest official in the land. He'll choose a woman of noble blood to be his wife, not a servant's daughter."

The tears Miriam had tried so hard to control spilled down her cheeks against her will. "I know. I don't expect anything for myself.

But Joshua promised that my brother Nathan could come back home and be his son again if—"

"Don't believe him, Miriam. Your brother will only get a glimpse of what a respectable life is like, but he'll never be allowed to live it. I know because that's what happened to me. You heard Joshua's reaction when I asked to marry Dinah. And it will be the same for Nathan. Joshua will never give Nathan his own name. Believe me, it's better if your brother never tastes that way of life because it will be denied him in the end."

A final call was made to the passengers as the ferry finished loading and was preparing to cast off.

"I need to go, Hadad."

He caught her arm roughly. "Wait for the next boat."

She watched the sailors release the mooring lines and push away from shore, then she turned to Hadad again. "What's the real reason you don't want me to go?"

For a moment he looked startled, as if her question had caught him off guard and he didn't have a ready answer. Then his anger returned. "Because it's too dangerous. You're risking your life for nothing."

"If it's so dangerous, then why is Dinah going?"

Hadad quickly turned his face away as if he had something to hide, but Miriam couldn't imagine what it was. "Believe me," he finally said, "I'm against the idea. But Amariah insisted that Dinah come with us, and Joshua finally gave in to him."

Miriam had a hard time imagining the prince insisting on his own way, much less standing up to Joshua.

"Miriam, please reconsider," Hadad said. "Let Joshua find someone else to accompany Dinah."

"Since when do you care so much about my life?"

"There is a very good chance that this mission will fail. If it does, we'll all be killed. I don't have much to live for now that Dinah is lost to me, but you do. If you could only see Joshua's heart for what it is . . . if you could just get over him, Miriam, you could have a decent life, a husband, a family."

"Can you stop loving Dinah," she asked softly, "even though you know she'll never be yours?" She saw that she had struck a vulnerable spot, poking a wound that hadn't healed.

Hadad vented his pain with anger. "How can I convince you to stay here? It's much too dangerous! This mission may not end with one battle, Miriam. Even if we kill Manasseh, there's still Zerah to contend with and—"

"Who's Zerah?"

"Manasseh's palace administrator. He's a very dangerous man, and he has a powerful hold over the king. He's always hovering beside Manasseh, caressing him and gazing at him with his sinister crossed eyes. He gave me the creeps, Miriam. But Manasseh has given Zerah a great deal of power for some reason, and even if we kill the king, Zerah could easily rally the troops and proclaim himself king in his place."

"What does Joshua say about all this?"

A strange expression crossed Hadad's face. The anger and vulnerability she'd glimpsed quickly vanished, replaced by the eerie deadness once again. "Joshua knows all the risks. But I'm sure he didn't explain any of them to you, did he?"

Miriam didn't reply. She watched a second ferry approach the shore and tie up at the dock.

"Is there any way at all that I can talk you out of going?" Hadad asked.

Miriam considered his question for a moment, and when she finally answered him, her voice was a soft murmur. "The first time I met Joshua he was sick with a fever. He might have died if I hadn't nursed him back to health. Then my father and I helped him escape from Jerusalem. It cost Abba his life. After the explosion at the Temple, if I hadn't gone back to look for him, Joshua wouldn't have survived. If anything happens to him on this mission and I'm not there to help him, I'll never forgive myself."

The ferry arrived; the passengers from the mainland filed off. As Miriam moved to join the line of people waiting to board, Hadad walked beside her. He stopped her just before she boarded and took her arm again.

"He isn't worth your life, Miriam. Joshua will never love you the way you love him."

"I know, Hadad. I know Joshua can't change. But neither can I."

8

"IT WAS RIGHT ABOUT HERE." King Manasseh pointed to the place where he thought the beggar woman had once read his and Joshua's palms, years ago, when they had been boys. Zerah had insisted that they walk down to the Kidron Valley, hoping that a return to the site would help jog Manasseh's memory of her prophecy. His men had searched for the woman, but it had happened too long ago—more than ten years. She was probably dead.

Everything seemed different to Manasseh, the trees bigger, the road narrower, the surrounding fields shrunken. "It was cold and raining that day," he began. "Joshua was the one who first stopped to talk to her. He wanted to give her some money, but he'd forgotten his pouch so I gave her a piece of silver. In return, she read my palm. She had no idea I was the king."

"Are you sure?"

"Yes, I'm sure! She was nearly blind. Besides, I wasn't wearing royal robes and I had no entourage. We were just two schoolboys, out for a stroll in the rain."

"Try to remember her exact words."

Manasseh sighed. They had been over this story a dozen times. "She told me I would have great power someday and hold many lives in my hand. I would achieve great fame. I don't remember what else. Then I made her read Joshua's palm. He fought me, saying he didn't want his fortune told because it violated the Torah. She took one look at his hand and dropped it like a hot stone, crying, 'Danger!' He was a danger to me. She said our lives would go in opposite directions and he would destroy everything I did."

"Were those her exact words? *He would destroy?*"

"I don't know . . . maybe she said he would *try* to destroy, I can't remember. But she said he wasn't my friend. He was my enemy."

"Is that everything?"

"I think so . . . no, wait. She also said that the power belonged to me but that Joshua would be more powerful." Manasseh thought about that for a moment. "How can that be, Zerah? I remember wondering at the time how that could be true. I'm the king. I'm the royal heir of King David, not Joshua. I wish I had gotten rid of him that day when I still had the chance. I wish he had died from his cursed breathing attack."

A crowd started to gather, curious to see what business the king had in the Kidron Valley. Zerah glanced around nervously. "Let's go back."

Manasseh knew Zerah hated to be seen in public. He usually left the palace only to attend the religious ceremonies at the Temple, and then only at night, when he would be well hidden by the cover of darkness. As they walked up the ramp, Manasseh planted his hand on Zerah's shoulder. "When are you going to tell me what the omens say about killing Joshua?"

"As soon as I figure out what they mean. They're unclear, Your Majesty."

"How can they be unclear? Either my enemy is destroyed or he isn't. Either I win or he does."

"The omens promise you the victory, but it will be only a partial one."

"I don't understand."

"I don't either, Your Majesty."

The months of planning and waiting had seemed endless to Manasseh, filled with the strain of anxiety. He wanted to defeat Joshua so badly it made him ill at times to think of failing. He knew that he would never feel safe again until his enemy was dead. Manasseh had entreated all the gods, offered countless sacrifices to win their favor, proffered innumerable petitions, sought multitudes of omens. But Zerah hedged, just as he was doing now, whenever Manasseh asked what the omens foretold.

When they reached the palace, General Benjamin was waiting for them in the council chamber. Manasseh would trust only his most experienced commander for this ambush mission, and he had called General Benjamin out of retirement to make certain that their plans were well laid and executed. The imposing general had served under King Hezekiah, taking charge of the defense of Jerusalem in General Jonadab's place during the Assyrian invasion. In peacetime, Hezekiah and Eliakim had entrusted Benjamin with the task of supervising their sons' military training.

Now nearing sixty, the general had maintained his powerful physique. Manasseh glanced at Zerah, aware that his administrator was frightened of the general. The king admitted only to himself that he had never fully outgrown his childhood awe of the man. Benjamin bowed low, then stood regarding Manasseh with eyes as cold and gray as stones, his weathered face as inscrutable as it had always been, revealing neither approval nor criticism of the task he had been assigned.

"Have you worked out all the details?" Manasseh asked him.

"I have everything under control, Your Majesty."

Manasseh relaxed slightly, knowing that the general was a man of his word. "Tell us the plan."

"Hadad chose an ideal location for the ambush, Your Majesty. I've handpicked the men who will escort your procession, and they are all highly skilled warriors. I am sending one hundred additional men into the area ahead of time, dressed in laborers' clothes. They will work in fields and vineyards during the day and hide in barns and storehouses at night so your enemies won't become alert to their presence. The day of the attack, the soldiers will leave their cover and begin to close the circle, completely surrounding the hill. By the time the procession approaches they'll be in position to cut off all avenues of retreat."

Manasseh sat forward abruptly. "Only one hundred men? That's not enough."

"Hadad assured us he would keep the attack force small."

"I want your guarantee that Joshua won't escape, General."

"He'll be completely surrounded. The roads will be blocked in every direction. The only way he could escape would be to jump off the cliff, and I assure you, I've examined the site and the fall would kill him if he tried it."

"Twice he has slipped from our grasp. Twice! I want your guarantee that it won't happen a third time!"

The general bristled slightly, reminding Manasseh of a guard dog with his hackles raised. "Very well, Your Majesty. I will station additional soldiers in each of the nearby towns, dressed in civilian clothes. They can cover every road leading out of the area. Believe me; no one will escape."

"Except Hadad," Zerah quickly added. "Remember, he promised to deliver Prince Amariah's body to us when this is over."

"Zerah's right, General. I don't want Hadad killed because someone screws up. Tell your men to watch for him. He'll be the only one who is clean-shaven. He looks Egyptian."

"I know what Hadad looks like," Benjamin said stiffly. "I trained Lord Shebna's grandson, just as I trained you and Joshua ben Eliakim."

"Have you chosen someone to act as my decoy, General?"

"I'll be inside the sedan chair myself, Your Majesty, dressed in your robes."

Manasseh pounded his fist on the arm of his chair and cursed. "I wish I could be there! I'd like to see Joshua's face when he realizes that I've defeated him!"

There was an immediate flurry of concern among Manasseh's bodyguards. "No, Your Majesty! It's much too dangerous! Anything could go wrong!"

Zerah rested his hand on Manasseh's. "If only the omens were clearer, my lord, but they're not."

"I know, I know," Manasseh sighed, shaking him off. "I'm just wishing, that's all. But if you can capture him alive, General, you'll be generously rewarded. I want to watch him die at my feet, begging for mercy."

Joshua stood on the ship's swaying deck, watching as the city of On came into view on the distant shore. It looked much like all the other Egyptian cities they'd passed—tightly clustered mud-brick homes, interspersed with palm trees and permeated with the stench of mildew and rotting fish. All of Egypt smelled the same to Joshua, and he could barely wait to inhale the clean mountain air of Jerusalem once again. The first leg of their long journey—the ten-day trip up the Nile to the delta—was almost over, his goal that much closer.

The day when their training had come to an end and they'd left Elephantine Island for this mission arrived too soon for Joshua. He had watched as Hadad drilled the men every day and had even joined with them to hone his own skills with bow and sword and spear, but none of the men seemed ready. His archers still weren't accurate enough at great distances. The swordsmen's reflexes were disappointingly slow. All of his volunteers were too green, their skills untried in real combat. He knew they needed more time, another month at least, before they'd be ready to face Manasseh's skilled soldiers, but they had run out of time. Their final squadron consisted of thirty-two men. Joshua wished for twice that number.

A spontaneous cheer went up from everyone on board when the ship docked in the city of On at last. The journey had been exhausting, the men unused to boat travel and the Nile rough sailing in flood stage. Joshua worried constantly about Dinah, who had been violently ill throughout the journey. He suspected that she was pregnant as well as seasick, but he was afraid to ask for fear of igniting Prince Amariah's anger. Joshua didn't know what they would have done without Miriam to take care of her.

He was as grateful as everyone else seemed to be to stand on dry land again. Hadad's soldiers milled nervously around the docks as the workers carefully unloaded bales of Jerimoth's cloth. All their weapons had been cleverly hidden inside the bolts of Egyptian cotton. But as Joshua stood watching beside his brother, he couldn't help worrying about the next stage of their journey. "Are you sure two days is enough time to hire a caravan and drivers?" he asked.

"How many times are you going to ask me that question?" Jerimoth answered irritably. "I've already told you it's a routine matter for me to hire animals and drivers."

Joshua knew that his brother's uncharacteristic anger was a symptom of his fear. He regretted involving him in such a dangerous plot, but he knew of no better way to smuggle men and weapons into the country.

"Listen, Jerimoth, everything depends on perfect timing. My men have to be in position before Manasseh's procession reaches the pass or else—"

Jerimoth's gaze was scorching. "Go see to your men and leave me alone to do my job."

A day and a half later, Jerimoth had loaded the caravan and was ready to leave as he'd promised. But the overland route north soon proved more exhausting than the river journey. Joshua didn't dare slow their pace even though the heat of full summer quickly drained their energy as well as their water supplies. They traveled together as far as Ashdod in Philistine territory, then split into three smaller caravans to cross the border into Judah using three different roads. Joshua didn't want to arouse suspicion by arriving in a large caravan.

"Remember," Joshua told his men before they separated, "if anything goes wrong, make your way to the village of Nahshon, two miles west of the ambush site. Jerimoth has hired a caravan of Ishmaelite spice traders for the return trip. Look for them."

Hadad and twenty of the men departed first to cross into Judah. They would deliver their load to Timnah, then make their way to the ambush site after dark to prepare the roadblock and dig entrenchments. Prince Amariah and the two women left in the second caravan to deliver their goods to Aijalon. Joshua had insisted that two soldiers accompany them to stand guard at the cave where they would hide. Once he'd killed King Manasseh, Joshua would send for the prince. His own caravan departed last to deliver the final load of Jerimoth's cloth to Beth Shemesh. Joshua would command their ten best archers from positions on top of the ridge overlooking the ambush site.

Crossing into Judah proved easy, but the sight of so many roadside shrines and high places shocked Joshua. He vowed that as soon as God granted them victory, the purification of his homeland would begin. The closer he got to the ambush site, the quieter the countryside seemed, the roads strangely deserted. He wondered why all the workers in the fields and vineyards appeared to be milling about, doing little work. Was it the heat?

When they arrived in Beth Shemesh the city was unusually crowded. All these men had probably come to watch Manasseh's dedication ceremony tomorrow. Joshua delivered his shipment of cloth to the marketplace without incident, then removed the weapons from their hiding places to wait until dark.

Late that night, Joshua and his men finally arrived at the ambush site. Hadad and his men were already there, working hard to create a natural-looking rockslide to block the road. They had already dug trenches along the road, covered with brush, to hide the men from view.

Joshua led his men up a narrow footpath to the crest of the ridge and worked by starlight to build earthworks. These would provide protective cover for his archers, while affording a clear shot of the procession. The men finished well before dawn.

"You may as well get a few hours of sleep," he told them. "I'm going to confer with Hadad one last time." He stumbled down the path in the dark, wondering if Prince Amariah and Dinah had made it safely to the cave.

Hadad's men had finished the roadblock and were also catching a few hours of sleep. "Where's Colonel Hadad?" Joshua asked the lone soldier standing watch. The guard led him to the trench Hadad had dug. It was empty.

"He was here a minute ago," the guard said. "He can't be far."

Joshua waited nearly half an hour, pacing restlessly in the deserted road, but Hadad never returned. "I need to get back up the hill," Joshua told the guard at last. "Tell Hadad I was just checking to see if everything is ready." Even in the darkness, Joshua could read the excitement in the young soldier's eyes.

"I assure you, my lord. We're prepared for battle."

But are you prepared to die? Joshua wanted to ask. "Be careful," he said instead. "And may God be with you."

9

Long after Dinah and Amariah had fallen asleep, Miriam lay awake in the darkness, tossing restlessly, wondering if the long night would ever end. The low-ceilinged cave was cold and damp, and it reeked of rotting vegetation and wild animals. The chill seemed to penetrate her heart. Tomorrow the battle would take place, tomorrow Joshua would assassinate King Manasseh—and fear for Joshua's safety lay in Miriam's stomach like a bitter tonic, preventing sleep. When they had parted ways in Philistine territory, she had wondered if she would ever see him again.

A rustling sound near the cave entrance startled her, and Miriam rolled over, straining to see in the darkness. Someone was rousing the sleeping guard; the last watch of the night must have begun. She lay listening to the murmur of voices outside the cave, waiting for the second guard to take his turn sleeping, but when she looked again she saw three figures silhouetted in the doorway. Was one of them Joshua? Miriam tossed the covers aside to hurry outside, wrapping her robe around her shoulders. The two soldiers were talking to Hadad.

"What are you doing here?" she asked him. "Is something wrong?" It seemed odd that Hadad pulled her aside, away from the guards, before answering her question.

"I came to check on you and Dinah," he said in a low voice. "I wanted to make sure you were both safe." A peculiar fire burned in his dark eyes, and his gaze darted among the shadows, not meeting hers. He seemed different from the Hadad she knew. Was it simply readiness for the approaching battle? Had the knowledge that he soon might die altered him this way? A thick canopy of trees and brush shielded the sky from view, and Miriam shivered in the gloomy darkness.

"Hadad, why—"

"Go back to bed, Miriam." His voice and hands were rough as he pushed her toward the cave. "Stay inside until this is over."

She did as she was told but lay awake listening to the murmur of voices outside the cave. Then all was quiet. Miriam waited, watching the entrance, but neither of the guards returned to the cave. When exhaustion finally won the battle with worry, Miriam slept.

The cave was lit by the approaching dawn when she awoke. Dinah was still asleep beside her, but Prince Amariah was up and moving carefully around the cave, stooping to keep from hitting his head on the low ceiling. When she saw that he was laying out food from one of their provision bags, Miriam scrambled off her pallet to help him.

"Let me fix breakfast for you, Your Majesty."

"This is for Dinah. She'll feel better if she eats something as soon as she wakes up."

"I know, my lord, but I can do it." She tried to take the bread and the knife from his hands, but he stopped her.

"I need something to do, Miriam. Waiting like this . . ." He exhaled. "Waiting is always the hardest part. I'll be so glad when this is over."

She let him finish his task, but even in the dim light she noticed the strain etched on his face and the tremor in his hands as he sliced the bread and cheese. In a few hours he might be the king of Judah, living in a palace again with servants to tend to his every need. Now he sought comfort in playing the role of a dutiful husband, tending his ill wife. Miriam couldn't imagine how it would feel to be part of a plot to kill her own brother.

Amariah glanced up, and when he saw Miriam watching him

he seemed embarrassed. "It was so good of you to come with us, Miriam. I don't know how I can thank you for taking such good care of Dinah. I've been so worried about her. If I'd had my way, neither you nor Dinah ever would have come."

His words surprised her. She repeated them to herself and found they didn't fit with what she had been told. "Wait a minute, Your Majesty. I thought it was *your* idea to bring Dinah."

"No! Never! I begged them to let her stay in Egypt, where it was safe, but Hadad insisted—"

"*Hadad* insisted? But he told me this was *your* idea."

"When did he tell you that?"

"Before we left Egypt. When he tried to talk me out of coming."

Amariah stopped what he was doing and stared intently at her. "Tell me exactly what he said to you."

The strength of his gaze flustered her. She struggled to remember Hadad's words. "He said that Joshua was just using me. He warned me that the mission would be dangerous and said that I shouldn't—"

Amariah shook his head as if to clear his thoughts. "Miriam, that doesn't make any sense. Hadad was the one who insisted that Dinah come with us. If he was concerned for your safety, why wouldn't he be even more concerned about hers?"

"But Hadad *is* concerned about her. He even came here early this morning to check on her."

"*What?* Hadad was *here*?" Amariah gripped her shoulders so tightly she winced.

"Yes, he was here just a little while ago. He talked to the two guards and—"

All the blood drained from Amariah's face as if someone had removed a stopper. "Stay here with Dinah." He pushed Miriam aside and hurried from the cave.

Miriam stared at the entrance in a daze. The fear in Amariah's eyes had frightened her, but she was unsure what it was she should fear. As she tried to untangle her thoughts, Dinah began to stir. Miriam quickly brought her the bread and cheese, grateful for the distraction of a familiar task. "Your husband thought you might like something to eat right away."

"Where is he?"

"Outside talking with the guards."

But Miriam heard no voices from outside the cave. Ever since they'd arrived, the guards had stayed close to the entrance, where they'd be hidden from view yet able to keep watch over the prince. Where had they gone? Hours seemed to pass before Amariah finally returned. When Miriam saw his bloodless face, she sprang to her feet. "What's wrong?"

"They've disappeared," he said breathlessly. "The two guards—I've looked everywhere for them. They're gone. So are all the weapons."

"But that makes no sense. Where would they go?"

He moved close to Miriam, peering intently into her face as if he didn't want to miss a word she said. "Miriam, tell me exactly what Hadad said this morning."

Miriam's heart leaped, and she didn't know why. Amariah was terribly afraid of something, and she seemed to hold the key to the mystery. She recalled the strange light in Hadad's eye and shivered.

"I asked Hadad why he was here, and he took me aside to talk to me so the guards wouldn't hear us. He looked different somehow—on edge. He said he came to make sure that Dinah and I were safe, then he told me to go back to bed. I heard him talking to the guards for a few more minutes, and when they were quiet again I fell asleep."

Amariah paced a few steps toward the cave entrance, deep in thought. "Both guards were awake?" he asked after a moment.

"Yes."

"They were supposed to sleep in shifts," he murmured.

"Someone came into the cave and woke one of them. I think it must have been Hadad."

Amariah closed his eyes and lowered his head, covering his mouth and chin with one hand. He stayed frozen that way for several long minutes, until Miriam thought she might scream from the tension. Finally he drew a deep breath and faced her again.

"Before we left Egypt . . . when Hadad tried to convince you not to come ... Did he tell you why it was too dangerous?"

The urgency in Amariah's voice told Miriam the importance of recalling every single word. Her heart galloped as she let her mind travel back to the ferry dock, remembering how Hadad had appeared out of nowhere, remembering how inexplicably frightened of him she had been.

"He told me that the battle might not end once Manasseh was dead. He said that Manasseh's right-hand man—the one with the strange, crossed eyes—might try to make himself king."

Amariah gripped her shoulders again. "He described Zerah?"

"Yes—that's what he said the man's name was. Hadad said Zerah gave him the creeps. That he was always hovering close to King Manasseh, always caressing him."

Amariah swayed, and for a moment, Miriam thought she would have to catch him.

"O God, help us all," he said. "It's a trap."

"What do you mean? What's a trap?"

"We're all walking into a trap!" Amariah's wide eyes seemed to fill his pale face. His breathing sounded as labored as Joshua's when he had one of his attacks. Dinah scrambled to her feet and took Amariah's arm as if to steady him.

"How do you know?"

"I feared this all along," he mumbled. "I tried to warn Joshua, but he was so intent on revenge that he was blind to all the warning signs, and now—"

"Amariah! How do you know?" Dinah shouted. She looked as ill as he did.

The prince forced out the words as if pronouncing a death sentence. "Because Zerah never leaves the palace. He's rarely seen in public except at night, and even then he's surrounded by bodyguards."

"But couldn't things have changed since you left?" Dinah asked. "Maybe Hadad saw him at a convocation ... or ... or at a—"

"Hadad could never have gotten close enough to see Zerah's eyes or to watch how he caresses my brother unless he was in the palace with them. And how else would Hadad know Zerah's name? No, Dinah, they must have plotted this together. It's a trap."

Dinah shook him, as if to bring him to his senses, to make him admit it wasn't true. "But why? Why would Hadad go to all this trouble? He could have killed you and Joshua himself if that's what he's after."

"No, no, don't you see? This is perfect justice to Hadad. We betrayed him, and now he wants to betray Joshua and me to Manasseh. It's the ultimate revenge. Hadad will come back here to kill me himself, I'm certain of it. That's why he got rid of the guards. And that's why he insisted that you come, Dinah. So he wouldn't have to return to Egypt for you."

"And I'm in his way," Miriam said. She fit all the puzzle pieces together—the strange way Hadad had acted, the odd look in his eyes, her inexplicable fear of him—and suddenly they all made sense. Hadad knew she would do anything to protect Joshua. He was afraid she would see through his lies. "Your Majesty, you're right—it is a trap!"

"Manasseh is probably nowhere near that procession," the prince said. "And he probably has hundreds of troops swarming all over the countryside, surrounding us. That's why we saw so many men in the village yesterday. They're Manasseh's men."

"What are we going to do?" Dinah asked.

"We need to warn Joshua!" Miriam said. "We need to tell him it's a trap!"

As Amariah drew a deep breath, Miriam was amazed to see that he was no longer panicked. He seemed surprisingly calm as he took Dinah's hands in his, speaking gently to her. "If you stay here, Hadad will very likely return for you. I'm certain he won't harm you. I'll understand if you want to go with him."

Fear and confusion battled on Dinah's face. "But I'm carrying your child."

"I know," he said quietly. "I promised you a royal son to replace the one Manasseh murdered. You don't have to stay with me any longer now that you're pregnant."

Miriam felt desperate. This was taking much too long. "Your Majesty, you need to run! Hadad will kill you if you stay here, and I have to warn Joshua that he's walking into a trap!"

Dinah looked as if she might faint. "None of this would have happened if it hadn't been for me."

Miriam suddenly saw the truth with perfect clarity, and it angered her. "You're wrong, Dinah. This is Joshua's fault, not yours. If he hadn't interfered, if he hadn't been so full of hatred and so intent on revenge, you would have married Hadad and none of this would have ever happened. Joshua manipulated everyone. Now he's caught in the trap he created himself."

"She's right, Dinah," Amariah said. "Let's not make the same mistake twice. Never mind what Joshua wants. Decide for yourself what to do about Hadad. Do you want to go with him?"

Dinah didn't reply. Miriam wondered how Amariah could wait so patiently when Hadad might return any minute to kill him. With no guards and only a bread knife for a weapon, the prince was defenseless against a vastly superior foe. Miriam felt a shiver of awe at his tremendous courage. Unlike Joshua's daring, which sprang from the desire to avenge himself, Amariah's courage was selfless.

As Dinah stood twisting her hands, Miriam wanted to shake her and scream at her to hurry. At last Dinah answered her husband. "Did Hadad pretend to be your friend just so he could turn you and Joshua over to Manasseh?" Amariah nodded grimly. "What about all the innocent men who volunteered for this mission? They trusted him as their commanding officer. Is he going to watch all of them die, too?"

"Yes. God help them," Amariah murmured.

"I thought I loved Hadad," Dinah said. "But I can't love a man who is capable of such treachery. Please, let's get out of here before he comes back."

The prince seemed to sag with relief. "Miriam, gather all the provisions you can find," he said. "I'll try to figure out how to get us back to Jerimoth's caravan in Nahshon. Manasseh probably has men everywhere, so we won't be able to take the roads and—"

"I'm not going with you," Miriam said. "I have to warn Joshua. Tell me which way to go. How can I find him?"

"Miriam, I can't let you do that."

"You let Dinah decide what she wanted to do. Give me the same right. It's my life, Your Majesty."

"Manasseh's troops have Joshua completely surrounded by now.

None of you will escape alive. I can't let you forfeit your life for him."

"You would have forfeited your life for Dinah."

"That's different. She's—"

Dinah touched Amariah's sleeve. "Let her go, Amariah," she said.

"Yes, please!" Miriam begged. "We're wasting time!"

At last he heaved a tired sigh. "If you go straight down the hill from the cave, you'll come to the road. Turn right and follow it east toward the sun. When you reach the roadblock . . . No, wait, that's no good. Hadad is in charge of the roadblock. He'll never let you through."

"Where's Joshua?"

"On top of the ridge above the road. But there's no way around the roadblock—that's the whole point of it. The hill borders one side of the road, and there's a cliff on the other side."

"Hadad might try to stop me, but I don't think he'll hurt me. I have to try, Your Majesty. You and Dinah go without me." Miriam bent to fasten her sandals, then moved toward the mouth of the cave. As she paused to look back at them, her heart told her that she might be seeing them for the last time. Dinah looked pale and frightened, the prince strangely calm and determined. She could think of so many things she wanted to say to them, but there wasn't time.

The prince rested his hand on her shoulder. "May God go with you, Miriam."

"And with you," she whispered.

Miriam hurried out of the cave and scrambled down the hill through the brush, searching for the road. It had been dark when they'd climbed the hill to the cave the night before, and it had taken Amariah and the soldiers a while to find it. Now she squinted in the brightness, and when her feet hit the rutted dirt track, she turned right and began to jog toward the sun.

Miriam knew she needed God's help. Lady Jerusha always assured her that God was always near, ready to answer; all she had to do was call on Him. It still sounded too good to be true, but then Miriam remembered how God had helped her find Joshua at the Temple, how He had helped Joshua survive the explosion, and she began to plead with Him in her heart as she ran.

O God, I know I'm not a worthy person. I know I was born in shame and disgrace. But I'm begging you . . . please let me get to Joshua in time. Please don't let him die.

The road climbed steadily uphill. After ten minutes of running, Miriam felt a sharp pain knifing her side. She had to slow down, but walking seemed much too slow—she would never get there in time. Tears of frustration blinded her as she began to jog again, ignoring the pain.

Joshua has done some terrible things, God. I know he has. But maybe if you give him another chance he could make it up to you. If somebody has to die, then why not let it be me? My life isn't worth much. I'm just a servant girl, but Joshua is the leader of your people. They need him. He knows your Laws, and he can teach everyone. Please, God . . . please . . .

The road snaked in switchbacks as it ascended the mountain. Each time she rounded a curve she expected to see the men guarding the roadblock, but the road climbed on, the sun rose higher. Miriam glimpsed the drop-off Amariah had described, visible through the trees on her left. The houses and animals in the valley below looked like children's toys. Nearly half an hour must have passed since she'd left the cave. If she didn't find Joshua soon, she would drop from exhaustion.

Then Miriam rounded another curve and saw what looked like a landslide spilling across the road ahead. A barren scar sliced down from the ridge marking the fallen boulders' path. There was no sign of Hadad or his men. Was this the roadblock or a genuine landslide? Staggering with fatigue, Miriam jogged toward the jumble of rocks. She couldn't go around them because of the steep slope on her right, the sheer cliff on her left. She would have to scramble over the boulders.

As she searched for the easiest route to climb, she glimpsed an abrupt movement on her right. Before she could turn her head, someone rammed into her side, knocking her to the ground in the middle of the road. Miriam would have cried out but a rough hand covered her mouth as a man fell on top of her, his weight knocking the wind out of her. She lay stunned, gasping for air.

"Don't struggle," he whispered. "Don't make a sound." Miriam was too dazed to struggle, too terrified to scream.

The man scrambled to his knees, then to his feet, pulling Miriam with him. He kept one hand planted over her mouth, the other clamped so tightly around her ribs she could scarcely breathe. With her head pressed firmly to her captor's chest, she couldn't swivel to see his face, but as he dragged her to the side of the road and rolled into the ditch with her, she caught a glimpse of the hand circling her waist.

Hadad's hand.

Miriam recognized his ring—the one that had belonged to his grandfather. He released her long enough to pull a clump of brush over the ditch to conceal them, but the weight of his body on top of hers pinned her in place. She couldn't move.

Hadad's lips brushed against her ear as he whispered through clenched teeth. "What are you doing here, Miriam?"

Prince Amariah regretted his decision as soon as Miriam left the cave. Hers was a suicide mission. For a moment he considered going after her, but Dinah's pleas brought him to his senses. "We have to hurry, we have to run. Hadad will kill you!"

The panic he saw in her eyes wrenched his heart. She was his wife; he was supposed to love and protect her. Instead, he had endangered her life by involving her in this mess. If he hadn't allowed Joshua and Hadad to bully him into bringing her, she would be safe at home in Egypt right now. Amariah silently vowed before God that if he escaped from Hadad's trap alive, he would never let Joshua or anyone else dictate to him again. He would take control of his life. He would be the leader God intended him to be. Starting now.

"Dinah, eat some bread and cheese before we go. You'll need strength to travel. It's going to be very difficult since we won't be able to travel on the roads."

"I can't eat anything. I feel so sick."

"Your stomach will settle if you eat something."

"But Hadad could come back any minute. We have to—"

"Hadad won't hurt you, Dinah. I know he won't."

"But he'll kill you!"

"Then eat some food for me, quickly. If not for me, then for our baby."

She ate the bread and cheese while he searched for a skin of water. The packs of supplies the soldiers had carried were gone. Except for the small amount of food he and Dinah had in their provision bag, they had nothing. He would have to recall everything he had ever learned about survival. Being a royal prince, he hadn't learned much. Miriam had helped him escape the last time, and once again he regretted letting her go. It was up to him. Dinah and their child were depending on him. He crouched beside her.

"Are you ready?" he asked.

"Promise me something." Her eyes darted from his face to the cave entrance in terror. "If the soldiers find us, promise you'll kill me. Don't let Manasseh capture me again."

His heart twisted at the thought of Dinah in his brother's hands. But he knew he could never kill her himself. "Dinah, I can't promise that. The baby—"

"Manasseh will kill our baby if you don't. Please, I'd rather die than go back to him."

"I'm going to do everything in my power to make certain we don't get caught."

"But what if we do?"

For a long moment Amariah couldn't answer. Then the words of David's psalm came to him from the past. The voice that spoke them was his father's. He gathered Dinah's hands in his and recited the words aloud.

"'He who dwells in the shelter of the Most High will rest in the shadow of the Almighty. . . . He will cover you with his feathers, and under his wings you will find refuge. . . . You will not fear the terror of night, nor the arrow that flies by day. . . . A thousand may fall at your side, ten thousand at your right hand, but it will not come near you. . . . For he will command his angels concerning you to guard you in all your ways; they will lift you up in their hands, so that you will not strike your foot against a stone.'"

As Amariah recited the words, all the panic and fear cleared from his soul. He knew exactly what he should do to save Dinah.

"We're going to find a safe place to hide until after dark," he told her calmly. "We're going to move carefully, without being seen, without leaving a trail." He held her at arm's length to peer intently into her eyes. "Will you help me keep watch as we go? Will you help me make certain there's not a footprint or a broken twig to show where we've been?"

She nodded fearfully, then threw herself into his arms, clinging to him as if to a plank in the sea. Amariah lingered in her embrace for a moment, savoring the bittersweet joy of it, then gently loosened her hold.

"We have to go now, Dinah."

10

Hadad's weight bore down on Miriam, crushing her into the dirt. His breath felt hot against her ear. She should have realized this might happen. Amariah told her that Hadad was guarding the roadblock. Why hadn't she thought of a better plan or approached the ridge by a different route?

"I'm going to uncover your mouth," Hadad whispered. "Tell me why you're here. If you make any sound louder than a whisper, I'll kill you."

She had mere seconds in her panicked state to invent a lie Hadad would believe. *Please, God . . . help me think!* What was the one sure way to deceive him, to convince him to set her free? He slowly uncovered her mouth.

"Dinah," she whispered.

"What about her?"

"She's deathly ill. Amariah sent me to find Joshua because the guards disappeared. If Dinah doesn't get help soon, she could die."

Hadad tensed. "What's wrong with her?"

"We don't know. She's burning with fever, vomiting blood."

Miriam sensed Hadad's indecision as instinct pulled him in two directions at once. His breath rasped in her ear. Time slowed to a crawl as she lay beneath him in the ditch, waiting for him to act. She used it to plan her next move. If only Hadad would believe her, if only he would drop his guard for a moment, Miriam could cry out a warning to Joshua. He was hiding on the hill above them somewhere.

Please, God . . .

"Hadad, let me go. You're hurting me. We need to hurry. We need to get Dinah to the closest city." He shifted his weight slightly. Again Miriam waited.

"All right," he said at last. "I'll go back to the cave with you." He scrambled out of the ditch, pulling Miriam to her feet. She was free.

Sky and earth and trees whirled around her dizzily as she stood by the side of the road, trying to get her bearings. She turned to face the ridge and drew a deep breath.

"Joshua, run! It's a trap! It's a trap! Hadad betrayed—"

Pain cut off her cries as Hadad tackled her again, smashing her to the ground with jarring force, cursing her below his breath. This time Miriam fought back. She knew she could never win, but desperation urged her to cause enough commotion to attract Joshua's attention. Maybe he could see this section of the road from where he was hiding. She prayed that he had heard her brief shout of warning.

Please, God, tell him to run for his life!

She wrenched one hand free from beneath Hadad and clawed at his face and eyes. He gasped in pain and released his hold over her mouth to pry her fingers off his face. She gulped air and screamed again, "Joshua, run! *RUN!*"

As Hadad covered her mouth again, Miriam fought with all her strength, kicking, twisting, ignoring the agonizing pain as his brawny arms squeezed her and the weight of his body crushed her.

Hadad rolled over and over in the dirt with her. She felt his feet scrambling for a foothold as he tried to stand with her. Miriam fought harder, trying to throw him off balance, trying to attract as much attention as she could before he could throw her into the ditch again, out of sight. He struggled to his feet, locking Miriam in a deadly embrace, face-to-face like lovers. Her feet dangled above the ground.

Then to Miriam's surprise, Hadad released her, pushing her

roughly away from him. She fell backward, arms flailing to regain her balance. Her feet searched for the ground but there was nothing behind her, nothing beneath her. The earth had simply disappeared.

Miriam screamed as she felt herself falling into a bottomless void.

From his vantage point atop the ridge, Joshua had watched as a lone woman jogged up the road toward the ambush site; then he stared in angry disbelief when he saw it was Miriam. What was that foolish girl doing here? Was this another one of her misguided attempts to help him? Why hadn't she done as she was told and stayed inside the cave until this was over?

He clenched his fists in frustration, knowing he didn't dare call out to her, hoping she had sense enough not to call out to him. When Hadad had tackled her, dragging her out of sight, Joshua breathed a sigh of relief. The morning fell quiet, the only sounds the chirping of birds, the droning of insects. The day would be hot.

One of his soldiers nudged him, pointing to a flicker of color and movement on the brief stretch of road visible between the trees a half mile behind them. The king's procession. A shiver of excitement raced through Joshua. In a few more minutes, Manasseh would walk into Joshua's snare. He drew slow, deep breaths as he prepared to kill his enemy at last. His life's work was finally coming to fulfillment. Once he'd avenged the murders of his father and grandfather, once he'd rid his nation of Manasseh, his work would be complete. Maybe then he could find the rest and peace that had eluded him for the past two years.

Suddenly, Miriam's cry pierced the quiet morning. "Joshua, run! It's a trap! It's a trap! Hadad betrayed—"

Joshua whirled around in time to see Hadad throw Miriam to the ground again. Foolish girl! She was going to ruin everything! All their carefully laid plans! Joshua had waited two years for revenge. What if Miriam's cries had alerted Manasseh's procession?

Joshua quickly scrambled down the hill to help Hadad subdue her. He had to convince her to be quiet and take cover. The procession was only a few minutes away.

By the time Joshua reached the road, Hadad had Miriam nearly under control. His hand was planted firmly over her mouth again. He pulled her to her feet. But they were teetering dangerously close to the edge of the cliff.

"Hadad, watch out!" he cried.

Before Joshua could sprint across the road to help him, Hadad suddenly released Miriam with a rough push. Joshua watched in horror as she tumbled backward and disappeared over the edge of the cliff.

Joshua froze in the middle of the road, too stunned to move. With breathtaking speed, Hadad drew his sword and whirled to face him. Joshua saw Hadad's blinding hatred. Too late, much too late, Joshua finally comprehended Miriam's words.

"It's a trap . . . Joshua, run!"

Blood oozed from the scratches she had made on Hadad's face, underscoring Joshua's mistake. Miriam wasn't foolish; she was level-headed, courageous. She had saved Joshua's life twice before. Why hadn't he heeded her warning? The horror of Miriam's death dizzied him. Joshua drew his own sword, his movements clumsy and slow.

Hadad stood with sword in hand, as if waiting for Joshua to make the first move. Joshua saw the intense concentration in his eyes, the slight smile on his lips. They both knew Hadad's skills were superior to his own. He was stronger, faster, more practiced. Joshua would lose in a duel against him.

Disconnected thoughts raced through Joshua's mind, and his head spun as he labored to make sense of them. The slow realization that he would never have a chance to kill Manasseh devastated him. It had all been a sham. He would never be able to satisfy his hunger for revenge. He had been tricked, betrayed, just as he'd betrayed Hadad. Joshua heard the blood rushing in his ears and felt the familiar weight settle on his chest, preventing him from drawing a deep breath. The sword felt heavy in his hand.

Hadad still hadn't moved. Surely Joshua's men on the ridge would notice this standoff. If Joshua ducked aside, maybe the archers could get a clear shot at Hadad. But the men were probably confused about what was happening. Hadad was their commanding officer. He had worked closely with them, lived with them, built them into a fighting team. Joshua was the outsider. None of the men was experienced enough to take command in a crisis. Hadad had made certain of that. In the next few minutes, Joshua was likely to die at his hands.

But Hadad continued to watch Joshua intently, his sword held level, ready to strike. Why didn't he attack? Suddenly Joshua remembered the approaching procession and understood. Hadad didn't have to kill him. He merely had to hold him at bay for a few more minutes until Manasseh's soldiers arrived. Joshua had two choices—fight a mismatched battle with Hadad, which he couldn't possibly win, or be captured by the soldiers and die at Manasseh's hands. His mouth felt as dry as desert sand.

"How does it feel?" Hadad said slowly. His voice was the satisfied growl of a predator who has cornered his prey. "How does it feel to be betrayed by a friend?"

"I already know how it feels. I was betrayed by Manasseh, remember?" But Hadad's question helped Joshua reach a decision. He would rather let Hadad kill him than be turned over to his enemy. He thought he heard the rumble of the procession in the distance above the thundering of his heart. He fought the panic of suffocation.

Concentrate.

Joshua pushed everything else from his mind to focus on what General Benjamin had taught him. *Exploit your enemy's weaknesses.*

As his eyes bored into Hadad's, watching for the first twitch of his muscles, Joshua summoned a mental image of Hadad sparring with his men in the practice yard. What were his weaknesses, his blind spots? He had a favorite offensive maneuver that he often used—feinting left, then swinging sharply to attack from the right—but as time slowly ran out, Joshua could recall no weaknesses.

Except one.

In an idea borne of desperation, Joshua allowed his gaze to wander from Hadad's for a fraction of a second, as if a sudden movement near the roadblock had caught his eye.

"Dinah, no! Stay back!" he shouted.

As Hadad turned his head to look, Joshua lunged. Either kill or be killed, he had instructed his men. That was the choice he faced. With his sword outstretched, Joshua threw himself at Hadad, driving the weapon into him with all the force of his weight, impaling him.

Hadad cried out in agony, badly wounded. Joshua had hoped to knock him off balance and topple him to the ground, but Hadad was too heavy, too strong. With the hilt of Joshua's sword protruding from his gut, Hadad lashed back convulsively, his eyes glazed in pain, blindly flailing his sword as if determined to take Joshua through the gates of Sheol with him.

Hadad's first crazed swing swished through Joshua's hair as he ducked, off balance. He couldn't move quickly enough. The second blow grazed his shoulder. Joshua tried to back away, but he stumbled. Hadad lurched toward him, faster than Joshua could move. He would never be able to get out of range of Hadad's frantic sword thrusts in time.

Instead, he surprised Hadad by lunging toward him again in a clumsy tackle. Joshua brought his right fist up, smashing it into Hadad's outstretched arm from below with enough force to break his grip. The sword flew from Hadad's grasp. Enraged, he coiled his left arm around Joshua's throat, forcing back his head with a jerk meant to snap his neck. Ordinarily he could have done it, but Hadad was weakening. Blood poured from him, soaking their clothes, pooling on the ground beneath their scrambling feet.

Joshua's arms quivered from exertion as he fought to pry off Hadad's arm before it crushed his windpipe. He couldn't breathe. His vision shrank until he peered through a narrow tunnel, illuminated by stars of light. In what he knew was his last desperate attempt, Joshua groped for the hilt of his own sword, still protruding from Hadad's stomach. When he found it, he twisted it savagely, pushing it deeper into Hadad's body.

Hadad screamed in anguish. He released Joshua and staggered backward, then sank to his knees while Joshua strained to fill his lungs with air again. Hadad found his own sword lying on the ground in front of him and swung it blindly, slashing Joshua's thigh. There was little strength behind his thrust. The weapon dropped from Hadad's hand as he toppled facedown in the dirt.

The rumble of the approaching procession was unmistakable above Hadad's wretched cries. Fighting nausea, Joshua cupped his bloodstained hands to his mouth and drew a breath to shout to his bewildered troops.

"Run! It's an ambush! Run for your lives!"

Even as he shouted, Joshua knew it was hopeless. Manasseh's army must have them all surrounded by now. He prayed that the men who had bravely volunteered for this mission would keep cool heads, that they would remember the evasive maneuvers they'd been taught, that at least some of them would escape to safety.

Joshua limped toward the edge of the cliff where Miriam had fallen and peered below. He expected to see her sprawled at the bottom but saw only rocks and brush. She had sacrificed her life for him, just as her father had. Her selfless act staggered him, humbled him, and he wanted to sink down in the dirt beside Hadad's body and weep at the senselessness of it all. But a more rational part of him argued that Miriam's act of love would be wasted unless he lived.

He saw only one way to escape from the snare that Manasseh's men had set for him. He wiped his bloody palms on the front of his tunic and picked up Hadad's sword, sheathing it in his own scabbard. Then, gripping whatever brush and outcroppings of rock he could find, Joshua lowered himself over the edge and began the precarious climb down the face of the cliff.

Inch by inch, Joshua slowly made his way from handhold to handhold—a clump of coarse grass, a jutting rock, a dried tree root. The descent seemed endless as his arms began to tire and his reserves of strength ebbed away. His mind urged him to hurry and yet exercise caution, and he wondered, *How can I do both?*

He found the next handhold, then dry dirt and dust showered down on him as he descended. It filled his nostrils, coated his hair and skin, and settled in his exhausted lungs until he choked helplessly, unable to stop himself. Would they hear him on the road above?

There's a toehold. See if it supports your weight. Good. Rest your arms a moment. Now keep going.

Suddenly he came to an abrupt halt. There were no more rocks or roots to cling to. He looked left, then right. He was trapped, pinned to the face of the cliff. Why hadn't he scouted his route more carefully? Now the only way down was to climb back up a dozen feet and look for a better way. He began to retrace his steps.

Sweat poured into his eye, stinging painfully, blurring his vision. Without thinking, he rolled his head to the side to wipe his face on his shoulder, then he gasped in agony as dirt and sweat rubbed into the fresh wound Hadad had given him. Pain shuddered through him.

Joshua lost his grip, found nothing to grab, and suddenly he was sliding—skimming down the cliff face, hands slipping, rocks pulling loose, feet scrambling. Jagged debris scraped his knees, his chin, ripped his clothes. Skin peeled from his fingertips as he dug them into the dirt to slow his momentum, to stop his fall.

O God, help me!

He groped for a jutting rock as he slid past it, and clung to it with one hand, swinging. It held, saving his life.

He gripped it with both hands as he carefully kicked a toehold in the dry earth so he could rest for a moment, catch his breath, and decide what to do next. His arms trembled with weariness, his shoulder throbbed and bled. He started down again, not daring to rest too long.

Find the next handhold. Now the next. A place for your foot. Keep going.

He never should have started down this cliff. It had been a bad idea. He couldn't go on. It was too far. There was so little on this sheer precipice to cling to. What if he fell again?

God of Abraham, how much farther?

He glanced down, then closed his eye to make the dizziness stop. The bottom still seemed a hundred whirling miles away. He would never make it down alive. But he had to. There was no other choice but to finish this treacherous descent.

Don't look down. Concentrate! Find something to grab onto.

On and on he went, necessity driving him, weariness dogging

him, until it seemed that the only thing there had ever been in his life was this never-ending cliff. Pain cramped his hands. The agony spread to his quivering arms, his shoulders. All at once Joshua's strength gave out, and with no place to plant his feet, he slid the last twenty feet to the bottom, landing with a jolt. His ankle twisted painfully as he smashed to the ground.

He tried to stand, collapsed, tried again, then lost consciousness as he slumped to the ground for the third time.

When Joshua first opened his eye, he didn't know where he was. Then he saw the mountain looming above him and he remembered the cliff. The endless cliff. God of Abraham, he had made it!

His knees were too weak to support his weight, so he rolled onto his back and slowly took stock of himself. No broken bones, but his limbs still trembled with fatigue. His clothes were covered with blood—some of it his own, most of it Hadad's. The cuts on his shoulder and thigh throbbed. So did his bruised hands and sprained ankle.

He decided to crawl to the nearest hiding place. When he spotted a thick clump of branches several yards away, he rolled onto his stomach and inched toward it. But something jutting from among the leaves and branches looked strangely out of place: a human hand.

Miriam.

She lay on her back, half hidden beneath a tree branch, her arms outflung. Joshua looked up and saw the tree where she had landed, growing from the side of the bluff. One of its branches had broken off beneath her weight.

He crawled to Miriam's side. Her body and dusty face were battered and scratched, her hair matted with dirt and leaves, but there was very little blood. She looked peaceful with her eyes closed, as if she might have been asleep. With no hope in his heart, Joshua felt her throat for a pulse.

The faint throb beneath his fingers stunned him. Was he imagining it? He slowly sat up and felt again.

"Miriam," he whispered.

When her eyes flew open, he jerked back, startled. She stared straight up at the sky, unseeing. Joshua gently turned her head to the side until he was in her line of vision. Recognition flickered in her glazed eyes. Her lips formed his name soundlessly. *Joshua.*

"Yes. I'm here."

Her eyes rolled closed again, as if the effort to keep them open was too great. She shook her head slightly from side to side, struggling to speak. He lowered his head to hear.

"Yes, Miriam?"

"It's . . . a trap," she whispered faintly. *"Run!"*

Then her body went still.

II

GENERAL BENJAMIN SAT INSIDE King Manasseh's covered sedan chair, gripping a dagger. As they neared the ambush site he was calm yet alert, ready to leap at Joshua son of Eliakim or whoever might attack him. Benjamin was a seasoned warrior, skilled in hand-to-hand combat, eager for the challenge of a good fight. He had trained Eliakim's son, knew all his faults and weaknesses, and knew that the lad would be a poor match for his own considerable skills.

The king's bodyguards on either side of him looked like hazy shadows through the curtains. They were spoiling for a fight, primed to kill, waiting for the first volley of arrows from the archers on the ridge, which would signal the attack. Benjamin wasn't worried about the impending battle. Hadad had assured him that Joshua's force would be small and inexperienced; Benjamin had chosen his finest skilled warriors. There would be no contest.

The procession emerged from a grove of trees onto an open stretch of road. Benjamin glimpsed blue sky and clouds on his right, the edge of the cliff a few feet away. This was it.

The procession slowed, then stopped abruptly. He tightened his grip on his weapon. "Why are we stopping?" he asked the aide walking on his left. "Have they fired on us?"

"No, General. The roadblock is just ahead, but there's something in the middle of the road. It looks like a body."

"Careful. It could be a trick."

Joshua may have been a poor soldier, but he possessed a clever mind. If he had changed Hadad's plans, the general would have no way of learning about it. He parted the curtain slightly and peered out, watching as one of his men advanced cautiously and kicked the body over with his foot. The soldier looked up in surprise.

"It's Hadad! He's dead!"

For the first time since leaving Jerusalem at dawn, Benjamin felt a seed of fear begin to take root. Something had gone horribly wrong.

"Everyone alert!" he shouted. "Take your positions!" As he emerged from the carriage, his men scrambled to form a protective circle around him, bows strung, swords drawn, shields raised. He crouched in the road and gazed into Hadad's staring eyes.

"This just happened," he murmured. "His body is warm; his blood hasn't thickened. Whoever killed him must be in the area."

Benjamin rose to his feet and inspected the abandoned trenches, where Hadad's men had planned to hide in ambush. They had fled hastily, without bothering to replace the loose brush that would have hidden them from view.

"Hadad must have given himself away at the last minute," he mused aloud. "This sword that killed him is Egyptian-made. It belonged to one of his own men." He shook his head. "Too bad. It was an excellent plan."

His men stood alert, watching him, waiting for orders. "Spread out! Quickly! They can't be far. Fan out in all directions until you meet with our forces closing in." He had spread a huge net around this hill. Joshua's men couldn't possibly escape. There was no place to go.

One of his men pointed to the cliff. "Could they have escaped that way? Down there?"

Benjamin peered over the edge. "There's no sign of life."

"Should we send some men down, just in case?"

Benjamin considered it, then shook his head. "Too dangerous without ropes. If our enemies made it down safely, they could easily kill us as we descend the cliff. We'll send a squadron by the valley road to search the area later."

"I wonder how the traitors learned it was a trap?" his aide asked.

Benjamin shrugged. "What worries me is that Hadad was an excellent soldier. He assured me that all of his men would be young recruits. How did he let himself take a sword in the gut like this? Someone knew how to fight."

"Maybe he had more than one attacker."

"Perhaps. But Hadad burned with enough hatred to fight an entire squadron by himself. And he took the fatal wound face-to-face, not in the back."

The general watched as his men began to fan out, combing the area in an orderly fashion, ascending the ridge, disappearing down the road. His seed of fear burrowed deeper. He knew one fact for certain: If he failed this mission, if he failed to capture King Manasseh's enemy, he would forfeit his own life.

"Hadad underestimated someone," he said slowly. "Let's not make the same mistake."

Joshua remained close to the base of the cliff, out of sight, until long after the road above him grew quiet again. It was safer to stay here than to venture out of hiding with hundreds of Manasseh's troops searching the area. He would stand a better chance of eluding them after dark.

How had his plans gone so terribly wrong? Why hadn't he been successful this time? He was doing his best to serve God, trying to win back the nation for Him. Now, inexplicably, Yahweh had abandoned him to this disaster. Alone in his confusion and grief, Joshua struggled to comprehend why God had failed to help him.

At first he thought the faint moaning he heard was a mourning dove. It took several moments for him to realize that it was Miriam. How could she still be alive? It was impossible.

He crawled out of his hiding place and shifted the tree branch that covered her body, shielding it from the soldiers' view above. Her eyes were open. Joshua called her name, and she slowly turned her head to face him. "It's a trap," she murmured again.

"I know, Miriam. I know. Hadad betrayed all of us."

"Run...."

Her unwavering concern for him moved him deeply, especially when he considered where it had led her.

"I'll run when it's time," he said gently. "After dark. I'm safe here, for now."

"Where... are we?"

"At the bottom of the cliff. Well hidden. Hadad is dead, and I think Manasseh's soldiers are finally gone." He lifted her lifeless hand and held it between his, stroking it gently. "You saved my life again. I wish I had more words to say than just 'thank you.'"

Her eyes filled with tears. "Am I going to die?"

Joshua looked up at the cliff, towering above them, then back at Miriam. He knew in his heart that it was hopeless to think that she'd survive, even if the tree had broken her fall. He couldn't bring himself to tell her. "Shh... don't think about dying."

"But I don't know what happens after I die." The terror in her eyes pierced his heart.

"We go to paradise and rest in Abraham's bosom," he answered gently.

"But will I be accepted there? My parents were never married.... My... my mother..."

"The Torah says that children aren't judged for their fathers' sins, nor fathers for their children's." As he repeated the familiar words, he realized for the first time how deeply ashamed she was of her background and how much he had taken his own parentage for granted. He had been highly esteemed because of who his father was, but he hadn't earned that good reputation any more than Miriam deserved to be tarnished by her mother's bad reputation. He thought of Hadad, who had been unfairly judged because of his father's sins. All he had ever wanted was a name.

Hadad's pain-filled cries echoed through Joshua's mind. Against his will, Joshua relived the moment he had run his sword through Hadad, then cruelly twisted it deeper, killing him. But Joshua knew that he had really killed Hadad months earlier at the Passover table. Now he was reaping the terrible consequences of his actions that night. He began to tremble until every inch of his body seemed to shake.

"I'm so scared," Miriam whispered. "I'm afraid to die."

"Shh, it's all right. There's nothing to be afraid of."

Words. Worthless, inadequate words. How many times had Miriam rescued him, waited on him, cared for his needs? Yet all he could offer her in return were meaningless platitudes. It *wasn't* all right. He feared death as much as she did. He groped for something better to say.

"It's written in the psalms, 'Though my father and mother forsake me, the Lord will receive me.' And it's true, Miriam. You can believe His promise."

"Joshua . . . will you hold my hand?"

He looked down at her hand, clenched tightly between his own, and dread filled his soul. "Are you in pain, Miriam? Tell me where it hurts, and maybe I can do something."

He watched her take stock for a moment, then her eyes widened in horror. "I can't . . . I can't feel anything! I can't move! My legs . . . they won't move! My arms—!" Her panic wrenched his heart as painfully as the sword had wrenched Hadad's. He couldn't imagine the terror of being paralyzed, of lying totally helpless.

"Shh . . . it's all right, Miriam. Everything's all right. It's God's blessing that you can't feel anything. You fell such a long way that you would be in agony. I couldn't bear that." He lifted her hand so she could see it between his. "I won't let go. I won't leave you."

"But they'll capture you if you stay here. I don't want them to capture you."

"I'm safe here, for now. I can escape when it's dark and meet up with the others."

"Will Amariah and Dinah be all right?"

He marveled that she could think about someone else when her own condition was so grave. "They have two guards to protect them," he said. "They'll make it back to the caravan."

"No, the guards left us. And Amariah didn't even have a sword."

"You mean he and Dinah are all alone out there?"

"He wanted me to stay with them, but I had to warn you."

Miriam's loyalty shamed him. There was no explanation for it, especially after the way he'd treated her and Nathan these past two years. He wanted to ask her why she had risked her life for him, but he was afraid to hear her answer. He feared it had something to do with Maki's loyalty to Joshua's family. And Miriam had no idea that Joshua had caused her father's death.

"How did you know it was a trap?" he asked instead.

"Amariah figured it out. I told him Hadad had come to the cave . . . then the two guards disappeared . . ." She closed her eyes and her voice trailed off as she lost consciousness again.

Joshua watched the shallow rise and fall of her chest, afraid that each breath would be her last. Dread and guilt consumed him, forcing him to face the truth: Miriam was dying because of him. His sister and Amariah were alone and defenseless because of him. It was his fault that Hadad had sought revenge.

He realized, then, that this disaster wasn't Yahweh's fault—it was his own. If this mission had been God's will, Manasseh would be dead and Joshua would be in Jerusalem by now, not huddled at the bottom of a cliff watching Miriam die. God didn't make mistakes—His purposes were always fulfilled. People made mistakes, and Joshua had made plenty. His biggest one had been not trusting God for vengeance but pursuing it himself. Striving for his own way instead of yielding to God's will was rebellion. That meant he had rebelled against God just as surely as Manasseh had.

Joshua punched the ground with his fist. Then why didn't God punish *him*? Why wasn't *he* dying instead of Miriam? She had never done anything wrong. He shuddered when he thought of all the other innocent people who would suffer because of his rebellion. Their blood was on his hands: the soldiers who had volunteered for this ill-fated mission; Prince Amariah, who faced arrest and execution as a traitor; Joshua's brother, Jerimoth; his sister Dinah. If Manasseh captured Dinah again . . . if Joshua had delivered her back into his hands . . .

He let out a strangled cry and fought to catch his breath, horrified at the enormity of all that he'd done, the terrible consequences of his mistakes, the innocent blood he had shed. But there was more, much more. He had killed Hadad, whose only crime had been falling in love with Dinah. Hadad would still be drinking wine in Moab, spending his grandfather's gold, if Joshua hadn't involved him in his rebellious quest for revenge.

And Miriam. Joshua's eyes filled with tears as he looked down at her. She had no business getting mixed up in all this. She shouldn't be lying here in his place. It wasn't fair. . . . God of Abraham, it wasn't fair!

"Forgive me," he murmured. "Please, Miriam . . . please forgive me!"

Her eyes fluttered open. "For what?"

He knew then that he had to confess everything. He had to ask her for forgiveness before she died. It was the only way he'd ever be free from his tormenting guilt. If only he could find all the others, too, and ask their forgiveness. He swallowed the lump in his throat so he could speak.

"Miriam, I need to ask you to forgive me for something that happened two years ago. It was my fault that your father died. I rushed out of the house too soon. Maki was—"

"I know," she whispered.

"You *know*?"

"Mattan told me the night after it happened."

"You mean all this time you knew I killed your father?" She nodded, her eyes fastened to his. He wanted to look away in shame, but he forced himself to face her. "But . . . but why don't you hate me, Miriam? How could you risk your life for me again and again if you knew that my mistakes killed him?"

"I forgave you."

Her words devastated him. He understood hatred and vengeance but not forgiveness. He would have understood if she wanted to avenge her father's death, but he couldn't understand her willingness to forgive his murderer. He shook his head in bewilderment. "I don't deserve forgiveness."

"No one does, but God forgives us anyway. Your mother taught me that."

"My mother?"

"Yes. Didn't she teach you, too?"

Of course she had. Jerusha had taught all her children about forgiveness when she'd told them the story of her life and how much she'd been forgiven. Joshua had always condemned Miriam for her mother's lifestyle, but he suddenly realized that his own mother had once lived the same way. Miriam knew all of this. She knew how he had caused Maki's death. And yet she forgave him.

He could no longer avoid the question he feared. "Miriam, why did you save my life? Why did you go back to the Temple for me a year ago? Why did you come back to warn me today?"

She uttered a weak sigh and closed her eyes. "I guess it doesn't matter anymore if you know." A tear escaped from beneath her lashes to roll down her cheek. "Because I love you."

Joshua groaned in despair. "No, that's impossible. You should hate me. You should be happy to let Hadad kill me. I used you. I used your father. It was my fault he died!"

She shook her head faintly, too weak to reply.

Joshua gazed at Miriam's pale face as she lay motionless and saw for the first time what a truly lovely woman she was, what a beautiful, unselfish heart she possessed. He had never bothered to see her, to know her. And now that it was too late, he realized that losing her would be his greatest loss of all. He pressed her lifeless hand to his lips and wept.

Amariah found a hiding place in a dense thicket at the bottom of a wide ravine and remained there all day with Dinah. By late afternoon, when they still hadn't seen any soldiers, he began to hope that they might escape alive. Amariah had insisted that Dinah eat the remainder of their food, and now he felt shaky with hunger.

"As soon as it's dark we'll find the village where Jerimoth is waiting," he whispered. "It's only three or four miles from here. We're going to make it, Dinah. This ordeal is almost over."

"What if Jerimoth isn't there?"

"He will be." Amariah chewed his lip, searching for a better way to reassure her. "Dinah, when the Assyrians surrounded Jerusalem, our fathers did everything they could, then they left the outcome to God. We have to do the same. We're in Yahweh's hands. Whatever happens to us is His will."

She huddled close to him in the cramped thicket, resting her face against his. "How did you end up with so much faith and Manasseh with none?"

He sighed. "I pity my brother. He was only twelve years old when he became king. I can't imagine that kind of pressure, can you? I've run from the responsibility of governing our tiny community of Elephantine, and I'm an adult, not the child that Manasseh was when he became king."

"But he had my father to help him."

"Yes, and I've had Joshua. Even so, I've never really faced up to the task. People's lives are at stake, Dinah, and I was so afraid of making a mistake that it immobilized me. It wasn't until I had no other choice—until the guards disappeared and Miriam left and I was faced with the responsibility of caring for you and our baby all by myself—that I finally decided to put my trust in God." He listened to the stillness around them, the rustling of the wind in the trees, the cry of birds in the distance, and felt strangely at peace.

"Amariah? Why didn't you run when you realized Hadad was coming back to kill you? You were willing to die for me."

"You're my wife. I'm responsible for you and our child."

"But you don't love me. Why would you sacrifice your life for me?"

He shifted so he could look into her eyes. "I don't think I really know the answer yet myself. Maybe when this is over we'll have a chance to sort out our feelings, but for now—"

"I know this was all my fault, and I'm so sorry. I loved Hadad. If I hadn't betrayed him, all of this never would have happened."

He pulled her close again. "Dinah, don't blame yourself. I could tell you all the reasons why this is my fault. I suspected Hadad's motives from the beginning. I should have stood my ground with Joshua and refused to have anything to do with his stupid plot. I certainly should have forbid you to come. I'm the community's leader, not Joshua. But I shirked my responsibilities, just as I've done all my life. My father would have used sound judgment and would have sought God's will. He never would have allowed his second-in-command to coerce him into—O God, no! Dinah, get down! Lie still!"

He pushed Dinah toward the back of the thicket and crouched over her protectively.

"What's wrong?"

"There's a soldier coming this way."

Amariah watched in horror as the man moved methodically toward them, using a spear to poke at clumps of grass and thickets like the one where they were hiding. The soldier carried a bow and a quiver of arrows on his back, a sword strapped to his side. In the distance, another soldier appeared on the first soldier's right, searching the same way. A third soon became visible to his left.

Amariah's heart raced as he tried to decide what to do. The first soldier was coming straight toward them, as if following their trail. He couldn't miss them. Amariah watched in frozen horror, praying that the man would veer to one side, bypassing them. In a few minutes he would spot them unless Amariah did something. He pushed the bread knife into Dinah's hand.

"Stay here," he whispered. "No matter what happens, stay hidden until dark. Then follow the road to Nahshon."

"Don't leave me!"

"I want you to live. You and our child." He leaped up and clawed his way out of the thicket, his robes tearing in Dinah's hands as she tried to stop him.

A moment later he was free. Amariah ran, dodging behind trees and rocks as if trying to escape the soldier's notice but doing it clumsily enough to attract his attention and draw him away from Dinah's hiding place. He knew he'd be captured, but it didn't matter as long as Dinah made it safely home. Funny, he thought of Egypt as home. When did that happen? And what did it matter now?

"Halt!"

An arrow whizzed past, barely missing Amariah's head. He dove to the ground, then crawled through the grass to take cover behind the nearest tree. His heart pounded in terror. When his limbs stopped shaking enough to control them, he stood and carefully peered out. Instantly, a second arrow sank into the tree trunk, inches from his face. The noise it made as it buried into the bark sounded like an explosion in the quiet forest. His knees went weak again, and he leaned against the tree for support.

Amariah waited. Except for his own gasping breaths, there wasn't a sound. Was the soldier creeping up on him or waiting for him to move, poised to fire again? Amariah's heart thrashed wildly in his rib cage. He prayed that Dinah wouldn't leave her hiding place, prayed that she and his child would escape to safety.

When the soldier suddenly leaped in front of him, Amariah cried out. A sword blade flashed in the sun, blinding him momentarily.

"Throw down your weapons!"

Amariah couldn't see his captor's face behind his shield. He raised his arms in surrender.

"I . . . I don't have any weapons."

The soldier's eyes narrowed as he stared at Amariah over the top of his shield, then they widened in amazement. "Prince Amariah?"

"Yes." The shield lowered, and relief washed over Amariah when he first glimpsed his captor. General Benjamin was his father's loyal friend. He had been Amariah's military tutor and guardian.

But Benjamin stared back with eyes as cold as slate. Clearly he worked for Manasseh now. Amariah was his prisoner, a traitor. Benjamin briskly searched the folds of Amariah's robes and glared in disdain when he found no hidden weapons.

"Where is your sword? Why aren't you armed?" He seemed angry with Amariah, admonishing him just as he had years ago when Amariah had struggled through military training. Back then, he had never been able to do anything right. Now he was alone, unarmed, clumsily trying to flee from hundreds of well-trained troops. Once again, the general seemed disgusted with his performance.

"I couldn't use a sword even if I had one," Amariah said quietly. "You know that better than anyone, General."

Benjamin surveyed the surrounding area warily. "Where are all the others? What kind of friends would desert you to die alone and unarmed?"

"I . . . I don't know."

The general shook his head in pity. "What are you doing mixed up in this plot in the first place? You're in over your head, son."

"I let myself be talked into this against my better judgment."

Again Amariah felt embarrassed to have performed so poorly in the older man's eyes. Benjamin had been a father to him, doing his best to train Amariah in spite of his ineptitude and lack of interest. But regardless of his humiliation, Amariah still had enough respect for the general to meet his gaze and confront him with a hard question of his own. "Why are you working for my brother? You know that the things Manasseh is doing aren't right."

"A soldier obeys his commanding officer and his king." Benjamin's voice was stiff and cold, as if he addressed a stranger, not someone he had helped raise from boyhood.

"So you'll blindly obey the king," Amariah asked, "even when he is wrong?"

"It isn't up to me to decide who's right and who's wrong."

"But surely you can see a difference between my father's reign and Manasseh's."

Benjamin didn't reply. He looked away, shifting his weight to the balls of his feet.

"You served under my father, didn't you, General? Do you remember him at all? I was only ten years old when he died, and sometimes I . . . I have a hard time remembering him. I have more memories of you and Lord Eliakim than I do of Abba. But I know that God's Law was important to him. . . . I know how hard he tried to live by that Law. And I know that my brother—" He couldn't finish. Amariah stared at the ground, ashamed to be fighting tears. For a moment, neither of them spoke.

"Your father was the greatest man I've ever known," Benjamin said. Amariah looked up, surprised by the gentleness in his voice. "You've always reminded me of King Hezekiah. Not your face, but the set of your shoulders, the way you stand. You have his hair. His voice."

Amariah nodded, still fighting ridiculous tears. "We both know that Manasseh is going to kill me. I won't ask for mercy, General, but will you do one thing for me? Will you tell me what you remember about Abba? It's been so long . . . and I need a piece of him to hang on to when my brother . . ." Amariah's knees gave way, and his back slid down the tree trunk until he slumped to the ground—hunger, exhaustion, and fear taking their toll at last.

"Poor kid," the general mumbled. He sighed and sheathed his sword, staring into the distance for a moment as if Amariah's distress embarrassed him. But when he finally crouched down to face him, the general's eyes were kind.

"What I remember most about King Hezekiah was his courage and his faith. They were fused together so tightly that you couldn't tell where one ended and the other began. I was very young to be in command, barely thirty-five years old when the Assyrians attacked Jerusalem. Hundreds of thousands of them. Everyone was terrified, certain we would all die by their swords or be carried off as their slaves like all the other nations had been. But your father defied them." A faint smile passed over his stony face. "He and Lord Eliakim walked through the streets, comforting everyone, telling us to trust God. I stood watch on the wall beside King Hezekiah all that night before the miracle. He never slept, never showed fear, just calmly recited King David's psalms and waited. He had surrendered to God, not to the enemy."

Amariah swallowed. "Then how can you . . . How can our nation—?"

"How can they tolerate King Manasseh?" Benjamin gave a humorless laugh as he rose to his feet. "Manasseh gives the people exactly what they want—anything they can imagine or lust after. Nobody wants moral laws; nobody wants to be told that his life is sinful. Why wouldn't they freely embrace a leader who abolishes all the rules? People don't want a leader whose purity puts them to shame. They want someone like themselves, maybe a little worse than themselves. Your brother is exactly the kind of leader the people want."

"I see. And what about you, General? Would you rather serve Manasseh than my father . . . or me?"

"I serve whoever happens to be the anointed king of Judah." His voice turned cold again. "I don't have the luxury of choosing who that is."

"Then let's get this over with." Amariah stood, shakily brushing the dirt from his robes, determined to face death as courageously as his father had. But Benjamin didn't move.

"Tell me where the others are, son. Where's Joshua?"

"I don't know. I haven't seen him since we split up yesterday."

The general glanced around nervously, as if considering something dangerous. For a moment Amariah had the insane hope that Benjamin was going to let him go free.

"Listen, son. I'll trade your life for Joshua's. Tell me what your escape plans are and help me capture him. In return, I'll convince King Manasseh that Joshua held you against your will all this time. I'll swear that I rescued you from him. For all I know, that's the truth. After all, you weren't even armed when I found you."

Amariah's pounding heart seemed to fill his chest as he considered Benjamin's words. The general wasn't offering freedom, but Amariah might win mercy at his brother's hands. He thought about continuing his life where he'd left off a year ago—living in the palace again, working for Manasseh and Zerah, worshiping idols at the Temple. He slowly shook his head.

"I wasn't held against my will. I was an accomplice in Joshua's plot."

Benjamin gave a snort of frustration. "King Manasseh doesn't know that. Listen, we'd be helping each other. I'm responsible for this mission, and if I don't capture Joshua, my life is over. I'll be sitting in the palace dungeon beside you. Why don't we help each other? Tell me where I can find him, son."

Amariah hesitated, tempted by the opportunity to escape certain death, aware that Joshua had manipulated all of them into this mess by his blind quest for vengeance. Then he remembered Hadad. "I can't do it, General. None of this would have happened in the first place if I hadn't betrayed a friend. I won't betray another one. You told me you admired my father's courage. Well, I'd also like to be remembered as a man of courage."

"But you're signing my death warrant as well as your own!"

"I know, and I'm sorry. Now let's get this over with."

Amariah had decided to accept his fate and face the inevitable consequences when suddenly, for the second time, he felt an absurd ray of hope.

"Wait a minute, General. I think I know how we can both get out of this alive."

"How?"

"Why don't you escape to Egypt with us?"

Benjamin glared at him. "And walk out on my sworn duty? Leave all my men?"

"We live on an island in the Nile, a military garrison. We could use someone with your experience and skill to help with the training. You swore allegiance to the House of David and to God—well, *I'm* an heir of David, the only one who's still faithful to God."

"I can't just walk away from—"

"From what? From evil? From immorality? What's keeping you in Manasseh's service besides fear?"

He witnessed the struggle being waged in General Benjamin's soul as decades of duty and loyalty battled his wish to live. Beads of sweat formed on his brow. "I can't leave my family."

"Who'll take care of them if my brother executes you? Listen, even if you capture Joshua, even if Manasseh lets you live, you'll forfeit your soul if you continue to follow my brother's orders. 'Above all else, guard your heart,' the Scriptures declare, 'for it is the wellspring of life.'"

Sweat trickled down Benjamin's face, leaving trails on his dusty skin. "I need time to think," he breathed.

Amariah sank down at the base of the tree again as hope turned his knees to water. "I can wait."

12

AMARIAH WAS STILL WAITING FOR General Benjamin to reach a decision when he spotted another soldier moving toward them. "Someone's coming, General."

He looked up. "That's my aide. I was supposed to meet him outside Timnah."

When Amariah saw the icy determination in Benjamin's eyes, fear pounded through him. "Do the right thing, General. Come to Egypt with us."

Metal hissed against leather as the general drew his sword. He turned and waved it high in the air to catch the approaching soldier's attention. The aide spotted him and waved in return, then began jogging toward them. Amariah stayed where he was, too weak with hunger and fear to stand, but Benjamin strode forward to meet his aide. They were too far away for Amariah to hear their words, but he saw the general gesturing broadly as he talked, and the younger man nodding, pointing behind him in the direction he'd just traveled. Amariah's chest ached from the relentless hammering of his heart.

Finally the two men parted—the soldier heading back the way he'd come, Benjamin returning to the tree where Amariah still sat. The general's face betrayed nothing as he sheathed his sword. "Tell me what our escape route would be. How did you plan to get out of Judah and back to Egypt again?"

"You're going with us?"

"I'll point my men in the wrong direction, then meet up with you and the others. Tell me where."

Amariah couldn't speak. What if he was walking into another trap? What if the general was using him to lead his men to Joshua? And what should he do about Dinah?

"We didn't have an escape plan," he finally managed to say. "Joshua never imagined that his plot would fail."

Benjamin shook his head impatiently. "I don't believe you. I trained Joshua better than that."

"I . . . I'm sorry, General . . . but how do I know this isn't a trick?"

He smiled slightly. "You're not as naïve as I always thought you were. And very wise to be suspicious. But you can trust me. A soldier is a man of his word."

"Hadad wasn't."

"I'm not Hadad. I won't betray you."

Amariah had never made a decision of this importance in his life without turning to Joshua or someone else for guidance. He didn't know what to do. So many people's lives were at stake, including his own. He thought he now understood how it had been for his father when he was forced to decide whether to trust God or surrender to the Assyrians. This was what leadership was all about—and what Amariah had always tried to avoid. He needed to make a decision. He would have to trust God to help him make the right one.

Benjamin gestured impatiently. "Look, we know you probably smuggled everyone into the country on a caravan—Hadad told us that much. I figure that's how you're getting everyone out again, right? What city are you leaving from and which caravan is it?"

Amariah whispered a silent prayer, then told him. "The village of Nahshon. We're leaving with Ishmaelite spice traders."

"Good. Now go back to your hiding place and stay there. I'll clear all my men out of this area so you can make it to Nahshon after dark. I'll meet you there early tomorrow." He was gone before Amariah could reply.

Uncertainty consumed him as he watched General Benjamin disappear over the rise. There was nothing more Amariah could do. He turned and slowly made his way back to the thicket where Dinah was hiding.

As the sun set and the first stars appeared in the sky, Miriam still lay unconscious. Joshua no longer considered leaving her as long as she was alive. If Manasseh's men found him, so be it. It was time he paid for his own mistakes instead of involving innocent people.

Hunger gnawed at him, and he realized that he hadn't eaten all day. His sword wounds, coated with dirt and dried blood, throbbed and burned like fire. He should cleanse them to avoid getting a fever, but he didn't have any water. Besides, if he was going to die of something, it would probably be of thirst, not his wounds. He couldn't recall ever needing a drink of water so badly. He'd lost both sweat and blood, then sat exposed to the sun all day with nothing to drink. He knew the dangers of going too long without water, but he hadn't wanted to leave Miriam's side, fearing she would awaken and spend her last moments of life alone.

He still gripped her hand as he'd promised. It had felt icy all day in spite of the warm afternoon sun. Now that the sun had set, the air would turn cool in the Judean hills. Joshua took off his outer robe and covered Miriam with it. Then he lay down beside her to share the warmth of his body with her.

He lost all track of time after darkness fell, but no matter where his thoughts wandered, they always seemed to drift back to Miriam. If he thought of his childhood—his home, his family—he would remember the crude shack Miriam had called home, the pitiful scraps of love she had been accorded. If he thought of the work he'd done and the praise he'd received for it, he would remember the hard, thankless labor Miriam had performed since joining his family two years ago, the indifferent way he'd treated her in return. Joshua had been given so much, Miriam so little. They had both faced enormous losses, yet hatred had emerged from his, love from hers. In spite of all she'd been through, her sweet, uncomplaining nature had never changed.

Miriam deserved better than a cruel death at the foot of a cliff. She deserved to live, to marry a man who loved her, to raise a family. Joshua knew that the odds against her survival were very great. But the odds that he would survive as a premature infant had been equally great. His father's prayers had beaten those odds. Joshua closed his eyes and cried out to God.

As the constellations marched across the sky above him, Joshua prayed harder than ever before, pleading for Miriam's life.

Joshua awoke with a start, angry with himself for falling asleep. It was still night. A pale moon had risen above the cliff behind him, bathing the valley with silvery light. He shivered in the chilly air and leaned on one elbow to check on Miriam. Her eyes were open. She turned her head to look at him, and a faint smile crossed her lips.

"You'd better pray that I die," she whispered.

"No, I'm praying that you'll live!"

"But the Torah says if you sleep with a virgin, you have to marry her." Tears shone in her eyes. "You were asleep. I heard you snoring."

He gaped at her, too stunned to speak. Her smile widened. "Don't look so horrified. It was a joke."

"A joke?"

"You do know what a joke is, don't you, Joshua?"

"Of course, but I—"

"Do you know that in the two years I've known you, I've never heard you laugh or seen you smile? I'll bet you have a nice smile, too. Like your mother's. She told me that 'A cheerful heart is good medicine, but a crushed spirit dries up the bones.'"

Joshua tried to smile, but his heart felt as if it were breaking. "Would it help you to heal faster if I laughed?"

She considered for a moment, then shook her head. "No, I think the shock would probably kill me."

He did laugh then, but it was bittersweet. He sat up and wiped the tears from her cheeks because he knew that she couldn't do it herself.

"You're right," he said. "I can't remember the last time I laughed. And I'm so tired of feeling this way. Grief has affected every area of my life—it's hamstrung my work, blinded my judgment, poisoned all my relationships—but I don't know how to shake it off. I can't get free of it."

"It isn't grief that did all that," Miriam said. "It's hatred."

"Why do you say that?"

"Because your mother's grief was every bit as deep as yours, but she never tried to kill anyone."

Joshua saw the truth of her words, and her insight stunned him. "I thought that if I killed Manasseh, if I could return to the life I once had, the pain would go away and I would be myself again. But now . . . now I know that I'll never get my old life back again."

"It wasn't your life that changed, it was your heart. You were so tender that first day Abba brought you home. You gave him your cloak and your shoes, you thanked me for nursing your fever, you bought salve for Mattan's leg, and you spoke so kindly to Nathan when you offered to be his father. You said, 'I know how much a father means to a boy. I'll try to be a father to you if you'll let me.' I still remember your words and the way that you said them."

"I didn't keep my promise, did I?" He felt the sick, dull ache of guilt when he remembered how poorly he had treated Nathan, how he had driven him from the island. And Miriam had known about Maki all along. When Joshua recalled how his grandfather had adopted Maki as a ragged urchin, deep shame settled in his soul. He hadn't followed the godly example Grandpa Hilkiah had set. Miriam was right; his heart had changed.

"Joshua, when you get back to Egypt—"

"You mean when *we* get back?"

She smiled slightly. "All right, when *we* get back . . . could you give my brother another chance? Please?"

He couldn't face her. "I think it would be more appropriate if I asked him to give *me* another chance."

"Promise?" she whispered.

He forced back the lump choking his throat. "I'll make it legal, Miriam. He'll be my son. I'll give him my name, I promise." He saw the relief on her face, as if a weight had been lifted from her.

"See? You do have a tender heart underneath it all," she said after a moment. "But you've grown so hard on the outside, like the crust on a stale loaf of bread. You don't let anyone get close to you, Joshua. In fact, everyone is afraid of you. It's as if you have a poisonous snake coiled inside you, and no one knows when it will leap out and strike."

Joshua groaned. "I know, but I can't help it, I can't control it. Do you have any idea how terrifying that is? I've ruined people's lives, people I loved. I've killed three men and I would have killed a fourth if someone hadn't pried me off him."

"And when your hatred has finished destroying everyone around you, Joshua, it's going to destroy you."

"God help me, it already has . . . look at me!" He touched his hated eye patch, then let his fingers trail down his scarred face. "And this is just the damage on the outside. But how can I stop it? How can I kill this monster before it kills me?"

Miriam was quiet for a moment, then said softly, "You have to stop feeding it."

"Feeding it?"

"It grows on your anger; it's hungry for vengeance. Don't store it up in your heart anymore."

"I wish I could get rid of it . . . but I can't forget what Manasseh has done."

"Of course you can't forget. But deciding to let go of the anger or hold on to it is a choice you can make every day. Jerusha says that if you give your hatred to God, He'll make something beautiful out of it."

He studied Miriam in the moonlight and thought she was the loveliest, most courageous woman he had ever known. "Have you been this wise all along, Miriam . . . and I never knew it?"

She had saved his life two times; now if only she would save him from himself. He twined his fingers in hers and lifted their joined hands so she could see them. "You can hold on to me," he told her, "if you'll let me hold on to you."

Her eyes filled with tears.

"What is it, Miriam? What's wrong?"

"I used to dream that someday you would hold my hand this

way. And now that you are, I can't even feel it."

Joshua wiped her tears away as they fell. "I'm sorry," he whispered. "I'm so sorry." Then, not knowing what else to do, he lay down beside her again and rested his cheek where she could feel it, against her own.

13

THE SKY WAS JUST TURNING LIGHT when Prince Amariah stumbled into the rented market stall in Nahshon with his wife. Jerimoth took one look at them and clung to his sister Dinah, weeping like a child. "I've been insane with worry, praying for a miracle . . . and here you are. Thank God, thank God!"

But Amariah knew they were still in great danger. One sole survivor from among Hadad's troops had staggered into the booth not long before them to tell Jerimoth how he had narrowly escaped the king's soldiers.

"Did you see any sign of Joshua or Miriam?" Amariah asked the young recruit.

"No. I was hiding in one of the trenches along the road when I heard Joshua yell for us to run—that it was a trap—so I ran. I don't know what happened to anyone after that."

"We'll wait for Joshua and Miriam," Jerimoth said firmly. "If one soldier made it . . . if you and Dinah made it . . . please, God, maybe the others will, too."

As fear and uncertainty consumed him, Amariah wondered for the hundredth time if he had made a mistake to trust General Benjamin. He studied Jerimoth's worried face and knew he had to tell him what he had done.

"Dinah and I didn't escape on our own. I had help. General

Benjamin captured me, and I talked him into defecting. He says he's coming to Egypt with us. He's going to meet us here in a little while."

"God help us." Jerimoth sank down on a bale of straw as if his legs could no longer hold him. "Can you trust him?"

"I don't know. It might be a trick. He wants to capture Joshua very badly. Look, maybe you and Dinah should leave now and start back to Egypt before the general comes. I'll wait here with the caravan in case anyone else escapes."

Jerimoth shook his head. "That won't do any good. If it is a trap, he'll be watching our booth."

"So I've betrayed us all?"

"Or saved us all. Only God knows which."

The marketplace came to life shortly after dawn. Two of the Ishmaelites Jerimoth had hired conducted business outside the stall, haggling loudly over their spices, while Amariah and the others waited behind the curtain in the rear of the booth. Jerimoth urged him to get some sleep, but Amariah was too tense. He nibbled on some bread and waited, his stomach a knot of anxiety.

When General Benjamin suddenly stepped past the curtain, armed and in his uniform, Amariah leaped to his feet. The general's features were inscrutable as he turned to Jerimoth. "Who are you?" he asked gruffly.

"I'm Jerimoth ben Eliakim. I own this caravan."

"Joshua's brother?" When Jerimoth nodded, the general turned his gaze to Dinah. "Who's she?"

Amariah was ashamed to admit to the general that he had entangled his wife in this mess. Only cowards involved women and children in their schemes. He put his arm around her shoulder. "She's my wife."

Benjamin studied her. "You're Lord Eliakim's daughter, aren't you? She's not your wife, Amariah. She's your brother's concubine."

Anger raced through Amariah so swiftly he could barely grab onto it and wrestle it down. "Dinah was kidnapped by my brother and held against her will! She freely consented to marry me!"

"Hadad told us she was dead. Is she the reason he betrayed you and Joshua?" The general's canny intuition amazed Amariah.

"Hadad was in love with her, yes."

Benjamin turned to the soldier. "You the only survivor?"

The abrupt change of topics surprised Amariah until he realized that this was an interrogation. The general wanted the entire story of their ill-fated plot.

"I'm the only survivor so far, sir."

"How many men were in your commando squad?"

The soldier didn't answer. Amariah's mind raced, looking for the snare. In the end, he couldn't see what difference it made for the general to know. "We had thirty-two men, not counting Joshua, Hadad, and me."

Benjamin was silent for a moment as he stroked his beard. "Twenty-eight of your men have been either captured or killed, so far."

The small amount of food Amariah had eaten rose to his throat. Twenty-eight stupid, senseless deaths. Even if Amariah made it out of Judah alive, how could he ever face their families? If only he had opposed Joshua and his insane idea.

"So do we leave now?" the general asked. "Or wait for Joshua and the last three men?"

Amariah realized that the question was addressed to him. Benjamin showed neither eagerness nor anxiety, and his calm control struck Amariah as out of character for a career soldier to whom loyalty was vitally important. He didn't act like a general who was about to desert his duty and his king.

Jerimoth stood. "You may all leave if you'd like, General, but I'm going wait for Joshua and Miriam."

Before anyone could respond, another one of Hadad's men suddenly stumbled into the booth. He was nearly weeping with relief until he saw General Benjamin.

"It's all right, the general is with us," Amariah assured him.

"Are you alone?" Benjamin asked. "Did anyone else escape with you?"

He shook his head, fighting tears, and Amariah realized that the soldier was even younger than he was. How could Joshua allow Hadad to pick such inexperienced men?

The general folded his arms across his chest. "Tell us your story."

"The king's soldiers are everywhere. Hundreds of them. They caught my brother Reuben and so I . . . I had to crawl most of the way on my stomach." He lost control and began to weep. "What happened, my lord?" he asked Amariah. "I was on top of the ridge, and I saw Joshua kill Colonel Hadad and then—"

"*Joshua* killed Hadad?" the general asked in amazement.

"Yes, then he told us to run. Was Colonel Hadad really a traitor?"

Amariah nodded. "He was working with King Manasseh to capture Joshua and me."

"But what about all of us? Colonel Hadad wouldn't let all of us die like that! He—"

"Did you see where Joshua went?" Benjamin asked abruptly.

The lad wiped his eyes and drew a shaky breath. "Over the cliff."

"Did he fall? Jump?"

"He climbed over the edge. That's the last I saw of him."

"What about Miriam?" Dinah asked.

The soldier looked at his feet. "Colonel Hadad killed her, ma'am."

"No!" Dinah cried. "She was Hadad's friend. He wouldn't kill her."

"I saw him push her over the cliff."

After all that she had endured the past few days, the news about Miriam's death seemed too much for Dinah. Amariah let her collapse into his arms and grieve. "I'm so sorry," he said. "I never should have let Miriam go. She would still be alive if she had stayed with us." He wanted to weep at the futility of her sacrifice. All of Hadad's men had been captured anyway, except for these two. "I hope you realize that you owe Miriam your life," he told his two men. "If she hadn't gone back to warn Joshua, neither one of you would be here." They nodded mutely.

General Benjamin walked to the door of the booth. "My men never searched the area near the base of the cliff. Joshua might still be there. I'm going to look for him."

"Wait!" Amariah leaped up to stop him. If the general captured Joshua, he would have no reason to fear the king, no reason to flee to Egypt with them, and every reason in the world to turn them all over to Manasseh. "Joshua is armed, General. He won't know that you're on our side. He'll fight like a wild man if he's trapped."

Jerimoth stepped forward. "Let me go look for him. I'll take the caravan and a few of the Ishmaelites. You stay in the background, General, and make sure your troops let us pass through."

Amariah couldn't read the general's face as he pondered Jerimoth's offer. "All right," Benjamin said at last. "I'll rejoin my men for a while longer so they don't become suspicious. I'll be back." He ducked out of the stall.

"Are you sure we can trust him?" one of the soldiers asked when he was gone.

Amariah sank down on the bale of straw. "No . . . but we'll have to. We don't have any other choice."

Joshua awoke after dawn, furious with himself for falling asleep again instead of praying. And he should have been keeping watch. It wasn't like him to be so careless. The sun was blinding, and his head ached from his need for water. His mouth felt as dry as sand.

He sat up and suddenly the earth tilted, whirling crazily, as if he had drunk too much wine. He closed his eyes and lowered his head, waiting for the sensation to pass. When he felt the dull throbbing of his shoulder and thigh, and saw how inflamed and swollen the wounds had become, he understood why he felt feverish. The wounds never would have made him ill like this if he had cleansed them right away.

His fever intensified his thirst. Joshua scanned the area where he sat, desperate for even a drop of dew clinging to a leaf or a blade of grass. The sun was already too high; if there had been moisture during the night, it had long since evaporated in the scorching heat.

He turned to Miriam and felt her throat for a pulse. His touch awakened her. Her face was as pale as death, her voice weak.

"Why are you still here?" she murmured. "You said you'd escape after dark."

"I know I did. But I can't leave you all alone out here."

"I want you to live."

"We'll either get out of this together, Miriam, or we'll die together. I'm praying that we'll live."

She closed her eyes and moaned. A thin veil of sweat shimmered on her forehead. "I'm not sure how much longer I can stand this pain."

"Are you in pain? Where?"

"My legs . . ."

"Miriam, do you understand what that means? You can feel something! Even if it is painful!" Joshua began to hope that she might live. God was answering his prayers. He uncovered her feet and massaged them gently. "Can you feel that? Can you feel my hands?"

"They're so hot! Your hands feel like they're on fire!"

He saw no reason to tell her it was from a fever. He continued massaging her feet and legs, silently praising God. "Does that help at all, or am I making the pain worse?"

"Yes . . . no . . . I don't know," she wept. "Do you really think the feeling will come back? And that I'll live?"

"Yes. I have faith in the power of God." Joshua felt so ill he wanted to collapse again and go back to sleep, but he continued to massage her limbs as his mind slipped toward delirium.

"I'm so thirsty," Miriam said after a while. Joshua licked his parched lips, craving a drink, too.

"I know, but I don't want to leave you all alone while I go look."

"I'll be okay. Please go."

"All right. Maybe I can find something to eat, too." As he stood, another wave of dizziness nearly felled him. He covered her with the broken tree branch to shield her from the sun and hide her from view. Joshua knew he was too sick to go, but for Miriam's sake he ignored his own pain and started forward on legs as stiff as planks, limping on his injured ankle as he skirted the base of the cliff.

He told himself to stay alert, to search for water, to watch for soldiers, but his mind wandered hopelessly from those tasks as he stumbled over the dry, rock-strewn ground. His head ached so badly that he wanted to lie down and close his eyes, but he wanted a drink of water even more. He willed his feet to keep walking. The arid ground was baked dry, waterless.

After too many fruitless minutes of searching, Joshua remembered that he had seen a road from the top of the cliff. Maybe it led to a village, to a well or a spring. He headed in what he hoped was the right direction, staggering through brown knee-high grass.

He found the road and—thank God!—there was a wide shimmering pool of water in the middle of it! He limped toward it, laughing and weeping, his feet tripping over each other. But the closer he got to the pool, the smaller it shrank until the mirage faded and vanished before his eyes.

Joshua sank to his knees, too weary to rise again, and crawled to the side of the road to rest in a patch of shade beneath a stunted bush. He couldn't think what to do. He must not give in to his fever. He had to find water, he had to get back to Miriam. It all seemed impossible. The sun's glare multiplied the agony in his head, and he closed his eyes to escape it. He awoke to the distant creak of wagon wheels, the rumble of hooves. The sun was high overhead. Joshua cursed himself for falling asleep. A frantic voice inside told him to take cover, to find a place to hide in case the figures moving slowly toward him were Manasseh's soldiers, but his body felt as paralyzed as Miriam's body was. He couldn't will himself to move. He watched in horrified fascination as the procession moved closer and closer, wishing only for a drink of water before the soldiers killed him.

As the men walking in front of the caravan drew nearer, Joshua saw by their brightly patterned robes and flowing keffiyehs that they weren't soldiers after all but Ishmaelites. He had a brief, feverish memory of making plans with Jerimoth to escape with a caravan of Ishmaelites if anything went wrong.

Everything had gone wrong! Hadad had betrayed them, Miriam had fallen, and Joshua had killed Hadad instead of Manasseh. But this couldn't be Jerimoth's caravan of Ishmaelites. They were traveling in the wrong direction. This road led to Jerusalem—Egypt was the other way. He wondered if the traders were friendly, if they would give him some water or sell him into slavery like Joseph. Did Ishmaelites still do that?

One of the men in an Ishmaelite robe resembled his brother. Jerimoth would give him a drink. Joshua knew it couldn't possibly be his brother, but he wanted so much for it to be him that he gripped the spindly branches of the bush and hauled himself to his feet. The surface of the road rocked and swayed like a boat on the sea. Joshua took a few stumbling steps, then collapsed in a heap in the middle of the road.

If it weren't for the dark eye patch, Jerimoth never would have recognized the battered, dusty man as his brother. "God of Abraham, thank you!" he shouted. "It's Joshua! Hurry! Hide him in the back of the cart!"

They lifted him into the wagon and Jerimoth climbed in beside him, ordering the Ishmaelites to turn the oxen around and hurry back to Nahshon. Joshua wept when Jerimoth gave him a drink of water. He was badly dehydrated and delirious, his filthy clothes stiff with dried blood. Jerimoth examined him for wounds and decided that most of the blood probably wasn't Joshua's. When he found the swollen gashes on his shoulder and thigh, he bathed the wounds as best he could in the jolting wagon, with water from his flask. The wounds were inflamed and festering and probably causing his fever.

"What have you done to yourself this time, little brother?" he murmured. Jerimoth knew this had all started on that disastrous Passover night. God alone knew when it would end.

"Miriam . . ." Joshua moaned. He called her name over and over as the cart rumbled down the long road back to the village. "Miriam . . ."

Jerimoth finally decided to tell him the truth to quiet him. "Miriam's dead, Joshua. Hadad killed her. Try to get some rest now. We're almost there."

"She's not dead . . . she's alive . . ."

"No, Joshua. One of your soldiers saw Hadad push her over the cliff." He wondered if Joshua had found her body at the bottom. Maybe that's what had disturbed him. "You're going to be all right, Josh. We're going to get the others, and we'll all be out of Judah by tonight. Try to rest."

"Miriam's alive! We have to go back for her!"

Jerimoth didn't know if Joshua was delirious or telling the truth. Could Miriam really be alive by some miracle? They would waste too much time going back for no reason, and even if she was back by the cliff, Joshua was in no condition to lead them to her. Jerimoth saw creamy stone buildings shining in the sunlight ahead of them; they were approaching the outskirts of Nahshon. "Joshua, we'll be entering the village soon. I'm going to cover you with this rug. You have to keep quiet."

Joshua pushed the rug aside and struggled to sit, gritting his teeth. "Please don't let her die. . . . You can't let her die! Miriam is alive. You have to believe me. . . . She's alive!"

Joshua's desperation convinced him. "Turn the caravan around!" Jerimoth shouted. "And God help us all."

It was long past noon when Jerimoth finally saw the cliffs in the distance again. He slid off the cart to walk beside it, watching for the place where they had found Joshua. One of the Ishmaelites spotted the trampled patch of grass where Joshua had lain beneath the bush. Jerimoth could faintly see the meandering trail Josh had made through the grass.

When the cart drew to a stop, Joshua struggled to sit up. "Miriam . . ."

"Stay here, Josh. We'll find her."

Taking a skin of water and a rug, Jerimoth and two of the Ishmaelites followed Joshua's trail to the base of the cliff. They combed the area, but there was no sign of Miriam. When Jerimoth realized their search had been a waste of time, he was angry with himself. They could have been across the border by now. He called to his men. "It's no use. Let's head back."

"Wait, Master Jerimoth! Look!"

They found Miriam lying hidden beneath a tree branch. Jerimoth knelt beside her and felt for a pulse. "She is alive!"

He raised Miriam's head to pour some water between her lips, and she opened her eyes and moaned. "Hang on," he told her. "We're going home." She cried out in agony when they lifted her onto the rug. "God of Abraham, please don't let us hurt her any more than she already is," he prayed. Jerimoth helped carry her back to the cart; they laid her beside Joshua.

"Miriam?"

"She's right beside you, Joshua. We found her."

Joshua groped for Miriam's hand and linked his fingers in hers. "Thank God," he wept. "Thank God."

Jerimoth turned the oxen around once more. "How fast can you make these animals go?" he asked the driver. "We need to hurry!"

The road back seemed endless, the journey slowed by afternoon travelers, herds of sheep, and farmers returning home from market. At last the grape arbors on the outskirts of Nahshon came into view, and they followed the winding road that led up to the village. Jerimoth ordered the driver to slow the cart while he hid Joshua and Miriam beneath a rug in the back.

"We'll only stop long enough to collect the others," Jerimoth told his men, "then we'll make a run for the border. We can still reach it by sundown if we hurry."

The cart labored up the hill, then bumped through the cobbled streets of the village, coming to a halt at last outside their rented booth. Joshua pushed the rug aside and tried to sit up.

"Where are we?"

"At the market stall in Nahshon. Stay here. I'll fetch the others."

"The others? Someone else made it?"

"Dinah and Amariah are here. And two of the soldiers."

A tear slid down Joshua's face. "Jerimoth . . . can you ever forgive me?"

Jerimoth's anger toward his brother had been smoldering since Passover night, increasing in strength each time Joshua demanded his own way or manipulated events with his rage. But as Jerimoth looked at his brother, lying bruised and broken, all his anger suddenly dissolved in a rush of pity. Joshua had paid dearly for his mistakes. His blind quest for revenge had done this to him. Jerimoth determined not to make the same mistake by allowing anger and unforgiveness to rule his life.

"Of course I forgive you," he said. "Stay here while I go inside."

The sacks of spices were still on display outside the booth, but the Ishmaelite traders who had remained behind to sell them were nowhere in sight. All at once Jerimoth froze when he remembered

General Benjamin. Had he just rescued Joshua so that Manasseh could murder him? He remembered his father's execution and began to tremble. He slowly parted the curtain to peer into the stall.

General Benjamin stood in front of him with four armed soldiers. His weathered face was impassive, his powerful frame immovable. Dinah and the others huddled behind him. "Did you find Joshua?" the general asked.

Jerimoth closed his eyes. "O God of Abraham," he prayed.

Jerimoth turned when he heard a noise behind him. Joshua had emerged from the wagon to stumble toward the booth. General Benjamin saw him, too.

"So there you are, Joshua. My men have searched everywhere for you. You're quite an escape artist."

"I'm the only one you want, General. Please, let all these others go."

General Benjamin gestured to the four soldiers. "I'd like you to meet my sons," he said. "I wondered if they would be welcome in Egypt, too?"

14

MANASSEH HUDDLED IN THE SHADOW of his mother's tomb, searching the constellations for his guiding star. A lone bat flitted like a shadow against the midnight sky, then vanished. He wondered if it was an omen. These days he seemed to wonder if everything was an omen, and he worried that he was going insane. When he recalled the blind woman's prophecy that Joshua would be more powerful than he was, he wanted to weep.

Hadad's plot had failed. Joshua had escaped from Judah for a third time. "That means something, doesn't it?" he asked suddenly.

Zerah eyed him impatiently. "What does, Your Majesty?"

"The number three . . . the fact that Joshua escaped from me three times?"

"It means nothing," Zerah said. He grimaced in disgust.

"That beggar woman told me Joshua would be too strong for me, and she was right. Now General Benjamin is gone. Now my enemy has a military expert, too, and I'm going to have to live on edge like this for the rest of my life, wondering what he'll do next, when he'll strike, whom I can trust."

"You don't know for certain that Benjamin was a traitor. They might have captured him or killed him for all we know."

"Don't be stupid—his wife and four sons vanished, too."

"The sorcerer who is meeting us here is very powerful," Zerah assured him. "He can tell us what the future holds."

But Manasseh refused to be comforted. "Did you see the emblem on their soldiers' shields? An ox! Don't you see how Joshua is mocking me?"

Zerah turned on him with a rare burst of anger. "Pull yourself together! He didn't defeat you, did he? You're still the king of Judah; Joshua isn't!"

"But I wanted to win. I wanted him to die."

"Listen to me. We tortured those men for every last shred of information before we executed them. They were Joshua's soldiers, and they were children! Your men captured all but two of them with no trouble at all, not even a scratch. I don't care what emblem he puts on his shields, your forces are stronger than his!"

"But General Benjamin—"

"Good riddance to the old mongrel. You're better off without him. Do you want him working against you inside your own barracks?"

"I suppose you're right." Manasseh was grateful for Zerah's strength and wisdom. He needed someone he could lean on, someone he could trust, a friend who would never betray him as Joshua had. He silently thanked the gods for sending Zerah to him.

"Now, I want you to calm down," Zerah soothed, "and forget all about your enemy for a while. This is an exciting night for you. Your mother's spirit will be summoned from beyond. She'll tell you everything you want to know. Think of it! You can talk to her tonight. How long has it been since you've spoken to her?"

"She died more than four years ago," Manasseh said quietly.

"Ah, look. . . . This must be the sorcerer coming now."

A line of torches bobbed up the path toward them, and Manasseh heard the faint bleating of goats. The thought of talking to his mother sent a shiver of excitement down his spine. Such power at his fingertips!

Sensing his excitement, Zerah moved closer to Manasseh's side. "If we're successful tonight, Your Majesty, perhaps we can conjure up King Hezekiah next time."

"No! Not my father! I'm not ready!" Manasseh heard the panic in his own voice.

"Why not?"

Manasseh wouldn't answer. He was unwilling to admit to Zerah that he was afraid to face his father. But long after the ceremony ended, Manasseh continued to ask himself why he feared him so.

"I see it hasn't taken General Benjamin long to set this place in order," Joshua said. He stood with Prince Amariah at the garrison on Elephantine Island, watching the soldiers spar in the courtyard, listening to the sound of clashing practice swords. In the two weeks since their safe return to Egypt, the general had already established a measure of order and discipline among the men that even Hadad had never achieved.

"Between General Benjamin and his sons, this will soon be Pharaoh's finest fighting unit," Amariah said. "Maybe now I can concentrate on governing instead of trying to train the men."

It struck Joshua as odd that Amariah had said, "*I* can govern" instead of "*we*," and he wondered what Amariah's reasons were for asking him to come to the fort. This was the first time he had seen the prince since their return two weeks earlier. Joshua had needed that much time to regain his health and strength.

"Let's talk inside," Amariah said suddenly. He led the way to his audience hall and took his seat on the modest throne, then motioned for Joshua to sit beside him. The prince seemed calm and serene, all his usual nervous gestures strangely missing.

"I've had a lot of time to think these past few weeks," Amariah began. "And I've decided to relieve you of your duties as my second-in-command."

For a moment Joshua's anger flared as if a spark had touched dry grass. Was Amariah trying to punish him by taking away his lifework? What other work was he supposed to do on this island? Then he remembered Miriam's warning that his rage would destroy him one day, and he battled to douse the flames.

"I understand," he said quietly. "I've made a lot of stupid mistakes and shown poor judgment by—"

"Hear me out, Joshua. This isn't about your past mistakes, it's about mine. I promised God that if Dinah and I got out of Judah alive, I would stop running away from my responsibilities. Governing this island community is God's will for my life. I understand that now. In the past I've depended on you more than on God to make my decisions. It's time I learned to depend on Him."

His words prodded the malignant lump of guilt that constantly devoured Joshua's peace. He needed to start cutting it away. His chest ached as he drew a deep breath.

"Amariah, I need to ask your forgiveness. I was wrong to force you to marry Dinah. And I was wrong to involve you in my quest for vengeance. I acted in rebellion—it wasn't God's will. Can you ever forgive me for what I've done to you?"

Amariah was quiet for a moment. When he finally spoke, Joshua was struck by how much his voice resembled King Hezekiah's—strong and resonant. "I've been angry with you for everything that happened, but I'm angrier with myself for allowing it. Even so, God taught me some valuable lessons. I do forgive you."

Joshua closed his eyes for a moment. The relief he felt was immense and absolute, like removing a heavy pack at the end of an exhausting, uphill journey. "I don't blame you for firing me," he finally said. "I understand completely."

"No, I don't think you do understand because I haven't finished yet. God brought us to Elephantine Island to preserve our faith and our worship—to be the remnant of true believers that Isaiah spoke of in his prophecy. We need to stop thinking of Egypt as our temporary home and build a permanent life here. When I was running from Manasseh's soldiers and I thought about going home, I thought of Elephantine."

Joshua wished the prince would deliver the scathing reprimand he knew he deserved and get it over with. He started to interrupt, then stopped when he saw Amariah's face. He had never seen the prince so bold and decisive, so calm and self-assured.

"What I'm trying to say," Amariah continued, "is that right now I need an architect more than I need an advisor. I want you to be in charge of building a temple for Yahweh here on Elephantine."

"You mean not just an altar? But an actual building?"

"Yes. Identical to the one in Jerusalem. The ark needs a permanent resting place. And we need a place where we can teach our children to celebrate all the sacred feasts and ... why are you smiling?"

"I was just imagining how amazed Manasseh would be if he could see what a strong leader you've become. You're going to make an excellent king, Amariah."

"I'm going to try."

"Firing me is the best decision you ever made. It took courage." He rested his hand on Amariah's shoulder. "You saved all our lives, you know. None of us would have made it out of Judah alive if you hadn't won General Benjamin over to our side."

"God changed his heart; I didn't. But you haven't answered my question. Will you be in charge of building the new temple?"

"I'd be honored, Your Majesty."

When he left the garrison late that afternoon, Joshua walked straight to the dock and boarded the ferry to the mainland. Now that he had direction for his own future, it was time to keep his promises.

The Egyptian forge where Nathan worked as a craftsman's apprentice was smoky and oppressively hot. Joshua's heart melted with pity when he saw Nathan standing close to the furnace, sweating like a slave as he labored to pump the bellows.

"Nathan!" Joshua had to shout to be heard above the clamor of the forge. "May I talk with you for a moment?"

Nathan continued to pump as he looked to his boss for permission. When the man nodded, Nathan laid down his bellows and slowly approached Joshua, his eyes filled with apprehension.

"Where's my sister?"

"At home. She wants to see you. I've come to bring you home."

"Why didn't she come herself?"

Joshua hesitated. "She's had an accident, Nathan. She can't walk very well yet. But she'd like to see you. Will you come?"

Nathan's stricken face revealed his alarm. He struggled into his tunic and abandoned his work without pausing to ask his boss. "What did you do to my sister?" he asked as they hurried toward the dock.

"I won't lie to you; the accident was my fault. She was injured while saving my life."

Nathan whirled on him, and his hands balled into fists as he lashed out at Joshua with all his strength. "I hate your stinking guts!" he shouted.

Taken off guard, Joshua endured a few painful blows to his stomach and ribs before finally pinning Nathan's arms. The strength of Nathan's hatred surprised him as much as his physical strength.

"Let me go!" Nathan cried, struggling.

"Listen to me first. I don't blame you for hating me, but I think you should know that Miriam doesn't hate me. She knows the truth about Maki—she's known it all along—and she forgives me. I need to ask you to forgive me, too. I promised to be a father to you, and I haven't kept my promise. Giving you food and a roof over your head didn't make me a father. Will you forgive me, Nathan?"

He didn't reply. Joshua released him, and Nathan turned away, jogging ahead to the ferry dock. When Joshua caught up to him, he paid both their fares, then found a place to stand beside Nathan against the rail. They faced forward as they crossed the river to Elephantine Island, and Joshua remembered Amariah's words: They were going home.

"If you'll come back to live with me, Nathan—if you'll give me another chance—I promise to give you more than food and shelter this time. I'd like to give you my name. You'll be Nathan son of Joshua, son of Eliakim, son of Hilkiah."

Nathan quickly turned his head away but not before Joshua saw how moved he was by his offer. Nathan was fighting to keep the wall he had erected between them intact, but the slim crack Joshua had glimpsed gave him hope.

"What do I have to do in return?" Nathan asked after a moment.

The question took Joshua by surprise. He didn't know how to answer. He remembered how Nathan had cut classes, stolen from the vendors, carved forbidden idols, and he knew he should make all the rules clear right from the start. As Nathan's father, Joshua had a responsibility to discipline him. He thought of his own Abba and took a deep breath.

"Nothing, Nathan. You don't have to do anything in return. Being father and son isn't a bargain we make. It's a relationship. I'll try to set a good example for you to follow, and I hope that you'll learn to respect me, to cherish the values that are important to me, maybe even to love me. But even if you don't—even if you defy me and shame me and hate me, I'll always be your father. You'll always be my son. Nothing can change that. I promise."

Nathan whirled away from him and pushed through the crowd, but not before Joshua saw the tears in his eyes. The boy crossed to the opposite side of the ferry deck, facing back toward the Egyptian mainland, and leaned against the rail. Joshua let him go, giving him the solitude he desired. But as he watched Nathan from a distance, he no longer saw a rebellious, disobedient urchin but a pitiful, wounded ten-year-old child who had never known the blessings of a father's love as he had. He realized what an awesome responsibility his own father had faced and what an excellent job he had done raising his four children. Joshua vowed to do no less.

As the ship drew near the shore, Joshua finally crossed the deck and stood by Nathan's side, resting his hand on his shoulder. Nathan flinched at his touch, but Joshua kept his hand firmly planted just the same.

"What do you say, Nathan? Will you give me another chance?"

Nathan wouldn't look at him. "I guess so," he finally mumbled.

Joshua squeezed his shoulder. "I'm glad because there's something else I need to ask, and I'm hoping you'll say yes to that, too." He waited until the boy's curiosity made him look up. "Nathan, may I have your sister's hand in marriage?"

He didn't wait for Nathan's answer but guided him by the elbow down the gangplank and through the streets toward home. He knew by the look of stunned disbelief on Nathan's face that he was incapable of uttering a single word.

Later, it was Joshua who felt tongue-tied when it was time to ask Miriam the same question. He carried her from the dinner table outside to the rear courtyard after the evening meal so she could practice walking. Her legs had grown slightly stronger, but she still couldn't stand or walk alone. Joshua knew it frustrated her that she didn't have the full use of her hands, either, and couldn't do her usual share of work.

He set her down outside the door, supporting her so she could walk the few steps to the bench. "Ready?" he asked.

She nodded, steeling herself. Joshua could only guess how much pain she endured to walk these few faltering steps because Miriam never uttered a single complaint. "You're very brave, you know," he told her. "I marvel at your lack of self-pity."

"It frustrates me to be so dependent on everyone."

"Miriam, we've all been dependent on you for two years. It's about time we repaid you. We would have starved to death if Tirza or Sarah had to cook all our meals . . . not to mention the fact that we'd still be wearing the same filthy clothes all this time."

He had hoped to elicit a smile, but her jaw remained clenched in determination, her brow furrowed as she concentrated on her task. "I won't be this helpless forever. I'll walk again, you'll see." She reached the bench in the center of the yard and sank down on it, exhausted.

"As stubborn as you are, Miriam, I don't doubt for a moment that you will walk."

When she looked up at him and saw him grinning, her face softened. "I knew your smile would be nice," she said.

"Will you marry me?" he asked suddenly, then laughed at the look of disbelief on her face. "You know, Nathan had the same look on his face this afternoon when I asked him for your hand."

"What did he say?"

"Come to think of it, he never gave me an answer. And neither did you."

Her eyes filled with tears, and he knew from her expression that they were tears of sorrow, not joy. "Please don't joke," she said.

He crouched in front of her. "I'm not joking. I want to marry you."

"You're only asking out of pity and guilt."

"You're wrong. I don't pity you. You're one of the strongest people I've ever met. And it can't be guilt because you forgave me, remember? The truth is, I need you. You're not afraid to confront me with my faults. You're probably the only person who can help me change."

"Friends help each other, Joshua. You don't have to marry me."

"I know. But I *want* to marry you. I can't imagine living my life without you."

"You couldn't possibly want me. My mother was—"

"So was mine."

"But my father—"

"My grandfather loved Maki like a son. He would dance for joy at our wedding if he were alive."

"But you're an important official, the king's right-hand man, and I'm—"

"Actually, I'm not an important official anymore." A slow smile spread across Joshua's face at the irony. "Amariah fired me today."

"He *fired* you?"

"Yes. I'm just an ordinary builder again." When she had no reply to that news, he took her hand in his. "Miriam, will you marry me?"

She shook her head. "Joshua, look at me. I'm a cripple."

"So? I've been crippled by my own bitterness, but you loved me in spite of it. If you could look past my imperfections and fall in love with me, why can't you believe that I could do the same with you?" He lifted her hand to his face and let her fingers brush his eye patch, his jagged scar. "Do you love me, Miriam? In spite of this? In spite of how crippled I am inside?"

She lowered her eyes and nodded. Tears trailed down her cheeks.

"Then please believe that I love you, too. Please marry me."

After a long moment she lifted her face, and Joshua saw the answer he sought in her beautiful smile and shining eyes.

Part Two

[Manasseh] did much evil in the eyes
of the Lord, provoking him to anger.
He took the carved image he had made
and put it in God's temple.

---

2 CHRONICLES 33:6–7

Hide yourselves for a little while until his wrath
has passed by. See, the Lord is coming . . .
to punish the people of the earth for their sins.

ISAIAH 26:20–21

15

PRINCE AMARIAH STOOD BEFORE THE HIGH PRIEST, cradling his eight-day-old son in his arms. Today his firstborn would be circumcised, receiving the sign of God's covenant. Deep contentment filled Amariah, and his heart brimmed with love for the God of his fathers. His thank offering burned on the altar in front of him, sending the fragrant aroma of roasting meat heavenward. The priests had also slain his peace offering, and Amariah's guests would feast on it with him at a celebration following the ceremony.

He had chosen Joshua to stand beside him as his next of kin, to read the Torah passage from the scroll of the Law. Joshua's clear voice carried across the courtyard as he read the ancient words of scripture. "'Then God said to Abraham ... "This is my covenant with you and your descendants after you, the covenant you are to keep. ... For the generations to come every male among you who is eight days old must be circumcised."'"

The high priest's robes billowed in a swirl of bright color as he lifted his hands in prayer. "Blessed are you, O Lord our God, who has made us holy through your Law and has commanded that our sons should enter into the covenant of Abraham our father."

"Amen," Amariah breathed. He opened his eyes and looked down at his sleeping son's face. One miniature pink hand had escaped from the tight wrappings of swaddling cloth, and as Amariah caressed it, the tiny fist closed in a grip around his finger.

"What have you named this child?" Joel asked. As high priest, he would perform the ritual himself in honor of the community's new heir and future leader.

"His mother and I have named him Gedaliah—'Yahweh is honored,'" Amariah replied.

"Amen. O Lord our God, may Gedaliah son of Amariah, son of Hezekiah, live to honor you with his life and by his adherence to your Laws, as his father and his grandfather have done. Amen."

"Amen," the crowd echoed.

Amariah passed his son to Joshua. He accepted him awkwardly, unaccustomed to holding a small baby, then finally settled his nephew in the crook of his arm. He carefully unwrapped the layers of cloth. Amariah knew he himself might draw the child away from the flint knife in an instinct of protection, but Joshua would hold Gedaliah firmly in his embrace. Amariah watched Joel's face, not his son's, as the high priest performed the sign of the covenant. In a few swift, sure motions, it was over.

"Praise God for His blessings!" Joel shouted above the sound of Gedaliah's wails. "Yahweh has given us an heir. His love and His promises to Israel are faithfully delivered from generation to generation. Even in exile, the House of David will continue to reign over Israel as God has promised."

When the service ended, Joshua carried the baby to his mother for comforting while Amariah turned to greet his friends and family members. "I want to thank all of you for coming to celebrate with Dinah and me," he told them. "Please, join us at our home now, to share the feast of our fellowship offering."

As the crowd filed from the courtyard to walk the short distance to his house, Amariah waited for Joshua to fall into step beside him. "Thank you for standing as next of kin."

"It was a great honor. You must be very proud of your new son."

"You've always been like an older brother to me, Joshua. I'd like you to stand again at Gedaliah's dedication when he's a month old."

"When you redeem your firstborn . . ." The look of contentment on Joshua's face suddenly vanished. To Amariah, it was like gazing at a field that was bathed in sunshine one minute, then cast into shadow the next as the sun disappeared behind a cloud. "How could Manasseh sacrifice his firstborn when God has provided redemption?" Joshua said fiercely. "How could he have been so deceived?"

"Don't bring my brother's name into such a happy occasion."

"I'm sorry," Joshua mumbled.

Amariah glanced at Joshua's troubled face as they walked, wondering what else was bothering him. "I want you to know that Dinah and I have found happiness together," Amariah told him. "It's time you stopped flogging yourself with guilt because you coerced us to marry. I love her. I've tried to treat her with gentleness and consideration, and I think that after a year of marriage and the birth of our son, she also cares for me."

"I know she does, Amariah. Even if she hadn't told me so herself, I can see it in her eyes every time she looks at you."

Joshua raked his fingers through his curly hair, and the memory it evoked of Lord Eliakim made Amariah smile. Like father, like son. But Eliakim had possessed a peace of heart and spirit that was tragically missing in Joshua.

"Do you want to tell me what's bothering you, then?" Amariah finally asked.

"I don't know. . . . I guess the fact that you have an heir makes everything here so . . . so . . . permanent. I don't want it to be. I want to go home. To Jerusalem."

"I used to be miserable here in Egypt, too, but it was because I was resisting God. Once I saw that this is what He wanted me to do, and that He would give me the strength and wisdom to do it . . . well, everything changed."

"But you have a job to do here. I feel as though my work was finished after I helped all of you escape. I don't have a purpose anymore. When Hadad came up with his plan I was convinced that God was finally going to let me be His avenger. But I was wrong."

Amariah winced as he remembered the part he had played in the ill-fated conspiracy. He still thanked God every morning that he and Dinah had escaped. "I'm glad to hear you're not going to seek revenge again. But what about the temple we're building?" He turned to gesture to the courtyard in the distance behind them. "You're the only one among us with construction experience, and you have a God-given gift for engineering, like your father."

Joshua stopped walking. "Each block I raise on that temple makes living here that much more permanent. Whenever there is a construction delay or a problem at the stone quarry, I feel relieved. I think maybe this isn't God's work after all, maybe we can finally go home. Everyone else seems to be settling down in Elephantine, but I can't force myself to do it."

"You still want revenge."

"I can't help myself. All day long I ask God, 'Are you going to let Manasseh get away with murder and blasphemy? Let me do something! Let me fight for you!'"

"Joshua, you know the words of the Torah as well as I do: 'He is the faithful God, keeping his covenant of love to a thousand generations of those who love him. . . . But those who hate him he will repay to their face by destruction; he will not be slow to repay to their face those who hate him.' God doesn't need you to take revenge. He needs you to build this temple, to start a new Israel, here."

"But I want to go home."

"I think you've confused going 'home' to Jerusalem with seeking revenge. This is your home."

"It isn't, and I don't know how to change that. I have my family, my work, the temple foundation is almost dug, but I still feel so lost and restless—like I'm waiting for something to change. I wish I could wake up one morning and suddenly be able to accept God's will and live here happily. But nothing ever changes. I still long for Jerusalem. I still think about the view from the palace windows, the golden walls and gates, Yahweh's Temple—"

"You miss it the way it was, Joshua. But if you went back, you'd see how different it all is. You'd hate it. You have no idea what Manasseh has done. And you've been gone a long time. Things have probably gotten worse."

"That's the work I want to do. I want to change it back. I want to help cleanse it, destroy the idolatry, make Judah the way it's supposed to be—the way it was when our fathers governed."

In his own contentment, Amariah found it difficult to imagine Joshua's restlessness. "Would it help if I made you my palace administrator again?" he asked.

"You don't need a palace administrator. You can govern Elephantine alone. You're already doing an excellent job."

"And you're doing an excellent job with the temple. I'm just sorry you don't enjoy your work. When you're finished it's going to look as beautiful as the one in Jerusalem."

"Hardly!" Joshua's voice betrayed his bitterness. "I thought for a while that by recreating Jerusalem's Temple I could recreate my old life, but I can't. It's not the same." Their eyes met, and Amariah glimpsed his friend's profound sorrow. "Do you think we'll ever go home again, Amariah?"

"I haven't heard a clear word from God either way."

"But what's your personal opinion?"

"My personal opinion?" Amariah sighed and started slowly walking again. "I can't see myself ever living in Judah again. Maybe our sons or grandsons will return, but not us. That's why I'm convinced that we need to work to make this our permanent home."

"That feels like a death sentence to me. To die and be buried here? In this place? What about the Promised Land? God gave it to Abraham as our inheritance. That's where we belong. God could root out Manasseh with a flick of His little finger. Why doesn't He do it, Amariah? Why does He allow evil to flourish when it's within His power to change it?"

"Only He knows the answer to that."

Joshua exhaled in frustration, and Amariah could almost see the darkness closing in around his friend. "What can I do, Joshua? How can I help you?"

"Miriam asks me the same thing."

"She loves you deeply. You're blessed to have her for your wife."

"I know. Sometimes she's my only light, the only person who can keep the darkness away. I need her. . . . If anything ever happened to her . . ."

Amariah gripped his friend's shoulders and shook him slightly. "And I need *you*, Joshua. I don't think you realize how much. Take a good look at that temple you've started. Do you have any idea how important it is? How much our community depends on it for our survival? We can't possibly preserve God's remnant and remain faithful to His laws without it. The task God has given you is the most important one in the community. I'm just a symbol, really. But the temple is the substance of our survival as long as we're separated from our land. It's our link to God."

"Do you really believe that, Amariah?"

"Yes, I do. And I think the task of building that temple is much more important to God's plan right now than revenge. This is what He has called you to do. God says, 'It is mine to avenge; I will repay.' All of us would like to believe that we could accomplish one brave, selfless act for God and for His kingdom. But it takes greater courage to faithfully accomplish the daily, thankless tasks of everyday life for Him—being a father to our children, a good husband to our wives, building His temple one laborious block at a time."

As Joshua stared thoughtfully into the distance, Amariah couldn't tell whether or not his words were doing any good. He felt as if Joshua were drowning, and in trying to rescue him, Amariah was being dragged beneath the waves, as well. He longed to abandon his friend and return to dry ground, to eat and rejoice at his son's feast.

As if he had read Amariah's thoughts, Joshua straightened his shoulders and smiled slightly. "Aren't we supposed to be celebrating with your son?"

Amariah sensed how much the effort to shake off his depression was costing Joshua, and he was grateful. "Yes—my son." He drew a quick breath at the wonder of it. "In a time of exile and uncertainty, God has given all of us new hope for the future in my son."

16

AS DAWN LIT HIS SLEEPING CHAMBER, Joshua lay on his side, gazing at Miriam asleep beside him. He had awakened early, his mind turning with plans for the day and thoughts of the past, but as he focused on his wife's beautiful face, the world seemed manageable once more.

Miriam's eyes flickered open. She saw his tender gaze and smiled. "How long have you been lying there staring at me?"

"Let's see . . . a little more than three years now, isn't it? I figure since I ignored you for the first couple of years that I knew you, I need to make up for lost time." He pulled her into his arms.

"Did you have another rough night sleeping?" she asked.

"I woke early, that's all. I was thinking about Nathan's thirteenth birthday today, and how we'll be able to worship together for the first time. That started me thinking about Abba and grieving for him. So I decided to study you instead." He kissed her neck, her forehead, and finally her mouth, but Miriam returned his kiss impatiently.

"I wish you would have awakened me sooner. I have so much to do today. I should have been up hours ago." She freed herself from his arms and struggled to sit up, then pulled her deadened legs over the side of the bed. Joshua hurried to help her.

"Please don't overdo it, Miriam. Let Mama and the others help you for once."

"You fuss over me too much," she replied.

"That's because you never ask for anything for yourself."

He helped Miriam put on her robe and pin up her hair, then crouched to fasten her sandals for her. When she was ready, he helped her stand, fitting the crutches beneath her arms. After three years, neither of them pretended that she would ever get stronger or walk unaided. But when Joshua had offered to hire servants to wait on her, Miriam had stubbornly refused. He had used his ingenuity, instead, to redesign their house, adding railings for support, ramps in place of stairs, wooden conduits to channel water from the cistern, and low tables with benches so Miriam could work sitting down. He assigned Nathan the heavier chores such as carrying supplies from the marketplace or hauling water and fuel.

When Miriam was ready, Joshua put on his own clothes, pulling the leather patch into place over his eye. As he inspected himself in the bronze mirror, his scarred reflection reminded him—as it did every day—of Manasseh and the great debt of justice his enemy owed him. Like the Nile River beyond his doors, Joshua's grief and anger sometimes spilled their banks, threatening to overwhelm him. That was when Miriam became his island of refuge, the high ground to which he could cling.

"You look as handsome as ever," Miriam said, shooing him away from the mirror. "Go wake Nathan up. This is a big day for him. For both of you."

Joshua resisted the urge to help Miriam start breakfast, knowing it would only irritate her. He walked through their main living area to the alcove in the rear of the house where Nathan slept. As he gazed down at his son for a moment, he wished he felt the depth of love that he knew a father should feel. And he also wished for a sign of love on Nathan's part. They were still wary of each other, as distant as two strangers, in spite of Joshua's efforts these past three years to spend more time with him, engage him in conversation, and make a home for the three of them. Perhaps worshiping side by side today for the first time would finally knit them together.

"Nathan," he called gently. "Nathan, it's time to get up."

The boy bolted upright as if ready to flee. Awake or asleep, Nathan was jumpy and on edge. Joshua thought of the unchanging peace and security of his own boyhood in Jerusalem, of the love and laughter his family had shared, and was reminded for a second time of all that Manasseh had destroyed.

"Do you remember what day it is, son? You become a man today."

Nathan nodded and lay down again, draping his arm across his face. If he was filled with joy and anticipation at his passage into manhood, he hid it well. Joshua swallowed back his anger, praying as he did every day: *God, help me love him. Help me accept him the way he is.* He tossed Nathan his robe.

"Let's go, then. We don't want to be late."

He returned to the main room of their house, where Miriam was already hard at work, arranging food on platters for the small celebration after the sacrifice. He came up behind her as she sat slicing a melon and encircled her with his arms, bending to kiss her neck.

"I don't want you working too hard and wearing yourself out today. Wait and let Mama and Tirza help you."

"It's pretty hard to do much of anything with you hanging all over me like a gourd vine."

"Then maybe I'll have to hang on to you all day." Joshua smiled as he laid his hand on her stomach. "Can you feel my son kicking yet?"

"It's still too soon, silly. No one will even know I'm pregnant for another couple of months."

"They'll know. One look at your face and they'll know." He and Miriam had waited three years for a child, neither of them daring to voice the fear that she was barren.

She smiled up at him. "The only way they'll know is if you go spreading the news all over the island."

"No, I promised I would wait and I'll keep that promise. I don't want anything to take away from Nathan's special day."

In fact, Joshua dreaded telling him the news, fearful of his response. Nathan had been especially close to Miriam and still seemed jealous of Joshua, resentful of sharing his sister with him. How would he react to a baby?

Joshua moved his hand in gentle circles on Miriam's stomach. "Does every man feel this way when he finds out he's going to be a father for the first time?"

"And how is that?" she asked, laughing.

"Proud. Content. More complete, somehow, and—" Joshua saw a flicker of movement in the doorway and stopped. Nathan stood watching them, his face stricken. He had overheard them. Joshua released Miriam and took a step toward him, struggling to find the right words. "You, um . . . heard us talking just now?"

Nathan nodded. He pretended indifference, but Joshua saw the pain in his eyes and realized what he had just said: *a father for the first time*. If only he could take back his words.

"I'm sorry, Nathan. That wasn't how I'd planned to tell you the news, but . . . now you know. You'll have a new brother or sister by next harvest."

"Or is it a niece or nephew? I'm confused." Nathan's voice was cold with sarcasm.

Miriam pulled herself to her feet and hobbled toward them. "Nathan, please—"

"Congratulations. To both of you. I'm sure you're very happy," he said bitterly. He turned to leave, but Joshua stopped him.

"No one knows about the baby except the three of us, and it's going to stay that way. Today is your special day."

"Go ahead and announce it to the world. I don't care." Again, he turned to leave.

"Wait. We have something for you, son." Joshua retrieved the carefully folded bundle of cloth from where he'd hidden it and presented it to Nathan. The boy stared at it for a long time before unfolding the new embroidered prayer shawl. Joshua searched for a hint of pleasure in his eyes but saw none. When he recalled the time and money he had spent shopping for the flawless white linen, bargaining for the finest blue thread for the embroidery and tassels, hiring the best craftsman to do the work, he wished Nathan would show a little gratitude. It was so hard to love this difficult child.

"Try it on, son. Let Miriam see how you look."

"Later." He wadded it up and shoved it under his arm. "I just remembered something," he mumbled as he hurried away.

Joshua looked at Miriam helplessly. "I'm so sorry he overheard me."

"It's not your fault. He's been contrary all his life." She kissed his cheek. "You'd better hurry or you'll both be late. I'll have everything ready for the celebration when you come home."

Joshua retrieved his own prayer shawl and put it on, then stooped to tie his sandals. "Nathan, it's time to go," he called. As he waited by the open front door for his son, he heard Miriam rattling dishes, but no sound came from Nathan's room.

"Nathan, come on." He struggled not to reveal his impatience. "Nathan?" Silence answered him.

Joshua's stomach clenched like a fist as he went to Nathan's room. The new shawl lay abandoned on Nathan's sleeping mat. Joshua hurried outside to the rear courtyard where he and Nathan had set up tables last evening for the celebration, but there was no sign of him. The shofar sounded in the distance as Joshua ducked inside the house again.

"He disappeared, Miriam."

All the joy drained from her face. Joshua remembered how she had glowed with happiness before Nathan interrupted them, and he had to swallow back his anger. "Should I go look for him?" he asked her. "Where could he be?" For a moment Miriam seemed torn between the two of them, then she shook her head.

"No, go to the sacrifice without him."

"I don't want you to search for him, Miriam. It's too hard for you to get around." He hated reminding her of her handicap, hated being reminded of it himself, but he knew how stubborn she was. "You need to be extra careful because of the baby. Promise me—"

"I'll wait here. Nathan will come back when he's ready. Maybe he went on ahead to the sacrifice. Go on, Joshua. And don't worry. It wasn't your fault."

But as Joshua hurried to morning worship, he knew that it was his fault. He stood beside the gate to the men's courtyard as long as he dared, waiting to take his son through it for the first time, but Nathan never came. Throughout the sacrifice Joshua peered over his shoulder at the outer courtyard where Nathan usually stood beside Mattan and the other boys, but he wasn't there. The old, familiar anger billowed inside him like the smoke from the altar fire, some directed at himself, most of it at Nathan. He didn't hear a word of the liturgy. So much for their special day.

When the service ended, the friends who had been invited to Nathan's feast crowded around Joshua. Only Nathan's younger brother, Mattan, dared to ask the question Joshua saw written on all their faces.

"Where's Nathan? Why didn't he—"

Jerimoth cut him off. "Don't ask rude questions, son. Run ahead and tell Mama and Aunt Miriam we'll be along in a moment." He shooed Mattan and the other boys away.

"Yes, please go over to the house," Joshua told all the other guests. "Miriam and my mother have been cooking for days. I'll explain everything when I get there in a few minutes."

He and Jerimoth lagged behind as the courtyard cleared, walking in silence as far as the outer wall. Then Joshua stopped and leaned against it. "I can't do it, Jerimoth. I can't love Nathan the way I should. I've tried . . . I've prayed . . . I've asked God to help me love him as if he were my own son, but nothing ever changes."

"I believe that you do love him, Joshua, or you wouldn't keep trying so hard."

"I think I've only been doing it for Miriam's sake. I'd walk through Sheol for her, you know that. But this is just too difficult."

They listened to the sound of oxen and carts rumbling past on the street outside the enclosure, along with the shouts of vendors hawking their wares. "Do you feel like telling me what happened?" Jerimoth asked quietly.

Joshua sighed. "Miriam is going to have a baby."

"God of Abraham be praised! That's an answer to many prayers."

"We weren't going to tell anyone yet, but Nathan overheard us talking this morning. He also heard me say something stupid about being a father 'for the first time.' I didn't mean it like it sounded. I should have thought—" He stopped suddenly and looked at his brother. "That's not true, Jerimoth; I *did* mean it. I feel differently about my own child than I do about Nathan. God forgive me, but it's true."

"Josh, everyone sees how hard you try with Nathan."

"Is it the same for you? Do you really feel the same love for Mattan as you do for your own children?"

Jerimoth winced at his words. He took a moment to answer, staring at his feet. "Mattan was very young when I adopted him. He still had his milk teeth, for goodness' sake. He responded to my love like a flower to rain, and he was easy to love because he gave love in return. But even after all these years, Nathan has given nothing back to you. That's why it's so much harder for you."

"You haven't answered my question. Do you love Mattan the same as you love your own two sons and your daughter?"

"I feel no difference at all," he answered quietly. "Unless someone reminds me, I don't even remember that Mattan isn't my own flesh and blood. And Mattan doesn't think any differently, either. But Nathan has never forgotten that you aren't his father, and he won't let you forget. That's his fault, not yours."

Joshua smacked the courtyard wall with his palm, giving vent to his anger and disappointment. "I've waited for this day for months. I wanted everything to be perfect. I bought him a new prayer shawl, planned the feast . . . I couldn't wait to stand here with my son for the first time. Remember our first time? Remember going to the Temple with Abba and Grandpa?" Joshua knew he had to stop before his well of rage and grief overflowed. "I don't know what else to do for Nathan," he said hoarsely.

"Just love him," Jerimoth said.

"But what if I don't feel any love?"

"Love isn't a feeling; it's an attitude, it's actions. Like buying him the prayer shawl. Whether you feel anything or not, just do the loving thing."

"Sometimes that's very hard to do."

"No, it's impossible. At least in our own strength. Fortunately, Yahweh is the God of the impossible. He'll answer your prayers, in time. It's like this temple you're building here. Everything looks like chaos now, all torn up and heaped everywhere, but it will shine with beauty when it's finished. It's unfair to judge a work in progress. And that's what your relationship with Nathan is."

Joshua slid his fingers beneath his eye patch and rubbed the dust from his eye, then smoothed the patch in place again. "Do me a favor? Run ahead and cover for me. Tell Miriam to start the feast. I have to find Nathan."

By the time Joshua found him, nearly two hours had passed. The boy was wading through the marshes, several yards offshore, trying to spear a fish with a sharpened stick. His legs and the hem of his tunic were covered with mud, his sandals ruined. Joshua's lungs squeezed painfully as he fought off a breathing attack, but he kicked off his own sandals and waded out beside him.

"Nathan, you've been warned about playing in these reeds. The crocodiles—"

"There aren't any crocodiles around here."

Joshua gripped Nathan's arm and marched him back to the beach, silently praying for patience. He pushed Nathan down on the sand, then crouched beside him. "Do you have any idea how hard Miriam has been working to prepare this feast for you?"

"I never asked her to."

"Then why do you suppose she did it?"

Nathan shrugged.

"Because she loves you." He waited, but the boy stared sullenly at the ground. Joshua's anger tempted him to lecture and rage at his son, but he recalled Jerimoth's words and stopped himself in time.

"I want to tell you two stories," he said, his voice calm and controlled, "and when I'm finished we're going home so you can apologize to Miriam and all of our guests." Nathan rolled his eyes, but Joshua decided to ignore it. "The first story is one of my earliest memories—the day my sister Dinah was born. When Abba brought me in to see her for the first time and I saw the shiny-eyed way he and Mama looked at her, I hated Dinah with all of my three-year-old strength. I wasn't the baby anymore. Someone else was the center of attention. Then when Dinah started toddling around, learning to walk, I would push her down on her backside and make her cry every chance I got." He smiled faintly at the memory. "I was jealous. I loved my parents, and I didn't want to share the new baby with them. I can't condone your actions this morning,

Nathan. They were disgraceful. But I certainly understand them."

"I'm not jealous of—"

"The second story," Joshua continued, cutting him off, "took place the day I turned thirteen. My birthday is right before Passover, so I was doubly excited—I would be able to participate in the festival with the men that year. I barely slept the night before, and first thing in the morning, before the sun was even up, Abba gave me a new prayer shawl to wear, just like the one I gave you. 'Today you are no longer a child but a man,' Abba said. 'A father is responsible for the deeds of his son until he's thirteen, but starting today, you are accountable as a man in Israel.'

"I felt so proud walking up the hill beside my father wearing that shawl, I thought I would burst. At the Temple in Jerusalem, Abba always stood with King Hezekiah on the royal platform to worship, so I expected him to leave me with my grandfather and my brother, Jerimoth. But Abba stayed by my side. He gave up the honor of worshiping with the king of Judah to worship beside me that day. I realized then that it wasn't just a special day for me, it was a special day for Abba, too." Joshua paused, then added quietly, "I wanted it to be like that for us."

Nathan stared past Joshua for a long moment, gazing at the marsh. "I'll never be the son you want," he finally said.

"That's your choice, Nathan, not mine."

"Miriam's baby will be your real son."

"Is that what you're afraid of?"

"I'm not afraid of anything!" he shouted, turning to glare at Joshua.

"You must be because you've built a wall around yourself that's higher and thicker than the one I'm building around the temple grounds. You won't let anyone past it. I've tried, but you won't let me inside." He paused to take a breath, to ease the suffocating pain in his chest. "Why didn't you come today?" he finally asked.

"Rituals are stupid. I don't see why we need all that stuff."

"Those rituals act as a gateway into God's presence. We go to the sacrifices to find forgiveness for our sins. There's a gulf between God and us, Nathan. Can't you feel it? Can't you sense how far apart we are from Him? It's like you and me. We're so far from understanding each other, from getting inside each other's hearts—" He stopped again, unwilling to admit to Nathan how much it hurt to see the other men worshiping with their sons, knowing that he and Nathan weren't like them.

"You're doing this to hurt me," he said when he could continue, "but you're really hurting yourself. You're so afraid to let God inside your heart, so afraid He'll disappoint you like I have. Or worse, that like your real father, God won't be there at all."

"I don't have to listen to this." Nathan scrambled to his feet, but Joshua moved just as quickly and pulled Nathan into his arms. The boy struggled, trying to free himself, but Joshua held him fiercely, resting his face against Nathan's hair, praying that he would feel something besides anger and disappointment toward this child.

"Let me go!" Nathan shouted as he tried to break free.

"I won't, Nathan. I'm not giving up on you."

"When are you going to get it through your head that I don't need you?"

"Maybe I need you."

After a moment Nathan stopped struggling. When he sagged in Joshua's arms, sobbing, Joshua felt his own anger fade. He held him for a long time, until Nathan's tears finally subsided.

"We can worship together at the evening sacrifice," Joshua said softly. "Let's go home now, son."

The Egyptian sun blazed like a furnace in the afternoon sky as Nathan walked home with Mattan from their Torah lesson. He wiped his arm across his gritty forehead. "I don't remember it ever being this hot in Jerusalem," he grumbled.

"Quit griping," Mattan said. "You always talk as if Jerusalem was perfect, but it wasn't."

"It was better than this place. I hate being banished here." Nathan had lived in Egypt nearly half his life, yet he still hated everything about it. He carried with him an aching restlessness that seldom went away. "Don't you ever wish we could go home?" he asked.

"No. This is my home. I hardly remember Jerusalem anymore or—hey, you've got company."

They had entered the family compound through the rear courtyard, and Nathan saw Jerusha standing in the doorway of his house, talking to two other women. The cluster of adjoining houses where his extended family lived was usually tranquil this time of day, the children and servants resting to escape the heat. He heard Jerusha thanking the women as she said good-bye to them, and he sensed something was wrong. Jerusha's voice was hoarse with emotion, her eyes sorrowful and red-rimmed.

"What's wrong?" Nathan asked in alarm.

She hesitated much too long before answering. "Let's sit down in the shade where we can talk. I . . . I need to tell you both . . ." Jerusha's eyes filled with tears. Mattan took his adopted grandmother's arm and walked with her to the bench beside the outdoor oven. He sat beside her, but Nathan was too tense to sit.

"What's wrong, Mama Jerusha?" Mattan asked. "Who were those women?"

"They were midwives."

"Why? What's going on?" Nathan demanded.

"I don't know how to tell you this . . ." Jerusha's voice broke and she wiped a tear. "You know that Miriam is expecting a baby. Well, something went wrong . . . we don't know what . . . and the baby died in her womb. It happens to women sometimes, but it's especially sad because Miriam waited three years for a child."

Nathan's heart pumped with fear. "Is she okay?"

"The midwives said she'll be fine in a few days."

"I want to see her."

"Not right now, Nathan. Wait a little while. Joshua is with her."

Her answer infuriated him. How dare Joshua exclude him? "She's my sister!" he said angrily.

"I know," Jerusha said. "But Miriam and Joshua need time to grieve. Why don't you go to Mattan's house for a little while? Joshua will send for you later."

"Are you coming, too, Mama Jerusha?" Mattan asked as he helped her to her feet.

"In a few minutes," she said sadly. "I need to take care of a few more things first. You boys go ahead."

"Come on, Nate," Mattan said as Jerusha went back into the house.

Nathan didn't move. Two conflicting emotions battled inside him: immense relief that his rival for Miriam's affections was dead, and enormous guilt that he had wished for it. He'd been angry enough when his sister had married Joshua and he'd been forced to share her with him; the idea of sharing her with Joshua's baby had enraged him. He had hated that child since the day he'd learned Miriam was expecting and had wished it would die a thousand times over. Now his wish had come true. As Mattan took his arm to steer him away, Nathan jammed his elbow into his brother's ribs.

"Ow! What was that for? What's the matter with you?"

"I'm not going to your house."

"Fine. I'll go home without you. I don't care if you come or not." Mattan stalked away.

"It's my fault that Miriam's baby died."

Mattan stopped and slowly turned to face him. "How do you know that? What did you do?"

"I kept hoping that it would die. I wished for it. One of the gods must have answered my prayer."

"Don't be stupid. You know there's only one God. Why do you even talk like that?"

"When I lived with the Egyptians, they told me about the evil eye. They said that sometimes—"

"I'm not listening to any more of this." Mattan strode to the door of his house and opened it.

Nathan hurried to catch up. "I'm telling you I wished it! All I could think about was how much I wanted Joshua's kid to die. If he has a son of his own, he won't want me around anymore. Now his baby is dead, and I know it's my fault."

"My father had two more sons and nothing changed for me."

"That's different."

"How? How is it any different?" Mattan asked. "Abba adopted me the same day Uncle Joshua adopted you."

"Joshua isn't like your father. Besides, your parents were married when we met them, but Joshua and Miriam . . . I don't know, I can't explain it. Just forget it." He turned and strode away.

"Where are you going?"

Nathan kept walking without answering. The truth was, he didn't know. When he reached the street corner and glanced back, he was relieved to see that Mattan hadn't followed him. He wandered aimlessly for a while before reaching the riverbank, then gazed with longing at the distant forbidden shore, watching the ferry approach and tie up at the dock. The Jewish boys on Elephantine Island weren't allowed to mingle with the Egyptians or travel off the island without an adult, but Nathan suddenly had an overwhelming urge to visit the mainland.

It was much too easy for him to sneak on board the ferry without paying. Nathan hadn't stolen anything in more than three years, but as the boat shoved off with him onboard, he savored the familiar addictive rush of pleasure that came from getting away with it. He loved to take chances, to live on the edge, to flirt with getting caught. Nothing could compare with that feeling.

Once the boat reached the mainland, Nathan slipped ashore as easily as he had boarded and made his way to the marketplace. He wandered among the crowds for a long time before stopping to gaze at a display of Egyptian amulets—scarabs, the eye of Horus, ankh crosses. The craftsmanship was exquisite. He wished he could learn to carve that beautifully.

The owner interrupted his thoughts. "If you're not buying anything, Jew-boy, move along!"

Nathan knew that the way he dressed and wore his hair marked him as Jewish, strikingly different from the Egyptians. He fingered the long locks of hair on the sides of his ears, hating them. He looked like a freak because the stupid Torah forbid him to cut them off.

With anger and resentment building inside him, he wandered down the row of brightly colored booths, pausing in front of a display of knives. He could carve all kinds of beautiful things with one of those knives—except that Joshua had forbidden him to even own a knife, much less carve anything. The memory of how Joshua had banished him from the island for doing what he loved made Nathan angrier still. As an idea began taking shape in his mind, Nathan crossed the narrow lane to observe the booth from a distance. Out of sight of the owner, he decided which knife he wanted, then patiently waited for an opportunity to steal it.

After nearly half an hour, an Egyptian man finally approached the booth to haggle with the owner over the price of a dagger. When both men were engrossed in their bargaining, Nathan sauntered across the street, weaving between customers. He carelessly bumped into the display, lifted the knife from the table as he steadied himself, then slipped his prize into his sleeve. For the second time that day an exhilarating rush of excitement surged through his veins. He had done it! He forced himself not to hurry and draw unwanted attention, then turned the corner to blend into the crowd clustered around baskets of fruit, sacks of grain and spices, and cartloads of vegetables. The thrill of victory felt heady.

Eventually, the novelty and excitement of the marketplace began to fade and Nathan drifted away, wandering down a narrow side street. A group of Egyptian boys a few years older than himself crouched in the dirt, playing a game of *senet*. The wooden board was homemade, with flat stones for markers and a pair of knucklebones for dice. He stood on the sidelines watching as each pair of contestants moved their stones in an S-shaped path around the board. One boy, whom the others called Hassan, won every game. Nathan had learned to play the game during the months he had lived on the mainland working for the Egyptians. He'd watched the older men play during their lunch breaks; he still remembered a few moves that he hadn't seen Hassan use. When everyone else had been defeated, Nathan elbowed his way to the front.

"I'll play you next."

Hassan wrinkled his nose in disgust. "Look! It's Jewish scum! I thought I smelled something revolting." The others roared with laughter.

Nathan planted his hands on his hips. "What's the matter? Afraid a Jew might beat you at your own game?"

"Not even in your dreams."

Nathan brandished his new knife, dangling it in front of Hassan's face before tossing it in the dirt beside the senet board. "Then let's make the game interesting. My knife against your amulet."

Hassan fingered the ivory eye of Horus that he wore on a leather thong around his neck while the other boys goaded him to accept Nathan's challenge. "Come on, Hassan, take the Jew's knife. He can't beat you."

Hassan slowly untied the amulet and laid it in the dirt beside the knife. "All right, show us how Jews lose."

Nathan played calmly, coolly, enjoying the rapt attention as all eyes focused on the contest. Hassan began to sweat once he glimpsed Nathan's speed and skill. When Nathan triumphantly removed the last of his seven pieces from the board, five of Hassan's remained. Nathan scooped up the knife and the amulet with one hand.

"That's how Jews win!"

In an instant Hassan leaped on him, smashing his fist into Nathan's jaw, knocking him to the ground. Nathan fought back with a vengeance, unleashing all of his pent-up anger and rage. They rolled over and over in the dirt, pounding each other. Nathan gave blow for blow and might have defeated him in spite of the older's boy's size if Hassan's friends hadn't joined in the brawl. Four of them pinned Nathan to the ground while Hassan beat him viciously. When Nathan was nearly unconscious, Hassan used the new knife to cut off Nathan's sidelocks for a prize, pocketing them along with the knife and the amulet. He sauntered away with his laughing friends.

Nathan longed to sink into oblivion. It hurt to breathe, let alone move, but he knew he had to leave before Hassan and his friends decided to come back and beat him some more. He struggled to his feet and limped toward the ferry dock, barely able to see out of his swollen eyes. Blood and dirt smeared his torn clothes. He ached all over, his stomach and ribs so badly bruised that he could barely stand erect. The gods had punished him justly. He deserved much more than a beating for wishing Miriam's baby would die. Hassan should have killed him.

When he reached the river, Nathan was in too much pain to try to sneak on board the ferry again. Instead, he spotted a lone Jewish man standing in line and hobbled up to him.

"I've been robbed," Nathan said through swollen lips. "Can you lend me the boat fare home?" The man nearly dropped his goods.

"Heavens, boy! Who did this to you? And they even cut off your locks? We need to report this to the Egyptian authorities."

"No, just help me get home. My family will take care of it."

"What's your name, son?"

"Nathan, son of Joshua ben Eliakim." He felt a shiver of pleasure at the look of awe and respect on the stranger's face.

"Oh my. Did he send you here to the mainland on an errand?"

"He doesn't know where I am."

It would cause a scandal when word of his disobedience spread across the island. Nathan smiled slightly, aware that he had evened the score with Joshua for wanting a son of his own blood.

The man not only paid Nathan's fare but insisted on delivering him to his doorstep, refusing payment for the ferry. Joshua answered the door himself, and when Nathan saw the look of shock and anxiety on his face he thought it was almost worth suffering the pain of his injuries to produce such a reaction.

"Nathan! What happened to you? Where have you been?"

"As if you care." He brushed Joshua's hand away as he fingered the stubble that remained of his sidelocks. "Go cry for your real son."

Joshua grabbed him as he tried to push past. "Answer my question!"

Nathan folded his arms across his chest and stared back in defiance. As the silence lengthened, he noticed with satisfaction how pale and haggard Joshua looked, how hard he had to struggle for each breath. For reasons he didn't understand, Nathan enjoyed Joshua's distress. Even more, he enjoyed adding to it.

"Do you care at all what this day has been like for me?" Joshua said at last. "Miriam could have died, our baby *did* die, and now my son, who has been missing all afternoon, comes home beaten half to death and won't tell me what happened. I have no strength left for games, Nathan. Tell me who did this to you."

"A bunch of Egyptian kids."

"On the mainland? Why did you go to the mainland? You know it's forbidden—"

"Because I felt like it." He saw the color rise in Joshua's cheeks as the grip he held on his anger began to slip. Nathan couldn't resist a smirk of pleasure in spite of the fact that it made his lip crack and begin to bleed again. "Go ahead, beat me for disobeying."

Joshua drew a breath to speak and began to cough. Several moments passed before he could talk. "Don't say such stupid things. You know I've never beaten you, even when you've deserved it. Go get cleaned up, then we're going to the mainland to see the Egyptian authorities."

"I wouldn't do that if I were you." Nathan paused, prolonging the agony for Joshua, watching him steel himself for what would come. "The fight started over a game of senet. I was gambling with some stuff I stole in the marketplace."

Nathan expected an explosion of anger, but it never came. Instead, all the emotion drained from Joshua's face, replaced by the icy detachment of a stranger.

"I see. Then I guess you've already received the punishment you deserve." He turned his back on Nathan and walked away.

"When can I see Miriam?"

Joshua faced him again from the doorway, his words cold and deliberate. "Miriam is distraught after losing her baby. I didn't dare add to her pain by telling her you were missing. You're not going in to see her looking like that. You'll stay away from her until your face heals."

Nathan was so angry he wanted to punch Joshua. But he was in too much pain to fight with anyone. He had lost. Miriam could have died, and it was all his fault. He went to his room and lay down on his bed to weep, alone, in the dark.

17

MANASSEH COULDN'T BELIEVE THIS was happening to him. He watched the Assyrian delegation leave his throne room and felt too shaken to stand. The Assyrians had claimed they were offering a simple peace treaty but he knew better.

"This is the end of our sovereignty as a nation," he murmured. "The Assyrians are going to swallow us alive."

"You're looking at it all wrong, Your Majesty." Zerah shifted in his seat at Manasseh's right hand so the other assembled nobles couldn't hear his words. "The Assyrians are offering you a great political opportunity, and I think—"

"It's not a political opportunity, it's a threat—join the Assyrian Empire as their vassal or be annexed by their army!"

"Your Majesty, they said nothing about resorting to force. You know that Sennacherib's army was destroyed—right outside your gates, in fact."

"Wake up, Zerah! That was more than twenty years ago! They could give birth to an entirely new army and train them to fight in twenty years' time. And you can be sure that's exactly what Emperor Esarhaddon has done. Didn't you hear what his delegates just said? 'It's the dawn of a New Assyrian Empire.'"

"Then why not join them? Your grandfather, King Ahaz, made an alliance with Assyria and brought peace to our nation."

"My father always used King Ahaz as an example of how *not* to reign."

"But your father was controlled by factions that—"

"I want it quiet in my throne room!" Manasseh suddenly shouted. The agitated murmuring stopped instantly. It had rumbled through the audience hall ever since the Assyrian delegates had departed, but now the king's nobles and officials straightened in their places, their faces somber as they faced him.

In the hush that followed, Manasseh heard his guards talking among themselves outside his throne room door, but after a moment their voices stilled, too, as silence and fear spread like rising water. He could see by Zerah's tense posture that he had more to say.

"Finish with it, Zerah, before I lose my patience."

"I simply wanted to point out that your father also made alliances when it suited him. There's nothing wrong with treaties."

"My father's alliances were made between equals. They never required him to pay tribute. Assyria wants us as their vassal state like the rest of the nations around us. I'd be selling our freedom—a freedom hard-won by my father."

Zerah gave an elaborate shrug of surrender and slumped back in his seat. Manasseh knew him well enough to know that he wouldn't give up this easily. More arguments were sure to follow in the days ahead, before Manasseh was required to give the Assyrians his answer.

Elongated shadows stretched across the chamber floor, reminding him that it was late afternoon. The Assyrian petition and resulting discussion had consumed his entire day. Manasseh had eaten nothing since breakfast, and hunger added to his ill humor. The king gestured to the officials seated in front of him.

"Well, what about all of you—my so-called advisors? Let's hear your pearls of wisdom on the matter." No one spoke or moved. Manasseh folded his arms across his chest and waited. The silence and the tension, like Manasseh's nerves, stretched like drawn bowstrings. When the sound of the Temple shofar shot through the room, Manasseh stood. "Your sagacious advice will have to wait until tomorrow."

The relieved nobles bowed before him as he swept from the room, with Zerah trailing a few discreet steps behind him. "I'll have my evening meal in my chambers," Manasseh announced as he strode down the corridor. "Join me there when it's ready, Zerah. We have much to discuss."

"What about the evening sacrifice?" Zerah asked. "Aren't you going?"

"No. You'll have to worship in my place." Zerah appeared stunned by his uncharacteristic behavior but Manasseh kept walking, leaving Zerah to make his way to the Temple Mount alone.

As the door to his chambers closed behind him, Manasseh shrugged off his royal robe and let it drop to the floor. His suite was dark, the shutters closed against the afternoon sun, and the rooms felt cooler than the stifling throne room had.

"No, don't open them," he told his valet, gesturing toward the windows, "and leave me alone until my food is ready."

"Shall I light the lamps for you, Your Majesty?"

"No. Just go."

Manasseh stood in the darkened room, savoring the solitude. The world would be a much better place without all the people in it—except for a few to wait on his needs. He smiled at the thought, then quickly grew serious again when he remembered the Assyrians.

Things had been going so well in his kingdom until this crisis. And he knew without a doubt that it *was* a crisis, in spite of Zerah's assurances that the Assyrians wanted only his friendship. Manasseh had hoped that he would never have to face what his father had faced, but here he was—in the same room, confronting the same enemy, the same decision. He imagined Hezekiah pacing alone just as he was, weighing his options, considering the risks. He stopped when he suddenly remembered that his father had Eliakim and Shebna to advise him. For the space of a heartbeat, Manasseh wished he also had those two brilliant men and the experience and wisdom they could offer. Then he recalled that they had been traitors, serving the interests of a conspiracy, robbing his father of his rightful power. At least Manasseh was free to make his own decisions, even if the responsibility did unnerve him.

He remained alone until Zerah returned from the sacrifice, then they sat down together at the small table in his room while the servants heaped their plates with lamb, bread, and fresh fruit and filled their wine goblets. Zerah ate in silence, and Manasseh knew he was waiting for him to speak first. He had little appetite for the food in front of him, still upset by the Assyrians' visit.

"So, Zerah. You still believe Judah should become an Assyrian vassal?" he finally asked.

"I don't think the consequences will be as horrible as you imagine, Your Majesty. The annual tribute they require isn't much."

"Maybe for now. It will undoubtedly increase each year."

"It's not in their best interests to destroy our economy. Besides, what other choice do we have? You said yourself they might try to annex us by force if we don't join willingly."

"There's a third option, Zerah. We can refuse to surrender to their vassalage or to their army, just as my father did. That way I can preserve Judah's freedom."

Zerah laid down his bread and pushed his plate away. "Hold on. Your father paid a steep price for that freedom—forty-six cities destroyed, thousands carried into captivity. We would be an Assyrian vassal today if it hadn't been for a plague."

"Exactly! We'll fight them the same way my father did."

"With a plague?"

"My father's priests called on enormous powers to defeat his enemies. I want you to find out what spells they used and call on the same powers."

Zerah looked visibly shaken. "But . . . wait a minute. Surely you're not asking me—"

"No. I'm *ordering* you. When we met seven years ago, you assured me that you had access to the same ancient powers and spells that Rabbi Isaiah had."

"I do, but—"

"Then prove it!" Manasseh leaned across the table, challenging him.

Zerah started to protest, then stopped. As his eyes darted nervously, Manasseh noticed how close-set they were, how sinister they made him appear. Manasseh was surprised to discover that he suddenly distrusted him.

Finally Zerah smiled slightly and rubbed his hands together. "All right. But the only way I can do what you ask is if you let me consult one of the spirits first."

He looked too self-satisfied, too smug. Manasseh's suspicions multiplied. "Whose spirit do you want to consult?"

"King Hezekiah's."

Manasseh leaped from his seat, upsetting his wine. "You charlatan! You know very well I won't summon my father!"

"In that case, I'm powerless to help you."

Manasseh strode into his adjoining bedchamber, slamming the door behind him. He would never admit it to Zerah, but he was still ashamed of what he had done to his newborn son. Hezekiah had condemned child sacrifice and anyone who practiced it. Manasseh couldn't bear to face him.

He kicked a footstool, sending it spinning across the room, then picked up a table and hurled it with both hands, giving vent to his frustration. Did Zerah really need to consult Hezekiah, or was he disguising his lack of power behind Manasseh's fears? In all the years he had known Zerah, Manasseh had never mistrusted him until now.

When he had calmed himself a bit, Manasseh crossed to his window and opened the shutters. Now that the sun had set, a cool breeze blew through the room from the Kidron Valley below the palace. Ahaz's clock tower loomed in the courtyard beyond his window, and Manasseh recalled the story his father had once told him. As Hezekiah had lain dying in this room, Isaiah had called upon supernatural forces to heal him, then he'd made the tower's shadow move. The prophet had indescribable powers at his fingertips—and Zerah claimed to possess those powers. Was he telling the truth, or was Zerah a liar?

As Manasseh brooded, his doubts and fears multiplying, Zerah quietly slipped into the room and rested his hands on Manasseh's shoulders. "I'm sorry, Your Majesty. Please . . . let's not fight. I can't bear to have you angry with me."

"I thought you had access to spiritual power. You told me you knew the same spells that Isaiah used."

"I do."

"Then why won't you do what I ask? Call down a curse on the Assyrians for me! Destroy their army!"

"All right. But first we need to make sure that it's God's will. What was right for King Hezekiah may not necessarily be right for you."

"Kill a thousand sheep and cattle if you have to. Consult the stars. Seek guidance from the spirit world. Examine every avenue. I want omens that are clear and unmistakable, Zerah. I want your guarantee—" He stopped as an idea suddenly came to him. "Why don't you summon Rabbi Isaiah instead of my father?"

"I could try . . . if that's your wish . . ."

Manasseh spun around to face him. "How did my father reach his decision to defy the Assyrians? What did he base it on? He didn't believe in omens or guidance from the stars. How did he know it was God's will?"

"I assume he sought the advice of men who did have access to the hidden things."

"You mean men like Eliakim?"

"Yes."

"Then how did Eliakim know? I governed by Eliakim's advice for almost ten years, and he never even noticed the stars, much less consulted them. He did everything by the Torah. It was tiresome. He would make me consult the Law if I wanted to spit on the ground. From what I recall, my father stuck pretty close to the Torah, too. You've spent the past seven years convincing me that the Torah is just a bunch of useless, outdated laws designed to enslave me. I agree with you. Now show me how I can know God's will—with certainty—without it."

"The omens will reveal—"

"But I'm dependent on you to interpret them for me!"

Zerah's face went rigid. "You don't trust me? You think I'm deceiving you?" When Manasseh didn't reply, Zerah's eyes filled with tears. "I don't believe this! How can you doubt that I'd want anything but the best for you? For us?"

"I want the certainty my father had."

"Then let me summon him. Ask him yourself how he knew what to do."

"No!"

"Listen, you were a child when your father died. You don't know how *certain* he was. You don't know if he had doubts or fears, much less if he really knew God's will."

In an instant, memories of Hezekiah returned to Manasseh as clearly as if Zerah had summoned his spirit. He recalled Hezekiah's strong hands and sweeping gestures, his deep voice resonating with power, the way his dark, probing eyes would soften with love when he looked at Manasseh. Hezekiah's scent seemed to fill the room again, the way it had before he died. Manasseh struggled to cling to these snatches of his father's memory before they slipped away, fitting the pieces together, recreating the man he had loved so deeply. When the last memory finally faded, he was left with one conviction.

"My father knew God's will, Zerah. My father knew God."

They stared at each other in silence for a long time before Zerah spoke. "What do you want me to do?"

"You're a priest; put me in communication with his God. Get answers for me. And swear to me that you'll tell the truth."

"It hurts that you doubt me."

"Too bad. This decision is much too important for me to be concerned about your feelings. It's almost dark enough for the astrologers to work—send them up to King Ahaz's tower to study the skies. Then go up to the Temple and start sacrificing animals for omens. I'll join you in a little while. I want answers, Zerah."

"Yes, Your Majesty. We won't disappoint you."

Zerah left to do what he'd commanded, but as Manasseh sat alone in the room once again, staring at the remnants of his meal, he found that he couldn't get his mind off the men who had served his father. He wished he could summon the spirits of Eliakim or Shebna or Isaiah to advise him, but then he recalled that they were traitors and realized that he couldn't trust what they said. Their spirits might try to deceive him, too.

Suddenly he had a better idea. Manasseh may not be able to talk to the prophet, but perhaps Isaiah's writings contained a clue about what he should do. He summoned his servant.

"Several years ago I confiscated all of Rabbi Isaiah's personal papers," he told him. "Find my secretary and tell him to get those documents out of the archives and bring them to me."

When the servant returned with Manasseh's secretary they piled the prophet's scrolls on the table. "Help me look through these," Manasseh ordered. "I want to read all of the prophecies that haven't been fulfilled yet, especially the ones that might tell me what the Assyrians are up to." As his servants lit more lamps, Manasseh snatched up the closest parchment and sank down on his couch to read it.

Then Isaiah said to Hezekiah, "Hear the word of the Lord Almighty: The time will surely come when everything in your palace, and all that your fathers have stored up until this day, will be carried off to Babylon. Nothing will be left, says the Lord. And some of your descendants, your own flesh and blood who will be born to you, will be taken away, and they will become eunuchs in the palace of the king of Babylon."

Manasseh stopped reading and looked up.

"What is it, my lord?" his secretary asked.

"Is Babylon still an Assyrian vassal?"

"Yes, Your Majesty."

"Good. Then this doesn't concern me." He tossed the prophecy on the floor and picked up another one. He scanned through it quickly, then slowed as he came to these words:

When men tell you to consult mediums and spiritists, who whisper and mutter, should not a people inquire of their God? Why consult the dead on behalf of the living? To the law and to the testimony! If they do not speak according to this word, they have no light of dawn.

Manasseh dropped the scroll and sprang to his feet.

"Are you all right, Your Majesty?"

"I don't have time to read these." He hoped his secretary didn't notice the tremor in his voice. "Finish reading them for me. Leave all the ones I should see, and take the rest back to the archives. I'm going up to King Ahaz's tower."

By the time Manasseh had climbed the last winding step to the top, his fear had transformed into anger. He took little notice of the magnificent star-filled sky or the luminous quarter moon perched above the distant horizon. "Where's Zerah?" he demanded. The royal astrologers looked up from their charts and scrolls in surprise.

"I don't know, Your Majesty."

"Didn't he tell you I was coming?"

"Yes, Your Majesty. We've just finished reading your stars this very minute."

"Well, what do they say?" He sank onto the stone seat that his grandfather had built into the tower wall. Ahaz had always needed to rest when he reached the top.

The chief astrologer consulted his clay tablet of notes. "The stars say that this is a good time for setting goals, Your Majesty, and for making solid plans to achieve them. A struggle could result in a commitment if it rests on a firm foundation. Carefully made plans should go almost as expected, but be prepared for some resistance. Stay alert and you may solve a puzzle if—"

"What in blazes are you talking about? Your gibberish is the only puzzle that needs to be solved!"

"I'm sorry . . . we—"

"Abstractions! You haven't offered me a single concrete word of advice!"

The astrologer eyed the armed bodyguards accompanying Manasseh and dropped to his knees in front of him. His associates quickly did the same.

"Forgive us, my lord. We didn't realize you needed an answer to—"

"Didn't Zerah tell you about the Assyrians?"

"He didn't want to tell us too much or it might influence our readings."

"The blind leading the blind, is that it?"

"I'm not sure I understand, Your Majesty."

"That's my point! If you don't know what my question is, how in blazes are you going to give me an answer!"

"My lord, if you could give my colleagues and me a few minutes—"

"There's not a cloud in the sky!" Manasseh said, sweeping his arm across the horizon. "The stars are shining for everyone to see! Can you read what they say or can't you?" The astrologers huddled in consultation for a moment, comparing notes, then the leader gingerly stepped forward again.

"You are entering a fortuitous time for making agreements that involve stability and security. But expect a few surprises. There may be more going on than you know about. Watch and listen. Important changes may be starting that could alter the shape of your destiny. Seek out the powers behind these changes and work with them. The objective is to have everybody win, so don't exclude an opposing faction if—"

Manasseh interrupted him with a storm of cursing. "What kind of worthless mumbo jumbo is that? I need specific guidance!" It took every ounce of restraint he possessed to keep from ordering his guards to hurl all four astrologers off the top of the tower. Instead, he turned away, descending the steps in a blind rage, then headed up to the Temple Mount to find Zerah.

The scene at the top of the hill resembled something from a nightmare, with flickering fires and slaughtered animals and chanting, shadowy figures. Zerah dominated the eerie tableau, and the firelight danced across his face and illuminated his frizzy hair and beard like a halo as he stood beside the massive altar. He had rolled up his sleeves to examine a sheep's liver, and his arms were soaked to the elbows in blood that looked glossy black in the dim light. A dozen priests hovered near him, slaughtering animals and ripping the skins from them. Grotesque, disemboweled forms dotted the courtyard around the men as blood drained in a dark pool at their feet. The gore made Manasseh's stomach reel. He couldn't remember ever seeing so much blood; Yahweh's priests and Levites had always slit the animal's throat, catching its blood in a basin.

Zerah took one look at Manasseh's face and dropped the sheep's liver into the basin. "Manass—I mean, Your Majesty, what is it? What's wrong?"

"Your astrologers are worthless! I want clear answers—do's and don'ts! All they're doing is mumbling vague abstractions!"

He shivered as he recalled Isaiah's prophecy: *"When men tell you to consult mediums and spiritists, who whisper and mutter . . ."*

Zerah rinsed his hands in clean water and dried them on a linen towel. "You had do's and don'ts when you had the Levites ordering you around. You're way beyond all that now. Why would you ever want to go back to dogmatic rules when your own inner guides can help you make the right decision?"

Again, Manasseh recalled Isaiah's words: *". . . should not a people inquire of their God?"*

"Consult the Urim and Thummim for me," Manasseh said.

Zerah's bushy eyebrows met in the middle in a frown. "Are you certain you want to do that?"

"Why not? Is this bloody mess of sheep guts going to tell me whether or not I should sign an alliance with Assyria?"

"My omens will serve as a guide. Like the stars, they'll help *you* reach the decision that's right for you. With Urim and Thummim the decision is given to you—yes or no. Are you sure that's what you want?"

"I'm prepared to do God's will if I ever find out what it is!"

"I can arrange for this to take place tomorrow after—"

"Tonight, Zerah. I want to seek Urim and Thummim tonight. That way I'm in control."

Manasseh expected another pouting comment from Zerah about his sudden lack of trust, but Zerah simply said, "As you wish," and headed toward the Temple chamber where the high priest's ephod was stored. Manasseh followed, grateful that the Levites hadn't taken the ancient breastpiece with them when they fled six years ago.

As soon as Zerah brought out the wooden box and opened the lid, Manasseh reached into the pocket behind the twelve precious gems and made certain it contained two stones—Thummim for "yes," Urim for "no." They were identical in size and shape but one was black, one white. He would take no chances that Zerah might trick him.

"Is there a ceremony involved?" he asked. "Where are we supposed to do this?"

Zerah slipped the ephod over his head and fastened the chains that held it in place. "There's no ceremony," he said, replacing the stones. "We can do this wherever you'd like. Why don't we go back to the courtyard by the altar?"

As they walked side by side across the Temple grounds again,

Manasseh recalled the stories his father had told about how King David consulted the Urim and Thummim for guidance. Maybe King Hezekiah had consulted it, as well. Maybe that was his source of certainty. Manasseh's heart pounded with excitement as he prepared to hear God's answer and know His will with certainty, just as his father had.

By the time they returned to the main courtyard, Zerah's priests had cleared everything away except the basins containing the omens. The sacrifices had all been placed on the altar to burn, filling the courtyard with their sweet aroma. Manasseh's nerves tingled with excitement. "What am I supposed to do?" he asked Zerah.

"We've already offered enough sacrifices for you. Just ask your question. But keep it simple—yes or no."

Manasseh considered all of the things he wanted to know—was he right in deciding not to become an Assyrian vassal? Would Esarhaddon send his army to attack Jerusalem if he defied him? Would God provide a miracle for him as He had for King Hezekiah? But even as Manasseh pondered all of these questions, the thought of following in his father's footsteps and facing hundreds of thousands of Assyrian troops brought an icy sweat to his forehead. He decided to begin with the simplest question.

"Should I sign this treaty with Assyria and become their vassal?" he asked.

Zerah closed his eyes and lifted his hands, beseeching the gods in prayer. Manasseh was too overwrought to focus on any of Zerah's words. The prayer seemed to last until dawn. Finally Zerah ended with *amen*—so be it. Manasseh held his breath as Zerah reached inside the breastpiece and drew out a stone.

It was Thummim. Yes.

The answer stunned Manasseh. "What? That's it?" he cried. "God wants me to become an Assyrian vassal?" The courtyard seemed to sway beneath his feet. "I don't understand. Why is God abandoning me? Why won't He help me stand up to them the way He helped my father?"

"Those aren't yes or no questions, Your Majesty."

"I-I don't want to be an Assyrian vassal! What about our sovereignty?"

"I tried to warn you to decide for yourself."

Zerah started to return the stone to its pouch inside the breastpiece, but Manasseh snatched it from him. "Let me see that." He stared at the stone as if willpower alone could make it change color in his hand, giving him the answer he wanted. "I don't understand," he murmured again, then closed his fist around it, longing to hurl it into the giant altar's flames.

Zerah took Manasseh's hand and gently uncurled his fingers to remove the stone from his grasp. "You need to get some rest, Your Majesty. You've had a long, trying day."

He nodded mutely. He felt drained of strength. God wasn't going to help him as He'd helped his father. There would be no miraculous plague. He would have to forfeit his sovereignty, pay tribute.

Why wouldn't God help him? What about all the sacrifices he'd made, all his devotion?

"Isn't there anything else I can do?" he pleaded.

Zerah shook his head. "The answer is clear, Your Majesty."

Manasseh turned his back and allowed his bodyguards to lead him down the hill to his palace.

As soon as King Manasseh was out of sight, Zerah hurried inside the Temple storage chamber and sank down on a bench as his trembling knees finally gave out. If Manasseh had discovered the tiny dot of hardened wax no larger than a pen stroke, it would have cost Zerah his life. Thankfully, the crisis had passed. Manasseh hadn't noticed the bead of wax that marked the Thummim stone, nor would he ever know that Zerah had placed it there in order to distinguish it from the Urim if the need ever arose. He was glad he'd had the foresight to mark one of the stones in case of an emergency—such as the one tonight.

The ordeal had been grueling for Zerah, but in the end, using the ephod had turned out to be the quickest way to accomplish what Zerah had intended all along—signing the treaty with Assyria. It spared him the time and trouble of slowly leading Manasseh to the same conclusion with omens and sorceries. Zerah had dreaded the exhausting work of exploiting his relationship with Manasseh, manipulating the strings of his emotions. Now everything could continue as before.

Zerah had faith in his gods and in his own spiritual power—up to a point. In spite of his assurances to the king, he had no idea which spirits or spells Isaiah had called upon to summon the plague on the Assyrians, nor would he know how to control such lethal powers if he did succeed in conjuring them. The king expected the impossible.

He caressed the Thummim one last time before placing it inside the breastpiece. Then he unfastened the high priest's ephod and returned it to the box, closing the lid until next time.

Miriam sat at her table beside the outdoor oven, humming to herself as she kneaded bread for their noon meal. Her body rocked in rhythm with her song as she repeated each step—folding the dough, pushing it with the heel of her hand, spinning it a quarter turn, folding it again. She enjoyed breadmaking because it was one of the few daily tasks she could still do. So many other jobs, such as wringing laundry and weaving cloth, were impossible with her crippled hands.

She shielded her eyes and glanced up to gauge the sun's height. There was plenty of time for the bread to rise and then bake. It would still be warm when Joshua arrived home for lunch in a few hours. She covered the dough with a cloth when she was finished and placed it in the sun to rise, then wiped the flour off her hands. She heard the back gate creak open, and when she looked up she was surprised to see Joshua. He stood in the courtyard as if carved from stone, staring into space with a vacant gaze, watching a scene she couldn't see. Her immediate fear was that something had happened to Nathan. She groped for her crutches and struggled to her feet.

"What's wrong?"

He gave a start, as if he hadn't noticed her until then. "I just came from a meeting with Prince Amariah," he said slowly. "Our homeland is gone."

"What do you mean, it's gone?" She hobbled over to him and reached up to touch his face, trying to draw him back to her, back from the place inside himself where he so often retreated. He brushed her hand away in an absent gesture, as if shooing a fly.

"We just received the latest news from Judah. King Manasseh has forfeited our sovereignty to the Assyrians."

"But why? Was there a war or something?"

"No. That's what's so ironic. Not one Assyrian soldier ever left Nineveh. Their emperor announced that he was building a new empire, and Manasseh signed up as his willing vassal."

Joshua's voice was calm, almost dreamy, but Miriam saw the repressed rage in his clenched jaw and rigid shoulders, heard it in his wheezing lungs. She needed to help him douse the flames of his anger before they burned up everything that was good in him.

"What will this mean?" she asked.

"It means that our country has lost its independence. It means that everything my father worked for, all of his prayers, his faith, were for nothing. One of the greatest miracles in the history of our nation has been canceled with one stamp of Manasseh's royal seal. . . . And it means that we'll never be able to go home now, unless we're content to be Assyrian slaves."

"Is Egypt in danger? Could the Assyrians come here?"

He shook his head as if the question was irrelevant. "Pharaoh has armed garrisons like this one all across the nation. He's ready for the Assyrians."

"Then what's wrong, love?"

"I don't want to fight for Pharaoh, I want to fight for my own country. Manasseh never should have given in. We could stand up to the Assyrians just like Abba and King Hezekiah once did. I begged Amariah to send our men and me to Jerusalem. Pharaoh would give us all the weapons we needed. We could convince plenty of other Judeans to join us and fight for our freedom. God would surely give us the victory."

"What did Prince Amariah say?"

"He won't do it. He thinks this is God's revenge, that God is using the Assyrians to punish Manasseh."

"Isn't that what you wanted, Joshua? Didn't you want God to punish Manasseh?"

He shook his head slowly from side to side, his gaze turned inward again. "No. I wanted to punish him myself." He moved away from her like a man walking in his sleep.

"Joshua, where are you going?" He didn't answer. Instead, he drifted out through the courtyard gate, leaving it to swing open in the breeze behind him. "Joshua, wait! Can't you talk to me about it?" He didn't seem to hear her.

Miriam knew that he was heading to the nearby riverbank to be alone. She also knew from experience that being alone was the worst possible thing for him. He couldn't pray when he was this upset, and his anger would slowly grow and swell like the rising bread dough, with no release. She considered sending one of the servants to the marketplace to find Jerimoth, then decided that it was her job to console her husband, not Jerimoth's.

Joshua was such a complex man, and so much smarter than she was. Miriam looked at life in simple terms, while Joshua made everything complicated. He tried too hard to analyze and organize everything, even things he couldn't change. Why had God ever put them together? Could it be that Joshua sometimes needed her practical, commonsense approach to life as a balance?

It would take her nearly thirty minutes to walk the same distance he could walk in five, but she steeled herself for the long, arduous trek over rough terrain to the riverbank, dragging her useless legs. Three times her crippled limbs gave out and she fell, struggling alone like an overturned turtle until she righted herself. When she finally found Joshua he was standing close to the shore, staring downriver toward the sea, his shoulders slumped in defeat. He didn't see Miriam limping toward him until she staggered up behind him and collapsed to the beach in exhaustion.

"Miriam! What are you doing here?" he said angrily.

"Following you."

He sank to his knees beside her, and she felt his hands trembling with fury when he gripped her shoulders. "You know you can't walk this far over rough ground! What a stupid, dangerous thing to do! What if you fell?"

"I did fall—three times!"

"You could have hurt yourself."

"Then don't run away from me, Joshua. Share your problems with me."

All at once the anger drained from his face, and he clasped Miriam to his chest, clutching her tightly. "I'm sorry . . . I'm so sorry."

"I want to help you, Joshua. It breaks my heart to see you so unhappy. I don't know what to do for you."

"I don't know, either."

He sat back with a sigh and turned her around so she could lean comfortably against him, cradled in his arms. She listened to the gentle lap of water against the shore and the slow thudding of his heartbeat as she rested to recover her strength. The air wheezed through his chest as he struggled to breathe.

"What's it like there?" she asked after a long silence.

"Where?"

"That place where you go, inside yourself. Where you mourn and grieve."

"It's horrible, Miriam. You don't want to know."

"But I need to know. . . . You go there so often."

"I don't want to drag you there with me. That's why I left the house."

Miriam felt her own anger rise as she turned to face him. "It's not *your* life and *my* life anymore, it's *our* life. We're *one* flesh. That means we share everything—the sorrows as well as the joys. If you won't take me there, how can I help you find your way back to me?"

He didn't reply, and Miriam sensed the struggle he was waging with his demons of depression. "What goes on inside of you, Joshua? If you explain it to me in simple terms that I can understand, maybe you'll understand it better yourself."

He sighed and settled her against his chest again, his hand tracing idle patterns on her shoulder. "Did I ever tell you about my father's tunnel?" he asked.

"I don't think so."

"He carved it out of solid rock beneath the mountain in Jerusalem to channel water from the Gihon spring to the Pool of Siloam. He took me inside it once when I was nine or ten years old. We had an oil lamp with us, but as soon as we rounded the first curve and the light from the entrance disappeared, the darkness tried to swallow every shard of light. I could feel the weight of all that darkness, and the weight of the mountain above my head, closing in on me, trying to crush out my life. With every step I took, the water seemed to grow deeper and colder, and I didn't think we'd ever find our way back to the light again. I was terrified, but I was too ashamed to tell Abba. The only thing that made it bearable at all, the only thing that got me through it, was Abba's presence beside me."

He folded her hand between his own.

"That's what it feels like, Miriam. Like a mountain of darkness that I can feel, darkness that tries to swallow every bit of light and crush me beneath its weight. It's like I'm wading through water that's cold and deep, and it keeps rising—to my waist, to my chest, to my chin—until I feel myself being sucked under and I'm about to drown." His wheezing worsened, and she worried that he wouldn't be able to catch his breath.

"God keeps closing all the doors," he continued. "Hemming me in, taking away more and more choices, forcing me to wander deeper and deeper into the mountain. I'm terrified. Lost. What if I can't find my way out again? And Abba's gone. He isn't beside me anymore."

"But God is still with you."

"That's the most terrifying part of all. God seems a long way off. Sometimes it feels like I left Him behind in Jerusalem. I can't feel His presence here among all these foreign gods."

She studied his face, desperate to help him. Miriam knew that false cheer and easy answers wouldn't help him; only the truth. "You know what I see, Joshua? The darkness comes every time you get angry with God. You're angry with Him today because of what happened in Judah. He didn't work things out the way you wanted Him to. But He doesn't leave you—you walk away from Him, away from His light. You enter the tunnel yourself every time you find it impossible to go in the direction He wants you to go, impossible to accept His will for your life."

"How can I accept His will when I don't understand it? Why does He keep taking away everything I love? You know what my biggest fear is? That He'll take you away from me, too. He's taken so much already."

"I could get angry and depressed for what I've lost, too—not only is our baby gone, but I can barely walk, and my hands don't work right, and I'll be crippled like this for the rest of my life. I've always been so independent. I never wanted anyone to be in charge but me. But maybe that's why God allowed me to be crippled—so I'd see how much I need other people. So I'd learn to lean on them, to trust them. Maybe it was the only way I could learn to trust God. Don't you ever wonder what He wants you to learn from all this, Joshua?"

"I guess I thought I was finished learning."

She leaned into him, nestling closer. "I trust your love, Joshua. I trust that you would never do anything to harm me, that you only want what's good for me."

"It's true, Miriam. I'd give you my own arms and legs if I could."

"Then you have to believe that it's the same with God. If the Assyrians take over Judah, if we live on Elephantine Island for the rest of our lives—whatever happens—it's for our own good and for His purposes." As he toyed with a lock of her hair, she noticed that his breathing had eased a bit.

"How many times have you saved my life now?" he asked. "God must have put you on this earth just for me."

She smiled. "Maybe that's why He hasn't given us a baby. Maybe my hands are already full taking care of you."

He kissed her then, and Miriam knew that he would find his way out of his dark tunnel again, into the light.

18

NATHAN AWOKE FROM THE NIGHTMARE with his heart pounding, his body drenched with sweat. It was his running dream, the one in which someone pursued him down dark, lonely streets while he tried to flee on legs as heavy and awkward as tree stumps. He had no idea what he was running from. In his panic, he never dared to glance over his shoulder and see. The familiar dream should have lost its power to terrify him after all these years but it hadn't, and at age eighteen, his childish fear embarrassed him.

He rolled off his sleeping mat and stumbled out to the courtyard to wash, squinting in the glare of the dawning sun. When his limbs finally stopped trembling, he went back inside for breakfast. Miriam was usually up by now, fixing their morning meal, but Joshua sat in her place, slicing cucumbers into thick, uneven pieces.

"Want some?" he asked, holding out the plate.

Nathan shook his head. "You didn't cut off the peels. Miriam always does."

"I guess I forgot."

"Where's Miriam?"

Joshua carefully laid down the knife and plate and rose to face Nathan as if he had something important to say. It pleased Nathan that he had grown nearly as tall as Joshua and could almost look him in the eye. But he knew that no one would ever mistake them for father and son. Nathan was thin and wiry and couldn't seem to gain weight no matter how much he ate. Everything about him seemed paltry and insignificant compared to Joshua, from his thin brown hair and scraggly new whiskers to his stringy muscles, which were as streamlined as a long-distance courier's. Joshua walked with the proud bearing of royalty, and his thick, curly hair and full beard were the rich color of ebony. To Nathan, Joshua's aristocratic posture seemed pretentious on a man who was as bronzed and solidly built as the Egyptian slaves he ordered around all day. And it annoyed Nathan that Joshua paused to wipe his large, callused hands on a towel before answering his question.

"The midwives were here yesterday to check on Miriam's pregnancy. They think it would be wise for her to stay in bed."

"All day?"

"Until the baby is born."

"You mean for the next six *months*?" Nathan thought of the frustration he would feel at being confined to his bed for that long and knew that Miriam would feel the same. But he also felt afraid for his sister. Why did she even want a baby if it was going to cause her so much trouble?

"It has taken five years for her to get pregnant again after losing the baby," Joshua continued. "We don't want to take a chance that she'll lose this one. She's going to need both of us to help her out. Can I count on you, son?"

"What do I have to do? Bake the bread?" He meant it as a joke, but he saw by Joshua's scowl that he had misunderstood. The man was a walking storm cloud, spreading darkness and gloom wherever he went. Nathan wondered how Miriam could stand him.

"No, of course not," Joshua said. "I'll hire extra servants for that, and my mother will help, too."

Nathan poked among the bowls of food Joshua had spread out on the table, looking for something else to eat.

"Here . . . are you looking for the bread?" Joshua handed him a small loaf left over from yesterday. Nathan knocked it against the table to show Joshua how stale it was.

"I'll crack a tooth on that stuff. I'm going over to Mattan's house for breakfast."

Joshua's frown deepened. "Well, I suppose it would be all right this morning . . . but I don't want you moving in over there. Your uncle Jerimoth has enough mouths to feed as it is."

"So? He can afford six kids. He makes more money than Pharaoh does." Once again, Joshua failed to smile at his attempted humor. He gazed at Nathan with a mournful expression as he idly fingered his stupid eye patch.

"Don't be disrespectful, Nathan. Your uncle Jerimoth works very hard for a living and he—Please don't roll your eyes at me like that."

Nathan couldn't help himself. It was an automatic response to Joshua's endless lectures. "Can I go now before they clear away all the food?"

"What about the morning sacrifice? I thought we—"

"I'm pretty sure Uncle Jerimoth can find the way. He's been to the sacrifices once or twice before. I'll follow him."

"Nathan, you know I hate it when you're sarcastic—"

"Sorry." He resisted the urge to roll his eyes again and slipped out of the back door, quickly crossing the courtyard to Mattan's house. Not only would the food be better than anything Joshua might attempt to fix, but the atmosphere at jovial Uncle Jerimoth's house would be an improvement, as well. Nathan could already hear laughter before he opened the door. Mattan sure won the luck of the draw when he got Jerimoth for a father. Nathan was stuck with the King of Gloom. Again he wondered how Miriam could stand him.

Miriam. He hoped his sister would be all right.

Nathan had a lot of time to worry about her as he waited for the boring sacrifice to end. Ever since he had learned that Miriam was pregnant again, he had tried not to wish that the baby would die this time. Now he wondered if maybe he should do something more for her. He owed it to her after causing her first baby's death, yet he wasn't sure what he should do. He shifted from foot to foot, thinking about his sister as the Levites droned the liturgy. By the time the service finally dragged to an end, he had formulated an idea. He drew his brother, Mattan, aside, knowing he would need his help.

"Come to the mainland with me, Matt. There's something I need that I can't get here."

"I'll have to ask Abba for permission. I'm not allowed to—"

"If you help me we can be back before he even knows you're gone."

Mattan gave him a hard shove. "What's wrong with you? I'm not going to disobey my father. I'm going to school."

"Jerimoth isn't your father."

"Yes he is!" Mattan stood with his hands on his hips, daring Nathan to contradict him.

"All right, then. He is. But I still need your help. Your father will never even know you were gone. Come on. It's important."

"I don't understand you at all," Mattan said, shaking his head. "Your father loves you. Why do you keep defying him all the time?"

"He's not my father."

"You're going to go too far one of these days, and he'll finally give up on you. Then you'll realize how stupid you've been—after it's too late."

As Mattan stormed off, Nathan realized that he should have borrowed some money from him for the boat fare. His mission on shore was too important to risk being caught as a thief or a stowaway. Now he would have to return home and scrounge for some loose silver. Joshua had arrived home from the sacrifice first, so Nathan hid behind the courtyard wall, watching from a distance as Joshua carried Miriam outside, where she could rest in the shade. As soon as Joshua left for work, Nathan crept into the house and looked around for Joshua's silver pouch. There wasn't much in it—enough for the ferry but not enough for Nathan to buy what he wanted. He chose two small pieces that Joshua would never miss then left the house as quietly as he'd come and hurried to the ferry dock.

Nathan hadn't been to the mainland by himself since his disastrous trip five years ago, but he didn't have time to savor the exhilarating taste of freedom. He could talk his way out of being tardy for his lessons, using his sister, Miriam, as an excuse, but not for missing his lessons entirely. As soon as the boat landed, Nathan went straight to the marketplace, scanning all the booths until he found the one he wanted—the one where all of Egypt's gods were on display. Some of the idols were carved from ivory, some from wood or stone, but the expensive ones, made of gold and silver, perched on a shelf in the rear where only the owner could reach them.

When Nathan had lived on the mainland, the craftsman he'd been apprenticed to had worshiped a collection of household gods and goddesses every morning and evening. He had explained to Nathan which goddess had blessed him with four strong, healthy sons—Taweret. Maybe the goddess could help Miriam deliver a strong, healthy son, as well. An ivory image of Taweret was on display near the front of the booth. Nathan knew it would be difficult to steal the image by himself with no one to distract the owner, but he had no choice. He sauntered up to the booth, cursing Mattan beneath his breath for not coming along to help him. The merchant glared at him.

"What are you looking at, Jew? There's nothing here you want. Move along!"

Nathan bowed politely, adopting the humble pose he had perfected on his dim-witted Torah instructors. "Excuse me, sir. I'm an apprentice for an Egyptian bronze caster here on the mainland. My master sent me—"

"You're a lying Jew, aren't you! Be off with you!"

Nathan remembered the beating he'd endured at the hands of filthy Egyptian pigs like him, and his temper soared out of control. He didn't have the time or the patience to work one of his con games on this fool. In a fit of desperate anger, he pointed to the shelf behind the man's head.

"It's going to fall! Look out!" When the owner whirled around to see, Nathan snatched the idol from the display and ran.

"Stop! Thief! That Jewish boy is a thief!"

Nathan knew it had been a stupid, clumsy way to steal something, but the man's contempt had driven him to it. Now there was nothing he could do but run through the unfamiliar streets, searching for a place to hide. Stunned shoppers stared at him as he pushed them aside and sprinted past. Nathan hoped that the idol merchant would give up the chase, but he continued to shout an alarm as he ran behind him.

"Stop him! He's a thief!" Several bystanders tried to grab Nathan, but he twisted out of their grasp and shoved them to the ground. More men joined the merchant, taking up the chase. Nathan was tempted to toss the idol aside so they would have no proof of his theft, but Miriam needed it. Fear for her and for himself kept him going, desperate to escape. As he ran on and on, with his pursuers close behind, Nathan realized with horror that he was living his nightmare.

Just as he was ready to drop from exhaustion, he suddenly remembered the junkyard full of slag and debris behind the foundry where he had once worked. On his last reserve of strength, he staggered into the deserted dump and dove beneath a pile of scrap wood. The narrow hiding place was impossibly small. They would never look for him there. A moment later he heard his pursuers' shouts as they ran into the yard behind him.

"There's no way we'll ever find him in this mess," someone said. "We've lost him."

"I don't care. Search anyway!" Nathan recognized the idol merchant's voice. He heard the men tossing pieces of junk around as they searched.

"We'd better send some men to watch the dock," the idol merchant warned. "He'll have to take the ferry if he wants to get home to Elephantine Island."

Nathan's heart sank like a stone in the Nile as he realized that he was trapped on the mainland. He lay unmoving, barely breathing, as the Egyptians combed the scrapyard. Hours seemed to pass before they finally gave up the search. Nathan stayed hidden until he was certain they were gone, then chose the largest chunk of wood he could carry and carefully made his way out of the village. A mile upstream, he waded into the river and began to paddle, clinging to his makeshift raft. With any luck, the current would carry him downstream to the southern tip of the island. Joshua had warned him that there were crocodiles in those waters, but Nathan would sooner take his chances with crocodiles than risk getting caught by the Egyptians.

He seemed to float in the filthy water forever, and by the time a Jewish fisherman pulled him into his boat, just offshore from the island, Nathan was exhausted from paddling and thoroughly sick from vomiting all the muddy water he had swallowed.

"What happened to you, boy? You fall overboard?"

"I was spearing fish when I fell in. The current took me away." The fisherman looked doubtful but didn't question Nathan's lie.

It was late afternoon when Nathan reached home and slipped inside without being seen. The idol had miraculously survived the ordeal tucked inside his robe, and he hid it beneath his sleeping mat. Then he peeled off his ruined clothes and crawled beneath the blankets. The next thing he knew, Joshua was shaking him awake.

"Nathan? What's wrong, are you sick?" His callused fingers touched Nathan's brow.

"I never made it to my classes. I've been in bed all day. I'm sick to my stomach."

"Are these your clothes? I'll take them outside. They smell bad." He bent to pick up the dripping bundle. "Nathan, they're soaking wet!"

"I tried to wash the vomit off. I guess I didn't do a very good job."

Joshua held them at arm's length as he gazed down at Nathan. "Are you going to be all right? Can I get you anything?"

Before Nathan could reply, there was an urgent pounding on the front door. He closed his eyes as his heart pounded in reply. Joshua dropped the clothes again. "I'll be right back."

Nathan sat up, straining to hear who it was, wondering if he should run while he still had the chance. The voice at the door sounded somber, official.

"Good afternoon, my lord. We're sorry to disturb you, but we would like to have a word with your son if he's home."

"Nathan? He's sick in bed. Why? What's this about?"

"The Egyptian authorities have come over from the mainland. One of their merchants reported a robbery this morning, an idol carved from ivory. They said the thief was a Jewish teenager."

"Are you accusing my son?"

"He has a reputation as a thief."

"That was—how long ago—five years! Don't you dare call Nathan a thief unless you have proof!"

Nathan crawled from his mat to listen beside the door to the main room, scarcely able to believe that Joshua would defend him. Again, he had the urge to run but knew he wouldn't get far on an island.

"I'm sorry," the elder continued, "but we checked with the rabbi before we came to see you. He said Nathan skipped his Torah class today."

"I already told you he was home, sick."

"Yes. And there is a simple way to prove if that is true. This is the captain of the ferry. He says that a Jewish boy was one of his passengers this morning, and he thinks he can identify him. We'd like to question Nathan if you don't mind."

"I do mind. I resent your accusations."

Nathan stepped through the doorway into the room. "Ask me anything you want." He didn't know why he had come forward, exactly, but he did know that it was useless to try to hide. But more than that, he wanted to hurt Joshua, to see him humiliated in front of these men. He needed to prove to himself that Joshua was a liar, that he didn't love him like a real son, that he would give up on him if pushed to the limit.

"That's the boy," the ferryman said, pointing. "He rode over on my ship."

Nathan recognized the other men as three of Elephantine's elders. "What were you doing on the mainland?" their leader asked.

Nathan glanced at Joshua, expecting an explosion of anger like the one he had received the last time he'd stolen something. Instead, the pain he saw on Joshua's face stunned him. His father seemed to age twenty years as he rested a trembling hand against the wall to steady himself. Nathan had a sudden premonition of Joshua growing old, dying. He felt a stab of fear.

When Joshua's anger finally did come, it was directed at the elders, not at Nathan. "You have no right to come into my home and accuse my son like this. I'm his father. It's my duty to question him and to discipline him if he's done anything wrong."

"But if a member of our community is accused of theft, it reflects on all of us. We have to clear this up and let the Egyptian authorities know that the thief has been caught and punished. We have to assure them that it won't happen again."

"Do you trust me to handle my household according to the Law?"

"No one questions your honesty or integrity, Joshua."

"But you question my son's?" The elders didn't answer. "I'd like you to leave so I can speak to Nathan alone," Joshua said calmly. "You can wait for us at the city square. If he's guilty, you'll have his confession. If he's innocent, we'll expect an apology. Good day."

Joshua closed the door behind them and turned to face Nathan, leaning against the door for support. Nathan's heart raced faster than it had when fleeing from the idol merchant. He couldn't read the emotions etched on Joshua's face and had no idea what to expect next. Joshua continued to gaze at him without speaking until Nathan's insides turned to water. He could no longer stand the silent suspense.

"Aren't you going to ask me if I did it?"

Joshua shook his head.

"Why not?"

"Because I couldn't bear it if you lied to me, son."

Nathan had been in confrontations with Joshua before, but he felt something different this time, something he couldn't quite identify. It wasn't exactly fear—he wasn't afraid of Joshua, nor did he fear a beating. He had been beaten before and knew he could take it. No, it was something else . . . a fear he couldn't define.

"How long are we going to stand here looking at each other?" Nathan finally asked, unable to bear the strain.

"That's up to you."

Nathan suddenly remembered Mattan's warning that one day he would push Joshua too far, and he felt his stomach twist again. Was he afraid that Joshua would kick him out? No, he knew he could get by on his own. He had done that before, too. He didn't need Joshua. He wasn't afraid.

But he was.

Joshua's patience was maddening. If he had ranted and raved, Nathan could have fought back, but he didn't know how to fight the pain and disappointment he saw in Joshua's eyes, the empty silence that stretched endlessly between them.

"What do you want from me?" Nathan shouted.

"The truth," Joshua said hoarsely. "Just the truth."

"You believe them, don't you? You think I did it."

"I have no way of knowing if you did it or not. But I do know that I taught you right from wrong. I taught you what the Law says about stealing and about lying. I taught you that idolatry is a grave sin." Nathan watched Joshua's Adam's apple rise and fall as he swallowed. "If you tell me you're innocent, then I'll defend you against your accusers. If you've made a mistake, Nathan, and you're sorry for it, then I'll forgive you."

"I don't believe you."

Joshua lowered his head as a wave of stunned sadness washed across his features. Nathan's heart raced faster. When Joshua finally looked up, Nathan was amazed to see that he was fighting tears.

"Have I ever lied to you, son?" His voice was so low it was almost a whisper.

Joshua's words couldn't possibly be true. He would never forgive Nathan. He would abandon him forever if he knew the truth. Nathan wanted to prove him a liar.

"I did it. I stole the idol."

Joshua closed his eyes. He didn't speak.

"You're not surprised, are you? You knew I took it."

"Bring it here, son."

As Nathan returned to his room to fetch the idol, he had the urge to run out of the house and just keep going. Joshua wouldn't care. He would have a child of his own in a few more months. Nathan was nothing but a troublemaker. He never would amount to anything. This whole affair just confirmed what Joshua had believed about him all along.

Nathan retrieved the image from beneath his mat and stared at it for a moment, turning it over and over in his hands, examining the beautiful carving, the smooth, flawless ivory. He had wanted to help Miriam, but everything had gone wrong. Now he was in serious trouble. Once again, he was tempted to run, to steal a boat and let the current carry him away. But if he fled he would never know if Joshua really would have forgiven him or if it was all a lie. He longed to find out. He returned to the main room and found Joshua standing exactly where he'd left him. When he saw the idol in

Nathan's hands, Joshua lowered his face again and covered his eyes.

Blind terror, worse than in his nightmare, coursed through Nathan. He tried to tell himself that it didn't matter what Joshua thought of him, that it didn't matter if Joshua abandoned him, but it wasn't true. He did care. Again, Nathan faced the maddening silence as Joshua battled his emotions. When Joshua finally looked up, he spoke only one hoarse word.

"Why?"

How could Nathan explain his fear for Miriam's life, the guilt he felt for causing her first child's death, his longing to help her somehow? Suddenly it was important to Nathan that Joshua know the truth.

"I took it for Miriam's sake," he blurted. "I know how much she wants a baby, and I didn't want this one to die like her last baby did. The goddess Taweret protects women who are pregnant, and I thought maybe this time I could help Miriam." The idol felt heavy and clammy in his sweating hands. He waited for Joshua's angry tirade, but it never came.

"What is the idol made out of?" he asked quietly. It seemed like an odd question.

"Ivory. From a hippopotamus."

"And where is the animal now?"

"I don't know. Dead, I guess."

"Powerless? Unable to protect itself?"

Nathan shrugged.

"Then how can it protect Miriam's baby?"

"I didn't think it would hurt to try. Your God isn't answering any of your prayers. Her last baby died!"

"God did answer my prayers, Nathan. If you could have seen how far your sister fell eight years ago, you'd know that she should be dead. I prayed that she would live, and God answered me. I know Miriam would like a child, but it's not the most important thing to me. I'd rather have Miriam than a baby. I already have a son who bears my name."

Nathan didn't trust himself to speak. He didn't want to be moved by Joshua's words, didn't want to admit even to himself the fierce emotions raging inside him. He watched Joshua warily, fearing that he would try to embrace him. Part of Nathan wished that Joshua would hold him, but another, harder part knew that something vital to his survival would break if he did. He quickly turned his back and walked to the far side of the room.

"What happens now?" he asked.

He heard Joshua sigh. "You and I need to go see the elders, son."

The walk with Nathan from their home to where the elders were assembled in the city square was the longest Joshua had ever taken. He felt devastated with shame. How could his son do such a terrible thing? Joshua's own failure as a father was now exposed for all to see. But far worse than his own shame was his staggering fear for Nathan's soul. How had he lost his son to idols? How could he draw him back to God?

The city officials paced restlessly as they watched him and Nathan approach, as if anxious to finish with this business before the evening sacrifice. When Joshua saw the Egyptian authorities standing to one side, he knew he couldn't face this ordeal alone.

"Send someone for Jerimoth," he said. His brother would remind him of their father's example. He would help Joshua do what Abba would have done. He tried to draw a deep breath to calm himself but couldn't. He remembered the aching numbness he had felt for weeks after the Temple explosion, as if he had been slapped by a giant hand. But this pain was deeper, more paralyzing than any physical pain.

Jerimoth was panting slightly as he came to stand beside Joshua and Nathan a few minutes later. His gaze traveled from Joshua's face, to the idol in Nathan's hands, to the Egyptian authorities standing in the background, and Joshua saw that he understood. "O God of Abraham, help us all," Jerimoth whispered.

"How does your son plead?" the chief elder asked. His voice was kind, not accusing.

"Guilty, my lord." Joshua took the idol from Nathan and handed it to him. The elder carried it to the Egyptian authorities as if it harbored an infectious disease, then he faced Joshua again. Fear for

Nathan swelled inside Joshua, making it difficult to breathe.

"The Law says that a thief must pay back what he stole plus an added restitution of twenty percent. Are you willing to pay your son's fine?"

"Of course. But I think it would be better for Nathan if he worked to pay the fine himself. I'll loan him the silver in the meantime." The elders nodded in agreement as Joshua untied his silver pouch. He prayed that this ordeal would soon be over, but one of the Egyptian authorities suddenly stepped forward.

"Just a minute. How old is your son?" he asked.

Joshua felt a rush of fear. He pressed his fist to his chest to ease the pain. "He's eighteen, my lord."

"Then he is of age. We demand that he be flogged according to Egyptian law."

"No, please . . ." Joshua breathed. Jerimoth gripped his arm, bracing his body against Joshua's to support him as the elders quickly crowded around them to confer.

"You're not in a position to argue with them," the chief elder said in a low voice. "The crime took place on the mainland, not on our own island this time."

"Please, I'm not arguing . . . I'm begging. Tell them I'll make sure he never returns to the mainland. Explain that he's only a boy."

"This isn't his first offense. Under the circumstances, since it's more than a simple theft, since it involves bringing an idol to our island . . ."

"No, listen, *please!*"

"We agree with the Egyptians, Joshua. Nathan needs to suffer the consequences of his actions."

"I'll punish him. I'll—"

"If he had been caught on the mainland, they would have flogged him on the spot," the elder said in a whisper. "And if they knew that he has stolen before, they would cut off his hand."

"Then I'll take the lashing for him. It's my fault for not being a better father when he was younger. I should have—"

"I can take my own punishment," Nathan said suddenly. His face was the color of ashes. "Just do it and get it over with." He loosened his belt and shrugged off his outer robe.

Joshua tried to cry out as they led Nathan to the lashing post, but he couldn't draw any air into his lungs. It took what little strength he had to wrestle with his brother as Jerimoth tried to steer him out of the square.

"You should leave, Joshua. It would be easier for both of you."

"Let go of me! Nothing can make this easier! I'm his father! I have a right to be here!"

Tears blurred Joshua's vision as the elders stripped Nathan to the waist and fastened his wrists to the post. He was so thin. There was no meat on his back. Joshua could count each rib, each vertebra. He rubbed his eye with the heel of his hand and forced himself to watch, counting each blow.

One . . . two . . . three . . .

The lash whistled through air and snapped sickeningly against Nathan's flesh. Joshua felt each painful strike shudder through his own body.

Four . . . five . . .

It took Jerimoth and three of the elders to hold him back. Joshua no longer cared that everyone saw him weeping.

Eight . . . nine . . . ten . . .

Nathan groaned after each stroke but didn't cry out. The torture seemed endless. "That's enough . . ." Joshua moaned. "Make them stop. . . ."

Thirteen . . . fourteen . . .

When it was finally over, Joshua gently untied his son and hefted him over his shoulder, careful not to touch his bloody back. Jerimoth led him home; Joshua was unable to see where he was going, his vision blinded by tears. Nathan was in shock and only semiconscious when Joshua laid him facedown on his sleeping mat. Then Joshua stumbled outside to the courtyard for a basin of water and clean cloths to bathe Nathan's wounds. Jerimoth followed him.

"Joshua, why are you torturing yourself like this? It's not your fault. You *have* been a good father to him. It was Nathan's own choice to steal. There was nothing more you could have done for the boy."

Joshua set the basin down again and covered his face in despair. "Why did God give Nathan to me? Why not to you? You're a much better father than I am. Look at Mattan; look how he turned out.

You could have helped Nathan, changed him. Why did God give him to *me*?"

Jerimoth rested his hand on Joshua's shoulder. "Because you understand him so much better than I ever could."

He looked at his brother in bewilderment. "*Understand* him?"

"Yes, Joshua. Nathan is just like you. Both of you are filled with anger. Both of you rage at circumstances in the past that you cannot change. Both of you mourn and question the loss of your fathers. Both of you are furious with God."

Joshua leaned against the wall as he struggled to comprehend his brother's words.

"I don't say these things to criticize you," Jerimoth continued. "God knows how different you and I are. But look closely at Nathan's anger and rebellion, and see your own. God *did* give him to the right father—the father who could recognize the pain in Nathan's heart and understand exactly how he feels."

Deep in his soul, Joshua suspected that his brother's words were true. But if he thought about them now, his heart would break. Instead, he ladled clean water into the basin with deliberate concentration.

"I'm going home," Jerimoth said softly. "Nathan has been punished enough. Let him know you love him, you forgive him."

Joshua nodded, unable to speak, and carried the basin into the house. When Joshua sat down beside him, Nathan turned his face to the wall.

"Go away and leave me alone."

"I can't do that, Nathan."

"I don't want you here!"

"I'm sorry, but I have to be here. You're my son. Your suffering is my suffering." And as he spoke the words, Joshua was stunned to discover that they were true.

In the months that followed Nathan's whipping, Joshua was well aware of his need to battle against the darkness of depression. He relied on Miriam's love and patience as he struggled to believe that God was still by his side. He had endured two painful blows: the loss of Judah's sovereignty to the Assyrians, and the unmasking of his own failures as a father. His fears for Nathan's soul consumed many sleepless nights, leaving him unprepared for a third blow when it came.

"Joshua, I think you should send for the midwives," his mother told him one morning. "I'm worried about the swelling in Miriam's legs and feet." Joshua went numb at his mother's words. Miriam hadn't seemed well for several days, but she'd stubbornly insisted that she was all right.

"I'll get the women myself, Mama." He left the house at a run, barely aware of his surroundings as he sprinted across the island to fetch the two midwives.

"Does she have any other symptoms besides the swelling?" they asked as he hurried back to his house with them again.

"She complained of a bad headache last night," he said. "This morning she still seemed groggy from it. Disoriented." He saw them exchange glances, and he began to walk so fast they had trouble keeping up with him. When he burst through the front door, out of breath, Nathan met him.

"What's going on? Why are they here? Isn't it too soon for the baby?"

"Miriam's not in labor . . . she's . . . I can't explain." He brushed past Nathan and hurried into the bedchamber, followed by the women. "Miriam, I'm back. I brought—" He stopped, staring in horror at his wife as her body suddenly went rigid. Then her spine arched, her eyes rolled, and she began to convulse. "Do something! Help her!" he cried, but there was nothing any of them could do. Joshua watched helplessly until the convulsion finally ended and Miriam lay still. His mother and one of the midwives hustled him out of the room.

"What's wrong with my wife? Tell me what's wrong with her." He struggled to pull air into his lungs.

"Your wife's condition is very serious," the midwife said. "Unless we do something soon, she will go into a coma and die. It has happened before to other women with the same symptoms."

Joshua listened as if trapped in a bad dream. "Do whatever you have to do."

"The only thing we can do is start her labor. Once the baby is born, Miriam's condition will probably improve."

"But it's too soon for the baby," Nathan blurted. Joshua had forgotten that he was there.

"Yes, it's too soon by several weeks," the midwife told him. She paused before saying, "The child will likely die."

"She wants that baby!" Nathan cried. "You can't let it die again!"

"Nathan, please," Joshua said. "This doesn't concern you." Nathan turned and stormed from the house, but at the moment Joshua was much too upset to deal with him.

"If Miriam doesn't give birth soon, she could die," the midwife continued. "I'm sorry. I understand what a difficult decision you have to make."

"There's no question—save my wife. Do whatever it takes, but don't let Miriam die."

"Are you sure you understand that your child—?"

"I was born almost a month too soon, and I survived. Please, don't let Miriam die!"

"Shh ... If she hears you, my lord, if she thinks there's a choice ... most mothers want to give their lives for their babies."

He thought of Miriam's unselfish love, the many times she had willingly risked her life for him, and he knew that the midwife was right. "I want you to start her labor right away," he said.

"All right. But once we break the sac of waters and labor begins, there will be no turning back."

"Do it!" He paused to cough the air from his lungs, then drew a ragged breath. "What can I do? Tell me what I can do."

His mother took his arm and steered him toward the rear courtyard. "You can stay out of their way, Joshua. They have work to do. You'll make everyone a nervous wreck by hovering around, barking at everyone. Trust God. Let His will be done."

But as the hours passed, and then one day of labor turned into two, Joshua discovered that trusting God was impossible. In the past His will had been incomprehensible and had brought devastating losses. What if he lost Miriam? As the fear and tension in the household soared, Nathan vented his frustration on Joshua.

"This is your fault! It's your child that's making her suffer! Do something!"

"Nathan, I wish I could, but . . . look, I feel as scared and helpless as you do."

"If she dies, it'll be your fault!"

"Son, wait—" But Nathan slammed out of the house, and once again Joshua felt the devastating anguish of failure. His son should be coming to him for consolation. They should be comforting each other.

"I can't take this waiting much longer," he told Jerimoth, late on the second day. "Neither can Miriam. She's suffering."

"Women often cry out during childbirth."

"But for so long? It's been two days. I need to know what's going on."

"My Sara is helping inside. Maybe she can put your mind at rest." Jerimoth sent for her, but when Sara emerged from the bedchamber, one look at her distraught face sent fear racing through Joshua before he even heard her terrible words.

"Miriam isn't able to help with the delivery because of her paralysis. She's almost at the end of her strength. If the baby isn't born soon, the midwives say that—"

Jerimoth cut her off. "Never mind what they say." He spun Joshua around and pushed him toward the front door. "We're going to the temple to pray. Send for us if you need to."

"No, I can't leave her," Joshua insisted. "I need to stay here."

"You need to pray. That's the best thing you can possibly do. Right now it's the only thing." Jerimoth propelled him forward against his will, through the door and into the street, heading toward the temple grounds. Joshua was dimly aware of seeing other people going about their lives—bartering for food, feeding their livestock, walking home from the river with a string of fish—and it seemed unfair to him that life should continue with such indifference while Miriam suffered . . . while his child, his wife, struggled to live.

"I can't pray, Jerimoth. I'm afraid to pray. God has already taken everything I loved. What if He takes Miriam, too?"

"Is that how you picture Him?" Jerimoth asked in surprise. "As a cruel, heartless God who wants to hurt you?"

"I don't want to imagine Him that way, but it seems like all I've received from His hand is senseless suffering and loss. Miriam is the only good thing He's ever given to me to make up for all that He's taken."

"That's fear talking, not faith. You know God isn't like that."

"Can't you understand why I don't trust Him? Don't you see how terrified I am that I'll lose Miriam, too?"

"Yes. I do understand. That's why we need to pray. Come on."

They reached the gate to the temple site and went inside. The priests were going about their duties as if nothing was wrong, and again Joshua wondered why everyone else's life seemed tranquil except his own. Jerimoth nudged him into the men's court and dropped to his knees by the altar, pulling Joshua down beside him.

"You've told me how you feel, Josh. Now tell God. He understands." Jerimoth closed his eyes and lifted his hands.

At first the only words Joshua could pray were, "Please, Lord . . . please don't take Miriam." He repeated them silently over and over as Jerimoth prayed silently beside him. As time passed and Joshua's panic lessened he began to bargain with God, promising to build Him the finest temple in the world, promising to dedicate his life to making Elephantine their home—anything God asked—if only He would spare Miriam's life. But when even a lifetime of dedicated service didn't seem like enough, Joshua decided he had to pledge the one thing he'd refused to relinquish all these years: "O God," he prayed, "if you give Miriam back to me, I'll cancel the debt Manasseh owes me. I'll sacrifice my need for revenge, I'll lay aside all the hatred I feel for him, I'll put Manasseh out of my heart and my mind forever in exchange for Miriam's life." It was all he had to offer.

Hours later, Jerimoth tugged on his sleeve. When Joshua looked up and saw their mother signaling to them from the women's courtyard, his heart stood still. He scrambled to his feet and ran toward her. "Mama, no . . . please don't tell me . . ."

"Miriam is asking for you."

"Is she going to die?"

"She might. She's very weak from losing so much blood."

"I need to see her." He turned, ready to take off at a run, but his mother stopped him.

"Joshua, wait. I'm sorry, but the baby was stillborn."

He took a moment to absorb the painful truth. "You mean all that time, all that suffering . . . for nothing?"

"I'm so sorry."

His child was dead. And Joshua had made the decision to bring him into the world too soon. "Does Miriam know about the baby?"

Jerusha nodded. "You need to give her a reason to hang on, Joshua. She's suffered terribly, and now she wants to give up. She wants to go to paradise with her baby son."

"No! She can't die!" Again he started to leave, again his mother stopped him.

"Wait, son. I need to tell you something else." Joshua's heart raced as he steeled himself for more. "The midwives said that if Miriam lives, there can't be any more pregnancies. She will never be able to deliver a baby because of her paralysis. This birth nearly killed her. She must not get pregnant again."

He stared, unable to speak. *If* she lives?

"Go to her, son. She needs you. Jerimoth will walk me home."

Joshua ran blindly through the streets, too incoherent with grief and fear to pray. When he stumbled through the door, he saw one of the midwives holding his tiny, shrouded baby in her arms. She looked up at him with sorrowful eyes. "I'm so sorry, my lord."

"I'd like to hold my son," he said.

"That isn't wise. . . ."

"Give me my son." He spoke the command quietly, but he knew that his rage was apparent in the deliberate way he pronounced each word. The midwife unwound the swaddling cloths so Joshua could see his son's tiny gray face. He looked peaceful in spite of losing his two-day struggle for life. Joshua lifted him from her and settled him into the crook of his arm. He remembered holding Amariah's son at the circumcision ceremony and feeling the warmth and life in the infant's body. His own child felt stiff and cold. The midwife turned her face away at his tears.

"I'm sorry," he whispered to his son. "I'm sorry. I wanted you to live . . . but . . ." He couldn't finish. He gently handed the baby to the midwife and turned away to wipe his eyes before going into

Miriam's bedchamber. What could he say to his wife? How could he explain the death of the child she had longed for when he didn't understand it himself?

Miriam's face was whiter than the linen sheets, her body as cold as their son's. He lifted the blanket and lay down in the bed beside her, drawing her to himself. She felt small and fragile in his arms, with no strength to hold him in return.

"Don't leave me, Miriam. Stay with me. Please."

"I don't think I can...."

"Remember what you told me? It's not your life and my life anymore, it's our life."

"I can't give you children."

"You're more important to me than children."

"No—"

"It's the truth, Miriam! Don't call me a liar!"

A tear rolled down her pale cheek. "I hate my broken body ... my twisted legs, these useless hands..."

"I love you. Every inch of you, just the way you are."

"How can you? Other women are whole and—"

"Do you see me as a monster with a scarred face and a mangled eye? I see you as my precious wife. You're not crippled to me. I love you for who you are, not because you'll give me children."

"But I want you to have a son. If I die, you can marry—"

"Don't make choices for me, Miriam! If you love me, give me what I want! I want you! I already have a son!" He hugged her fiercely, angry with himself for shouting at her, desperate to convince her to live. "O God ... Miriam ... if only I could give you my strength, my body.... Please don't leave me. The darkness will swallow me alive if you go. I'll never find my way out. Stay with me, please stay with me."

"I'll try...."

"You will! ... God of Abraham, please! You will!" He held her in his arms until she fell asleep, willing his life into her body, pleading silently with God to spare her.

At sundown on the third day, Joshua was still keeping his exhausted vigil, sitting beside Miriam's bed, refusing to leave her. He was only dimly aware of the midwives coming and going, taking care of her, as he waited for Miriam to come back to him. Finally his mother knelt in front of him and took his face in her hands.

"Son, look at me. It's over. You can let go of Miriam's hand now."

"No . . . she wants me to hold it—"

"It's time to let go."

"Miriam might—"

"She's asleep. She isn't going to die. But you need some fresh air. You need to go watch the sunset and see that there's still a world outside this room. If you hurry, you can make it in time for the evening sacrifice. Miriam is out of danger. I promise you that she will live." It took a moment for his mother's words to penetrate, for him to finally understand that God wasn't going to take Miriam as He'd taken everything else. "Go make a thank offering, Joshua. God answered your prayers."

He ran all the way to the temple grounds. The other men were clustered around the altar, watching the priests slay the evening sacrifice, but Joshua remained at a distance, surveying the jumble of debris surrounding his partially built temple. He knew that the only thing that had delayed its completion was his own ambivalence.

He waited until the service ended before crossing the courtyard to stand before the blazing altar. He whispered a prayer of gratitude for Miriam's life and renewed his vow to build an enduring monument to God in his new homeland. Then he drew a deep breath, remembering his other vow.

Joshua knew that forgetting everything that Manasseh had done and giving up his own right to revenge would be the hardest of his vows to fulfill. But as the sacrifice burned on the great altar in front of him, Joshua knelt before God and finally laid all of his hatred, all of his vengeance at Yahweh's feet.

19

NATHAN INHALED THE PUNGENT AROMA of roasting meat as he hurried across the crowded city square. The temple that Joshua and the other men had labored for years to build was finally complete, and the entire community had gathered to dedicate it as they celebrated the Feast of Pentecost. Nathan didn't care about the new temple or Pentecost, but he was looking forward to the chance to drink and celebrate with his friends. The sound of music and laughter, the roar of voices raised in celebration rang in his ears as he slid into his seat at the banquet table between his brother, Mattan, and sister, Miriam.

"You're late," Miriam chided. "We had to start eating without you. Where have you been?"

"With some friends from my platoon." He reached for the platter of meat, turning his head so she wouldn't smell his breath and discover that he and his friends had also shared a cask of Egyptian beer. He was high from it but not quite drunk.

"You should have changed out of your army uniform," Miriam said. "You know Joshua hates to see you come to a Jewish feast in Egyptian clothes."

"I don't care. He isn't sitting with us anyway." He gestured to the head table, where Joshua sat beside Prince Amariah. "He's much too important to sit with us."

"This is a momentous day for your father. Please don't ruin it by being difficult."

"He isn't my father," Nathan mumbled, but he had a mouth full of bread and hoped Miriam couldn't hear him.

Uncle Jerimoth and his growing family filled the remainder of the places at their table. "Have some melon, Nathan," Jerimoth said, passing a bowl of fruit. "It's delicious. You must be very proud of your father and what he has accomplished. I know I'm proud that he's my brother."

"I wonder what he'll do with himself now that his precious temple is finished."

Jerimoth smiled patiently. "It's not his temple; it's God's."

"Don't kid yourself. That building is his obsession. He lives for it." Nathan knew that Joshua would have lectured him for his surly tone of voice, but Uncle Jerimoth was perpetually cheerful.

"It belongs to all of us, Nathan," his uncle said. "It's going to be the centerpiece of our life here."

"It's going to be an anchor, weighing us down. Joshua used to talk about going back to Judah and fighting for our homeland. Now he'll never leave this island. He'll never tear himself away from his masterpiece. And just when I'm finally old enough to fight, too."

"Is it such a hardship for you to live here on Elephantine?" Jerimoth asked kindly.

"It's a prison sentence! I'm sick of this place. There's a whole world out there, full of interesting people and places, but I'm stuck here in the past, anchored to a bunch of rituals that were old and moldy five hundred years ago."

Uncle Jerimoth's smile vanished as he studied Nathan with concern. "What's wrong, son? Why are you so bitter?"

"I'm not bitter! I'm bored! I spent the first eight years of my life scrounging for a living in Jerusalem. Now I've been stuck on this miserable island in the middle of nowhere for eleven years. Except for the year we lived in Moab, I've never seen anything of the world."

"Does your father know how you feel about living here?"

Nathan almost said *he's not my father* but stopped himself in time. "He doesn't care."

"Now, I know that's not true. Listen, Nathan, you shouldn't hold your feelings inside for too long. You need to talk to Joshua. If you bottle them up, they'll only fester and ferment until they spew out in the wrong way and at the wrong time."

Nathan simply nodded and finished his meal in silence. Later, as Joshua strolled among the tables, greeting people and acting important, Uncle Jerimoth waved to get his attention. "Joshua ... over here!"

He moved toward them, grinning, walking on air. The sight disgusted Nathan. But before Joshua had a chance to greet him, one of Jerimoth's sons stopped him with a question.

"Uncle Joshua, isn't your temple exactly like the one in Jerusalem? My brother Mattan says it isn't."

Joshua crouched beside him. "I keep forgetting that you were born here. You've never seen Solomon's Temple, have you? Well, you're both right, in a way. This temple has the same dimensions as the one in Jerusalem, and I built it to look exactly the same, right down to the two pillars in front. But instead of facing east, I've aligned it to face Jerusalem. The limestone that we quarried from the cliffs along the Nile isn't exactly like Judean limestone, either, but see the roof? That's the biggest difference. The roof of Solomon's Temple is covered with gold. And our courtyard is smaller, too. There was no need to make it any bigger since not as many people will be coming here to worship."

"Abba says from now on we're going to celebrate all the feasts exactly the same way as they do in Jerusalem," the boy said.

"That's right. According to the Torah . . ." Joshua then noticed Nathan, slouched in his seat. "Why did you come to the feast dressed like an Egyptian?"

"Because I felt like it."

Joshua stood to face him, and Nathan scrambled to his feet, too, feeling the dizzying effects of all the beer he had drunk. Jerimoth stepped smoothly between them. "Let it go, Joshua. Nathan and I were talking during dinner, and I think he's still a little upset."

"What on earth does he have to be upset about? I've given him everything he could possibly want."

"You don't even know what I want! I want to get off this island!

I want to travel, meet people. I'm going stir crazy here."

"You can't leave until you finish your military training."

"I need a break from it."

He saw the color rise in Joshua's face. "A *break*? That's what you said about your other studies. You never finished those, either."

"I don't care. I want to see something different for a change."

"The world out there has nothing to offer but temptation," Joshua said in the superior, all-knowing tone that Nathan hated. "Everything you need to be happy can be found right here on this island." Before Nathan could reply to that ridiculous comment, a knot of city elders surged up to the table to congratulate Joshua.

"Nathan, let it go for now," Jerimoth whispered as Joshua spoke with the other men. "When I advised you to talk to your father, I didn't mean right now. He's exhausted. He has barely had time to sit down all day."

"He never has time."

When the elders finally drifted away, Joshua turned to him again. Nathan saw how weary he looked, but he plunged ahead anyway. "Listen, I'm not a kid anymore, I'm twenty years old. Let me travel with one of Uncle Jerimoth's caravans for a couple of months. Let me see the world."

"This is hardly the time or the place for this discussion," Joshua said coldly.

"Oh, I get it. You have more important things to do."

"That's not what I meant. I—"

"My lord, Prince Amariah is waiting for you," one of the elders interrupted.

"I'll be there in a minute." Joshua turned to him again. "Nathan, I don't know where this crazy idea about traveling came from, but you can just forget it."

"See?" Nathan said to Jerimoth, "I told you he never listens to me." He stalked away in search of his friends and another cask of Egyptian beer.

Torches lit the courtyard that evening as Mattan watched the men dancing in the city square with the Torah scroll. He scanned all their faces, searching for his brother Nathan, but he was nowhere in sight. The Feast of Pentecost was such a joyful occasion, with music and dancing and tables piled high with food from the first harvest. And the dedication of the new temple had given them even more reason to celebrate. But Nathan had come close to ruining the feast for everyone by arguing with Uncle Joshua at the dinner table. Mattan didn't understand his brother at all. Why was he always so unhappy?

He was still looking for Nathan when two of Mattan's younger brothers ran up to him and began tugging on his hands. "Come with us, Matt. We're going to go get some more date cakes."

"Not right now. I'm full. Maybe later." He was proud that they looked up to him, but he was worried about Nathan. Then the crowd parted for a moment and he spotted him across the square, laughing with a gang of his friends from the barracks. Mattan shooed the youngsters away. "Go find Abba. He'll take you for more sweets."

He sauntered over to Nathan. "Where have you been all night? I haven't seen you since you left the dinner table." He decided not to mention Nathan's argument with Uncle Joshua.

Nathan looked up at Mattan with unfocused eyes. "Having a private party of my own. Want some of this?"

Mattan sniffed the mug Nathan offered him. "Is this Egyptian beer? Where did you get it?"

"What difference does it make? Here—have some."

Mattan knew by the way Nathan slurred his words that he was drunk. He also knew that his own Abba would be very disappointed in him if he ever got that drunk—and so would Uncle Joshua if he knew about Nathan. Mattan took the mug that Nathan shoved into his hands in order to avoid an argument. He pretended to sip as he listened to him and his friends laughing and bragging about their army training and life in the barracks. The gathering seemed harmless enough, but as time passed, Mattan could tell that his brother was growing restless.

"This party's winding down," Nathan said as he downed another beer. "Time for some excitement."

"What do you suggest?" one of the others asked.

"How about a trip to the mainland?"

Mattan was too stunned to speak. When most of Nathan's friends began to argue against the idea he was relieved. Even with too much beer in their stomachs, clouding their judgment, they remembered the consequences. "It's forbidden, Nate. We'd better not."

But Nathan wouldn't give in. "So what! In the first place, your fathers are so wiped out from a day of celebrating they'll never even miss you. And in the second place, I can guarantee it will be worth the risk."

"What's on the mainland besides trouble?"

Nathan grinned. "Egyptian girls. They're celebrating the festival of Osiris this week."

"How come you know so much about pagan festivals?"

"I lived with the Egyptians for a while. They can really hold an orgy, too—not like our stuffy festivals. Anything goes with them. That's how they celebrate over there."

"Forget it, Nate. One look at us and they'll know we're Jews. They won't have anything to do with us."

"You're forgetting that we're soldiers in Pharaoh's army now. Our uniforms will impress them."

"I don't know . . . count me out."

"Yeah, me too." All but three of Nathan's friends wandered away.

Mattan hoped that Nathan would finally give up the idea, but he grinned at his remaining friends and asked, "So . . . are you with me?"

"Yeah! Let's do it!" they all agreed. Then they looked at Mattan, who had remained silent.

"Your brother isn't going to rat on us, is he?" one of them asked.

Nathan slapped Mattan's back good-naturedly. "Nah, he's all right. You won't tell on us, will you, Matt? Hey, I know! Why don't you come along, too? Find out what women are all about."

"It's a bad idea, Nate. You've had a little too much beer. Let's go see if there's any food left. Come on."

Mattan set down his mug and headed toward the food tables,

hoping that Nathan would give up his crazy idea and follow him. Matt was tired and ready to go home. The best thing he could do for his brother was to convince him to go home, too, and sleep it off. He glanced back to see if Nathan was following him and saw him hurrying away from the square with his friends, heading toward the ferry dock. They rounded the corner and disappeared into the night.

Nathan wasn't that stupid, was he? But then Mattan remembered how drunk his brother was and decided he'd better follow him. He turned to retrace his steps, but the mob in the crowded square slowed Mattan's progress.

"Where have you been hiding all night, Matt?" one of his friends asked, stopping him. "Want to join us?"

"I can't . . . I have to go . . ."

"Go where? What's your hurry?"

How could he explain? It took several minutes to disentangle himself, and by the time Mattan finally reached the dock, Nathan was gone. Mattan saw a small papyrus boat halfway across the channel, silhouetted in the moonlight, and heard his brother's drunken laughter carry across the dark water.

"You won't tell on us, will you, Matt?"

He slowly walked back to where his father was seated at their table. Mattan's youngest sister was asleep in his lap, and he was rocking her gently, tapping his foot in time to the music.

"Abba?"

"Yes, son?" His father's eyes glowed with contentment as he looked up. Mattan loved the way Abba said the word *son*, conveying so much pride and love in a single word. Mattan remembered the first day they had met in Jerusalem and how he had fled to Abba's open arms for solace. Jerimoth's arms had been open for him ever since. At age eighteen, Mattan was too old to curl up on Abba's lap. But the knowledge that he could, if he needed to, comforted him.

"Did you have a question, son?"

"Abba . . . how do I know whether or not it's right to do something?"

"The Torah is always your best guide."

"I'm not sure if the answer is in the Torah. And I'm not sure if..."

"Tell me as much or as little as you want, son. I promise I won't pry for more information." He smiled his warm, familiar smile, and Mattan knew he would keep his word.

"Abba, is it wrong to tell on someone if they're trusting you not to?"

"If you made a vow, then you must keep it."

"I didn't make a vow."

"Hmm ... Then it's more complex, isn't it?" He stroked his beard thoughtfully. "The Torah says we must always seek to do our neighbor good and protect him from harm. Will keeping this secret harm someone? Or protect him?"

"Both. I mean, if I mind my own business everything could turn out all right. He won't get into trouble unless he gets caught."

"And if you tell what you know?"

"Then he's certain to get into trouble."

"Suppose you were in this person's place. Which action would be more helpful to you? I don't mean the immediate consequences, but in the long term? Is he making a mistake that could hurt him for the rest of his life?"

"Yes."

"Can you prevent that damage?"

Mattan nodded slightly. "Thanks, Abba."

He turned and wandered slowly away, scanning the faces in the crowd. When his younger brothers skipped up to him and began pulling on his arms again, he gently pried them off. "I need to talk to Uncle Joshua. Have you seen him?"

"Over there," they said, pointing.

Joshua looked content as he sat beside Prince Amariah, watching the festivities. This had been a memorable day for him with the dedication of the new temple. Ever since Miriam had almost died, Uncle Joshua had been a different man—more focused in his work, more at peace. Nathan had been involved in the usual minor incidents of youth since his flogging two years ago but certainly nothing as serious as going to a pagan orgy on the mainland. If Mattan just kept quiet, maybe Nathan wouldn't get caught. Maybe he could sneak home in the morning with nothing worse than a bad hangover, and Uncle Joshua would never know that he had been to an Egyptian worship festival.

While Mattan watched, Joshua suddenly threw his head back and laughed at something the prince said. Mattan turned away. He couldn't tell him. He couldn't ruin this joyous day for him. But then he realized that he wasn't ruining it, Nathan was. Why did his brother want to hurt Uncle Joshua this way? And why was he so hell-bent on destruction? The Torah commanded Mattan to protect his brother from harm. He turned around and slowly walked to his uncle's table.

"Uncle Joshua, may I talk to you?"

"Certainly. Excuse us, please, Your Majesty." He stood and began strolling away with him, resting his hand on Mattan's shoulder. His uncle was a good man, a kind man. He didn't deserve to have Nathan causing him so much trouble. At that moment Mattan hated his brother.

"What is it, Mattan?" Joshua asked as they walked.

"Nathan drank a little too much Egyptian beer. He . . . he and three of his friends decided to go to the mainland."

Joshua halted, swaying slightly as if the earth had suddenly jolted to a stop. Mattan wondered if he was remembering Nathan's last trip to the mainland and picturing the vivid cross-hatched scars on Nathan's back. When Joshua finally spoke, his voice was a monotone of pain. "Did he tell you why?"

"The Egyptians are celebrating the festival of Osiris. He said he wanted to go . . . you know . . . for the Egyptian girls."

"Do you know which three friends went with him?"

"Colonel Simeon's son and the sons of Reuben and Caleb, the Levites." Mattan saw Joshua scanning the crowd and knew he was searching for the three men. They would have to be told. "Uncle Joshua?"

"Yes?"

"Did I do the right thing?"

He nodded almost absently and squeezed Mattan's shoulder. Then he wove through the crowd and Mattan saw him draw Reuben the Levite aside.

When Mattan glanced back toward his family's table he saw his father watching him. Abba's expression was sorrowful, but when their eyes met, he nodded.

"God of Abraham," Mattan whispered, "please don't ever let me hurt Abba this way."

For Joshua, the trip to the mainland seemed to take three days. The two Levites on either side of him gazed silently across the dark river, as paralyzed by what their sons had done as he was, but Colonel Simeon lashed out at Joshua during the entire voyage.

"Your son is behind this! Nathan has been a troublemaker on this island from the very first day. Lying. Stealing. Dabbling with idols!"

Joshua was too numb to feel any more pain. He knew Simeon was right; Nathan had done all of those things and more. As the harsh words rained down on him, he could only ask God to forgive him for not listening to Nathan earlier tonight, for not loving him as a father should. Then he prayed for the grace to love him now.

"Your son coaxed the others into this; I know he did. They're basically good boys, but Nathan is a no-good, disobedient rebel! He—"

"Enough," Reuben finally said. "All of our sons are guilty."

"But not as guilty as his son! I demand justice! I'll see that Nathan is stoned to death for his disobedience, just as the Torah decrees!"

"No one stones their rebellious children anymore," Caleb said dully.

"Well, maybe they should! Look what happened to our homeland. We shouldn't allow sinners and idol worshipers to live!"

"Then our sons would die, as well," Reuben said.

"Our sons deserve a second chance. They've never done anything like this before, but Joshua's son has been in trouble before. He's the instigator. At the very least he should be banished from our island for good. If he wants to go out in the world and frolic among pagan gods, let him. But keep him away from my children!"

Joshua leaned over the rail of the boat, fighting nausea. He remembered how he had brought Nathan back home after making him work on the mainland ten years ago and how he'd given him his name. But in spite of all his efforts to love him, Nathan had rebelled again and again. How had Joshua ever imagined that God could use him to reclaim Judah from idolatry when he couldn't even restrain his only son?

He heard the roar of the celebration and the throb of pagan drums long before the boat finally docked. The temple of Osiris, god of the Nile, stood in a plaza near the river. Yahweh had placed His temple, His sanctuary, in the middle of the heathen river god's domain. Joshua wondered how the next generation of their tiny remnant would ever resist the fatal lure of idolatry after the generation of men who had fled Jerusalem with him were all dead.

He stepped off the boat like a man in a daze and followed the sounds of revelry. But when he finally entered the torchlit square, Joshua jolted awake. The Egyptian festival was so vile and disgusting, it took every ounce of willpower he had to keep from turning away and running back to the boat. He waded through the depravity with only one thought—this was the work of the Evil One. Joshua had to rescue his son from him.

Nathan and his friends were easy to spot among the beardless Egyptians. The three men who had come with Joshua quickly grabbed their sons, who were watching the orgy in astonishment from the edge of the crowd. Nathan was the only one participating. He was locked in an embrace with a young Egyptian girl.

The force of Joshua's fury nearly blinded him. It wasn't directed at Nathan but at the sin that had ensnared him and would eventually destroy him. Joshua had seen the devastation that sin had wrought on Manasseh. He had witnessed the resulting enslavement of his people. He wouldn't let the Evil One claim another victim. Especially Nathan.

"You can't have my son!" he cried as he wrenched Nathan from the girl's grasp. A hush rippled through the crowd for the space of a heartbeat as Joshua hauled Nathan to his feet.

Nathan was startled, angry, and very drunk. "What do you think you're doing? You have no right—"

"I have every right! I'm your father!"

"No you're not! You're not my father!" He stumbled drunkenly, too disoriented to resist, as Joshua dragged him out of the square and toward the ferry dock. The pagan orgy quickly resumed behind them. But as they neared the boat, with the others already on board ready to depart, Nathan halted.

"I'm never going back there with you!" He took a wild swing and caught Joshua by surprise, his fist smashing painfully into Joshua's jaw. Without thinking, Joshua struck back with a blow to his son's gut that knocked him backward. Nathan stumbled and nearly fell, but when he regained his balance he lowered his head and rushed at Joshua, fists flailing. Joshua blocked most of his blows, then planted a punch on the side of his son's face. Nathan sprawled to the ground, blood streaming from his nose.

"That's enough, Nathan!"

He was much too drunk to fight, but he scrambled to his feet and came at him again. Joshua landed another blow that split his lip. When Nathan still wouldn't quit, Joshua leaped on top of him and wrestled him to the ground. He didn't want to hurt him, but Nathan had turned into a madman. There was no other way to subdue him except to fight. They rolled over and over in the dirt, pummeling each other.

Nathan fought recklessly. He was quick and strong from his military training, and he brawled with the scrappiness of youth. But Joshua was heavier, more muscular, and unwilling to lose his son to idols. He finally managed to pin him to the ground, planting his knee in Nathan's back, twisting his arm behind him.

"You know better than to commit adultery! I taught you! The priests taught you! And you certainly know better than to worship with pagans! There is *one* God, Nathan—ONE! Say the Shema!"

"Let me go."

"Not until you say it. 'Hear, O Israel . . .'"

"I hate your guts!"

"Fine. Hate me. I can live with that. But I won't let you hate God. I won't let you defy Him and show contempt for His laws. *Say it,* Nathan!"

Instead, Nathan cursed.

The river was only a few feet away. Joshua stood and hauled his son to his knees, then lifted him by his tunic and threw him into the water. He waded in after him, pushing his head under, holding him there until Nathan flailed in panic.

"Are you crazy?" he gasped when Joshua brought him to the surface. "You want to kill me?"

"You're killing yourself. 'The evil deeds of a wicked man ensnare him; the cords of his sin hold him fast. He will die for lack of discipline, led astray by his own great folly.' Now *say* it!"

"Why don't you disown me and get it over with! Then you can get out of my life!"

"I can't do that. I'm your father."

"You're not my—"

Joshua pushed him under, holding him beneath the black water with trembling hands. When he finally let him up, Nathan gagged and coughed, gasping for air.

"Help . . . stop!"

"Do you want me to drown you?"

"No . . . don't . . . !"

"You should fear God half as much as you fear me right now." He plunged him under and held him down for almost a minute before pulling him up. Nathan vomited river water and beer.

"You're going to kill me!"

"Living a sinful life and defying God's laws are going to kill you. But that's a slow, painful way to die. I'll save you the trouble and drown you quickly." Nathan clawed frantically as Joshua forced his head under one more time. "Now say it!" he demanded when he finally brought Nathan to the surface. "'Hear, O Israel . . .'"

"'Yahweh is God . . .'" Nathan wept, "'Yahweh alone. . . .'"

Joshua dragged him to shore and dropped him on the sand. But when he looked down at his son—bloody, sick, and shivering with fear—he sank to his knees beside him and gathered him into his arms.

Nathan passed out after Joshua helped him onto the boat. Thankfully, Colonel Simeon was silent on the return trip to the island, as if too deeply shocked by what he had witnessed on the mainland to speak. One of the men helped Joshua carry Nathan home, and they deposited him on his sleeping mat, unconscious.

Joshua couldn't sleep. The pain in his heart had swelled until it seemed to fill every inch of him. His bruised jaw ached where Nathan had punched him, and he held the poultice Miriam made against his cheek as they sat outside together, talking until dawn.

"Maybe you should let him go, Joshua. Let him leave the island."

"If he goes—even with one of Jerimoth's caravans—he'll never come back."

"You've done everything you can for him. It's not your fault that he turned out this way."

"I made a vow to be a father to him—"

"And you've kept that vow, time after time. Rebelling was Nathan's choice."

"What will become of him?" He took the poultice off and stared at it blindly. "What in the world will become of him?"

Not long after sunrise, Joel, the high priest, arrived at their house. Joshua knew that he had probably volunteered to come in place of one of the elders because he was a family member.

"Nathan's trial will be held this morning, right after the sacrifice," Joel said, his voice somber. "The other elders and I have been talking with Caleb, Reuben, and Colonel Simeon since . . . well, all night, I guess."

"What's going to happen, Joel?"

"The three men were all eyewitnesses, Josh," he said with a sigh. "There's no doubt that Nathan is guilty. Colonel Simeon is demanding justice. He says the punishment for a son who continually rebels is stoning."

A shudder rocked through Joshua. "And the other council members?"

"Divided. Many of them are afraid. They don't want their sons corrupted, but I don't think they will go as far as the death penalty. Most of them think Nathan should be banished from the island. I've been counseling them to reserve their final judgment until you've had a chance to plead Nathan's case."

Joshua gestured helplessly. "There's no case to plead. Nathan knew the Law, and he disobeyed it. The other boys were just watching, not participating the way he was. You know the Law, too, Joel. You know the trouble Nathan has gotten into before. What defense can I possibly offer?"

"I don't know. . . . I'm sorry. I did what I could for you, Joshua."

After Joel left, Joshua wandered into the house to change his clothes, pausing to look in on Nathan. One of his eyes was black-and-blue from the beating Joshua had given him, his face swollen and caked with dried blood. Miriam had stripped off his wet clothes, but his hair was matted with mud and weeds from the river. Joshua remembered being angry enough to drown him, and he was filled with remorse for losing control. He thought about all the trouble and heartbreak Nathan had caused through the years, and he wanted it to end. But he realized that the pain wouldn't end once Nathan was banished from the island. He had been part of Joshua's life for more than twelve years. Nathan would remain in his heart even if they were separated forever. The knowledge brought tears to his eyes.

As Joshua stood looking down at him, Nathan rolled over and opened his eyes. When he saw Joshua he groaned and draped his arm across his face as if trying to hide. Joshua sank to the floor beside the mat, leaning wearily against the wall.

"How much do you remember from last night?" he asked.

Nathan's mumbled reply was soft. "More than I'd like to."

"I lost my temper. Some of my discipline was . . . Some of it was done in anger. I'm sorry." Nathan didn't respond. "The elders are meeting in a little while to decide what to do," Joshua continued. "I'm supposed to present your defense."

Nathan gave a harsh laugh. "Good luck."

"Is there anything you want me to tell them?"

"I was drunk out of my mind."

"That's a contributing factor, but it's not a defense."

Nathan uncovered his face and stared up at the ceiling. "They probably won't believe me, but I wasn't worshiping idols. I just went there to . . . because I . . ."

"You wanted an Egyptian girl."

Nathan closed his eyes. "I'm so bored here."

"I understand. But boredom doesn't exempt you from obeying God's Laws."

"There are too many laws! Life here is just too stinking strict. I'm hemmed in with rules and 'thou shalt nots' until I feel like I'm suffocating. I can't stand it anymore! Why can't I have a little fun like everyone else in the world?"

"Do you really want an answer, son? Or are you just blowing off steam?"

Nathan sat up, propped on his elbows. His eyes met Joshua's. "No, I really want an answer. Why can't we be like everyone else?"

"Because we're God's chosen people, His covenant people. The psalmist says, 'He has revealed his word to Jacob, his laws and decrees to Israel. He has done this for no other nation; they do not know his laws.' I made you say the Shema last night. Did you really believe those words, Nathan? Do you really believe there is only one God?"

"Yeah, I believe it. It's just that sometimes it seems like the priests made up all those rules, not God. Other religions don't have so many laws."

"Moses wrote, 'Who among the gods is like you, O Lord? Who is like you—majestic in holiness, awesome in glory, working wonders?' Our God is holy—none of the pagan gods is called *holy*—and we're made in His image. He demands holiness of us because it's the only way we can have fellowship with Him. The Law is there to remind us to be holy in everything we do—the way we dress, what we eat, how we live. It's true that other gods don't have laws for people to follow. That's what makes them so appealing. And it's also what proves they're false. Man creates those gods in his own sinful image. People don't want rules and laws; we don't want holy living. Tell me—if you were going to invent a god and a book of rules to live by, would you invent one that is as demanding as Yahweh?"

"His laws are impossible to keep."

"Yes, they are. That's why He gave us the Temple and the sacrifices; that's why a lamb dies in our place every time we sin. You've been sheltered here. You only see the immediate rewards of sin, the instant gratification it can bring. But if you went out in the world for a while and saw the long-term results of adultery or covetousness or living a life apart from God, you'd see how sin eventually destroys us. All that fun and freedom you witnessed last night are illusions to lure you away from the truth. Shall we go back to the mainland this morning and see the consequences of last night's fun? Most of those men probably feel as sick and miserable as you do right now. And what about the long-term consequences? Some of those women probably became pregnant last night. Do you know what the pagans do with the children they conceive at their orgies? Do you know what that girl last night would have done with a child of yours? She would sacrifice him in the fire. In fact, if your mother had been a pagan instead of a Jew, she would have sacrificed you. Children are loved and cherished among our people because they're precious to God. Do you still want to call the world's way 'fun' and our way too strict?"

"There must be a compromise somewhere in the world."

"There isn't. This is a struggle between life and death. Yesterday at the Feast of Pentecost we celebrated the giving of God's Law at Mount Sinai. That's to remind us that 'man does not live on bread alone but on every word that comes from the mouth of the Lord.' His word offers us life and protects us from the sin that will destroy us. The Evil One wants to enslave us to sin, but God gave us the Law because He wants us as sons. Moses said, 'Take to heart all the words I have solemnly declared to you this day. . . . They are not just idle words for you—they are your life.'" He tried to meet his son's gaze, but Nathan wouldn't look at Joshua. He sat with his head lowered, staring down.

"I know why you want to leave Elephantine, Nathan. You think you can leave all your problems and your unhappiness behind, but you can't. The problems are inside your own heart. You'll be taking them all with you wherever you go. You never got over your past and the fact that your father abandoned you. I admit I wasn't a very good example for you because I had trouble forgetting the past, too. I was angry with God for allowing Abba to die. But God knew he would die. And God knew exactly what kind of a home you would be born into. Can you forgive Him for allowing that? Can you accept His will? Because everything that happens in our lives can help shape us into the persons God wants us to become. Yes, He allowed my father to die and your father to abandon you—but He gave us each other. We've both been so busy mourning what we've lost that we've failed to see all that He has given us in return."

Nathan continued to stare down at his sleeping mat, tugging on a loose thread in the blanket. Joshua waited for him to speak, wondering what he was thinking.

"I know I haven't been the father you wanted or needed," Joshua finally said. "I couldn't fill that empty place he left when he abandoned you. But you've been looking in all the wrong places, trying to fill the hole he left. It won't work. Only God can fill that place. He's the Father you've longed for all your life."

The room fell silent. "Nathan, look at me," Joshua said softly. He waited until Nathan looked up. "Do you still want to leave the island? Leave Miriam and me?"

"No," he whispered.

Joshua swallowed the lump in his throat. "Then I'll try to convince the elders to let you stay. . . . Is there anything you want me to tell them?"

Nathan's eyes swam with tears. "Yes . . . tell them I'm sorry."

Joshua nodded. "You need to get washed up. Then it's time for us to go, son."

The elders and Levite judges sat waiting in Joshua's newly built hall of justice on the temple grounds. Joshua felt a growing tightness in his chest as he stood beside his son, listening to the charges against him. Nathan had stolen a boat and gone to the forbidden mainland. He had taken part in idolatry. He had broken Yahweh's commandments to honor his father, to flee from adultery, to worship no other god but Yahweh. There was nothing Joshua could say in Nathan's defense. Reuben, Caleb, and Colonel Simeon testified against him, and Joshua knew all the charges were true. But to Colonel Simeon, the worst crime Nathan had committed was to entice other young people to sin.

"In the past Nathan has acted alone," the colonel stated, "but now he poses a threat to all of our children. The Torah clearly says that if our very own brother entices us to worship other gods, we are to show him no mercy. We are to stone him to death!"

Joshua shuddered when he remembered how he had used the same Torah passage to justify assassinating Manasseh. He stared at the ground, unable to face Nathan's accusers, knowing that his own sin and rebellion had set a poor example for his son.

"The Torah also says," Simeon concluded, "that if a man has a stubborn and rebellious son who does not obey him, if he is a profligate and a drunkard, 'Then all the men of his town shall stone him to death. You must purge the evil from among you. All Israel will hear of it and be afraid.' If you're too cowardly to obey the Torah, then the very least I demand is that Nathan never sets foot on this island again! We must purge the evil from among us!"

As Simeon's shouts echoed off the walls and died away, Joshua finally looked up. "Sin isn't 'out there' somewhere, Simeon . . . on the mainland . . . among the pagans . . . in my son. Sin is inside each one of us. You can banish Nathan from Elephantine Island or even execute him, but that won't protect your sons from sin. The Evil One will always seek a way to tempt them away from God. It happened to the generations that came before us—it happened to our own brethren back in Judah—and it will happen to the generations that come after us, too. The answer isn't to shelter our children from every bad influence that might lead them astray. The answer is to allow them to experience God's goodness and faithfulness for themselves. Let them ask difficult questions, then stand back and allow God to work in their lives. Let your children 'taste and see that the Lord is good.' Our generation experienced God's deliverance firsthand, and so we have a relationship with Him based on faith. But we can't pass our relationship on to our sons. We can point them in the right direction, but they must experience God themselves and decide whether or not to embrace Him. Do you want your sons to make that choice out of fear? Because they're afraid they'll be executed or banished like my son was?"

"I want that boy off this island," Simeon shouted. "There is no room here for anyone who rebels and disobeys God!"

"Then why didn't you banish me? I disobeyed God. I rebelled when I sought vengeance against King Manasseh. My sin led to the deaths of thirty of your sons. Why wasn't I banished from the island? Why didn't you condemn me to death?" None of the men would look at Joshua. "I repented of my rebellion. I asked God and all of you for forgiveness. If Nathan confesses his idolatry and his sin like I did, if he offers his sacrifices at the temple, God will forgive him . . . right?" When the Levites didn't answer, Joshua felt his temper soar. "You're Yahweh's servants—you should know the answer! Does He forgive our sins when we repent, or doesn't He?"

One of the chief Levites finally nodded. "If the repentance is genuine, yes, He forgives us."

"And aren't we commanded to forgive one another?"

Simeon spat with fury. "I don't believe that his so-called repentance is genuine. That boy is a liar and a thief! He deserves to be executed! I saw him at that festival. I saw everything with my own eyes."

Joshua lowered his head in shame. "Yes, I saw him, too. My son is guilty. I know that justice demands punishment." He slowly sank to his knees in front of them. "But I'm begging you—"

Appalled, the elders quickly stood and tried to drag him to his feet. "Joshua, don't beg. Stand up. . . . Don't do this. . . ."

He shook them off as tears streamed down his face. "I'm begging for mercy. I'm begging for forgiveness. 'As a father has compassion on his children, so the Lord has compassion on those who fear him.' Please have mercy on my son."

The elders gave up their attempts to get him to his feet and decided to gather in a huddle to discuss a verdict. "Give us a minute, Joshua."

He heard only the mumble of voices as they turned their backs to him and left him kneeling, alone. In his mind he could imagine Nathan turning his back, as well, heading out into the world alone. In spite of all the pain his son had caused him, Joshua knew that he couldn't bear to lose him. How could he live the rest of his life never knowing what had become of him? He struggled to draw a breath, and in his pain he was suddenly aware that God had answered his prayer. For more than ten years he had prayed for a father's love for Nathan, prayed to love him as if he were his own flesh and blood. Now he knew that God had answered. The grief he felt was a father's grief for his beloved son. He was about to lose Nathan—his son—and he couldn't bear it.

He was still slumped on his knees when the elders returned with their verdict. He heard their words as if they stood at a great distance.

"When someone sins repeatedly then claims to repent, only a change in his actions will prove that his repentance is genuine. Has Nathan truly turned away from his sin and turned toward God? He will have six months to convince us. But this will be his final chance."

Joshua looked up at Nathan and saw tears falling down his bruised face. Then Joshua covered his own face and wept.

20

MIRIAM STRUGGLED TO BE BRAVE, to hold back her tears as she limped into Jerusha's darkened bedchamber. The unthinkable was happening: Mama Jerusha lay dying. The physicians had all said it was so. Now she had asked to speak with Miriam alone.

"What am I going to do without you, Mama?" Miriam asked as she took her mother-in-law's hand in her own. "I need your advice to know how to live, how to be a good wife. I need your wisdom."

Jerusha smiled faintly. "I don't have any special knowledge, my daughter. Wisdom comes from God. He'll give you all that you need to guide this family for me."

"For you? But I could never take your place."

"You're taking your own place, Miriam, continuing the role God gave you years ago when He brought you into our lives. You kept us all alive and moving forward through our grief back then. And I know you'll do the same after I'm gone."

"But what about your daughters? Tirza is the oldest, surely she—"

"I love all of my daughters, but you're the one who's the most like me. Tirza and Dinah were raised in luxury and spoiled shamelessly by their father. . . ." Jerusha smiled the way she always did whenever she remembered Eliakim. "I know my children think of me as a nobleman's wife, but in my heart I'll always be a poor farmer's daughter. You and I are simple, practical women. And that's what this family needs to hold everyone together. You're the strongest one, Miriam. I'm leaving my family in good hands."

Miriam could no longer halt her tears. Jerusha had said that she was the strongest one, but Miriam knew it was only because she was the weakest. She bent to hold Mama Jerusha in her arms one last time.

"You taught me so much about Yahweh and about living by faith. . . . Whom will I turn to?"

"Turn to God," Jerusha whispered.

Two days later Miriam stood with her husband beside Jerusha's grave, unable to comprehend that she was gone. Joel recited the prayers for the dead, and as Miriam listened, she studied each of Jerusha's children, gathered to mourn her. They were her legacy, so different from one another, yet so much alike. Jerimoth, the successful merchant, stood with his enormous brood of offspring. Tirza cradled the newest of her five priestly sons in her arms. Dinah, who was pregnant with another child of royal blood, clung to her husband, weeping softly. Joshua, the architect and leader, clasped Miriam's hand so tightly it ached, as he battled his own grief. As Jerusha had so often reminded her, they had their tasks to do for God, and Miriam had hers.

When the service ended, Joshua released Miriam's hand and bent to toss a handful of dirt onto Jerusha's grave. The other family members did the same. Miriam was grateful that her crippled body prevented her from bending. She couldn't bring herself to bury Jerusha, even in a symbolic gesture. While everyone else said their farewells and left for home, she and Joshua lingered beside the grave. Miriam saw by the slump of her husband's shoulders, the lines of sorrow around his eyes, that she needed to lay aside her own grief for a while to comfort him.

"I'm so glad Mama is buried beside our baby," she said. "It helps me remember that they're together now."

"She should be buried beside my father. I don't even know where he was buried—or if he was buried."

She recognized the old bitterness trying to draw him into his private darkness, and she leaned against him to keep him from slipping away. "What difference does it make, Joshua? Your mother isn't inside that discarded body anymore. She and your father are together, resting in Abraham's bosom."

"I wish you could have known Abba."

"But I do know him. He was part of you and part of Jerusha, part of your whole family. His love helped make you the people that you are. He's as real to me as your mother is."

He took her hand again and held it tightly in his. "Why don't you ever doubt or question God? Don't you ever wonder why your legs never got stronger? Why our child is lying here in this grave? Why Mama is? You're always helping others, always giving, and now here's another loss, something more God has taken from you."

"Do you remember what your mother always used to say? 'I will thank Him for all that He has given me, not curse Him for all that I've lost.' She taught me that God doesn't always give us what we want, but He always gives us what we need." She looked up at his solemn, handsome face and watched as he rubbed his hand across his eyes, then smoothed the patch into place again. "Sometimes I wonder what you see in me, Joshua. My mind is so different from yours, with your deep thoughts and probing questions. I'm just a simple woman. And my prayers and my faith are simple, too."

"But that's exactly what I love about you. In spite of all my years of Torah study, I think your faith is much stronger than mine in the end."

"Why? Because you ask questions and I don't? It takes a very strong faith to ask hard questions of God."

He sighed and ran his fingers through his hair. "I don't want to get into another wrestling match with God over Mama's death, and yet . . . and yet I can't pretend that I accept it. I know how much you loved Mama, too. What's going through your mind now that she's been taken from us?"

"I loved her. I miss her already. But I accept that Mama's death was God's will even if I can't see what the reason is. And you will, too, just as you learned to accept your father's death." A tear rolled down Miriam's cheek, but she didn't wipe it away. "I know that with all of the reading and studying you've done, you see God's hand shaping the nations. But sometimes you forget that He also cares about you and me. Everything that happens in our life is under His control and serves His purpose. Your mother taught me that. She always said that even when she was captured by the Assyrians it served His purpose. And she used to say that someday we would understand why we've had to struggle so with Nathan."

"But what can possibly be the purpose in Mama's death? Why now? Why so suddenly?"

"See how very different we are?" she said, gazing up at him. "I don't need to know the reason; I simply trust that there is one. But I'll pray that God will show you why."

He searched her eyes as if he might read the secret of her faith in them, and she saw the heaviness of his grief. Then he wrapped his arm tightly around her, supporting her as they began the slow walk home.

King Manasseh paced in his private chambers, waiting for Zerah and his bodyguards to arrive, waiting for the daily round of court business to begin. His officials would already be filing into the throne room to await his entrance. Zerah needed to brief him on today's court business and give him the morning agenda, but Zerah was late. When he finally did arrive, he entered the room alone and quietly closed the door behind him. He was unable to disguise his apprehension.

"What's wrong?" Manasseh asked.

"You'd better read this, Your Majesty. It arrived this morning."

Manasseh recognized the letter Zerah handed him as an official communiqué from Assyria. His fear soared. "What do they want?"

"The Assyrians are marching this way. They're expanding their empire again, and they intend to conquer Egypt. They need more tribute from us to help pay for it."

Manasseh read the message, then tossed it to the floor in anger. "Cancel my court for the day. Send everyone home."

"What about your advisors?"

"I don't need them. I don't trust them. You and I will handle this by ourselves." When Zerah didn't move, Manasseh grabbed him by the tunic and pulled him close, whispering urgently in his ear. "If word leaks out that the Assyrians are marching, it could start more riots like the ones we had a few years ago when we first signed the treaty with them, remember?"

"But we executed everyone who opposed the Assyrian alliance."

"We executed the ones we discovered—what if there are others? I'm not taking a chance that it will happen all over again." He shuddered when he remembered the violent anti-Assyrian protests and the fear under which he'd lived until all of the protesters had been rooted out in a purge. For months, blood had flowed ankle deep in the streets and in his execution pits. The ranks of his nobility had been decimated before his army had finally restored law and order.

"I won't go through that again, Zerah. You and I will figure out a way to meet these tribute demands ourselves. And this time we will seek omens first and learn which days are favorable for us before we act."

When court had been canceled and everyone sent home, Manasseh met with Zerah in the inner chamber of his suite, far from prying eyes and listening ears. It was the only place he felt safe enough to voice his fears and concerns. Zerah sank into a seat, but Manasseh restlessly walked the floor as he confessed his alarm. "Our nation can't afford to pay these extra taxes to fund the Assyrian war machine. They will ruin us."

"With over half a million men marching, we can be grateful that the Assyrians aren't mobilizing for war against us, Your Majesty."

"They may as well be. The cost is nearly as great."

"At least we're still a free country."

"Yes, but we're paying a terrible price for our freedom. Look at this." Manasseh waved the list of demands in Zerah's face. "They're demanding everything: rations of wheat, barley, oil, wine; iron and bronze for weapons; countless cattle and sheep; gold and silver payments. And we have no choice but to pay. I wouldn't blame the people for rebelling. They just harvested their crops and now everything will be going into Assyrian stomachs. Are we supposed to live on scraps until the next harvest just so Emperor Esarhaddon can conquer Egypt?"

"Be practical, Your Majesty. No matter how much they demand, it's still better than captivity and ruin."

"Our nation will be destitute. We'll have nothing to export or trade."

"Don't panic—"

"I'm not panicking!" But Manasseh knew how guilty he still felt about reversing his father's courageous stand against the Assyrians and serving as their vassals. His failure had haunted him ever since he had signed the treaty, and he could no longer bear to look down from his palace window and see the Kidron Valley, where the Assyrian army had been slain. All of his life Manasseh had feared not living up to his father's stature, and now that he knew how far short he had fallen, he couldn't admit to Zerah or anyone else how ashamed he felt. He turned away from the window, away from the view of the valley where the miracle had occurred, and grabbed a skin of fermented wine. As he poured himself a cupful, much of it sloshed on his shaking hand. He quickly drained the glass.

"There's really only one answer." Zerah's voice, so practical and down-to-earth, brought Manasseh back from the edge. "We'll divide the nation into territories and assign overseers to be in charge of taxation and forced labor."

"That's not going to be popular with the people."

"We'll tell them to think of these payments as a loan. When the Assyrians defeat Egypt—and they surely will—all of Pharaoh's wealth will pour back into the empire, with added profits for nations like ours who helped fund his victory."

But Zerah's cheery prediction did nothing to lift Manasseh's gloom. "I thought we still had our freedom, Zerah, but we're Assyria's servants. We'll be enslaved to them forever."

Three weeks later he and Zerah met in secret once again after they received a report that one of their new overseers had been murdered. "This is what I feared," Manasseh said. "The riots are going to start all over again."

Zerah rested his hand on Manasseh's shoulder to comfort him. "There won't be any riots if we act swiftly and send out the troops. We can stop the rebellion before it spreads."

"Do you think Joshua is behind it?"

"Oh, come on!" Zerah gave him a look of disgust as he drew back. "Don't start worrying about him again! It's been years since he last surfaced. Surely you can forget about him by now. He's obviously forgotten about you. In fact, he's probably dead—we put enough curses on him, he should have died of something by now."

"Hadad said they were living on an island in Egypt. He has the ark, my brother, my army general, and all my priests. What do you suppose he's waiting for?"

"I'm not going to humor your idiotic fantasies about Joshua ben Eliakim. We need to appoint a new overseer."

"I need an heir," Manasseh said suddenly. Zerah stared at him as if he'd proposed something utterly ridiculous. "Don't look at me like that! It's only a matter of time before my enemies stop attacking my overseers and come after me."

"Now you're being paranoid."

"If they kill me, there's no son of David to take my place. I need an heir, Zerah."

"You need someone you can trust by your side, not a faithless woman who will stab you in the gut when you least expect it."

"I'll make sure she comes from a loyal family, one that is beyond suspicion." But Manasseh saw by Zerah's flushed face and tight frown that he was growing upset. "Listen, there's no need for you to be jealous. . . ."

"I'm not jealous!"

"She would simply be a means to an end. The woman would mean nothing to me."

"Why now?" Zerah asked angrily. "What's your hurry after all these years?"

"I'm nearly forty years old, Zerah. Don't you think it's about time I had an heir?"

"Your father was forty-two when you were born."

"Look, I'm sorry I mentioned it to you. I can see that you're not the one to help me find a concubine. I'll ask my secretary to find—"

"You're making a big mistake." Zerah's voice was so ominous, so menacing, that Manasseh froze. With all of the upheaval in his nation, the last thing he needed was for Zerah to turn against him, too. Zerah had great power at his disposal—evil power.

"You're right," Manasseh said after a moment. "Maybe I am being a bit hasty about this." He drank the remainder of his wine in one gulp. "Will you help me seek omens to determine the best time to father an heir?"

Zerah smiled coldly. "Certainly, Your Majesty."

21

"Assyria has invaded Egypt?" Joshua asked in disbelief. He read through the message from Pharaoh Taharqo a second time, still unable to believe what he was reading. Comprehension dawned slowly, and with it came a growing impatience. "They've finally done it. The Assyrians have marched into Egypt."

Prince Amariah nodded glumly as he shifted on his throne. "And my orders from Pharaoh are to be prepared to mobilize the Elephantine garrison. We have to be ready to defend the nation at a moment's notice."

"Pharaoh should have seen this coming," Joshua said. "The Assyrians made vassals out of all the smaller nations in their path. No other enemy stands between them and the Egyptian border."

"Sit down, Joshua. You're making me nervous pacing around like that." Amariah gestured to the seat beside his throne.

Joshua sank into it reluctantly. The audience hall seemed dark and oppressive to him, the space too small and confining to contain his restlessness. "I don't want a government position, Amariah. I don't want to sit here on Elephantine Island now that we're at war. Pharaoh asked for all able-bodied men. I want to train with the others. I want to fight."

Amariah sighed. "When we moved here all those years ago and I pledged to fight for Pharaoh and Egypt, I never imagined that we would actually have to do it. Judah is one of Assyria's vassal states. That means if we get called to war, we'll be fighting against our own nation."

"No, we're fighting *for* our nation. When Pharaoh wins, when we push the Assyrians back to the other side of the Euphrates, we can march into Judah and set it free."

"I thought you'd finally given up your desire to avenge Manasseh."

"I did. But I'm not manipulating events this time. I'm just taking advantage of the opportunity God is providing. It's all coming together at last, can't you see? This is what we've been waiting for all these years."

"I think you're getting a little ahead of yourself and ahead of God. Let's wait until the Assyrians are defeated before we plan our strike against Manasseh."

"Fine. But in the meantime I want an army commission. I can handle a regiment, I've kept up my reserve training, and if I drill every day for the next few weeks—"

"You don't have to convince me, Joshua. I know you're an able commander. But why do you want to go to war? You're forty years old; you have a wife who needs you. Stay here and help me govern the island."

He shook his head. "I've been waiting too long for this opportunity. I have to fight!" He stood again, unable to remain seated.

"How long do you think it will take to mobilize all the men?" Amariah asked, but Joshua ignored his question as a sudden fear shot through him. He turned to face the prince.

"I don't want Nathan to go. If we get called to fight, promise me you'll use your authority to have Nathan assigned to the home guard. Miriam needs him."

"But Nathan is—"

"I'll train, I'll gladly go to war . . . but not my son."

"What about Nathan's wishes? He isn't going to be content to stay home while all his friends go to war."

"I know I'm being selfish, but I can't help it. I don't want to lose him. Suppose he was your son? Suppose Gedaliah was old enough to go?"

"You know that a royal son would never be called to fight. I'll never face that choice, so I can only imagine how you feel. But in fairness to Nathan, I can't—"

"You have three more sons besides Gedaliah and two daughters. Nathan is the only son I have. Please, Amariah. Don't make me beg."

He saw the prince's reluctance in his furrowed brow, heard it in his hesitant voice. "I'll talk to his commanding officer," he said at last, "and see what I can do."

All afternoon Joshua pondered the best way to break the news to Miriam that he had volunteered to go to war with the Elephantine Island garrison. He decided, after the evening meal, to walk with her to visit Jerusha's grave. A gentle breeze from the river swept the night air clean, and a radiant moon rose above the palm trees, making it difficult for Joshua to comprehend that his adopted country was already at war far to the north. He tightened his arm around his wife's waist as he looked down at his mother's grave.

"God answered your prayers, Miriam. I think I understand why God took Mama." She waited, standing utterly still. "The Assyrians have attacked Egypt. God knew Mama couldn't face another invasion. She had already been through enough with the Assyrians for one lifetime."

"Will they come this far south?" Miriam asked after a moment.

"It's very unlikely."

"Then what else aren't you telling me?"

He marveled at how well she knew him, how easily she could read his moods. And he knew her well enough to know that his decision was going to cause her a great deal of pain. "I'll be given a commission. I'm going to fight."

"You *have* to go? Or you *want* to go?"

"Both."

"I see. And if Mama was still alive, would you have gone to war?"

He hesitated, seeing where Miriam was leading him. "The Assyrians were her lifelong enemies," he said slowly. "She couldn't have endured the thought of losing me to them."

"But I can?"

He caressed Miriam's cheek as if trying to smooth away the pain and anger he saw on her face. "Miriam, nothing is going to happen to me. I know because I can see God's plan so clearly in all of this. King Manasseh is Assyria's ally. Once we've driven the Assyrians back to Nineveh, Judah will be ours. We can all go home."

"We *are* home," she said softly. Her eyes filled with tears. "Joshua, please—"

"Don't!" He quickly covered her lips with his fingers. "Don't ask, Miriam. You know I would do anything for you, but please don't ask me to stay here. I have to fight. I have to."

Her tears spilled down her cheeks. "But who's going to take care of you this time? Who will watch out for you and save your life? I can't come with you like I did all those other times."

"God will watch over me . . . and over you."

She closed her eyes and shuddered, then opened them again a moment later. "Maybe this is why my legs have never healed. Maybe God wants to keep me on my knees."

Nathan bristled with excitement as he hurried up to the barracks with his friend Saul. "They said our assignments would be posted this afternoon. I hope we're together."

"Are you sure we'll actually get to fight the Assyrians?" Saul asked. "Aren't we too far south to be called into battle?"

"Listen, I'm not supposed to know this," Nathan said, "but I overheard Prince Amariah talking out in our courtyard last night and—"

"You were eavesdropping?"

"Yeah, so what. He said the Assyrians are pounding the Egyptians. Pharaoh's troops are getting pulverized. They're desperate, and they're sending for every man they can get."

"So we'll get to see some action?" Saul asked.

"Guaranteed. They're mobilizing all the troops, including our regiment."

"I was beginning to think we'd never be real soldiers. We're finally going to get off this island and fight!"

"We'll chase those heathens all the way back to Nineveh!" Nathan vowed.

When they reached the barracks, a crowd of soldiers had already gathered near the wall where the assignments had been posted. One by one, Nathan's fellow recruits cheered as they read the listings, as eager as he was to enter the battle. Saul, who was a few inches taller than Nathan, craned his neck for a closer look.

"Hey, your father has been given a commission. He's the commanding officer of my regiment. But I don't see your name here."

"They wouldn't put me in his unit. Let me see." Nathan elbowed his way to the front and quickly scanned the lists of names. Then he read them again. He couldn't find his name on any list. "Hey, what's going on?" he shouted.

"I found it," Saul said, "over here." He pointed to a list that was pinned separately from the others. Nathan saw his name, then read the heading on the top of the page in disbelief.

"Home guard! They can't do this to me!" He unleashed a stream of curses.

Saul tried to lead him away as everyone turned to stare. "Shh . . . calm down, Nate. If our commanders hear you, they'll—"

"I don't care! What more can they do to me? They've already denied me a chance to fight! And I'll tell you right now, I'm not going to take it!"

"Nathan, wait. Don't do something stupid."

But in his fury Nathan was beyond reason. He stormed into the barracks and tracked down his former drill instructor, taking the man by surprise as he confronted him.

"Why did you assign me to the home guard? How could you do this to me? I don't deserve the home guard! I'm every bit as good as the other guys, and you know it!"

"We need good men to guard the home front. It's an honor—"

"I want to fight! Reassign me!"

"Those are your orders, Nathan. A good soldier obeys without question."

"You know as well as I do that the Assyrians will never get this far south. I'll never get a chance to fight. Change my assignment *now*!"

Nathan's angry demand seemed to push the drill instructor over the edge. He swiftly crossed the room and shoved Nathan against the wall, planting his hand on his chest to pin him there. "You watch the way you talk to me! Right now you're dangerously close to a charge of insubordination!"

Nathan barely resisted the urge to fight back. The man finally released him. "Just for the record, I had nothing to do with your assignment. In fact, I recommended you as a squad leader."

"It was Colonel Simeon, wasn't it? I'll bet he's behind this. He never forgave me for what happened at the Feast of Pentecost. He thinks I'm a bad influence—"

"That's enough!" the man shouted. "Colonel Simeon had nothing to do with it, either."

"Then why won't they let me fight like everyone else?"

The instructor hesitated. "I like you, Nathan. You're a fine soldier, but you have a rotten temper, and I don't want you to get yourself into trouble over this. I'm going to tell you where the order came from, but only so you'll see why you'd better drop it, understand?" Nathan waited. "Prince Amariah made the request."

Nathan felt as if all the air had been punched from his lungs. He knew then that Joshua had requested the assignment. He was so stunned, so furious, he couldn't speak.

"Are you okay, son?" the drill instructor asked. Nathan barely nodded. "As I said, it's an honor to be assigned to guard the prince. He asked for you personally, and—Hey, where are you going?"

"Home." Nathan stormed from the barracks, jogging through the streets, his fury mounting.

He found Joshua in the rear courtyard of their house, sharpening his dagger on a whetstone. To see him preparing for war, eager for it, made Nathan angrier still. Joshua looked up in surprise as Nathan slammed the outside gate behind him.

"You pulled strings, didn't you? You got me assigned to the home guard!"

Joshua carefully slid the dagger back into its leather sheath before answering. "Yes, I made the request," he said quietly. "They didn't have to honor it, but even your commanding officer saw the wisdom in—"

"Because I'm a rebel? A thief? Am I going to carry those labels around for the rest of my life?"

"Calm down, son. Your past had nothing whatsoever to do with this decision."

"Like blazes it didn't! You're afraid I'll ruin discipline and lead everyone astray or maybe damage your precious reputation again."

Joshua lowered his voice. "I asked for you to be posted here partly for Miriam's sake. She's raised you since you were a baby. If she lost you—"

"She has Mattan. He's too young to go. I want to fight!"

"Nathan, I also asked for my own sake. You're my only son. Who will carry on my name if anything happens to you?" He tried to rest his hand on Nathan's shoulder, but he twisted away.

"I don't really care what happens to your stupid name. Either change my orders so I can fight, or else I'm leaving right now. I'll join one of Pharaoh's other regiments on the mainland. I've finished my training; they won't turn me away. That's your choice!"

"Why does everything have to be a confrontation between us? Why can't you try to understand me? Or understand why I asked for this?"

"Why should I bother when you make no attempt to understand me? Now, thanks to you, I'm going to be stuck here on this stupid island for the rest of my life." Nathan was angry enough to punch Joshua, but he knew from past experience which one of them would win that fight.

"I used to hate it here, too," Joshua said, "but once I saw that it was God's will—"

"Let me fight!" Nathan shouted.

"You could be killed, Nathan. Many of our men will be. The Assyrians are highly skilled warriors."

"I'm already dying here. Suffocating! Fighting is the one thing I'm good at. Let me go! I'm tired of living in your shadow. Let me have a chance to make my own name, to see who I really am."

"You already have a name and an identity as my son, as part of my father's family and his father's family. You've had that identity ever since I gave you my name."

"I'm *not* your son!" Nathan knew how much those words

would hurt Joshua, but he took aim and fired them as his only remaining weapon. "You're not my father! Change my orders or say good-bye to me."

Joshua gazed at him, his face creased with sorrow. "Either way I lose you, don't I?"

"That's right. So decide how you want it to be."

Joshua sighed deeply, and for the second time in his life, Nathan had a premonition of him as an old man, dying. He had to remind himself that Joshua was barely forty years old.

"You win, Nathan," he said at last. "Come up to the fort with me. I'll get your orders changed."

Miriam stood on the dock, staring upriver at the swirling water long after all of the troop ships had departed, long after all of the other soldiers' families had returned to their homes. With Joshua and Nathan both gone, she had no reason to return to an empty house.

How would she ever cope with the long, lonely months of waiting that stretched ahead of her? How could she stand the uncertainty and dread that would stalk the empty silences? She let her crutches fall onto the wooden pier, then collapsed beside them, not even caring that she had no way to pull herself to her feet again. She tried to pray but no words came. She felt utterly alone.

After a long time, the pier began to rock slightly as someone walked out to the end where she sat. Miriam turned and was surprised to see Prince Amariah. He stopped beside her and stood with his hands on his hips, gazing silently into the distance for a long moment. Then he crouched beside her.

"Mind if I sit with you?"

When she shook her head, he sank down with a sigh, dangling his feet over the edge of the pier. The silence stretched comfortably between them. Miriam thought of all the memories they shared and how much time had passed since they'd first met. She knew the prince had been thinking the same things when he suddenly said, "We've been through a lot together, haven't we, Miriam? It seems like a very long time ago that I paid thirty shekels of silver for you in Jerusalem."

"You paid fifty. Don't forget the twenty you gave my mother."

"That's right," he said, laughing softly. "I forgot about that. But I've never forgotten how you helped me escape from Jerusalem."

"Dressed in women's clothing."

"Yes, in women's clothing." He shook his head in mock dismay. "I violated the Torah shamelessly dressing like that."

"It wasn't my idea, it was Joshua's—" As soon as she said his name, Miriam's tears were unleashed. She covered her mouth to stifle her sobs, but nothing could stem the flow of grief that washed down her cheeks. Amariah wrapped his arm around her and pulled her close, allowing her to weep. She didn't realize how much she needed the release, how badly she needed to be held, until her tears were spent and she sat quietly beside him once again. "I'm sorry," she whispered.

He hugged her gently. "Don't be. Each of us is alone in some way, living with circumstances that no one else can understand." He let his arm drop from her shoulders. "Do you feel like talking?"

"You go first."

He exhaled slowly. "You know, Miriam, this royal blood flowing through my veins is such a mixed blessing. Today it kept me from going to war with all the other men—and it will keep my sons here, too, where it's safe. But it's flowing slow and heavy with guilt right now, like the Nile when it's loaded with silt. I feel relieved that I don't have to fight, but I feel guilty because I'll be safe while better men than me have to suffer and die." He glanced at her anxiously, as if afraid that he'd said the wrong thing; then he looked down at the river again. "But would my life have any meaning if I didn't have King David's blood? Am I being ungrateful when I despise this special gift from God? Sometimes I try to imagine how different my life would have been if I was just an ordinary man, but it's hard to imagine something I've never experienced."

"And you can't miss something that you never had," she said softly. "You know what I've been thinking? It was better for me before—when Joshua didn't love me. I had nothing, but I also had nothing to lose."

"You don't really mean that, Miriam. Would you honestly give back these last ten or twelve years that you and Joshua have shared? Do you really wish you'd never known his love, just to avoid the pain you're experiencing right now?"

Miriam recalled Joshua's tenderness and his passion, the peace and joy she felt in his arms, knowing that she was utterly loved and cherished by him. The memories brought fresh tears, then suffocating panic at the thought that she might never see Joshua or feel his arms around her again. She took slow, deep breaths to combat her panic.

"I never wanted to play the part of a cripple," she said shakily. "I never wanted to weigh Joshua down with the burden of my helplessness. And so I couldn't tell him how much I needed him. I couldn't beg him to stay or tell him just how alone and scared I feel sometimes, how terrified I am of my own helplessness. When his boat pulled away from shore I wanted to scream, 'How can you go? How can you leave me all alone like this?'"

Amariah rested his hand on top of hers. "He went for your sake, Miriam. He had to be the man you fell in love with."

"That's crazy! He's already a hero for marrying me, for loving me even though I can't give him children. I don't need him to play the part of a brave warrior for my sake."

"But he needs to play it, Miriam. It's who he is. You'd lose him forever if you made him stay here. He was very concerned about you, though. He asked me to assign Nathan to the home guard for your sake."

"Nathan would have hated that. It would kill him to stay here while everyone else went to war."

"I know. And he and Joshua are very much alike, aren't they?" She nodded slowly. "If you understand why Nathan had to fight, then you can begin to understand why Joshua did, too. He agonized over leaving you, but he did the loving thing, Miriam. It's better for you to lose a whole man than to hang on to a bitter, empty shell."

"The darkness would swallow him," she said, finally understanding. "I would lose him to his private darkness if he stayed home." She looked up at Amariah as a sudden realization struck her. "I finally understand how Joshua feels. I know how he suffered all these years after God stripped him of everyone and everything that he loved. I know what it means to feel so alone and yet so afraid to trust God because He sometimes gives hard answers to your prayers."

"Miriam, you can trust God's love. He'll do what's best—"

"No. That's the answer I've always given Joshua—'Trust God; He won't do anything to hurt you'—and now I can't accept it any more than Joshua could. I'm still a cripple. I've lost Abba, Mama Jerusha, and both of my babies. If I lose Nathan and Joshua, I'll have nothing left. And if I trust God and it's His will to take them, then I might lose my faith in Him, too."

She saw the sorrow and understanding in Amariah's eyes as he met her gaze. "I have no answers for you, Miriam. I'm sorry."

"Waiting will be the hardest part. Waiting and not knowing what will happen. That's what Joshua always said—he was so tired of waiting for God to act." She turned to stare into the dark river again, watching the reflections of the clouds on the water. "O God, I want Joshua to come back. . . . I need to tell him how sorry I am."

"For what, Miriam?"

"For telling him he shouldn't question God. For never really understanding the terrifying darkness that haunted him—until now."

"Miriam, I promise you won't be alone while he's gone."

"I know." She listened to the lapping water for a moment before asking, "How bad is this battle going to be? You've been through some life-and-death ordeals with me; you know I can handle the truth."

"You're one of the strongest women I've ever met." He smiled slightly, but it quickly faded. "The Assyrian army is the best in the world. That's why they've conquered most of it. But none of their emperors has ever been able to annex Egypt."

"Could they conquer it this time?"

"They've already advanced farther than they ever have before. They are career soldiers with the finest organization and equipment in the world. Our soldiers from Elephantine are probably no match for them. But David was an unlikely match against Goliath, too. In the end, the outcome rests with God." He stood and offered

Miriam his hand, helping her to her feet. "Dinah and I will always be here for you. Just ask."

"Promise me you'll tell me what you know about the war, whenever you hear something?"

He bent to retrieve her crutches. "I promise, Miriam. It's the very least I can do."

22

THE SUN BLAZED IN THE COPPER SKY, as pitiless and unrelenting as the enemy. Nathan doubted he would ever live to see nightfall. He was in Sheol itself; or if not Sheol, then certainly the valley of the shadow of death. He could never have imagined such unending horror.

They were losing the battle. The Assyrians raged against them, as numerous as grains of dust in a sandstorm, burying them beneath their weight, blotting out hope like the sun. Nathan's friends were falling all around him, cut down ruthlessly with sword and spear. He wondered why he was still standing. He gripped his sword as if his hand were welded to it and swung it until his arms trembled with fatigue, but still the Assyrians surged forward.

As stinging sweat streamed into his eyes, blurring his vision, he thought of Joshua—forced to fight half blind, his perspective distorted, his field of vision limited. Nathan longed to be with him, to draw sanity in all this horror from Joshua's rocklike strength and faith, but he doubted if he would ever see him again. More than likely they would both be dead before nightfall. Nathan wasn't sure how he had survived this long.

War didn't bring the glory and excitement Nathan had dreamed of—only unending terror. One mistake, one momentary lapse of vigilance would cost Nathan his life. He no longer fought to defeat the enemy but simply to stay alive—stabbing, killing, spilling blood without end, without choice. For every Assyrian he slaughtered, three more appeared out of nowhere, streaming forward ruthlessly, driving him back inexorably. He saw hatred and bloodlust in their black eyes and swung his sword again and again. He was so exhausted he considered lying down and feigning death, but the Assyrians mutilated their dead, then rode their chariots roughshod over the bodies. If he was this weary with fatigue and thirst, how could Joshua possibly survive this massacre?

As his will to survive staggered toward lethargy and resignation, Nathan suddenly heard the trumpet signaling retreat. He gazed in amazement at the handful of men still standing with him, not certain he'd really heard correctly; then he turned and ran from the enemy along with all the others, weeping with relief at the sound of his salvation. Only Nathan's commanding officer continued to fight, vainly trying to stem the flood of enemy forces until his men had a chance to escape. It was something Joshua would do.

The fact that the enemy chose not to pursue them was the only thing that prevented every last man from being butchered. Instead, the Assyrians left to join the main body of their forces fighting at Memphis, while Nathan staggered with his comrades back to their encampment, helping the wounded, leaving the thousands of dead and dying behind. He was weary, splattered with blood, quivering with exertion, but miraculously unharmed.

How is this possible? He didn't deserve to be alive. Better men than he had fallen.

After a long, exhausting walk, Nathan finally reached camp, sagging to the ground in front of his tent. He wanted to go home—to Elephantine Island. He would be content to join the ranks of the home guard now, and he realized that Joshua hadn't been trying to punish him by making the request but instead spare him. He must have known what hell this was, and he'd acted in love. Nathan longed to tell him he was sorry.

Slowly, his regiment gathered to regroup. So many were missing, so many wounded, that the survivors huddled together in a daze of shock, many of them weeping. Two out of every three men had died. Nathan's body shook uncontrollably, as if trying to shed the horror of this day of combat as a dog shakes off water. Scenes of the battle replayed endlessly in his mind like a waking nightmare, and he shrank from the thought that he would have to go back and fight the Assyrians all over again tomorrow.

"You fought well and very courageously," Nathan's only remaining officer said as he tried to boost morale. Nathan hadn't felt brave but terrified. He and the others stared at the ground in guilt, wondering why they were alive when so many of their comrades were dead.

As the horror-filled events of the day seeped deeper and deeper into Nathan's soul, he found himself longing to talk to Joshua. Only his wisdom and keen sense of perspective could help Nathan cope with the brutal reality of war or help him find the courage to face it all over again tomorrow. When he'd eaten a little food and regained some of his strength, Nathan decided to walk down the road to where Joshua's regiment was encamped.

"I'm looking for your colonel—Joshua ben Eliakim," he told the standard-bearer. "Do you know where I can find him?"

The man shook his head wearily. "No one has seen him since the battle. Colonel Joshua and both lieutenants are among the missing."

The slippery, sick feeling of dread crawled through Nathan. "Hasn't *anyone* seen him?"

"Ask them," he shrugged, gesturing to the listless soldiers. Joshua's regiment had fought closer to the front lines and sustained even more losses than Nathan's had. With no officer to regroup or comfort the men, they sat slumped like corpses, lacking the will to eat or quench their thirst or even to tend their wounded.

"Have you seen Colonel Joshua? Do you know what happened to him?" Nathan wandered through the camp, asking again and again, his voice growing louder and more desperate, until he'd questioned nearly every man that had survived. No one seemed to know.

"Are you in this regiment?" one of the survivors finally asked. "Was the colonel your commanding officer?"

"No, he's . . . he's my father." Something broke inside Nathan as he spoke the words for the first time in his life. He began to weep. *Joshua was his father.* Why had he waited so long to acknowledge it? Why now, when it was probably too late? "He's my father," he murmured again. He barely comprehended what the other soldier was telling him.

"The colonel fought beside me for a while. He was wounded and bleeding pretty badly. When we heard the call to retreat, he kept fighting. He stood his ground so we could all get away. That was the last I saw of him."

No, God. Please.

It shocked Nathan to discover that he was praying. He repeated the prayer in an endless refrain as he made his way to the makeshift field hospital to search for Joshua among the wounded. Hundreds of blood-soaked men lay sprawled on the ground while the Egyptian physicians tended them with a mixture of medicine and sorcery. The air was filled with moans, with pleas for something to ease the pain, with the anguished cries of those who feared death. Nathan wandered among them in a daze, searching the faces for his father's familiar eye patch. The torn and mangled bodies that were spread across the earth barely seemed human. Nathan was in a nightmare, and he longed to wake up.

"I'm looking for my father. His name is Colonel Joshua ben Eliakim. Have you seen him?" he asked one of the medics.

The man seemed as weary as his patients. "We don't have time for names."

"He lost his right eye a long time ago. He wears a black eye patch."

"We look at wounds, not faces. . . . There are so many. Can you give us a hand?"

"I have to find my father first."

With nowhere left to search, Nathan started down the long road of retreat, back to the battlefield, back to hell itself. He would never be able to accept his father's death unless he gazed at his familiar, scarred face one last time and held him in his arms. He needed to say good-bye. And that he was sorry.

All along the way the wounded and dying who had fallen beside the road begged for his help. At first Nathan tried to give drinks of water, words of encouragement, but there were so many dying men . . . too many. He saw several of his friends among the dead but not Joshua. Nathan walked for nearly an hour as if treading water—seeing the same mangled soldiers begging, dying—until he finally came to the field of trampled flax where the battle had taken place. It was strewn with thousands and thousands of bodies and discarded weapons, like flotsam along the banks of the Nile after a flood. The hot, stagnant air was filled with an eerie silence now that the battle was over, and the stench of decay filled his nostrils. The only movement was the rustle of wind through the grass and the slow circle of vultures wheeling overhead.

So many dead. God of Abraham, so many. Please help me find him.

It was like trying to find one drop of water in a vast ocean of slain. Heart-weary, Nathan staggered forward, turning over bloated bodies, gazing into staring eyes, searching for his father's familiar face and black leather eye patch. It devastated him to realize that in all the years since Joshua first offered to be his father in the shack in Jerusalem, Nathan had never once called him "Abba."

"God of Abraham . . . help me find him," he wept. "Let him still be alive. Please give me a chance to call him Abba . . . just one time . . . just once. . . ."

At last, after hours of fruitless searching, grief and exhaustion and loss overwhelmed Nathan. He sank to his knees and retched. He wished he could heave all the pain and sorrow from his heart, as well, but it was bottomless. He wept uncontrollably as he had so long ago in Jerusalem, a small, lonely boy crying for his abba.

He remembered the day he'd turned thirteen and had cried in Joshua's arms, so afraid of losing him to the new baby; the day he'd been flogged and his father had begged to take his punishment, then carried him home and tended his wounds; the night his father had dragged him from the pagan worship festival, then fallen at the elders' feet, pleading for mercy for his son. All those years, Nathan had denied that Joshua was his father, but now he finally understood; Joshua had loved him as much as any flesh-and-blood father ever could. Nathan had found his real father—and lost him.

"I'm sorry, Abba," Nathan wept. "Please forgive me . . . I'm so sorry." He knew he was no longer talking to his earthly father but to God. *He's the Father you've longed for all your life,* Joshua had once told him. *Only God can fill that empty place inside you.* Nathan had rejected God and rebelled against Him all his life, just as he'd rejected and rebelled against Joshua.

"I know it's too late to make things right between me and my father," Nathan prayed, "but please give me another chance with you, Lord. Let me try to be your faithful son."

As Nathan bowed his head to the blood-soaked ground, even the breeze suddenly seemed to grow hushed all around him. In the unnatural stillness, he heard Joshua's familiar voice in his heart, repeating the words he'd vowed so long ago: *I won't let you go, Nathan. I won't give up on you. I promise.* His father had been true to his word. In spite of all that Nathan had done, his father had never stopped loving him. And Joshua's love and faithfulness were mere shadows of God's.

Nathan lifted his head as the sun slipped over the horizon in a wash of vibrant color. He knew—as surely as he knew that it would rise again in the morning—that God loved him, that He had forgiven him. After twenty years of searching, Nathan had found his true Father at last.

Stars filled the sky by the time Nathan staggered back into camp. He wanted nothing more than to fall into bed and sleep to forget the horror of this day, but the moans of the injured and dying carried across the field to him in the night. Remembering his promise to come back and help tend the wounded, Nathan made his way to where the exhausted medics were still hard at work.

"I'd like to help. Tell me what I can do."

"The men are hungry. You can distribute food and help the ones who can't help themselves."

Nathan ladled rations by torchlight and made his way in the dark among the rows of men, serving food to those who could sit and eat. Then he returned with more rations to help feed those who couldn't. He crouched beside a bedraggled soldier who had one leg and both hands bandaged.

"Are you hungry? Here, let me help you sit." Nathan lifted the man's head, then froze when he saw his father's face. "Abba?" he whispered.

Food spilled to the ground as Nathan clutched his father in his arms. A moment later he felt Joshua's crushing embrace in return. "Nathan! Thank God!"

"Abba . . . Abba . . ." It was all he could manage to say, but he thanked God that he could finally say it.

At last Nathan released his father and leaned back to look at him, staring as if at a mirage. Joshua's uniform was ripped and tattered into rags, and his eye patch was gone. Nathan barely recognized him without it. His hands trailed over Joshua's face, his shoulders, his chest. "Are you all right, Abba?"

"I'll live," he said, wiping his tears. "What about you? What are you doing here, son?"

"I came to look for you. I had to find you . . . I had to tell you . . ."

The wall Nathan had erected around his heart suddenly toppled to the ground, crumbling as if struck by an Assyrian battering ram. He fell into Joshua's arms again.

"I love you, Abba."

Miriam was surrounded by the other women of her family, but she felt utterly alone. All of their husbands were exempt from battle: Joel, because he was the high priest; Amariah, because he was royalty; Jerimoth, because he was too old to become a soldier. All of their sons were too young to fight. Only Miriam risked losing both of the men she loved.

In spite of her loneliness, she refused to move out of her house; she needed the memories it held of Joshua and Nathan. Each time she went to the sacrifices, Miriam would gaze at the beautiful buildings, searching for memories of her husband in the temple he'd constructed. Her brother Mattan, who came often to help her, was touching in his devotion to her, but she hadn't raised him to manhood as she'd raised Nathan. Prince Amariah came faithfully to share any news he had: the troops had arrived safely; they had joined Pharaoh's other forces; a major conflict was expected soon.

Then came the day Miriam had dreaded; Amariah's grim expression told her he had come with bad news. "There's been a battle, Miriam. I'm told that our casualties were enormous. We'll have to wait for names." A week later he reported a second battle, equally devastating for Pharaoh's forces. "The Assyrians have pushed deep into Egyptian territory, inflicting tremendous losses against the Egyptians. Still no names, but some of our wounded will be returning home soon."

Miriam hobbled to the dock each day to watch for the first ships. When they finally sailed into the harbor, neither Joshua nor Nathan was on board. Amariah questioned the survivors and told Miriam that both men had survived the initial battle, but no one knew about the second.

Weeks passed, then months with the same disheartening story, the same maddening uncertainty—more battles, more losses, no word if either Joshua or Nathan still lived. Miriam spent hours waiting for ships at the dock or kneeling at the temple, praying for their safe return—or for the strength to cope if they didn't. She remembered how Jerusha had remained steadfast in her faith, even after the devastating loss of her husband. Miriam prayed for the courage to follow her example.

Nearly ten months after the war began, Amariah came to Miriam's house one evening before the sacrifice. She saw the mixed emotions playing across his features and waited, holding her breath. "The war is over, Miriam. The Assyrians have captured Memphis. Pharaoh Taharqo surrendered and has been taken captive."

"What's going to happen now?" she whispered.

"The Assyrians will leave occupation forces behind, but I doubt if they'll come this far south. Except for higher tribute payments, we'll probably be able to live much as we did before."

"No wonder God moved us so far upstream," she murmured.

"I had the same thought." He smiled faintly, then turned serious once again. "Some of Pharaoh's troops have been taken captive as spoil. The Assyrians will deport them to other lands. I'm told that they usually choose officers rather than enlisted men."

"Joshua?"

"Maybe. God alone knows. But the rest of our men will be coming home."

Over the next few weeks, the boats started to return with Elephantine's soldiers. Neither Joshua nor Nathan was among the first to arrive home. Miriam waited and prayed, watching every day for their ship.

After two weeks of anticipation and dread, she finally spotted a tall figure wearing a dark eye patch standing against one of the ships' rails. As the ship drew closer, Miriam scarcely dared to hope that it was her husband. But no other man from their island had the same proud stance, the same unruly black hair and scarred beard. It was Joshua! Tears blurred her vision, but not before she recognized the wiry figure standing beside him—Nathan!

Miriam quickly scrubbed the tears from her eyes and looked again. They were alive. They were together. She stared in disbelief at the easy manner they had with each other, the casual, affectionate way Nathan hooked his arm over Joshua's shoulder. God not only had brought them back to her but had somehow brought them to each other. They were father and son at last.

Nathan spotted Miriam first and pointed to her for Joshua. They waved joyously, leaning so far over the rail that Miriam laughed, certain they would both topple overboard. Before the sailors could tie the ship to the dock, Joshua leaped across the gap to shore and ran to her, swinging her into his strong arms, crushing her in his embrace, mingling his tears with her own.

"I'm home, Miriam! I'm finally home! And I never want to leave you again!"

Part Three

But Manasseh led Judah and the people
of Jerusalem astray, so that they did
more evil than the nations the Lord
had destroyed before the Israelites.
The Lord spoke to Manasseh and his people,
but they paid no attention. So the Lord
brought against them the army commanders
of the king of Assyria. . . .

2 CHRONICLES 33:9–11

23

"Come look at this ship, Nathan." From the small rise where Joshua worked to build a new addition to the military garrison, he had a clear view of Elephantine Island's harbor and the magnificent vessel that was sailing into it. "What do you make of it, son?" he asked when Nathan climbed up to join him.

Nathan whistled appreciatively. "Quite a sight! It's flying Pharaoh's banners. But I think I see Assyrians on board, too."

"You're right. It must be on some sort of diplomatic mission, but I can't imagine why they've come here."

"You'd better run home and take a bath, Abba," Nathan said, grinning. "They'll never believe you're one of Elephantine's leading elders dressed like that."

Joshua squeezed Nathan's shoulder. "Keep a close eye on the Egyptian laborers until I get back."

As he hurried home to bathe and change his clothes, Joshua tried to shake off the vague sense of foreboding that had sailed into his heart at the strange ship's approach. Since returning from war several years ago, he had finally found peace and contentment for the first time since leaving Jerusalem, and he didn't want anything to disturb it. He whispered a silent prayer that whatever this official mission might bring, it wouldn't bring an end to the way of life he'd grown to accept.

Joshua had been much in demand on the island as an architect and builder in the years that followed the war, and he was especially proud to be in partnership with his son. A gifted sculptor, Nathan added the artistic flourishes and embellishments that set their work apart. Their distinctive building style earmarked most of Elephantine's finest structures.

Joshua's apprehension didn't diminish once he'd bathed and changed his clothes and joined Prince Amariah and the other elders in the audience hall. The visiting delegation was composed of a mixture of Egyptians and Assyrians along with countless slaves, but the central figure in the drama was a lavishly dressed Assyrian who carried himself with the air of royalty. Joshua shifted restlessly in his seat beside Amariah as he waited for all the rituals of protocol, the diplomatic pleasantries, the exchange of gifts and compliments, to finally come to an end. Pharaoh's ambassador introduced the Assyrian dignitary.

"This is Shamash-Shum-Ukin, viceroy of the Assyrian province of Babylon. He is also Emperor Ashurbanipal's brother. Pharaoh thought you might be interested in what he has to say."

"We are honored by your visit, my lord," Amariah said, bowing slightly. "And very interested to hear what brings you such a great distance."

Joshua had to listen closely to follow the viceroy's long, rambling speech, rendered in poorly pronounced Hebrew by a translator. The Assyrian complained in unflattering terms about his brother's reign and the hardship his policies had brought to vassal states and provinces such as Babylon. But when the viceroy finally reached the point of his lengthy discourse, his words astounded Joshua.

"I've come to propose a revolution against my brother Ashurbanipal's harsh reign. I will lead the revolt myself, with all of Babylon's rich resources at my disposal. The leaders of many beleaguered vassal nations—including the new Egyptian pharaoh, Psammetichus—have already pledged their support. I was hoping for yours, as well."

For a moment, Amariah gaped at him speechlessly, then he eyed the Egyptian officials warily. "I am honored that you would travel all this way to confer with me, my lord, but I'm afraid you have a greatly exaggerated view of my importance. I am the leader of only a small band of expatriates from Judah, nothing more. And I govern this island only by the gracious consent of Pharaoh."

"Your humility is admirable, *Prince* Amariah," the viceroy said, "but the truth is, we have a great deal in common. You long to rebel against your brother's reign as much as I long to rebel against mine."

Joshua could no longer stay seated. "Excuse me, how did you know—?"

"That he is a son of King Hezekiah? An heir to the royal dynasty of King David? It's simple—Pharaoh Psammetichus told me."

"We've known the truth about your identity for a long time, Prince Amariah," the Egyptian ambassador said. "When King Manasseh learned you'd sought refuge with us, he requested your extradition as a traitor. Pharaoh Taharqo refused, as did the current pharaoh. You Judeans have proven yourselves loyal subjects and valiant soldiers."

"Both are qualities I'm looking for," the Assyrian viceroy added.

Joshua was still on his feet, struggling to comprehend this astounding turn of events. "Excuse me once again, but I need to know . . . have you asked King Manasseh to join your rebellion?"

"I've been careful to approach only those leaders who have clearly displayed anti-Assyrian sentiments. Judah's king is not among them. In fact, he has launched several very bloody purges among his own nobility, executing anyone suspected of disloyalty to the empire. I also happen to know that there is a great deal of discontent among the common people of your nation because of the heavy taxation my brother Ashurbanipal has imposed on them. They lack only a legal heir of David—such as Prince Amariah—and a trained military force—such as the one he commands here—to rally them to revolt against Manasseh."

"God of Abraham," Joshua murmured as he groped for his seat. "You're finally going to let us go home." He listened to the remainder of the meeting as if in a dream.

"I've come to ask you to sign a treaty of alliance with me, Prince Amariah, and join my rebellion. When we are victorious, you will be the king of Judah, an independent state in a confederation of states with myself as the leader."

"When would this revolution take place?" Amariah asked quietly.

"I am in the final stages of planning a coordinated strike—perhaps within a year's time. My plan is to ignite so many small fires of revolution throughout the empire that my brother will be unable to extinguish them all at once. I could use a stronghold such as Jerusalem in the very heart of the western vassal states, cutting Ashurbanipal's lines of communication and supply. If you decide to join me, Prince Amariah, you would have ample time to prepare your forces, plan your strategy, then await my signal to liberate your homeland."

"God of Abraham, thank you," Joshua murmured.

Long after the viceroy had left the assembly with his delegates to await Amariah's decision, Joshua and the other elders sat in stunned silence. "Could this be God's plan to win back the nation?" Amariah finally asked.

"We've waited so long for this," someone said. "I have children and grandchildren who don't know any other home but Elephantine."

Joshua said nothing. Unlike their last assassination plot, which Joshua had forced on Amariah by bullying and coercion, this plan would come to pass without his interference. He was certain that joining the rebellion was God's will, that the long season of exile was over at last. He had sacrificed his right to revenge as part of his vow to save Miriam's life, but Manasseh's crimes demanded justice, and Yahweh was a God of justice.

"I'm no longer the legal heir," Amariah said. "We know that Manasseh has a son. The boy must be nine or ten years old by now. I won't plot to kill him."

"I agree with you," Joshua said. "But you could serve as co-regent with him until he is old enough to reign alone. After living under Manasseh's influence, I'm sure he'll need a great deal of guidance."

The prince turned to the high priest. "Could I hear your thoughts on all this, Joel?"

"I don't know what to think," he said, shaking his head. "The viceroy may well be on our side, but he's still an Assyrian. No doubt he's as ruthless and cold-blooded as his brother and all the rest of them are. Would God really use a pagan to help us?"

"Yes, I think He might," Amariah said. "I've studied all of Rabbi Isaiah's prophecies, and he insists that the Assyrians are God's instruments of judgment." The prince paused, scrutinizing his advisors' faces, inviting their comments. As hard as it was for Joshua to remain silent, he determined not to pressure Amariah. God's will must be done. When no one spoke, the prince drew a deep breath. "Going to war means putting ourselves, our brethren, and our sons at risk. I won't do it unless I'm certain this is what God wants. Joel, would it be appropriate to seek God's word with Urim and Thummim?"

"Yes, Your Majesty. That's why we made a replica of the ephod—for decisions such as this one."

Long before the priests made the appropriate sacrifices, long before they offered prayers for divine guidance, Joshua knew which stone God would lead Joel to select from his ephod. Yahweh had clearly orchestrated all these events to bring them to this day of judgment against King Manasseh. Joshua felt no surprise at all when Joel drew Thummim, only a deep sense of satisfaction and peace.

"This opportunity is from God," Prince Amariah announced. "We're going to sign the treaty and join Viceroy Shamash-Shum-Ukin's rebellion."

In the months that followed, all but the most essential business came to a halt on Elephantine Island as Joshua helped the exiles prepare for the coming revolution and the liberation of their homeland. While the soldiers honed their fighting skills, Joshua sent spies into Judah to gauge the extent of support they could expect from their countrymen. The men returned with encouraging reports of widespread discontent under the Assyrians' domination, along with shocking stories of the wickedness and idolatry that had spread throughout the land under Manasseh's evil reign.

"It's time," Joshua assured Prince Amariah. "God's judgment is long overdue. We've lived more years on Elephantine Island than we lived in Jerusalem. My son, Nathan, was a child when we left and has grown to manhood here. I'm about to become a grandfather, like Abba was the night this all began. It's time."

"I know," Amariah said. "My sons were all born here. To them, the Promised Land is only a place they learned about in school."

Joshua spent long hours with Amariah and General Benjamin's sons, planning the approaching invasion. With promises of weapons and support from Pharaoh and the Assyrian viceroy, he felt confident that his well-trained regiments, experienced in battle, could easily overpower Manasseh's forces. Joshua himself would lead the commando squad that would infiltrate Jerusalem ahead of time, opening the gates for the invading troops.

As he waited restlessly for the Assyrian viceroy's signal, the contentment Joshua had finally found on Elephantine Island rapidly disintegrated. Everything he had learned to accept about life in Egypt began to irritate him, from the grainy beer they were forced to drink in place of wine, to the stench of rotting fish that seemed to permeate every inch of the island.

"Do you know how long it's been since I've tasted good Judean wine?" he asked Miriam. "Or eaten an olive fresh-picked from the tree?"

"I remember how steep the streets of Jerusalem were," she said, laughing. "I wonder how I will ever manage with my crutches."

"It won't matter, Miriam. When we return to Jerusalem, we'll all be walking on air."

Joshua was at home one evening, changing his clothes before the sacrifice, when Prince Amariah arrived unexpectedly at his door. Joshua appraised his pale face and strained features and knew that the moment he'd long awaited had finally arrived.

"The rebellion has started, hasn't it!" Joshua was stunned when the prince shook his head.

"Can I sit down?" Amariah sank onto the nearest bench before Joshua could reply. "I haven't told any of the others this news. I needed to talk to you alone, first."

Joshua felt a wave of dread. He drew a deep breath, afraid that the stones would soon begin to pile onto his chest. "What happened?"

"The viceroy's rebellion has ended before it ever began. Emperor Ashurbanipal learned of it somehow, and he executed his brother as a traitor."

"No . . . that isn't possible!" Joshua's limbs began to tremble with rage and disbelief. "You've heard wrong! This was God's will . . . we sought His word. . . ."

"It's true, Joshua. The Assyrians sent announcements throughout their empire. The viceroy is dead. The rebellion is finished. I received word about it from Pharaoh himself."

"No," he moaned, struggling for air. "I don't understand! Why would God raise all of our hopes like this, just to dash them again? What is He doing to us?"

"I don't know," Amariah replied. "I don't know what to think."

"But we can still go ahead with our plans, can't we?" he said in desperation. "People in Judah are fed up with King Manasseh. They'll join our rebellion."

"You know that's impossible. The emperor will be expecting trouble. His troops will be ready to quell any disturbances as quickly as they spring up. We'd never stand a chance on our own, and Pharaoh can't help us, either."

"Is God in control or isn't He?" Joshua shouted. "Why did everything fall apart? We prayed! We sought His will! He said yes!"

"Joshua, the Urim and Thummim said only that it was His will to join the rebellion, not that we'd win our homeland back."

"But what was the point of it? Why join a rebellion that God knew would collapse?"

"I wish I knew."

"O God of Abraham, *why*?" he moaned. "I've been trying to be patient all these years, trying to settle down and be content here, but He's kept me waiting like a petitioner outside His throne room, waiting for an audience, waiting for justice! Won't I ever see it? How long, God? How long?" He bent over with his hands on his thighs, gasping for air, certain he would suffocate.

"Are you all right?" Amariah asked in alarm. "Where's Miriam? Shall I get her?"

"No, don't . . . she's not here. . . ." He wrestled to control his terrible rage, knowing that it was choking off his life. "I'll be okay . . . in a minute. . . ." He managed to stand straight again just as the shofar announced the evening sacrifice.

"I'll walk with you," Amariah offered, but Joshua shook his head.

"I can't go. . . . I can't praise God. . . ."

"Joshua, don't do this to yourself. Don't turn away from God. Let's seek Him for answers together."

"I'd be a hypocrite if I set one foot in that temple," he breathed. "Go without me. I want to be alone." He turned his back on Amariah and stumbled out of the rear door, heading toward the riverbank, hoping the prince wouldn't follow.

He found the beach windswept and deserted, as barren and desolate as his own soul. His plans and dreams had been cruelly crushed. There would be no freedom from exile on Elephantine Island, no judgment or punishment for King Manasseh. Once again, God had slammed a door of hope in Joshua's face. He stood alone for a long time, watching the sun set over the Nile, waiting for the terrible darkness to slowly close in around him.

24

KING MANASSEH STOOD BEFORE THE BRONZE MIRROR, admiring his reflection as his servants dressed him in his royal robes. What he saw pleased him. True, he had put on weight over the years as he'd slipped into middle age, but he thought the extra bulk, along with the strands of silver in his dark hair and beard, gave him added dignity. As he turned to leave his chambers for his daily omen-reading, his secretary stopped him.

"I thought you would want to know right away, Your Majesty. A runner has just reported that a large brigade of Assyrian soldiers crossed our border shortly after dawn. They are headed for Jerusalem and should arrive soon."

Manasseh didn't have time to wonder why. "Quickly, tell Zerah to make plans. We must greet our unexpected guests with a lavish welcome."

When the Assyrians arrived, Manasseh was surprised to learn that Emperor Ashurbanipal had sent his personal spokesman, the rabshekeh, who requested an immediate audience. Manasseh greeted him with all the pomp and splendor he could afford, aware of what an honor he was being paid by this visit.

"I know that only the most urgent business could have brought such an important man as yourself this great distance," Manasseh gushed. "I hope you won't think me rude if I express my curiosity.

Why am I being paid such an honor?"

The rabshekeh eyed him coolly. He seemed to take his time answering. "Did you receive Emperor Ashurbanipal's notice about the rebellion led by his brother, viceroy of Babylon?"

"I was shocked by the news, of course, but very pleased to learn that the emperor has successfully quenched the rebellion—praise be to the gods."

The rabshekeh wore a mocking expression as he applauded softly. "A fine performance, King Manasseh. You are a very good actor. But we have proof that you participated in the viceroy's plot."

Fear turned Manasseh's blood to ice. "Never! It isn't true! I didn't know anything about the rebellion until I received the emperor's notice!"

"You're lying. The viceroy didn't have time to destroy all of his documents before we captured him. We found a list of co-conspirators. One of them was you—the ruler of Judah, son of King Hezekiah, heir to the dynasty of King David."

"But it's not true! It has to be a mistake!"

"The document bore King David's seal—your seal. It was unmistakable."

Manasseh glanced around in horror, noticing for the first time how many Assyrian soldiers had crowded his throne room, how menacing they appeared fully armed. His own bodyguards had vanished, and the Assyrians were blocking all of the doors. He felt the terror of being trapped with no escape.

"You . . . you have to believe me," he stammered. "I never joined any rebellion!" He was sweating and nauseated, certain he would faint. He had to do something! The rabshekeh had to believe him! Then Manasseh suddenly realized how he had been framed. "Wait a minute. I'm not the one you want, it's my brother . . . it has to be! He's a traitor who fled the country years ago. He was still wearing a royal signet ring on his finger. He's in league with my enemies. They've been plotting to topple my government for years. You have to believe me—this is all a mistake!"

"Nice try, Manasseh, but I don't believe you. According to our records, your nation has a long history of rebellion. Your father,

King Hezekiah, rebelled against Emperors Shalmaneser and Sennacherib."

"Then your records will also show that I've faithfully paid tribute to Emperors Esarhaddon and Ashurbanipal—"

"Yes, while conspiring with Ashurbanipal's brother. The Egyptians were also part of the rebellion, and we know that your son is named Amon, after Egypt's most important god."

Manasseh's stomach twisted like wrung cloth. Was this how Joshua would finally defeat him? "Please, I can explain. The Egyptians have been harboring my enemies and my traitorous brother for years. I named my son Amon in order to gain the Egyptian god's favor against them. Tell him, Zerah."

"It . . . it's the truth." Zerah's shaky voice was barely a whisper. He had the deathly pallor of a corpse.

"Please," Manasseh begged, "tell your emperor that I can explain. You see, my enemies—"

"Save it for your trial." The rabshekeh motioned to his men, and they moved toward Manasseh with barbed hooks and bronze shackles. He was afraid he was going to scream.

"What are you doing to me? You can't . . ." They hauled Manasseh to his feet to strip off his royal robe. "No . . . stop!" He tried to resist, but there were too many of them, they were too strong. As he vainly tried to cling to his garments, one of the blue tassels tore off in his hand and he clutched it to his chest as if it could save him. They ripped away his tunic, as well, until he stood clothed in only his undergarments. He felt naked and exposed.

Manasseh stood shivering with fear and shame as the soldiers clamped cold metal shackles around his wrists, then his ankles. "Please don't do this to me . . . please . . . I beg you to believe me!" The bonds felt heavy on his limbs, as if they would never come off again.

"Merciful mother Asherah, save me!" Zerah cried as the Assyrians tore off his clothes.

One after the other, every nobleman in the room was being stripped and shackled as Manasseh had been. He stood frozen in terror, listening to their pitiful pleas for mercy, but he saw no way out of this nightmare for any of them.

"I'm innocent! You're making a mistake. I've never been part of a conspiracy. You're arresting an innocent man!" Like words from a dream, Manasseh suddenly recalled how Isaiah and Eliakim had stood in this same throne room, repeating his very words. He understood the helpless outrage they must have felt at such a monstrous injustice.

"Save your defense for the emperor's ears," the rabshekeh said. "You'll get your day in court in Babylon."

"You're not going to take me all the way to Babylon!" Terror filled Manasseh as he suddenly recalled Isaiah's prophecy: *one of Hezekiah's descendants would be taken in chains to Babylon.*

"Get him ready to go," the rabshekeh ordered.

Manasseh cried out as four soldiers suddenly forced him down into his chair, clamping his head against the back of his throne. Then a burst of fiery pain ripped through him as the Assyrians pierced his nose with a barbed hook. Hot, wet blood streamed down his face. He tasted it, bitter and salty on his lips. As the limp paralysis of shock prickled through him, he moaned, struggling to stay conscious.

How could this be happening? He wasn't a traitor. He was the king of Judah, a loyal subject of the Assyrian emperor. He remembered how Isaiah and Eliakim had proclaimed their loyalty, too.

Beside him, Zerah struggled against the soldiers holding him down. He was too old for this kind of treatment. He cried out in anguish as the Assyrians drove a hook through his nose, as well. Manasseh felt the helpless despair of being unable to save someone he loved.

"Zerah, call down your gods!" he pleaded. "You have power!" But when the soldiers stepped aside, Manasseh looked at Zerah's bloody face and saw that he was unconscious.

Manasseh was certain that neither he nor Zerah would survive the long journey to Babylon. Many of his noblemen didn't. The Assyrians gave them enough food and rest to keep them moving but not enough to prevent them from arriving weeks later in a horribly weakened condition. Manasseh's skin blistered and peeled from hours beneath the burning sun, and his ankles chafed and bled after being rubbed raw by his shackles. He and his secretary had to support Zerah between them for the last leg of the journey after he became too weak to walk alone.

Every moment that he was conscious, Manasseh beseeched the gods for help, reminding them of his zeal and devotion, enumerating the shrines and altars he had built, the countless sacrifices he had slain for them. "Have we slighted one of them?" he asked Zerah. "Angered one? Did the priests neglect one of the rituals to bring this disaster upon us? Surely the stars would have foretold a calamity such as this. Why didn't the omens warn us?"

Zerah's laughter held a tinge of hysteria. "The minds of the gods are ever-changing and capricious. We have become pawns in their rivalries, Manasseh. Playthings for their amusement."

"What about your powers, Zerah? Use your powers!" But as Manasseh watched his friend grow weaker each day, his hope drained as steadily as his own strength. They were both going to die in chains. Rabbi Isaiah had once caused the sun to move, but even he had been powerless to save himself after Manasseh had shackled him as they now were.

Manasseh saw Babylon, sprawled on a great plain, long before they reached it. A wide, shimmering moat surrounded the city, along with walls as high as two of Jerusalem's walls piled one on top of the other. The great ziggurat towered higher still, crowned by a temple to Babylon's gods. The Assyrians marched the prisoners through one of the city's one hundred bronze gates, making examples of them as traitors, parading them through the streets of Babylon in chains, as they had paraded them through Jerusalem. Thousands of people thronged to watch. Too humiliated to lift his gaze, Manasseh saw little of the magnificent city except the ground beneath his aching feet. He had commanded Isaiah to tell his future; now he had fulfilled the very words of his prophecy.

Manasseh was still supporting Zerah when the soldiers led them into a squat, mud-brick barracks, then down steep, narrow stairs to the jail, deep underground. At first Manasseh was grateful to be out from under the pitiless sun until he glimpsed the dank, airless dungeon that would be his prison. The door to his cell was a crude hole in the rock wall near the floor, barely two feet in diameter. He struggled in panic as the Assyrians forced him to the ground and made him crawl through it on his stomach. Inside, four barren, rock-hewn walls enclosed a windowless space barely eight feet square. There was no pallet, no bedding, only a hole in the corner for a toilet. High above his head, three holes no wider than his fist allowed light and air to filter in. The guards pushed Zerah into the cell behind Manasseh, then bolted a wide iron bar in place over the opening, leaving only a narrow slot at the bottom to pass food and water through. The sound of the great iron nails being driven into the rock, sealing him permanently inside, brought the terror of suffocation.

"I can't take this!" Manasseh wept. He curled into a tight ball, hugging himself, as he battled hysteria. "Do something, Zerah! Help us both, or I'm going to go insane in here!" But Zerah appeared to be in a stupor as he slumped in the corner, staring blindly at the wall. He rocked slightly, as if cradling a baby, and uttered a soft, keening sound.

Manasseh crawled across the floor to him and took his face in his hands, forcing him to look at him. "Zerah, look at me! Say something! Talk to me!" Zerah's glazed eyes were unseeing. Manasseh clung to him and wept until the cell grew dark and he finally fell into an exhausted sleep.

He awoke to the dim light of dawn and the sound of their food being slid beneath the bar into the cell—a bowl of water and a plate of cold table scraps. Manasseh felt the fiery heat of Zerah's body and realized that he was burning with fever. He scrambled across the floor on his hands and knees, hampered by the shackles that still chained him hand and foot, and pleaded with the guard through the narrow grate.

"Please, my friend needs a physician. Have mercy, I beg you. Don't let him die in this terrible place." His voice echoed and died in the silent jail. As if in a dream, Manasseh suddenly recalled the night his soldiers had brought the badly beaten body of Joshua's grandfather to him. Hilkiah had needed a physician, too, but Manasseh had condemned him to a prison cell to die. Were the gods playing games with his mind, reminding him of the past? Were they punishing him for his sins? But no, he wasn't a sinner. Sin was an illusion.

"I'm going crazy," he murmured as he crawled back to where his friend lay. "You have to get well, Zerah. You can't leave me all alone in this place. I'll go mad." He lifted Zerah's head to give him a sip of water, but he couldn't swallow. Water dribbled from the corners of his mouth into his beard. Manasseh held him in his arms, helpless to do more.

As the cell grew lighter he noticed the huge, festering sores on Zerah's ankles where the shackles had rubbed his flesh raw. They weren't healing as Manasseh's blisters were but had turned a sickly greenish color, with darker streaks radiating up his legs. The heavy bonds, still in place, bit deeply into Zerah's wounds. During the night Zerah's insides had turned to water, but there was no way to clean him or change his clothes. The stench killed any appetite Manasseh might have had, and he watched, uncaring, as rats brazenly carried away their food.

For several days, Zerah was incoherent with fever. Manasseh hoped he was reciting incantations to bring healing or to get them out of this stinking prison, but he knew in his heart it was mindless babbling. He swatted the flies that swarmed around Zerah's sores, but as time passed, he eventually gave up the impossible task.

Their food came only once a day, and Manasseh soon learned to eat it before the rats did. Using the meager bowl of water to cool Zerah's fever had proved futile; instead, Manasseh carefully rationed it between them. By the end of the week his friend's body had grown so foul that Manasseh didn't want to be near him anymore, let alone touch him. But the guard continued to ignore his pleas for help.

As death approached, madness overpowered Zerah. His eyes rolled back in his twitching face, and his body convulsed the way a sorcerer's did when a spirit took possession of him. He screamed obscenities, cursing the very gods he had once worshiped for not helping him. At times he howled and snarled like an animal, clawing at invisible assailants and lashing out with surprising strength. Manasseh huddled in a far corner in terror, waiting for the end.

After what seemed a very long time, the babbling ceased. When the sun rose in the morning and the cell grew light, he saw that Zerah was dead. Manasseh was alone. He covered his own face and wept with hopeless grief.

Joshua leaned against the half-finished wall of his latest project and stared into space as Nathan ordered the workers to their various tasks. His son had asked him to visit the site, insisting that he needed his advice, but Joshua recognized it as a ploy to try to reignite his interest in their work. He knew Nathan could easily complete the project without him.

For months, ever since the viceroy's rebellion had failed, Joshua had been unable to find joy or satisfaction in anything he did. *"Hope deferred makes the heart sick,"* the proverb said, and Joshua lived those words. He had successfully battled the flames of his anger and rage, but in the aftermath, Joshua's life seemed dull and flat and gray, as barren as a charred landscape. Worse, he still couldn't go to the temple or pray.

As he watched his laborers erect the new scaffolding, he slowly became aware that Nathan was speaking to him. "Abba? You haven't heard a word I've said, have you?"

"I'm sorry, son. I don't have the energy for this. I'd better go home." He turned to leave just as a boy came running up the path to the worksite. It was Jerimoth's youngest son.

"Uncle Joshua, wait," he said breathlessly. "Abba sent me to get you. He says you need to come and talk to him and Prince Amariah right away."

"Do you know what he wants?"

"One of Abba's caravan drivers has brought news. Abba thinks you should hear it."

Joshua sighed in exasperation, certain it would prove to be another ruse to try to help him shake his apathy. Nevertheless, he followed his nephew to Amariah's audience hall.

"Sit down," Jerimoth insisted, hovering nervously around him. "You need to be seated to hear this." Joshua obeyed, too weary to argue. Jerimoth spoke slowly, hesitantly. "Listen, Joshua, the last thing in the world I want to do is raise your hopes, but my driver is a reliable man. He was an eyewitness. We can trust him to tell the truth." He nodded to the man. "Go ahead. Tell him what you told us."

"My trading ventures took me to Jerusalem four months ago. While I was there, a battalion of Assyrians arrived one morning in full battle array. Everyone bolted for home at the sight, believe me, and I stayed holed up in my booth in the caravansary. But eventually they blew the shofars and ordered the entire city into the streets to watch a procession. I couldn't believe my eyes. The Assyrians had King Manasseh and all his noblemen in chains and shackles, parading them through the streets with hooks in their noses."

"And you're certain it was the king?" Jerimoth prompted.

"Yes, my lord. I recognized King Manasseh even in his undergarments, without his crown and fancy robes and bodyguards. Besides, they announced his name all through the streets as they made him march, saying he was a traitor to the empire, telling us they had proof that Manasseh had conspired with the emperor's brother to take part in a rebellion."

Joshua opened his mouth to speak but couldn't utter a sound.

"When they finished making an exhibition of him," the driver continued, "they deported the king and all the nobility to prison in Babylon."

"All of his officials?" Jerimoth asked.

"There weren't that many, my lord. King Manasseh murdered all but a handful years ago when they opposed his treaty with Assyria."

"Who's governing the nation?" Prince Amariah asked.

"No one. Chaos reigns. Every man is doing as he sees fit."

Joshua didn't realize that he had stopped breathing until his brother pounded him on the back, seconds before he would have fainted. Someone thrust a cup of water to his lips and made him drink. The room reeled as Joshua struggled to comprehend what he'd just heard. *Manasseh has been imprisoned by the Assyrians! He's been stripped and hauled away with hooks and chains!*

"O God, make him suffer!" Joshua cried out when he could finally speak. "So many have suffered by his evil hand! Pay him back *double* the pain he has inflicted on others!"

Everyone stared at him. Joshua sat trembling in his seat, as stunned by the force of his hatred as they were. It pumped through every inch of him, darker than blood, more bitter than gall. After all these years, his desire for revenge had suddenly sprung to life again, from deep within his heart. He had starved it, held it down in shackles as he'd vowed, but it had remained alive, curling around his soul like a writhing serpent—inert but alive.

Amariah's astonishment made Joshua defensive. "Didn't King David wish the same for his enemies? 'Repay them for their deeds and for their evil work,'" he quoted. "'Repay them for what their hands have done and bring back upon them what they deserve.' That's all I'm asking for—justice!"

Amariah frowned. "I know, Joshua, but how can you wish for anyone to fall into the hands of the Assyrians?"

He slowly realized what Amariah meant. God had placed Manasseh in the hands of the Assyrians—masters in the art of cruelty and torture. They would inflict far more pain than Joshua could ever imagine. Manasseh would die a slow, agonizing death.

"Yes!" he shouted, fists clenched. "You have no idea just how much I've wished for this very thing!" Joshua slid his hand beneath his eye patch to wipe the tears of joy and triumph from his eyes.

Prince Amariah turned away. The vehemence of Joshua's hatred seemed to unnerve him. "I know this news has shaken all of us—especially me," he said. "It seems that by joining the viceroy's rebellion I unwittingly brought about my brother's death."

"Wasn't that the reason you joined?" Joshua said angrily. "To de-throne Manasseh? What's the difference whether we went back and killed him or the Assyrians do it? Either way God is finally judging Manasseh's wickedness."

"I know, I know," the prince said with a heavy sigh. "But the Assyrians torture their prisoners horribly. . . ." For a moment he couldn't speak. He cleared his throat. "Anyway, I think I should return to Judah as soon as possible and see what's become of our homeland. If it's truly without a leader, then perhaps God wants me to step in."

"What about the Assyrians?" Jerimoth asked.

"I'll need to see if they're still there, of course. And if they're still a threat. I'll survey the situation, then wait for God to lead me."

"I'm going with you," Joshua said.

Amariah studied him. "All right," he said after a moment. "I'd appreciate your help."

When Joshua finally left the throne room, he didn't wait for Jerimoth or anyone else but hurried straight to the temple. He wanted to offer a thank offering, but when he reached the gate to the courtyard, shame and guilt stopped him short. He had turned his back on God in anger these past months, questioning His wisdom and goodness. He had refused to pray. But God had been in control all along. Manasseh was finally paying for his crimes. Joshua knew he wasn't worthy to enter the temple courts, guilty as he was of doubt and unbelief.

"I'm sorry, Lord," he prayed, gazing with longing at the altar. "Can you ever forgive my lack of faith?"

He felt a hand on his shoulder and turned to face Joel. "I haven't seen you here in a while," the high priest said gently. "Are you going in?"

"I've been a fool, Joel. A stubborn, unbelieving fool."

"Well, as the psalmist has written, 'There is no one who does good, not even one.' But God provides forgiveness if we ask." He gestured to the altar, then guided Joshua through the gate into the courtyard.

As Joshua knelt before the fire that consumed his sin offering, renewed energy and zeal coursed through his veins. He remembered the proverb he'd been living and realized that the second half of the verse was also true: *"Hope deferred makes the heart sick, but a longing fulfilled is a tree of life."*

25

MANASSEH NEVER KNEW THAT DAYS and nights could be so endless. He wasn't sure which was worse: the long, tedious days spent pacing in the stifling cell or the never-ending nights, lying awake on the hard stone floor, waiting to hear his jailer's footsteps at dawn. They were the only sounds of life that he ever heard, apart from the scurry of rodents and his own echoing cries.

"Talk to me, please! Say something," he pleaded with his captors through the slot beneath the door. "Let me hear another voice before I go insane!" But the owner of the dark hand that shoved food through the hole disappeared day after day without a word, leaving Manasseh with only a parting glimpse of sandal-shod feet. He remembered doing the same thing to Dinah—ordering the servants to give her the silent treatment to wear down her resistance. He studied the jagged wounds she'd made on his arm and stomach and knew that if there was such a thing as divine retribution, then he was paying for his crimes. He had not only left Dinah alone in silence like this during the day, but he'd returned each night to brutalize her. He could no longer remember why. Unable to face what he'd done, he closed his mind against all memories of the past, as if sealing the door to a part of a house he no longer wanted to use.

Over the days and weeks and months that followed, Manasseh's life settled into a nightmarish routine. Horrible dreams filled the restless nights, and he would awaken dozens of times to find the cell still dark—as black as the endless night in his soul. He longed for the dawn, for light to filter through the three holes near the ceiling, but with it would come the terrible heat. Within hours of sunrise, his clothes would be soaked with sweat, his throat parched, and he would have to force himself not to guzzle his meager bowl of water in one gulp. They had arrested him in late winter; he'd arrived in Babylon in early spring. The long, hot months of summer stretched ahead.

His food arrived once a day at dawn, and Manasseh often lay awake in the dark hours before sunrise dreaming of what the guards might bring. Images of platters loaded with delicacies filled his mind: lamb and quail, roast venison and fattened veal; fruit and vegetables of all kinds: cucumbers, melons, olives, grapes, dates, figs, lemons, and pomegranates. He longed for a taste of dark bread, warm from the oven and dripping with honey. But when his daily scraps appeared with numbing uniformity—dry, tasteless, often inedible—he was forced to seal his mind against such fantasies, closing yet another door.

All day long Manasseh stared at the four walls, the ceiling, the floor, until he knew every crack and stone. He began to imagine shapes of animals in the rough-hewn surfaces the way a child sees figures in the clouds. Eventually even those became unchanging, and he stopped looking for them. The barrenness of his world sucked the very life from him, the monotony of gray rock deadening his mind. He longed for color, beauty, pattern, texture. But even his skin and linen undergarments had turned the same dingy gray as the stones.

The only spot of color that remained in his world was the blue tassel from his royal robes, which he had miraculously clung to all these months. He treated it like a treasured prize, handling it carefully to keep it clean, rationing the rare glimpses of it he allowed himself, so he would have something to look forward to. It became his talisman, his touchstone with reality, reminding him that a world had once existed outside these four unchanging walls. But he couldn't bear to dwell on those memories too long, either.

Manasseh spent part of each day pacing in his tiny cell,

exercising his aching muscles so they wouldn't grow weak and stiff. The chains between his ankles dragged back and forth across the cell, scraping the floor as he walked while his mind spun endlessly, going nowhere, like a donkey treading a mill wheel. He had been born under the sign of the lion, born into the tribe of the lion. But what had it all meant? That he was destined to end up here, pacing like a caged lion? Signs and omens had once been so important to him, but now he couldn't make sense of any of them.

Gradually his mind became blank to all thoughts but his present misery. He was imprisoned, his freedom lost forever. Manasseh had always been in control of his life, but now other people decided his fate and there was nothing he could do about it. The anger and frustration he felt at his lack of control consumed him, but with no way to vent his rage, it eventually transformed into hopelessness. Despair seemed a living thing to him, following him around the cell as he walked during the day, lying next to him at night, damp and clammy like an unwelcome bed partner. He would never know freedom again. He was going to die here. His mind was slowly unraveling.

One morning the footsteps outside Manasseh's cell sounded different, lighter. After so many months he had memorized the sound of the guard's familiar tread, and he knew before he glimpsed the feet outside the grate that this was a different man. The hand that slid his food through the hole was slender, the flesh pale.

"How much longer am I going to be imprisoned here?" Manasseh cried. "When will I receive my trial?"

"Soon," a soft voice answered. The footsteps retreated.

Manasseh wept on and off for most of the day, but whether it was from the sound of another human voice at last or from the words of hope that voice had offered, he didn't know. Perhaps it was both. He awoke long before dawn the following day to wait for the guard, unwilling to risk being asleep when he returned. Tears filled his eyes when he heard the same light footsteps as the previous day.

"Please . . . you said my trial will be soon. How soon?"

"Very soon, I think."

"When? Can you find out when? Can you let me know tomorrow?" he called to the retreating steps.

Now the endless days seemed longer still as Manasseh waited with renewed hope for each dawn. Day after day, the guard's reply was the same, spoken in a voice that was warm and soothing: "Your trial is coming very soon." At first Manasseh didn't care that this promise never changed; the human contact alone was enough to sustain him. But slowly, he grew impatient.

"Try to find out the date," he begged one morning. "I need to know how soon!"

He had said the wrong thing. The new guard turned as silent as the first one had been, day after day, reducing Manasseh to such a state of despair that he lay on his stomach with his arms extended through the slot, weeping and pleading with the man every morning. "I'm sorry I was impatient. It won't happen again. Please talk to me! Please say something!"

His pleas were met with silence. Then, after several weeks of unending silence had passed, the guard suddenly spoke to him one morning. "I have good news. You will be set free soon."

Set free!

For the first time in many months, Manasseh remembered what hope was. He sobbed uncontrollably. His ordeal would end soon. He would be set free. The part of his mind still mired in despair urged him not to believe it, not to let the guard raise his hopes, but the man's voice was so gentle, so filled with compassion, that he couldn't possibly be lying. Manasseh dreamed of what it would be like to crawl out of his cell, to be a free man again. Thoughts of freedom consumed his waking hours.

Day after day the guard spoke the same promise, "Very soon you will be set free," until once again, Manasseh lost control.

"When?" he screamed. "You have to tell me when! When will I be set free?" The guard rewarded his outburst with so many days of silence that Manasseh eventually lost count of them. Little by little he stopped begging, stopped reaching his shackled hands beneath the bar as he waited in vain for the man to speak again. Instead, Manasseh greeted the sound of his footsteps with pathetic sobbing.

Then one day the guard spoke again. "Tomorrow," he said. "You will be set free tomorrow."

Manasseh repeated the word over and over like a chant throughout the long day and endless night.

Tomorrow . . .

Tomorrow!

When dawn finally arrived, Manasseh sat huddled by the opening, waiting for his freedom at last. His heart pounded wildly when he heard the approaching footsteps. His friend would pry away the bars. He would set him free.

Instead, the slender hand shoved a bowl of water and a plate of food beneath the crack.

"No! Wait!" Manasseh cried. "You said I'd be set free!"

"Yes," the voice said. "Tomorrow."

In spite of his devastating disappointment, Manasseh believed him. He needed to believe him. And so he did.

But after endless days of repeated torture, repeated promises of "tomorrow" that went unfulfilled, Manasseh finally understood. The guard had been playing a cruel game from the very start. "You lied to me," Manasseh screamed. "You kept saying tomorrow, but you're never going to set me free! It's a lie!"

"Yes, I lied," the voice said softly. "And now that you know the truth, they will take you out and execute you. Tomorrow you will die."

"No! That's another lie! It isn't true!" But as the footsteps retreated, Manasseh began to wonder if it were true. As he waited in terror throughout that long day and night, images of Assyrian executions tormented him—slow, painful tortures. Being impaled, flayed alive. The sleepless night flew past too quickly. Too soon, the cell grew light. When he heard the footsteps descending the stairs they seemed different. He listened in horror and recognized the heavier tread of the first guard.

Manasseh backed away from the cell door, his heart leaping in panic. He trembled from head to toe. When the feet paused outside his door, he began to whimper like a frightened animal. "I don't want to die. . . . Please . . . please . . . I don't want to die. . . ."

Bowls of food and water slid beneath the crack, then laughter echoed in the passageway outside his cell. Manasseh felt his grip loosen as he slipped toward madness. He slid down the wall of his cell and curled into a ball on the floor.

"I can't take this anymore! I can't!" he screamed. He was hanging on to sanity by his fingertips, and as his strength slowly gave way, he took the only escape route left to him—he unlocked the door that led to his memories of the past.

Manasseh closed his eyes and he was a child again, nestled beside his mother. He saw her beautiful face, smelled her rich scent. She began to rock him in her arms, and her sweet voice soothed him as she sang her favorite psalm. *"'Praise the Lord, O my soul; all my inmost being, praise his holy name. . . .'"*

Miriam sat across the table from her husband, watching him devour his food with gusto. Her plate sat before her, untouched. Like a man newly released from prison, Joshua seemed happier and more alive than he'd ever been in his life. It worried her. Sometimes when he didn't know she was watching, he would close his eyes, as if murmuring a prayer of gratitude, and a slow smile of triumph would spread across his face. Miriam would shudder, knowing he had imagined his enemy's torture.

"Is there more food?" he asked after he'd cleaned his plate. "That was delicious."

"Here, take mine." She shoved her plate across the table to him.

"What's wrong?" he asked. "Why aren't you eating?" His tone was curious, not concerned. The relaxed expression of satisfaction never left his face.

"There's nothing wrong. I'm not hungry, that's all."

"Don't you feel well? Are you sick?"

She decided to confront him with the truth. "Yes, I'm sick with worry—over you."

"Miriam, why?" he asked, grinning. "I've never felt better in my life! And if you're worried about my safety after I return to Jerusalem, I've already told you—"

"It's not fear for your physical safety that concerns me as much as fear for what's happening in your heart."

"Did you like me better when I was depressed?" He seemed mildly amused, as if he didn't take her seriously. He moved his own plate aside and began eating the food on hers.

"No, you know I hate to see you depressed. But your joy is all out of proportion, Joshua. It seems wrong for you to gloat like this over another man's suffering."

"Manasseh was my enemy, and justice brings satisfaction, especially after I've waited so long for it. Don't you suppose our forefathers rejoiced and celebrated when 144,000 Assyrians died in the night? Or when Goliath fell? Or when the walls of Jericho came down?"

"I'm worried about what might happen to you if you're disappointed again—if your hopes all fall through like they did when the rebellion failed."

He looked at her in surprise. "But that's ridiculous. How could I be disappointed?"

"Because you have everything all figured out in your mind—what's going to happen, how God is going to work—and if things don't end up exactly the way you think they will, you'll be angry with God again."

Joshua used a piece of bread to mop the plate clean, then popped it into his mouth, shaking his head as he chewed. "The Assyrians arrested Manasseh as a traitor," he said after swallowing. "He'll be executed, just like the emperor's brother was. In fact, he's probably already dead." He couldn't suppress a smile. It made Miriam ill.

"What about the rest of your plans? What if you and Amariah can't win control of our country again?"

"We'll take it one step at a time, Miriam. First we need to slip back into Jerusalem and survey the situation for ourselves, then—"

"I'm going with you."

For the first time, his smile disappeared. "You know that's impossible."

"Why? You're traveling by ship, aren't you? Then by caravan? I can easily ride along. Besides, no one will suspect that you're spies if you bring a crippled woman along."

He rose from the table. "I'm not even going to discuss this, Miriam."

She rose, as well, grabbing her crutches in case he walked away from her. "When you came back from the war you promised that you'd never leave me again, remember?"

"It's only for a month or two. Besides, you won't be alone. You'll have Nathan's wife and baby to fuss over." He walked around the table to her as he talked, then wrapped her in his arms. "Look, would you feel better if Nathan didn't come with me? If he stayed here with you?"

"I'm going with you," she said firmly. The decision brought Miriam peace of mind for the first time since Joshua began making plans to go. "You can leave without me, Joshua, but you can't stop me from boarding the very next ship and following you to Jerusalem. If you're not around to pick me up when my crutches slip, I'm sure someone else will do it for me."

"Miriam, you're being stubborn—"

"Does that surprise you? Didn't you once say it was one of the reasons you fell in love with me?"

Joshua's arms dropped to his sides as he exhaled in frustration. His contented look had vanished completely. "And just what do you think you can do for me in Jerusalem?" he asked angrily.

"Probably the same things I do here—cook your meals, soothe your temper, save you when you get into trouble."

"Look, I'm not the only one going on this trip. Joel and Amariah will never agree to let you come."

She gave a short laugh. "They'll agree to anything you say. You and Nathan are the only ones who can use a sword."

"You're not going!" he shouted. She knew he raised his voice only because he had run out of excuses. She turned her back to him and began clearing the table.

"I'm going to Jerusalem, Joshua. So you'd better start writing me into your plans."

26

EVERY DAY, BEGINNING AT DAWN, Manasseh opened the door to his memories of the past and left his prison cell to journey to another place in a different time. He decided to start with his earliest memories of childhood and relive every moment he could recall of his life. He knew that many of those memories would be painful, but pain was good—it meant that he was alive and still clinging to his sanity.

The sound of his mother's voice, singing to him, was his first memory. He hummed the tune that had been Hephzibah's favorite over and over to himself and felt the warmth of her arms, smelled the flowery scent of her perfumed skin. He wandered the halls of the palace nursery and felt safe, secure, and utterly loved.

Before long, his brother toddled through the rooms behind him, shouting, "Wait, Ma'ssah . . . wait!" Manasseh remembered how Amariah would look up to him, his big eyes pathetically hopeful, longing for his friendship. But he had been cruel to Amariah as a child, shoving him roughly aside, and even more cruel to him as an adult, pressuring him to embrace all of Zerah's changes. *"Amariah cries out in his sleep sometimes,"* Zerah had once told him. For the first time Manasseh understood that his actions had driven his only brother into exile.

Slowly, the memories became harder and harder for Manasseh

to face as Joshua entered his life. For years they had been inseparable, doing everything together from the time the morning sacrifice began until the evening one ended. He smiled when he remembered how serious Joshua had always been, how he'd hung on to every word Rabbi Gershom had uttered in their Torah lessons, and how clumsy and inept he'd been with a sword. Joshua, his best friend, had grown up to become a traitor conspiring to usurp his throne—hadn't he? In the silence of his prison cell, Manasseh closed his eyes and heard Joshua struggling for air, the painful wheezing of his breathing attack after Manasseh had left him stranded in the rain. *"You know I'm not your enemy, Manasseh. . . . We're best friends, aren't we?"* He wondered which of the lies he had believed were true and which truths had been lies.

As the long days passed and Manasseh's journeys continued, he came at last to the memories he feared the most—the ones of his abba. He thought it strange that he should fear his father's memory, because he had loved Abba deeply and had been so completely loved by him in return. He remembered how tall his father was, how he had to look up and up to see the familiar warmth in his eyes. He remembered the slight limp in his step from his scars, the scent of aloe balm and incense on his clothes. Manasseh could linger for hours over these memories, but when Abba opened his mouth to speak, Manasseh drew back in fear, knowing what his first words would be.

"Hear, O Israel. Yahweh is God—Yahweh alone. Love Yahweh your God with all your heart and with all your soul and with all your strength."

The memory brought Manasseh back to his prison cell with a jolt, shaken out of his reverie by the force of his father's voice. Think about something else, he told himself. Think about the mountains and valleys that surround Jerusalem. Think about all the things you learned in your studies: the history of Israel beginning with Abraham and Isaac; the stories of Joseph and Moses and the exodus from Egypt; recite all of the nation's kings, starting with Saul and David and Solomon. As he recited, Manasseh realized he was part of that history. He had taken his place on Judah's throne as his father had before him, fulfilling the prophecy spoken to King David that a descendant would always sit on his nation's throne.

He closed his eyes and saw Abba, seated on his throne in splendor with Eliakim on his right, Shebna on his left. He saw the judgment hall filled with people, bowing before King Hezekiah, seeking his wisdom, his justice. But there was no pride or arrogance in his father's posture as he reigned, only a quiet humility that somehow made him seem more powerful. He saw his father striding up the royal walkway to stand on the platform at the Temple, a sovereign king of authority and strength. But then his father, who had never bowed a knee to any Assyrian overlord, fell down on his knees—on his face—before God, humbling himself in obeisance to his King and Lord. He heard the passion and awe in his father's voice: *Yahweh is God—Yahweh alone.*

Manasseh had to stop. The memory of his father's unshakable faith caused him too much pain. He stared instead at his barren cell, at the flies swarming around his empty food bowl. As he toyed with the hook that pierced his nose, he tried to count how many flies there were. But even that was impossible. They moved too fast. And there were too many of them.

Hours later, when he was ready to journey again, Manasseh traveled back to the royal platform, only this time he was the king, striding up to the Temple with Zerah beside him. *"Sin is an illusion, Manasseh. Remember, you're the sovereign ruler of Judah. You are accountable to no one."*

The Temple Mount looked very different than it had when his father had stood on the platform. Manasseh saw the carved image he had made standing in front of the sanctuary; the altars to the Baals and the starry hosts in both courtyards; the booths for male and female shrine prostitutes; the altar for divination; the Asherah pole.

Yahweh alone.

Where had all those altars and images come from? Manasseh remembered placing them there, but he could scarcely remember why. His mother had worshiped Asherah—that was one reason. But why hadn't she ever told him? *"'Praise the Lord, O my soul . . .'"* she had sung. *"'He does not treat us as our sins deserve.'"*

His father had been deceived and manipulated by the priests, Zerah had said. Manasseh must return to pure worship—acknowledging the god in everyone and everything in creation. But had King David been deceived and manipulated, too? And Abraham? And Moses? Manasseh tried to recall when he had made all the changes at the Temple and decided that it was after he had discovered the conspiracy, after he'd learned how Isaiah and Eliakim had plotted against him. But now he wondered who he should believe—Zerah, who had died cursing and blaspheming his gods? Or Eliakim, who had looked Manasseh in the eye before he died and said, *"I want you to know that I forgive you."*

Manasseh groaned in confusion and despair. He was too weary to sort through all these thoughts. He simply wanted to journey back to happier times and be a child again. He closed his eyes and padded barefoot into his father's chambers to say good-night to him. Abba sat in front of a small table, sorting through a pile of documents by lamplight. He put them down when Manasseh entered and drew him close to his side.

"Tell me what the rabbi taught you today, son."

Manasseh shivered, afraid suddenly that he might forget something or mix something up. But Abba's hand rested gently on his head, caressing his hair. His fears subsided.

"I'm learning the Ten Commandments, Abba." His childish voice sounded innocent and sweet. "They begin, 'I am the Lord your God, who brought you out of Egypt, out of the land of slavery. You shall have no other gods before me. You shall not make for yourself an idol in the form of anything in heaven above or on the earth beneath or in the waters below. You shall not bow down to them or worship them; for I, the Lord your God, am a jealous God, punishing . . .' "

Manasseh's eyes flew open, and the barren gray walls of his prison cell confronted him. *Punishing.* He was in Babylon, in a prison cell, in chains, as Isaiah had warned. All the gods he had pleaded with—Baal, Asherah, Molech, Amon—hadn't saved him. He had broken God's commandment and worshiped idols, and now he was going to die here as punishment.

He looked down at his body and wept at what he'd become. At least six months had passed since the Assyrians had shackled him with hooks and chains, six months since he'd bathed or washed his hair or trimmed his beard. His skin was black with grime from his own sweat and filth, his fingernails were jagged claws, his clothes mere rags. One of his teeth had fallen out after he'd chewed a leathery piece of gristle, and the others were just as rotten. He was mere skin and bones, barely human, unable to bear his own stench.

Memories poured down on top of him, thousands of them, like garbage piled in a dump. He thought of the people he had murdered: Rabbi Isaiah, tortured to death; Eliakim, scourged and stoned; his infant son hurled into the flames. Those were only the first murders. How many hundreds had followed? He recalled all of the vile, disgusting things he had done while worshiping false gods, his uncontrolled lust and depravity, and he shrank from himself in shame. Manasseh didn't blame God for punishing him, for abandoning him here. He could find no comfort, no consolation as he faced the naked ugliness of his sin and guilt; only deep self-loathing and horror. He was going to die here, and he deserved it.

He slowly uncurled his fist and stared at the blue tassel that had torn from his royal robes the day he was arrested. God had commanded the Israelites to sew tassels on their clothing to remind themselves of His laws. *"You will have these tassels to look at and so you will remember all the commands of the Lord, that you may obey them and not prostitute yourselves by going after the lusts of your own hearts and eyes."*

Manasseh sank deep into despair, his mind and his spirit exhausted from his memories. His crimes against other people were bad enough, but his worst sins had been committed against God. He had broken His laws, offended His holiness. When he saw himself as God did, Manasseh grieved, weeping uncontrollably, wishing for death. His soul was as filthy and loathsome as his flesh had become, the stench of his sin reaching to the heavens.

"I can't take this anymore," he wept. He could no longer confront his past and all the evil he had done. He couldn't abide his present, confined like an animal in this stifling cell. He couldn't face his future, existing day after day without hope. And he couldn't face himself, knowing what a wretched creature he had become. Separated from other people, from God, and from himself, Manasseh knew he was already in hell.

As demons of madness danced around him, beckoning him to join them, Manasseh ran to the only refuge that remained. He closed his eyes and huddled in the safety of his mother's arms, allowing her song to drown out insanity's taunting cries.

"'Praise the Lord, O my soul; all my inmost being, praise his holy name. Praise the Lord, O my soul, and forget not all his benefits—who forgives all your sins and heals all your diseases, who redeems your life from the pit and crowns you with love and compassion.'"

As Manasseh sang the beloved words, they slowly penetrated his tattered soul. The song described what Yahweh was like, what He had promised. Manasseh had lived with false idols, false ideas about God for so long that it was as if he had never heard these words before. They washed over him like drops of life-giving rain on his parched spirit.

"'The Lord is compassionate and gracious, slow to anger, abounding in love. He will not always accuse, nor will he harbor his anger forever; he does not treat us as our sins deserve or repay us according to our iniquities. For as high as the heavens are above the earth, so great is his love for those who fear him; as far as the east is from the west, so far has he removed our transgressions from us. As a father has compassion on his children, so the Lord has compassion on those who fear him; for he knows how we are formed, he remembers that we are dust.'"

Manasseh fell prostrate before God as his father had done, bowing before God's majesty, pleading for his mercy. "O Lord Almighty, God of my ancestors," he prayed. "I know that you alone made heaven and earth, and that all things tremble before your power. Your glorious splendor can't be contained, and your wrath toward sinners can't be endured. Yet your promised mercy is immeasurable and unsearchable, for you, O Lord, are a God of great compassion. You are long-suffering and very merciful, and you have pity on human suffering.

"O Lord, according to your great goodness you promised forgiveness to those who sin against you. And in the multitude of your mercies you allow sinners to repent, so that they may be saved.

"You, O Lord, have not appointed repentance for the righteous, for Abraham and Isaac and Jacob, who did not sin against you, but you have appointed repentance for me, a sinner. For the sins I have committed are more in number than the sand of the sea. They are multiplied, O Lord, they are multiplied!

"I'm not worthy to look up and see the height of heaven because of the multitude of my sins. I am so weighed down with them that I can't even lift my head because of them, and I have no relief. For I have provoked your wrath and have done evil in your sight, setting up abominations and multiplying offenses.

"But now I bend the knee of my heart, begging you for mercy. I have sinned, O Lord, I have sinned, and I admit my crimes before you. I earnestly beg you—forgive me, O Lord, forgive me! Don't destroy me with my sins! Don't be angry with me forever or repay me for all the evil I've done. Lord, please don't condemn me to the depths of hell. For you, O Lord, are the God of those who repent, and in me you will show your goodness and mercy to all the earth. O Lord God, unworthy as I am, please save me by your great mercy and love...." Manasseh couldn't finish. He lay with his forehead pressed to the stone floor, weeping.

Then, for the first time since Zerah died, Manasseh was suddenly no longer alone in his cell. He felt God's hand of compassion reaching out to touch him, God's arms of mercy surrounding him. His tears of love washed Manasseh clean.

As the power of God's forgiveness slowly transformed him, Manasseh lifted his heart to heaven.

"'Praise the Lord, O my soul; all my inmost being, praise his holy name.'"

Then he slept in God's embrace, knowing true rest and peace for the first time in his life.

27

Joshua's caravan made the slow, winding climb to Jerusalem, and as the land of Judah unfolded before his eyes, the hills and valleys all seemed achingly familiar with their terraced vineyards and ancient olive groves—yet so horribly different. His homeland seemed as alien to him as Egypt had when he first moved there. Pagan shrines and high places now blighted the once-beautiful landscape. The smoke of Baal's altar fires rose like funeral pyres from every hilltop, proclaiming the spiritual death of his nation.

"Judah's idolatry is worse than Egypt's," Joel complained. The high priest averted his gaze to avoid the shrines and had no place to rest his eyes but the ground. "We certainly have a lot of work ahead of us."

"Yes," Amariah agreed, "and after all these years, I don't think we'll be able to change things overnight."

Joshua's first glimpse of Jerusalem stopped him in his tracks. "Miriam, look," he said in a hushed voice. "There it is!" The golden sunlight of early fall gilded the city's stone walls. Warm beams reflected off the Temple's roof like the radiant glow of a beacon, beckoning him home. From a distance, the city seemed bathed in an aura of amber light. "God of Abraham . . . I've forgotten how beautiful Jerusalem is!" he murmured.

The illusion quickly faded as they approached the gates, then entered the defiled city. In the marketplace, every wicked practice and unclean thing imaginable was for sale, from carved idols and fortune tellers to ritual prostitutes. Joshua gazed in horrified fascination at the vulgar images and mysterious amulets displayed on either side of the stall he'd rented, too stunned to look away. "How has Yahweh tolerated this for so long?" he murmured.

"I don't know," Joel said, "but thank God He shielded us and our families from it on Elephantine Island."

Joshua was eager to begin the reformation. His restlessness provided the drive necessary to get everyone through the first difficult days in their homeland. The stall they leased in the marketplace, piled with bolts of Egyptian cotton from their caravan, provided a convenient base from which to observe the city. Joshua managed to rent a tiny one-room house for Miriam and himself nearby, while Nathan, Joel, and Amariah slept in the rear of the booth. By the end of the first week, Joshua had gleaned enough information for them to take the first step in his plan.

"The greatest obstacle to your assumption of power doesn't seem to exist," he told Prince Amariah. "We've seen no sign of Assyrian officials or troops anywhere in the country. The only government officials that I can see are the city elders meeting at the gate, and even they don't appear to be very effective. But we'll start with them, first thing tomorrow."

Leaving Nathan in charge of their booth the next day, Joshua set out with Joel and the prince for the city gate. He had strapped his dagger beneath his robes, where he could reach it quickly. Prince Amariah waited for the elders to finish settling a dispute between two other men before stepping forward to repeat the words he and Joshua had rehearsed.

"Good morning, my lords," he began, "I was wondering if you could help me. I've been living outside of Jerusalem for many years, but I've recently learned that my older brother has died. I'd like to find out how I can redeem my father's inheritance."

"We have authority only in Jerusalem," the chief elder said. "Is your father's property within the city limits?"

"Some of it is. But tell me—who has authority outside of the city?"

The elder paused, glancing nervously at the others. "At the moment, no one," he said quietly.

"Well, isn't there someone at the palace I can petition?" Amariah asked.

The spokesman studied Amariah carefully, as if deciding how to answer. "You can leave your petition with a palace chamberlain, but . . . in case you're not aware . . . the king left Jerusalem some months ago and hasn't returned."

"What about his secretary or his palace administrator? Didn't he leave one of his officials in charge?"

The elder seemed reluctant to answer and irritated with Amariah for forcing the issue. "There is no one," he finally admitted.

Joshua's heart quickened with excitement. God had paved Amariah's way, making this easier than any of them could have imagined. When Amariah turned to him, his eyes asking an unspoken question, Joshua said, "Go ahead, tell them."

Amariah squared his shoulders and faced the elders again, his voice strong and decisive. "Very well, I'll begin with the part of my claim that is under your jurisdiction: my father's property here in Jerusalem. I am Prince Amariah, son of Hezekiah. My brother is King Manasseh." He extended his fist to display his royal signet ring.

The elders all seemed dumb struck, especially the chief elder. One of them had to sit down to absorb the news. Joshua watched them carefully, gauging each of their reactions. He had warned Amariah to expect suspicion and resistance, but as their astonishment slowly faded, the overwhelming reaction of all these men was fear. Joshua released his hold on the dagger handle as he breathed a sigh of relief. These elders wouldn't oppose his plans.

"If you require further proof of my identity," Amariah said, "feel free to question me."

The elder who was seated shook his head. "I would believe you, even without that ring. Your resemblance to your father is unmistakable. And I know who you are, as well," he said, pointing to Joshua. "You're Lord Eliakim's son."

"Yes, that's right."

"Like two ghosts from the grave," the chief elder murmured.

"You don't have anything to fear from us," Amariah said. "There has been enough bloodshed already during my brother's reign. We're here to help restore the government. I'm aware that Manasseh has a son who is his legal heir, but I'm not interested in challenging his claim. I only want to provide leadership until he's old enough to be anointed king. I'll serve as his palace administrator, Joshua as his secretary and advisor. From what you've said, I assume no one else lays claim to those positions at the moment."

"There's no one left to fill them," the chief elder said. "The Assyrians deported all of the king's officials along with him. Any noblemen who were lucky enough to escape are afraid to come forward."

"What about Manasseh's son?" Joshua asked.

"The boy is in hiding with his mother."

"Let him remain in hiding," Amariah said, "until you are confident that I mean him no harm." He crossed his arms, appraising the astounded men. They were unable to stop staring at him. "So, then. Can I count on your support for my claim?"

"We'll support you, Prince Amariah," the chief elder said quickly. "Heaven knows, we're desperate for leadership around here. But may I ask you a question? Why on earth would you want the job? Judah is an Assyrian vassal state. Do you have any idea what will happen to you if Emperor Ashurbanipal disputes your claim to the throne?"

"I can well imagine," Amariah said. "But I have King David's blood in my veins, and that gives me certain responsibilities to our nation. I have a healthy fear of the Assyrians, yes, but I also have faith in Yahweh. I believe that this is His will for me."

Joshua watched carefully, but the elders showed no response at all to Amariah's declaration of faith in Yahweh. He longed to astonish them further with the news that Joel was the anointed high priest of Yahweh and that they intended to reclaim the Temple as well as the government. But they had agreed ahead of time not to reveal Joel's identity. No changes at the Temple would be possible until Amariah was firmly in control of the nation.

"How soon can I reclaim my father's property?" the prince asked.

"You mean his palace? We can take you there now, if you'd like."

This was too easy. Joshua's mind raced ahead, searching for the trap. "Just a minute," he said. "What about Manasseh's guards?"

"The Assyrians rounded up every Judean soldier they could find, as well as the king's bodyguards. The palace is empty except for the chamberlains and a handful of servants."

Joshua finally agreed to let the elders escort them to the palace, unable to see any danger. But he remained alert for trouble, his dagger ready by his side.

When he reached the top of the hill, Joshua got his first glimpse of Manasseh's palace—they hadn't dared approach it since their return. The once-familiar structure now resembled a fortress with thick barricades surrounding it. Even if an enemy had breached the city walls, Manasseh would have been safe inside. Joshua smiled, aware that no barricade in the world could have shielded the king from God's judgment.

The guard booth beside the door stood vacant. Joshua and the others climbed the broad steps to the main doors and walked, unchallenged, into the palace. He wasn't prepared for the sudden swell of emotion that flooded through him. His dream of restoring his homeland was being fulfilled at last. He choked back the knot of emotion that filled his throat, praying that he wouldn't be required to speak.

An elderly chamberlain hurried toward them, his fearful gaze not on the strangers but on the chief elder. The old man looked tattered, unkempt, and vaguely familiar to Joshua.

Before the elders had a chance to speak, Amariah pushed forward to greet the man. "Ephraim! Is it really you?"

The chamberlain gaped at the prince for a moment, then recognition lit his face. He fell at Amariah's feet. "Your Majesty! ... Prince Amariah! Oh, you've come back to us!"

"Here, stand up, Ephraim, and let me have a look at you."

As Amariah helped the chamberlain to his feet again, Joshua suddenly remembered him as one of their favorite palace servants from childhood. He felt another rush of emotion, but a tidal wave of anger quickly consumed it, for if Ephraim was still alive, then he must have stood idly by years ago when Manasseh condemned Abba to death. He would have to pay for his cowardice. Joshua was imagining Ephraim's trial, the satisfaction of sentencing him to death, when Prince Amariah interrupted his thoughts.

"Ephraim, you remember Joshua, Lord Eliakim's son, don't you?"

Ephraim's eyes met Joshua's, but the hatred the old man must have seen in Joshua's expression made him back away. "Yes, of course," he said. "But you've changed, my lord, much more than Prince Amariah has."

"Will you show us around?" Amariah asked. "It's been so long, I'm not certain I can find my way anymore."

"I would be honored, Your Majesty," he said shakily. "I should warn you, though, that the Assyrians looted everything of value. We tried to fix things up and keep everything functioning in case King Manasseh returned, but . . ."

"It's all right, Ephraim. I'm sure you did your best."

They began a slow tour of the palace, beginning with the lower hallways, chambers, and council room. The palace administrator's office was so changed that Joshua had a difficult time believing it was the same room his father had used. When they entered the throne room, Joshua stared for a long time at his father's seat beside the king's throne, but he was unable to picture him there. This room was Manasseh's judgment hall—Abba had been unjustly condemned to death in this room.

Joshua wandered through the rest of the palace as if in a dream. Some rooms were still vaguely familiar, but most of it seemed so changed that he felt lost. Amariah grew more and more somber as they walked. Joshua recognized the prince's emotion as grief.

The hardest rooms for Joshua to view were the private living quarters—the king's chambers, where Manasseh had lived after Hezekiah died; the palace nursery where they had played together as children; the classroom where he'd spent so many hours with Manasseh and Rabbi Gershom. Joshua could only glimpse them briefly before turning away.

Throughout the tour, Ephraim eyed Prince Amariah nervously,

as if fearful of displeasing him. "Tell me which rooms you would like, Your Majesty, and I'll prepare them for you right away. The king's chambers are the most comfortable—"

"No, Ephraim, I'm not the king. My nephew is. I'm sorry, but I don't even know what his name is."

"It's Amon, Your Majesty."

"*Amon?*" Joshua repeated. "Like the Egyptian god?"

"Yes, my lord. But the boy isn't living here."

"I know," Amariah said. "When Amon returns, the king's chambers will be his. For now, the rooms I lived in before I left will suit me just fine."

"Which rooms would you like, my lord?" It took Joshua a moment to realize that the chamberlain was talking to him.

"I . . . I can't . . . I won't be living in the palace," he managed to say.

The prince turned to him in surprise. "Joshua, why not?"

"I can't live here. . . . Miriam and I will stay where we are for now."

"I understand," he said. "This is difficult for me, too. It's not my home anymore. I thought it would be, but it isn't. Most of my life has been lived on Elephantine Island."

"Maybe things will change once our families arrive," Joel said quietly.

Amariah shook his head. "I can't ask Dinah to live here. I don't even know if I can stand it myself. Manasseh is everywhere."

"I know," Joshua said. "Come on, let's get out of here." The tour ended near the door to the royal walkway, leading up to the Temple. None of them had gone up to see it since their return. "Does anyone feel like taking a look?" Joshua asked.

Joel sighed. "All right. The first time will be the hardest, no matter how long I avoid it."

When they reached the top of the hill, the three men could only stand outside the gate and stare in horror. Except for the sanctuary, the Temple Mount was unrecognizable. "God of Abraham," Joshua murmured. He had never witnessed such a sight. The courtyards were crammed with forbidden images. The royal sorcerers, astrologers, and shrine prostitutes all continued to practice their idolatry, going about their rituals as if the king had never left Jerusalem. The scene was so vile that none of them could bear to walk through the gate.

"Let's get out of here," Amariah said.

The triumph Joshua felt earlier as he'd climbed the palace steps had all faded, leaving sorrow and emptiness in its place. He wondered, as they walked down the hill again, if the task they faced would prove too great for them. "We have so much work ahead of us," he said. "We may as well accept the fact that it's going to take a long time—probably the rest of our lives."

Joel wiped his eyes with the heel of his hand. "I hardly know where to begin."

"I know what you mean," Amariah said. "I wonder if this is how my father felt when he began to reform the nation after King Ahaz died."

"This has to be worse," Joshua said, "much worse. Manasseh has reigned for a long time. If any man ever deserved God's wrath, it's him." He walked in silence for a moment, then said, "Ironic, isn't it? My father's first job for your father was repairing the Temple."

He had been chasing memories of Abba all day, but they had eluded him, darting out of sight every time he tried to picture his face. There were two more places he wanted to visit, but he needed to confront them alone. "I'll meet you later tonight," he told the others. "I want some time to look around the city by myself."

Joshua threaded his way through the jostling crowds, following the street that led to the Damascus Gate. Jerusalem seemed noisy and strident, the people he passed rushed and ill-tempered. He was surprised to find himself longing for the peace of Elephantine Island and the gentle sound of lapping water. When he reached the gate he paused, drawing a deep breath for courage. Then he hurried through it to face the king's execution pit.

The site was unchanged, a well-used testimony to the brutality of Manasseh's reign. Joshua stared at the scourging posts and the deadly stones that littered the ground, picturing them splattered with innocent blood. If he walked through the pit, he imagined that the earth itself would be soaked with it. Abba had suffered here, died here. Joshua didn't even know where he was buried. He found it difficult to live with the fact that he might never know. He hoped that Manasseh's suffering was ten times greater than what he had inflicted here.

The last place Joshua visited proved to be the most painful of all. He reentered the city and wandered through the broad streets of elegant houses that stood below the palace until he found his boyhood home. Like the execution pit, it seemed unchanged, except that someone else now lived there. He gazed at the front door for a long time, the ache in his throat so large he couldn't swallow. He thought of his mother's words: *"I will thank God for all that He has given me, not curse Him for all that I've lost."*

He would remember the good times, the happy memories: Mama sitting beneath the tree in their tiny garden, teaching him to count as they shelled dried beans; Abba crouching to greet his children after work, Joshua and Jerimoth both talking at once, Tirza and Dinah clamoring for his kisses. He imagined Grandpa Hilkiah returning home from the Temple in his prayer shawl, pausing to reverently kiss the *mezuzah* on the front door, his fingers caressing the box that contained the sacred law. Joshua peered at the doorframe, but the mezuzah, like his grandfather, was gone. He slid his fingers beneath his eye patch to wipe his eyes, then finally turned and hurried away.

As he made his way through the jumble of streets to his rented house near the marketplace, he silently thanked God for all that He had given him—for his peaceful life on Elephantine, for his infant grandson, for Nathan and for Miriam. Then he thanked God for Miriam's stubbornness. Because of it, he would find her waiting for him in their tiny home, ready to comfort him.

Manasseh's peace proved elusive; the warmth of God's presence, fleeting. As he sat in his prison cell day after day, sifting through the refuse of his life, condemnation and guilt continually buried him beneath their weight, leaving him alone with his devastating doubts. God couldn't possibly forgive him. His grace would never reach as far as this wretched pit. Despair forced Manasseh to sing the words of his mother's favorite psalm over and over until he believed them once again. "'He does not treat us as our sins deserve. . . .'"

His mother had worshiped Asherah for a time. Rabbi Isaiah had admitted it was true. At last Manasseh understood why this psalm had been so important to her. *"As far as the east is from the west, so far has he removed our transgressions from us. . . ."*

The only other measure of comfort Manasseh found was in prayer. It was through prayer that he eventually accepted the fact that he would live the rest of his life in this cell and probably die here. His life sentence no longer brought terror but quiet resignation. Even though God had forgiven him for all that he'd done, Manasseh still had to suffer the consequences of his sins. And that seemed right to him.

Slowly the months passed. Soon it would be a year since his arrest. As the nights grew colder and summer faded into fall, he begged the guard for a blanket against the chill. He lay huddled in the corner one morning, trying to keep warm, when he heard two sets of footsteps descending the stairs. Manasseh sat up in surprise, listening. He was astonished when the guards started prying the bar loose from the cell door, as they had when they'd removed Zerah's body. They must be giving him the blanket he had asked for. They must be removing the bar to shove it inside. He heard the bar fall to the floor with a loud crash, and he crouched near the door, ready to take the blanket.

"You may come out," a voice said.

Manasseh didn't understand. Did they want him to come out for the blanket? He couldn't seem to move.

"I said, you may come out, King Manasseh."

No. He remembered the taunting games the guards had played once before and refused to believe it. He waited for the joke to end, for his food and water to slide through the hole as they always did. But the hand that reached into his cell was empty.

"Come . . . take my hand. Let me help you."

The door to his cell stood open. The guard was telling him he could crawl through it. Manasseh had dreamt of doing it so many times that this seemed unreal, another dream. Slowly, he lay down on his stomach and inched forward, his eyes clamped tightly closed against disappointment. As soon as his shoulders emerged, two strong sets of hands gripped him beneath his arms and pulled him the rest of the way. Manasseh cried out in terror.

"It's all right, we're not going to hurt you," one of the guards said as they hauled him to his feet. Manasseh's knees wouldn't support his trembling legs. The men propelled him down the passageway toward the stairs against his will, away from the safety of his cell.

"Stop.... What are you doing to me? Where are you taking me?"

"We're setting you free."

"No ... no ..." he moaned. He refused to believe it, refused to trade his quiet acceptance and resignation for false hope and then despair.

When they reached the room at the top of the stairs, the huge, open space terrified Manasseh after being enclosed for so long. He felt as if he were shrinking. Strange, elongated shapes floated past him, and several moments passed before he realized that he was seeing people. He clapped his hands over his ears to escape the deafening sounds that clamored all around him. When one of the guards tried to pull his hands down, he resisted.

"Please," the guard said. "Give me your hands, King Manasseh. I want to take your shackles off."

He hesitated, afraid to believe him, then finally held out his trembling hands. The guard removed the heavy bronze fetters from his wrists, then his ankles, for the first time in nearly a year. Manasseh felt naked without them, his body so light he was afraid he might float. He rubbed his arms in disbelief, staring at the bands of skin that had remained cleaner beneath his bonds.

Someone took his arm and gently guided him into a smaller room close by. So much time had passed since Manasseh had felt another person's touch that the warmth of it brought tears to his eyes. Three servants waited for him beside a plastered *mikveh* large enough to immerse himself in; a fragrant scent he couldn't identify filled the room. As they stripped off his filthy rags and helped him into the hot bath, he wept. God's grace and forgiveness had stripped and cleansed him this same way. *"Wash me, and I will be whiter than snow...."*

Manasseh clung to his blue tassel, moving it from hand to hand as the servants scrubbed him clean. The water became so murky that he could no longer see the bottom. Afterward, they trimmed his hair and beard. He stared at the long strands that dropped to the floor, astonished to see that they were white. Finally, the servants made him lie down as they carefully filed off the bronze hook and removed it from his nose.

When Manasseh stood before a mirror, dressed in new robes, he didn't recognize the very old man facing him. He lifted a shaking hand to touch his sunken cheeks, his grizzled beard, and the man in the mirror did the same. "That's not me. . . . It can't be me," he murmured. He saw a dead man, pulled from his grave, with gray skin and black-rimmed eyes. Most terrifying of all was the glimpse of hell he saw in those eyes.

Someone took his arm again, and he floated, dreamlike, out of the building for the first time. How beautiful the world was! Manasseh wept aloud when he saw the azure sky, the billowing clouds, the radiant sun. And birds! He had forgotten about birds—how they sang, how they soared through the air. He stood in awe to watch a palm tree swaying in the wind, its long, graceful branches waving like green arms. Beautiful . . . oh, so beautiful! He lifted his face and the breeze caressed it like fingers, then ruffled through his hair. Everything he gazed at or touched seemed graced by the hand of God, a gift just for him.

They led him into another building, into a room with walls painted white and blue and ocher. Thick woven rugs covered the floor, and he stopped to kneel, to trace their swirling, multicolored patterns. He had to touch everything, feeling the nubby texture of the plastered walls, the fine weave of the linen tablecloth, the cool smoothness of the bronze lavers. He had nearly forgotten what colors were, but now they exploded all around him: pulsing crimsons, cool greens, dancing yellows. A woman entered with a tray of food, and he stared at her, transfixed. How astonishing a human face was! So soft, so delicate and perfect!

Then he smelled the food. When they seated him at the table laden with delicacies, he could only stare at it and weep, afraid that everything would disappear if he touched it, like the food always did in his dreams. He ate a few bites of each item they served him, but his shrunken stomach and starved palate were unable to tolerate more. One sip of wine made his head reel, and he pushed the cup aside, his senses already overburdened.

After the meal, Manasseh was reunited with the half-dozen of his nobles who had survived. They looked like walking skeletons, and he was terrified of them at first. His secretary was an ancient, crippled man, barely able to walk or speak. Together, they stood before the Assyrian rabshekeh.

"You're free to return home, King Manasseh," the rabshekeh told him. "Our investigation has found you innocent of all charges of conspiracy. Your record has been cleared. We will provide you with transportation so you can return to your homeland."

Manasseh couldn't understand what was happening to him. Experiencing God's forgiveness in his prison cell had been a far greater gift than he had expected or deserved. To be pardoned by the emperor, set free, allowed to return home, was beyond his comprehension. He fell at the Assyrian's feet, weeping at Yahweh's goodness.

That night he slept in a room with two tall windows and shutters that opened to the starry night sky. Manasseh stared in wonder at the heavens until the air grew too cold and he had to close the latches. He lay down on his bed and closed his eyes, but sleep wouldn't come. Instead, he traveled back in time on his final memory journey.

Abba had held his hand as they'd walked through the palace treasure house. The vessels of silver and gold, the caskets of precious stones and jewels left Manasseh awestruck. *"All of this will be yours someday,"* Abba had told him, *"but listen carefully, son. Don't let worldly goods or the praises of men fill you with pride. That's what happened to me. I did nothing to deserve all this wealth. Everything you see is a gift from God."*

Abba had tried to explain how he had sinned, but his words had repulsed Manasseh. He didn't want to believe that Abba could ever sin. His father was perfect. He could never do anything wrong. And so Manasseh had closed his ears to his father's confession, and to his warning. But Abba had made him memorize a verse from the

Torah, and now the words came back to Manasseh in his room in Babylon as if he had just learned them. *"When you are in distress and all these things have happened to you, then in later days you will return to the Lord your God and obey him. For the Lord your God is a merciful God; he will not abandon or destroy you."*

All his life Manasseh had feared living in his father's shadow, afraid that Yahweh wouldn't perform the miraculous feats during his reign that He had during Hezekiah's. But tonight Manasseh knew that God had performed an even greater miracle for him than slaying 144,000 enemy Assyrians. God had forgiven him, erasing the record of his sins.

The knowledge was too much for Manasseh. He fell to the floor on his face and worshiped God.

28

JOSHUA SAT BEHIND THE WORKTABLE where his father had once sat and stared at the documents spread out in front of him. After working nonstop for nearly a month, he still hadn't finished sifting through all the unfinished business Manasseh's palace administrator had left behind. So much of it was worthless garbage—pages of strangely worded omens and reports from the astrologers about which days were favorable to act and which ones weren't. He sat back and rubbed his eye, remembering Miriam's warning about straining it with too much reading.

After living more than half his life-span, Joshua was finally working at the job for which he had trained, beginning the work he once thought he'd spend a lifetime doing. Clambering around construction sites with the hot Egyptian sun on his back seemed to belong to a dream world from which he had finally awakened. But as Joshua gazed at the courtyard outside his window, he found that he missed the fresh air and sunshine more than he thought he would; missed the sense of accomplishment he felt as he watched a new building take shape. Most of all, he missed working with Nathan.

Joshua stood, compelled by a sudden urge to find his son and see how his work was progressing. They had assigned Nathan the task of removing the barricades from around the palace and restoring the facade. Joshua started toward the door, then stopped; he didn't want his son to think he was hovering over him, checking up on him. He returned to his seat again.

Maybe once they reclaimed the Temple Mount, he and Nathan could work side by side on the repairs. Nathan's original designs and expert craftsmanship would far outshine the gaudy idols that currently littered the Temple courtyards. But he couldn't begin the work; Manasseh's priests were still deeply entrenched there. Without a military force, Amariah and Joel weren't prepared for a power struggle with them yet. In fact, as Joshua and the prince quietly went about their work, most of the nation remained unaware that they had taken control of the reins of government.

Joshua was tired of sitting; he needed to stretch. He picked up two documents that required Amariah's seal and decided to deliver them himself. He found the prince in one of the council rooms, poring over lists of Assyrian tribute demands.

"Have you seen these accounts, Joshua?" he asked in astonishment.

"Not yet. Why? Are they in bad shape, too?"

"It's a wonder our nation isn't bankrupt!"

As Joshua skimmed the list Amariah handed him, a palace servant interrupted. "Excuse me, my lords, but a messenger has just arrived from one of our northern border outposts."

"Send him in," Amariah said. He looked up at Joshua, frowning. "Who would send us a message from the northern border?"

Joshua shrugged. "Who even knows that we're here?"

The disheveled messenger appeared as though he had come a long way in a short time and still hadn't caught his breath. He stared openmouthed at the two of them, as if he hadn't expected to find anyone in charge. Obviously, the border outpost hadn't received word of Prince Amariah's return, and that made the man's message an even greater mystery.

"Yes? What is it?" Joshua asked.

"I was sent ahead to tell the palace servants to prepare for the king's arrival."

"What do you mean? What are you talking about?" he asked irritably.

"You have to get everything ready. The king is coming!"

"The *king*? Which king? Who sent you here?"

"King Manasseh. He gave me the order himself."

Joshua opened his mouth to speak, but nothing came out. Amariah scrambled to his feet, then abruptly sat down again as if his knees had given way. "Is this some kind of a joke?" he asked.

"No, my lord. King Manasseh and his entourage arrived in Judean territory earlier this morning. They are on their way to Jerusalem right now. They are not far behind me, in fact."

"That's not possible!" Joshua shouted. "King Manasseh is dead!"

The messenger backed up a step. "He's not dead, my lord. The Assyrians escorted him as far as the border. I saw him myself. I talked to him."

"Was he still in chains?" Amariah asked, his voice a whisper. The messenger shook his head.

"He was wearing royal robes, my lord. You'll see for yourself. King Manasseh will be arriving shortly. I was told to run ahead—"

"NO!" Joshua's anguished cry was deafening. "God of Abraham, *no! No . . . NO!*"

Amariah closed his eyes. "You're excused," he told the messenger. "Go tell the other servants to get everything ready."

"This can't be true . . . it can't be!" Joshua couldn't catch his breath.

"I'm afraid it might be," Amariah said quietly. "Manasseh was arrested for treason, but he wasn't guilty, remember? The Assyrians must have found that out."

"O God of Abraham, how could you do this to me again!" Joshua collapsed to the floor and buried his face in his hands. "How *could* you?" The sound of his bitter cries filled the room.

When the anguish of his soul was spent, Joshua looked up at Amariah. "You realize that we're traitors once again. For taking control of the government when no one else would . . . for wanting to rid the country of idolatry, for wanting to turn people's hearts back to God. . . . We're traitors! He'll execute both of us."

"Not if we leave before Manasseh gets here."

Joshua shook his head. "I'm not running anymore. I'm tired of this game. I'm tired of working for a God who seems to be on my enemy's side. Let Manasseh kill me and get it over with." He covered his face again.

"What about Nathan and Miriam?"

"What?" Numb with despair, Joshua didn't comprehend Amariah's words.

"Your wife and son are in danger. Do you want Manasseh to kill them, too?"

How many years ago had he escaped with Nathan and Miriam? Nathan had been a skinny urchin, brazenly challenging the king's soldiers. Miriam had helped him escape the second time, too, after the explosion at the Temple. He remembered how she had unpinned her hair and tossed it over her shoulder as she courageously entered Asherah's booth. He and Miriam had escaped Manasseh's soldiers a third time, after the abortive assassination attempt. The thought of doing it a fourth time overwhelmed him.

"How could God put us through this all over again?" he questioned, struggling to breathe. "How could He let Manasseh go free when He had a chance to punish him? How could God let such an evil man parade back into town to carry on with his wickedness? I don't understand! I just . . . I . . ."

"Joshua, we have to get out of here before Manasseh returns."

He shook his head. "Do me a favor. Take Miriam and Nathan back to Egypt for me."

"You know Miriam isn't going to budge one inch without you. Now get up! We need to go!" Amariah took Joshua's arm and hauled him to his feet. They hurried through the main palace doors and found Nathan working outside.

"Abba! What is it? What's wrong?" he said when he saw Joshua.

"My brother has returned," Amariah told him.

"You mean . . . King Manasseh?"

Amariah nodded. "We've got to get out of the country. Do you know where Joel is?"

"He went to Anathoth to see what's become of his family's property. He didn't expect to be back until this evening. Do you want me to go get him?"

"No!" Joshua shouted. "How would you ever find him? No,

Nathan, I want you to get out of Judah, now! You have a wife and a child to think about."

Nathan seemed to study him for a long moment before saying calmly, "I'm not leaving without you, Abba. And we can't leave without Uncle Joel, either."

Joshua couldn't think what to do. The terrible injustice of Manasseh's release from prison so overwhelmed him that he lacked the will to fight. Nathan took his elbow and they started hurrying away from the palace.

"Abba, listen. I don't think we'll be in danger if we all wait at your house until Uncle Joel comes back tonight. King Manasseh won't know that you're here—hardly anyone does."

"The elders know," Joshua said. "And all the palace servants."

"But they've collaborated with us this past month," Amariah said. "If they reported us, they would be just as guilty as we are in Manasseh's eyes."

"How can Manasseh be back?" Joshua said with a moan. "This can't be true. God of Abraham, please let this be a mistake!" He was finding it more and more difficult to breathe.

"Nathan's right," Amariah said. "We'll probably be safe at your house for now. Neither the elders nor the servants know where you live. We can plan our escape while we wait for Joel."

"God of Abraham, *why*?" Joshua wanted to tear his clothes in grief, but he lacked the strength. "Why is God doing this to me again? Haven't I had enough of that man? Isn't it enough that he ruined my life?"

"Abba, shh . . . people are staring."

"I don't care." They reached one of the city's main intersections and had to push their way through the huge crowd jamming the streets. Excitement charged the air, as if the people awaited a momentous event. Joshua halted.

"What's going on here?" he asked a bystander. "What's everyone waiting for?"

"King Manasseh has returned. We're gathering to watch his procession."

Joshua stared, dumbfounded. It was true. His enemy had returned. How could God do this to him?

He swayed on his feet, and Nathan gripped his arm. "Let's get out of here, Abba," he whispered urgently.

"No. I want to see him."

"Abba, are you crazy?"

"He'll never recognize me after all these years. Especially in a crowd this huge."

Nathan turned to Amariah. "Can you please talk some sense into my father?"

"I want to see Manasseh, too," Amariah said quietly. "I think we'll be all right."

Nathan groaned. "At least take your eye patch off, Abba, so you'll be less noticeable."

Joshua untied the leather thong and tucked it under his belt, silently cursing himself for not wearing his dagger. If he had a weapon, he could disembowel his enemy before anyone stopped him. As he considered jogging home for it, the trumpets suddenly announced the king's arrival.

Deafening cheers rang in Joshua's ears as the people welcomed King Manasseh home. The sound even drowned out the clatter of hoofbeats as the Assyrian chariots swept the king into Jerusalem. Joshua was unaware of his own bitter groaning or that he was gnashing his teeth until he felt Nathan's comforting hand on his shoulder. When the first few chariots came into view, Joshua strained to see above the crowd. The drivers were Assyrian, and the procession resembled a royal escort, but he couldn't see Manasseh—the passengers were all elderly, white-haired men. Joshua searched for the king's dark hair and arrogant face in vain.

"Where's Manasseh?" he asked Amariah. "Can you see him?"

"No. These must be his officials. Maybe he's at the end of the procession." But after the last chariot rolled past, Amariah stared at Joshua in disbelief. "We must have missed him and didn't recognize him!"

"They were all much too old," Joshua said. "Maybe it was a rumor after all." The mob surged forward to follow the chariots, and Joshua felt himself being swept along with it.

"Please, let's go home, Abba," Nathan begged.

"Not yet. I have to see him." He took Nathan's arm so he

wouldn't lose him in the crowd and grabbed onto the back of Amariah's belt. The procession didn't stop at the palace but continued up the hill to the Temple. In the distance, Joshua saw the chariots halt outside the gates. The white-haired officials disembarked. "Come on, let's hurry," he told the others.

"We're not going inside the Temple grounds, are we?" Nathan asked.

"We won't stay for any pagan ceremonies; I just want to see him. He'll be on the royal platform." Joshua pushed his way forward, towing the others through the gate, into the Court of the Gentiles. When they reached the main courtyard, it was so tightly packed they could go no farther. Joshua craned his neck and caught a glimpse of the royal platform just as one of the old men mounted it.

"That's Manasseh!" Amariah cried.

Joshua stared at a thin, stoop-shouldered man with white hair and a grizzled beard. "No, it can't—" Suddenly the old man lifted his head and thrust out his chin in a gesture that was unmistakably Manasseh's. Joshua felt as if he'd been stabbed in the gut.

"O God of Abraham, why did you let him come back?" he moaned. *"Why?"*

"Abba, shh . . ." Nathan begged.

Gradually the cheering died away and a hush whispered through the crowd as they waited for King Manasseh to speak. Joshua had to hold his breath in order to hear him above the sound of his own labored breathing.

Manasseh faced the Temple sanctuary and raised his hands high in the air. "'Hear, O Israel,'" he said in a shaking voice. "'Yahweh is God—Yahweh alone! Love Yahweh your God with all your heart and with all your soul and with all your strength.'" Manasseh dropped to his knees. Then he fell prostrate before the astonished crowd. The sound of his loud weeping resounded in the silent courtyard.

"I don't believe what I'm seeing . . ." Amariah whispered.

It seemed to Joshua that a long time passed before Manasseh finally stood again. It was longer still before he could speak. The stunned crowd was utterly still, waiting.

"We've all been greatly deceived," Manasseh said. He gestured to the four-faced image in front of the sanctuary. "These are idols. Worthless idols! I want them out of Yahweh's Temple! And I want anyone who still worships them to get out, as well!" He sagged, as if his strength had given way. His officials caught him to keep him from falling off the platform, then hustled him down the royal walkway to the palace.

They all stood frozen for a long moment before Amariah spoke. "What do you make of that?" he asked.

"I don't believe any of it." Joshua closed his eyes, too weak and dizzy to think. The crowds buffeted him as they filed from the courtyard, but he couldn't move.

"I believe it," Amariah said quietly. "I'm going to go down to the palace to see him."

"Are you out of your mind?" Joshua cried. "It was your fault the Assyrians arrested him! He'll murder you!"

"I don't think so. Whatever happened to him in Babylon changed him, and not just on the outside. He was genuinely weeping just now. And he recited the Shema. He never would have done that the last time I saw him."

"Why not wait a few days," Nathan said, "and see if he's really sincere about cleaning up the idolatry?"

Amariah shook his head. "I think I should go now, while he's still overcome with the joy of being home. If I'm not back by the time Joel arrives tonight, leave for Egypt without me."

"What am I supposed to tell Dinah and your sons?" Joshua said angrily. "That you foolishly committed suicide? That you walked right into Manasseh's arms and let him execute you?"

"I honestly don't think that will happen," he said, "but I'm willing to take my chances." Amariah turned, and before either of them could stop him, he ran across the nearly empty courtyard and followed Manasseh down the royal walkway.

Amariah caught up with his brother inside the palace. Manasseh stood in the middle of the spacious throne room, gazing around in wonder—much as Amariah himself had done when he first returned.

"Everything looks the same," Manasseh murmured. "Who has been taking care of things for me while I was gone?"

"I have," Amariah said. "I hope you don't mind."

Manasseh whirled around. He gasped when he saw his brother and staggered backward, nearly falling over.

"I'm sorry, I didn't mean to startle you. It's me—Amariah."

"I . . . I heard your voice . . . and I thought . . . for a minute, I thought . . . You sound so much like Abba!"

Amariah could no longer contain his joy at seeing his brother. He ran forward and clasped Manasseh in his arms. He could feel his brother's body trembling. Manasseh felt pitifully thin, his embrace fervent but weak in return.

"Thank God, thank God," Manasseh wept. "I've prayed for this. . . . I've prayed that I would see you again. That I would have the chance to ask your forgiveness."

"I can't believe that you're alive! And that you've come home again!"

"Yes, I'm home. I've walked these halls so many times in my mind that it still feels like I'm dreaming." Manasseh seemed badly shaken.

Pity and love welled up inside Amariah as he helped his brother to his throne. "Here, you'd better sit down. Are you all right? Is there anything I can do?"

Manasseh looked up at him with tears in his eyes. "I know I have no right to ask this after all that I've done to you, my brother . . ." He rested his right hand on the seat beside him. "But I'll need your help if I'm ever going to undo all the wrong that I've done. Would you take your rightful place here, alongside me?"

Joshua stood in the open doorway of his rented house, staring into the street as if he could make Amariah appear by the force of his will. Joel had returned from Anathoth an hour ago, but there was still no sign of Amariah and no reason to delay leaving Jerusalem any longer.

"Abba, Prince Amariah isn't coming back," Nathan said. "Uncle Joel and I both think we should leave before they close the gates for the night."

"Why didn't I stop him?" Joshua asked. "This is my fault. I never should have let him go down to the palace."

"We've been over this ground a dozen times, Abba. Neither one of us could have stopped the prince. He was determined to go."

"But what am I going to tell Dinah? One of the reasons I came on this trip was to protect Amariah."

Miriam hobbled up beside him and leaned against his chest. "Maybe we should wait until tomorrow to leave. It's late, and we'll probably be just as safe here tonight as we will be out on the roads after dark."

Joshua drew a ragged breath and unconsciously clenched his fists. "Why isn't Manasseh in prison, Miriam? Why isn't he *dead*!"

"I was so afraid something like this would happen," she said softly. "You keep telling God how He should run things, and when He doesn't do it your way—"

"That's because nothing He does makes sense! I haven't understood Him my entire life, but I understand this least of all!"

Suddenly Miriam lifted her head and peered out into the street. "That looks like Amariah coming now. Joshua, he's here!"

"Thank God!" Joshua slumped against the doorframe in relief. "Get our things, Nathan; it's time to go."

Amariah hurried into the house and closed the door behind him. Even in the evening twilight, Joshua could see that his face was radiant with happiness. "Manasseh has changed," the prince said breathlessly. "He suffered terribly in prison, and now he has repented. He truly wants to worship Yahweh."

"You believe him?"

"Yes, Joshua. I do."

"Then you're a fool. He'll turn around and stab you in the back the first chance he gets. Are you ready to leave? We've been waiting for you."

"I'm not going."

"What?"

"Listen, I talked to Manasseh all afternoon, and I honestly don't think we need to run away. He wants to turn the nation back to God and start making restitution. He wants to celebrate the Day of Atonement later this month. We talked about cleansing the Temple, and he wants to see you, Joel. He needs your help."

Joshua was outraged. "You told Manasseh that Joel was here?"

"We have nothing to fear. My brother is sincere."

"You told him! You deliberately put Joel's life in danger!"

The high priest rested his hand on Joshua's shoulder. "It's all right. If I feared for my own safety, I would have stayed in Egypt. I came back to purify the Temple. Let's hear what Amariah has to say."

"Manasseh wants to talk to you about the Day of Atonement. He wants to offer the yearly sacrifice for the nation's sin and for his own. He wants you to officiate."

"How can you possibly worship God in that filthy place?" Joshua cried.

"I have to start somewhere," Joel said quietly. "Maybe everything won't be perfect at first, but if the king wants to make a fresh start, the Day of Atonement is certainly a good place to begin. What better opportunity than this for our people to examine themselves for sin, to repent, and to offer a sacrifice?"

"You're not seriously considering this!" Joshua said.

Joel spread his hands. "This is why I came back."

Joshua turned to Amariah, his anger barely contained. "I suppose you told him that I was here, too?"

"I did. He saw all the work we've been doing, running the government for him, and he's grateful. He asked to see you."

"I'm not walking into his trap."

"It isn't a trap, Joshua. If he wanted to capture you, he could have easily followed me here and done it by now. He just wants to talk to you."

"What about?"

Amariah hesitated. "I think he wants to tell you himself. Will you talk to him?"

The thought of meeting Manasseh face-to-face made Joshua's entire body tremble with rage. "No! I hate him too much!"

"Then this is your chance to tell him. You can choose the time and the meeting place—wherever you'll feel safe. He has already agreed that you can be armed, if you'd like."

"Isn't he afraid that I'll kill him?"

"He said he wouldn't blame you if you did. But I'll be there to guarantee that you don't. You'll have to kill me first. He's my brother, Joshua, and God's anointed king."

"Why don't you go see him, Joshua?" Miriam pleaded. "Confront your enemy like you've longed to all these years, and get it over with. Then we can go home to Elephantine Island and live in peace."

Joshua closed his eyes as he pondered the idea. "All right. Tell Manasseh I'll see him tomorrow."

29

JOSHUA AROSE BEFORE DAWN AND CREPT OUT of the house without waking Miriam. He hadn't slept. Rage and bitterness had robbed his peace and choked off his breath. He had agreed to meet with Manasseh before the morning sacrifice, in the meadow where the Gihon Spring used to be. Wary of being caught in a trap, Joshua arrived there first to make certain that Manasseh's men weren't lying in wait to ambush him. As he sat down on the low stone wall surrounding the olive grove, he almost wished his enemy would prove deceitful and provide him with an excuse to kill him. Joshua wore his dagger in plain sight, but after all these years, he hated Manasseh enough to kill him with his bare hands.

The sky above the Mount of Olives was already light by the time Manasseh emerged through the Water Gate. He brought no bodyguards with him—only Amariah. The prince looked healthy and robust in comparison as he walked beside him. Manasseh leaned heavily on his arm, and Amariah might have been the white-haired king's son instead of his brother. Joshua watched them make their way down the winding ramp and suddenly recalled the day Manasseh had raced him to the bottom, his body lean and muscular, his legs pumping effortlessly while Joshua had struggled to keep up. Now Manasseh's body looked thin and feeble, showing the ravages of his imprisonment. As his enemy drew near, Joshua saw the sickly gray pallor of his skin. His scarred nose appeared misshapen from the bronze hook the Assyrians had used. Joshua felt no pity at all. Manasseh deserved so much more. He deserved to die.

The king stopped fifteen feet away from Joshua. He looked subdued, all of his old arrogance gone. He cleared his throat nervously, and when he spoke, his voice was that of a very old man.

"Joshua . . . I can hardly believe—"

"I want to know where my father is buried!"

The question seemed to take Manasseh by surprise. "I . . . I don't know," he stammered. "I'm sorry . . . I never thought . . . But I'll ask. I'll find someone who was there, who remembers."

Joshua stepped closer. His lungs seemed as tightly clenched as his fists. "I hate you, Manasseh! I hate you with every ounce of strength I have! You have no idea how badly I want to kill you right now, so you'd better say what you have to say before I lose control and do it!" The king stared at him open-mouthed, as if too shaken to speak. Joshua grew impatient. "What do you want with me?" he shouted.

"I . . . I want to talk to you about the Day of Atonement. Rabbi Gershom taught us that we should confess and repent of all the sins we've committed against God and against other people . . . and I . . . when I remember all that I've done . . . I hardly know where to begin." Manasseh couldn't meet Joshua's gaze. His fingers moved restlessly while he talked, plucking at his hair, his beard, the folds of his clothes. His entire body had a slight tremor to it, his head wobbling continuously, like a man with palsy. "If it's possible, I'd like to make amends for all the pain I've caused you and ask forgiveness from you and all the other people I've hurt—"

"You don't deserve to be forgiven!"

"I . . . I know. . . . It's true. When I was in prison and all the props I depended on, like power and wealth and false gods, were taken from me, I was left with only myself—the real me—and I hated myself. If I were God, I wouldn't forgive me, either. I've ignored His Laws and offended His holiness for most of my life, and I could well imagine how great His anger and wrath must be as He prepared to punish me as I deserved. I was filthy with guilt. Unlovable, unworthy . . ." Manasseh's voice suddenly broke, and he paused. "But when I cried out to Him in desperation, He looked down on me—stinking, loathsome, and shivering with fear—and He lowered himself to that terrible prison where I lay waiting. He came down to me . . . and He took away my guilt and He washed me clean. Then . . . then He gathered me into His arms. God stood waiting for me all this time, not with wrath but with mercy, ready to forgive."

A picture formed briefly in Joshua's mind of Nathan shivering with guilt and fear as he lay on the Egyptian riverbank after the pagan festival. Joshua saw himself bending down in pity to gather his son into his arms. But before Joshua could bring the picture into focus, the scene was abruptly shattered by the sound of his enemy's voice.

"I want to repent. I want to change," Manasseh said, "but I don't know where to begin. I don't want to do the things I did before, but how do I stop? The old impulses are still there, the old habits. I've listened to lies for so long that I no longer remember the truth. And Zerah manipulated me for so long that I can't think for myself anymore. I know I need to start all over, but my life is an empty void without idolatry. Please help me, Joshua. Help me turn the nation around. It's so much easier to lead people into sin than it is to lead them back to God."

"I don't want anything to do with you or your evil reign!" Joshua said bitterly. "You deserve the same measure of mercy that you showed your son when you tossed him into the flames! The same mercy you showed my father and Rabbi Isaiah. You don't deserve a second chance, Manasseh, so don't ask me for one."

"You're right, I don't deserve mercy. When I was praying I imagined that the heavenly hosts had slammed all the doors and windows of heaven shut against my prayer so that God wouldn't hear it. Even the angels know that Yahweh is a God of mercy and compassion. They didn't want me to be forgiven any more than you do. But God opened a hole beneath His throne of grace to hear my prayer so that sinners for all time would know that no one is beyond the reach of His grace. If God could forgive someone like me—"

"I don't want to hear any more of this!" Joshua shouted. The weight on his chest had grown so heavy it threatened to suffocate him. "How can you expect me or any of the other people you've harmed to ever forgive you? How dare you even ask!"

"I know I have no right to ask you, any more than I had a right to ask God's forgiveness. But then I remembered the last words your father ever said to me."

Joshua held his breath, waiting to hear them, waiting to hear Abba speak to him one last time.

"On the day Eliakim died," Manasseh began, "on the day that I unjustly condemned him to death . . . he looked me in the eye and told me that he forgave me."

"You're lying!" Joshua cried out. "I don't believe you!"

Manasseh met Joshua's gaze for the first time. "Then you didn't know your father very well."

Of all the emotional blows Joshua had suffered over the past two days, this was the hardest one for him to endure. If Abba had forgiven Manasseh, then he would have wanted Joshua to forgive him, too. But Joshua knew that was utterly impossible.

"I don't believe any of it! Go look at what you've done to Yahweh's Temple and to this nation, then tell me how God could possibly forgive you!"

"I . . . I know—"

"He *didn't* forgive you, Manasseh, and I won't, either!"

Joshua couldn't bear to look at his enemy a moment longer. He couldn't listen to another word. He turned his back and ran down the path to the Kidron Valley, his vision blinded by rage.

Miriam watched helplessly as her husband struggled for air. Ever since his meeting with King Manasseh early this morning, his breathing had grown more and more labored as the day progressed. Joshua had talked of leaving to return to Egypt, but he was much too ill to begin the journey. He tried sitting, lying down, bending double, pacing the floor, but nothing seemed to help him breathe any easier. It was close to midnight, and neither of them had slept. The sound of Joshua gasping, coughing, and wheezing made Miriam sick with fear.

"Joshua, please let me send for a physician," she begged.

"It won't help. . . . They don't know . . . what to do . . . for breathing attacks. . . ."

O God, help him! she pleaded silently. She knew Joshua wouldn't pray. He had gone into his private tunnel, into the darkness, away from God. She was desperate to bring him back before his own bitterness killed him.

"You're doing this to yourself," she told him. "You have to get rid of your anger and hatred before they strangle the life from you!"

"How? The only way to get rid of what I feel is to kill him!"

"But that wouldn't be the end of it, Joshua. You're not just angry with Manasseh, you're angry with God."

Joshua sank down on a bench, then stood again a moment later, the struggle for air making him restless. "How could God forgive Manasseh?" he raged. "It's impossible! Manasseh didn't pay for all his sins or for all the innocent blood he shed. God's Law demands justice! His holiness demands justice!"

"Are there limits to God's forgiveness, Joshua? Are there some sins that He'll forgive and others that He punishes?"

Joshua's pale skin had a bluish tinge when he whirled to face her. "Do you want me to list all the sins Manasseh has committed? Murder, infanticide, idolatry, witchcraft, sorcery, divination, sodomy—" He began to cough and couldn't finish.

"If there is a limit we can exceed," she said when he was quiet, "if Manasseh can't be forgiven, then where does that leave all of us? We are all without hope."

"Why should he get a second chance? He didn't just murder my father and grandfather, he ruined my life!"

"Your own hatred did you more harm than Manasseh ever did. That's what's making you so sick right now. You're angry because God forgave him. And because God is asking you to forgive him, too."

"It's impossible! How can I forgive all the years of pain he caused me? Or the debt of justice he owes my family? I can't forget what he's done, Miriam."

"You're right; it's impossible. But God isn't asking you to forget. And He isn't asking you to condone it. He's asking you to forgive Manasseh *in spite of* what he's done." Miriam grabbed his heaving shoulders to make him stop pacing and forced him to look at her. "When you forgive someone, you make a choice to cancel the debt he owes you."

"Like you forgave me for killing your father?" he asked angrily. "That's what you're reminding me of, isn't it?"

"Forgiveness is costly, Joshua. We pay the price ourselves when we choose to cancel the debt."

Joshua's wheezing voice dropped to a whisper as he slowly suffocated. "Manasseh doesn't deserve forgiveness."

"Listen to you! I thought you wanted to serve God, like your father and grandfather did!" Miriam was sorry to be shouting, but she was desperate to save his life. "You can't serve God by doing the opposite of what He does! You have to forgive because God forgives! Otherwise, do you know what's going to happen? You're going to die separated from God while Manasseh, who did evil his entire life, will die reconciled!"

Joshua gazed at her in astonishment. "That's impossible. . . ." He sank into a chair, his shoulders slumped in defeat, his lungs rasping painfully. "Would you get me a drink of water, please?" he asked quietly.

Miriam blinked in surprise. Joshua never asked her to wait on him. "Of course," she said after a moment. She left him sitting there and limped outside to the cistern, unsure how she would manage to carry a drink and use her crutches at the same time. She solved the problem by searching for an empty wineskin with a leather strap, rinsing it out, and refilling it from the cistern. After looping the strap over her shoulder, she made her way back into the house. The room seemed darker to her. Then she noticed that one of the oil lamps was missing from its lampstand. Joshua was gone.

"O God, no!" she cried. Miriam could barely maneuver on Jerusalem's uneven streets in daylight; it would be impossible to follow Joshua at night, especially with no way to carry a lamp. Besides, she had no idea where he'd gone. As she wept with helplessness and fear for his life, she suddenly thought of Nathan. She had to find Nathan.

It seemed to take Miriam forever to hobble the short distance in the dark to the stall they'd rented in the marketplace, longer still for someone to answer her frantic pounding on the shuttered door.

Joel looked sleepy and confused when he finally opened it. "Miriam? What on earth . . . ?" He helped her inside. Nathan sat up on his pallet a moment later.

"What's wrong?"

"Joshua's having a breathing attack," she told them. "A bad one. But he's angry and upset and he left the house and I don't know where he went or where to look for him."

"Maybe it's better if you just let him go," Joel said. "Maybe he needs some time alone."

Miriam shook her head. "That's the worst thing I could possibly do when he gets this way. He goes inside himself, into his own dark tunnel, and he needs me to help him find his way out again."

Nathan scrambled to his feet. "I think I know where he might be."

"Where?"

"Stay here, Miriam. I'll find him."

Joshua held the oil lamp in his right hand, feeling along the clammy wall with his left as he slowly groped his way through the meandering tunnel. He had only been inside it once before, with his father, but the suffocating darkness, the weight of the rock closing in around him, the terrible heaviness bearing down on top of him, were all so familiar it was as if he had been inside this tunnel many times. The icy water grew deeper as he sloshed through it, the passageway narrower, like his lungs as he struggled to breathe.

He inched his way forward, searching for nearly ten minutes before he found what he was looking for: Abba's inscription. He held the light close to read the words his father had chiseled into the stone, feeling them with his fingers. *Behold the tunnel . . .*

Those were the only words he managed to read before a spasm of coughing overwhelmed him. As he fought to catch his breath, the lamp jostled in his hand. The wick sputtered and sank beneath the oil. The flame died. Joshua plunged into total darkness.

"Abba!" he cried out in panic. But his father was dead, and his heavenly Father was too far away to hear his cries. He knew that his own anger and unforgiveness had separated him from God. They were the true source of his darkness, just as Miriam had said. When he'd turned his back on God, he had walked away from the only Source of light.

Joshua's limbs went numb with terror. He wanted to run from this terrible black void, but he was too dizzy and disoriented to move. He shivered, shaken to realize that Manasseh had lived in this eternal darkness, this midnight of the soul, for most of his life; now Joshua was lost in it, too. How would he ever find his way out?

Suddenly, above the sound of his panicked gasps, Joshua thought he heard a noise. He held his breath, listening.

"Abba?"

At first he thought it was a ghostly echo of his own cry. Then he heard it again. "Abba? . . . Abba, are you in here?"

Joshua recognized Nathan's voice, heard the sound of his feet splashing through the water.

"Yes! Yes, I'm here, son." He slumped against the wall in relief, unable to draw enough air to shout again. Trembling all over, he waited for the bobbing light to appear. After the terrible darkness he'd endured, Nathan's puny lamp seemed to glow as brightly as the sun. Nathan's face creased with worry as he looked him over.

"Why are you in the dark? What happened to your light?"

"It went out. . . . I . . ." He couldn't finish.

"Abba, listen to you, wheezing like that. I don't think it's good for you to be wading around in this cold water. Come on, let's get out of here."

Joshua knew that if he tried to walk he would fall flat on his face. "Wait . . . there's something I want you to see. Shine the light on this wall. . . . There . . . can you read what it says?"

" 'Behold the tunnel,' " Nathan read. " 'Now this is the story of the tunnel—' "

"My father started digging at both ends," Joshua said, interrupting, "and the workers met here, in the middle. How do you suppose he did that? How did he ever get two separate, meandering tunnels to meet?"

"I don't know."

"They didn't meet at first," he said, remembering the story.

"Abba told me that one end was higher than the other. Hold the light up so you can see." Nathan lifted his arm to shine the light above their heads. The ceiling was higher than either of them could reach. "You see that? One tunnel had to be lowered to meet the other one—" Joshua suddenly felt the weight of angry tears pressing against his eyes. He cleared the lump from his throat. "You know what Manasseh told me today? He said that God *lowered* himself, down to the prison cell where he lay, to offer Manasseh His forgiveness. Can you believe that, Nathan?"

"Yes, I do believe it," he said quietly. "That's what God is like. That's what you taught me, Abba."

"When did I ever say that?" he asked angrily.

"You showed me. Day after day, year after year . . . you showed me. 'As a father has compassion on his children, so the Lord has compassion on those who fear him.' Remember how much I hurt you when I rebelled—stealing, making idols, turning my back on God's laws? Remember how much pain you felt when you had to watch me suffer the consequences of my sins? You didn't want me to be flogged and punished—you were willing to take my punishment for me. When I was lost among the pagans at the Egyptian festival, you searched for me and found me and carried me home again. Colonel Simeon demanded justice, but you didn't want justice for me, you wanted forgiveness. You didn't want me to be banished and to die separated from you."

"Of course not, Nathan . . . I . . ."

"Abba, you never gave up on me. You forgave me again and again and begged the council to forgive me. I know how much you longed for me to return your love all those years, yet you waited. It had to be my decision. But remember how you felt after the first battle, when you held me in your arms again? How you felt after so many wasted years, when I finally called you 'Abba'? That's how God felt when King Manasseh finally turned to Him. That's why God forgave Manasseh. He didn't want to see His son die for his sins any more than you wanted to see me die. 'As a father has compassion on his children.' That's what the psalm says, Abba. 'As high as the heavens are above the earth, so great is his love. . . .'"

Joshua stared at the reflection the lamp made on the water,

waiting until he could trust himself to speak. "Miriam told me that forgiveness is costly. She said I would pay the price if I chose to cancel Manasseh's debt."

"Abba, you were willing to pay my debt, willing to take my punishment and be flogged in my place."

He looked up at Nathan through his tears. "Does that mean that God is also willing to pay the cost and bear the punishment for all of our sins?"

"I guess it must," Nathan said softly. The tunnel was silent for a moment except for the sound of Joshua's labored breaths. "Abba, you're getting sick. This breathing attack is a bad one. You need to get out of this cold water. Do you want to carry the lamp?"

"No, you carry it." Joshua followed Nathan out of the tunnel, leaning against the wall for support, his knees still trembling badly. When they finally emerged, the night air was warm, the heavens splashed with stars. It seemed like a different sky than the one Joshua saw every night on Elephantine Island.

"I suppose you'll want to stay here in Jerusalem," Joshua said as they walked home.

"I want to live wherever you do, Abba."

"But I'll probably go back to Egypt. I know how much you've always hated it there."

"It's only a place. It doesn't matter where I live. I want to stay with you, work with you—if you'll let me."

Joshua stopped and pulled Nathan into his arms, holding him close. Was it possible that God had allowed all those years of struggle with Nathan just to show him His own heart toward His rebellious children?

"I love you, Nathan."

"I know you do, Abba. I know how very much you do."

30

THE BREATHING ATTACK WAS THE WORST ONE Joshua had ever had in his life. He feared that it might kill him. He tossed on his pallet, delirious with fever, as his exhausted lungs slowly filled with fluid. For days, he drifted in and out of consciousness, aware at times of Miriam or Nathan sponging him with water to cool his fever, propping him up so he could cough, or wrapping him in blankets when he shivered with chills. He grew so weary of his struggle to live that he longed to quit, but the sound of Miriam's voice always urged him to draw another painful breath.

At one point when he opened his eyes, he saw Joel kneeling beside him. "Joshua, do you want to make peace with God?" he asked kindly. "Do you want me to pray with you?"

Joshua knew what Joel was asking and why. *"You're going to die separated from God,"* Miriam had warned, *"while Manasseh, who did evil his entire life, will die reconciled."*

"Am I going to die?" he asked the high priest.

"You're gravely ill, Joshua."

"Yes . . . pray," he whispered, closing his eyes again. "Ask God what His will for me is. . . . Tell Him . . . I want to obey it. . . ."

He heard Joel's voice as he prayed aloud. It sounded soothing, but his words made no sense. He heard Miriam weeping.

Joshua fell asleep again and dreamed of his father. Abba took him in his arms and covered Joshua's mouth with his own, breathing life into him. But it wasn't air that Abba poured into him, it was words from the Torah. *"Do not seek revenge or bear a grudge . . . but love your neighbor as yourself."* In his dream, Joshua knew that the words would heal him if he inhaled them deep into his soul. He struggled to draw them in, to draw life from his father.

The next time Joshua awoke, his fever had broken. He began to hope that he would live. Gradually, over the next few days, it became easier and less painful for him to breathe, and his coughing eased. He could sit up when he wasn't sleeping, and eat a little food.

"How long have I been sick?" he asked Miriam.

Her face was drawn and pale, as if bereft of tears. "Nine days. I thought I was going to lose you."

"Come here," he whispered. He drew her into his arms and held her close, his love for her too deep for words. "I think God is going to let me stay a little while longer."

"Yes . . . thank God," she murmured.

Nathan crouched beside them. "Abba, if you're strong enough, will you come to the Temple with me tomorrow morning? It's the Day of Atonement."

Joshua covered his son's hand with his own. "Yes, I'll come."

The sky was overcast the next day, the streets damp with the first fall rains as Joshua entered the Temple courtyard with Nathan. Most of the pagan idols and shrines had been cleared away, and the air smelled of incense and freshly plowed earth. Joel stood beside Yahweh's altar, his brightly colored robes making vivid splashes of gold, blue, purple, and scarlet against the gray sky and wet pavement.

"Throughout these past days of fasting and mourning," Joel said, "God has led us to examine ourselves and to confess our sins. Now we bring those sins before Him as a nation so we can await His forgiveness."

Joshua knelt with the other worshipers and bowed his head, aware that he had no more right to ask God for forgiveness than Manasseh did. "Forgive me for my anger and my hatred," he prayed.

"Forgive me for wanting revenge and justice for my enemy more than I wanted your mercy. I've been angry with you, Lord, because your measure of mercy is as great as your measure of justice. I'm sorry. Now I need your mercy and forgiveness, too."

He stood again as the high priest cast lots for the two sacrificial goats. Joel slit the throat of the one selected to be sacrificed and drained its blood into a golden basin. He held up the blood for the congregation to see.

"'The Lord is my strength and my song,'" Joel recited, "'he has become my salvation. He is my God, and I will praise him, my father's God, and I will exalt him. . . . Who among the gods is like you, O Lord? Who is like you—majestic in holiness, awesome in glory, working wonders? . . . In your unfailing love you will lead the people you have redeemed. In your strength you will guide them to your holy dwelling.'"

Joel walked across the courtyard and disappeared through the doors of the sanctuary. Joshua knew he would carry the atoning blood into God's presence in the most holy place. A long rope trailed from his ankle. Only the high priest dared to stand before God once a year, and only after offering a sacrifice for his own sins earlier that morning. If God didn't accept the atoning blood, if He struck Joel dead in His wrath, the rope would be used to pull his body from the sanctuary.

Joshua waited in the silent courtyard for Joel to reappear and assure the worshipers that their sins had been atoned for. He listened for the faint tinkle of bells on the hem of the high priest's garment but heard only the plaintive cry of birds wheeling overhead. Joel seemed to be taking a long time. The people waited, watching the sanctuary doors. There was no sign of the high priest.

As the tension mounted, Joshua turned and glanced in the direction he had been avoiding all morning. King Manasseh stood on the royal platform, his eyes fixed on the sanctuary doors as he waited like everyone else for the high priest.

Joshua knew what he had to do if he wanted God's forgiveness. He pushed his way through the crowd until he came to the barrier that separated the congregation from the royal dais. He drew a painful breath, then stepped over the divide. Two of the king's officials rushed forward to stop him.

"Let me go. I need to speak to the king," Joshua insisted. He scuffled with them as he tried to break free. Manasseh looked down at the commotion and their eyes met. Joshua saw Manasseh's fear.

"Let him through," the king said in a shaking voice. But the guards didn't release their grip on Joshua's arms as they marched him to the foot of the platform. "No, let him go free," Manasseh said.

Joshua was face-to-face with his enemy, but he hesitated. He couldn't do this on his own strength. He hated Manasseh too much. He remembered praying for God's help to love Nathan, and he offered up a silent prayer. *Help me do this, Lord. I can't do it on my own.* His lungs wheezed loudly in the hushed courtyard.

"I forgive you, Manasseh," Joshua said quietly. Then he stepped forward to embrace his enemy. When Joshua did, it wasn't only Manasseh who was set free, but himself.

"Thank you," Manasseh wept. "Thank you . . . thank you . . ."

As Joshua stepped down again, the sun emerged from behind a cloud, reflecting off the Temple's golden roof. A murmur rippled through the crowd, and Joshua squinted in the glare to watch as the high priest stepped through the doors of the sanctuary.

Atonement had been made. Joshua's sins were forgiven.

He wiped a tear as the high priest laid his hands on the scapegoat's head. "We confess to you, Lord, all of our wickedness and rebellion. May the burden of our sin rest on this substitute that you have provided. And may all of our sins be removed far from us."

Joy filled Joshua's soul as he watched the scapegoat being led out of the gate, out of the city to be released into the desert—bearing his sins. As the peace of God flooded his heart, all the suffering of his life suddenly made sense to him. He understood the journey on which God had led him, bringing him here to forgive and to be forgiven. And he knew that for the remainder of his years, God wanted him to help Manasseh with his reforms. Joshua drew a deep breath—his first in many days—and crossed the courtyard to where Nathan stood waiting for him. He felt the sun of his homeland warming his back as he walked, a fresh breeze from the Judean hills caressing his face.

"I could use your help, son," Joshua said. "We have a lot of rebuilding to do here in Jerusalem." It seemed to Joshua that his words were an echo of what God was asking him to do.

Nathan looked up at him and smiled, his reply the same as Joshua's response to God: "Of course, Abba. I'll do whatever you need me to do."

When Christ came as high priest . . . He did not enter by means of the blood of goats and calves; but he entered the Most Holy Place once for all by his own blood, having obtained eternal redemption. . . . How much more, then, will the blood of Christ, who through the eternal Spirit offered himself unblemished to God, cleanse our consciences from acts that lead to death, so that we may serve the living God!
—Hebrews 9:11–12, 14

[Manasseh] got rid of the foreign gods and removed the image from the temple of the Lord, as well as all the altars he had built on the temple hill and in Jerusalem; and he threw them out of the city. Then he restored the altar of the Lord and sacrificed fellowship offerings and thank offerings on it, and told Judah to serve the Lord, the God of Israel.
—2 Chronicles 33:15–16

The Prayer of Manasseh

O Lord Almighty, God of our ancestors,
of Abraham and Isaac and Jacob and of their righteous offspring;
you who made heaven and earth with all their order;
who shackled the sea by your word of command,
who confined the deep and sealed it with your
terrible and glorious name;
at whom all things shudder, and tremble before your power,
for your glorious splendor cannot be borne,
and the wrath of your threat to sinners is unendurable;
yet immeasurable and unsearchable is your promised mercy,
for you are the Lord Most High, of great compassion,
long-suffering, and very merciful,
and you relent at human suffering.
O Lord, according to your great goodness
you have promised repentance and forgiveness
to those who have sinned against you,
and in the multitude of your mercies
you have appointed repentance for sinners,
so that they may be saved.
Therefore you, O Lord, God of the righteous,
have not appointed repentance for the righteous,
for Abraham and Isaac and Jacob, who did not sin against you,
but you have appointed repentance for me, who am a sinner.
For the sins I have committed are more in number than
the sand of the sea;
my transgressions are multiplied, O Lord, they are multiplied!
I am not worthy to look up and see the height of heaven
because of the multitude of my iniquities.
I am weighted down with many an iron fetter,

so that I am rejected because of my sins, and I have no relief;
for I have provoked your wrath
and have done what is evil in your sight,
setting up abominations and multiplying offenses.
And now I bend the knee of my heart,
imploring you for your kindness.
I have sinned, O Lord, I have sinned,
and I acknowledge my transgressions.
I earnestly implore you,
forgive me, O Lord, forgive me!
Do not destroy me with my transgressions!
Do not be angry with me forever or store up evil for me;
do not condemn me to the depths of the earth.
For you, O Lord, are the God of those who repent,
and in me you will manifest your goodness;
for, unworthy as I am, you will save me according to
your great mercy,
and I will praise you continually all the days of my life.
For all the host of heaven sings your praise,
and yours is the glory forever. Amen.

from the Apocryphal book The Prayer of Manasseh (NRSV)

Author's Note

In 1961, archaeologists uncovered the ruins of a temple on the island of Elephantine in Egypt. Aligned to face Jerusalem, it was identical in size and construction to the Jerusalem Temple and had been built by Jewish priests and Levites fleeing the persecution of King Manasseh's reign. Records unearthed with it revealed that a full schedule of sacrifices and feast days had been celebrated there. Since no other temple was ever built by exiled priests or Jews, some scholars have concluded that the Ark of the Covenant might have been rescued during the time of Manasseh and housed in Egypt, as well. My novel *Among the Gods* is based on this premise.

King Hezekiah did have a second son named Amariah. In the book of Zephaniah (1:1), Amariah and his son Gedaliah are listed as the prophet's ancestors.